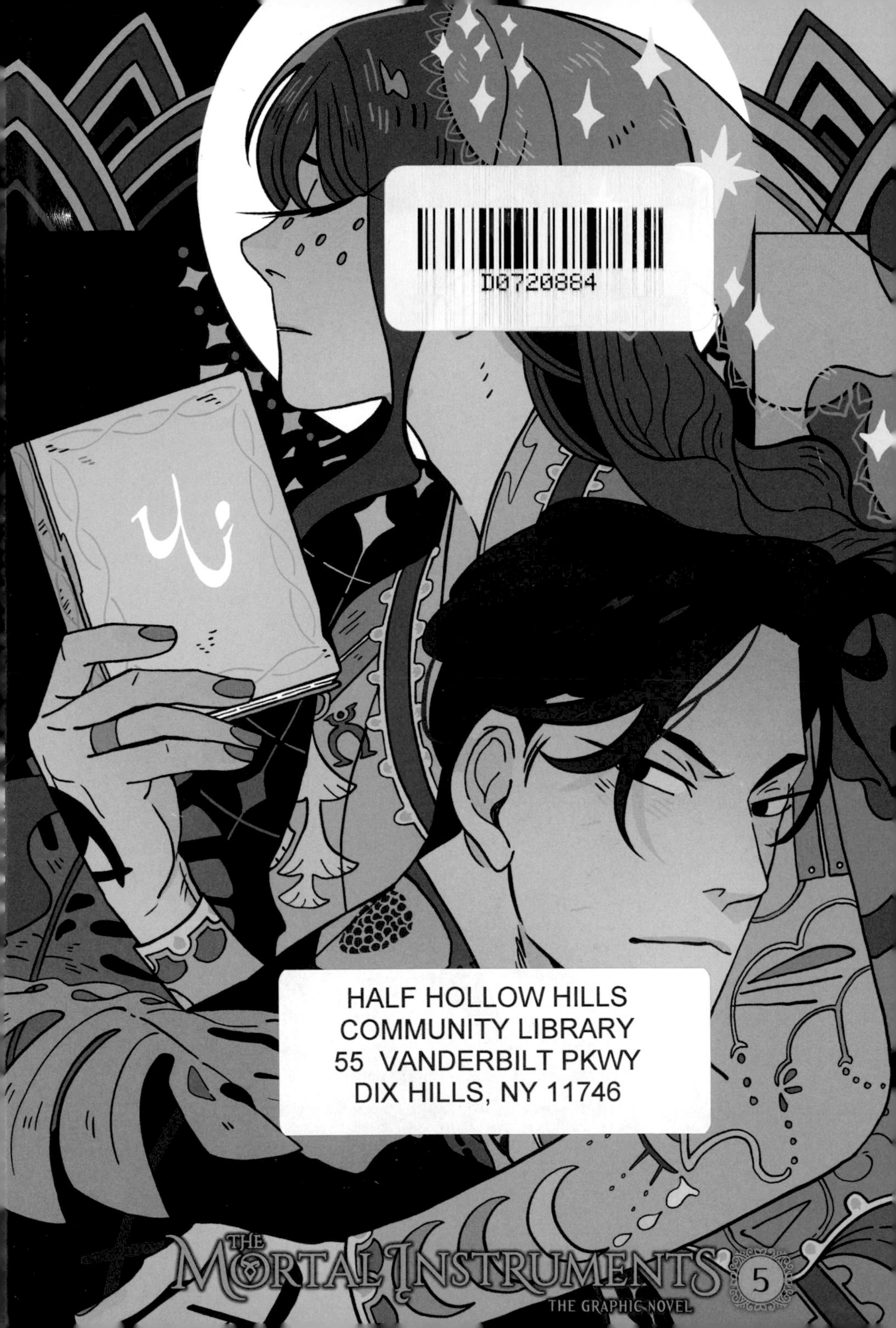
THE MORTAL INSTRUMENTS
5
THE GRAPHIC NOVEL

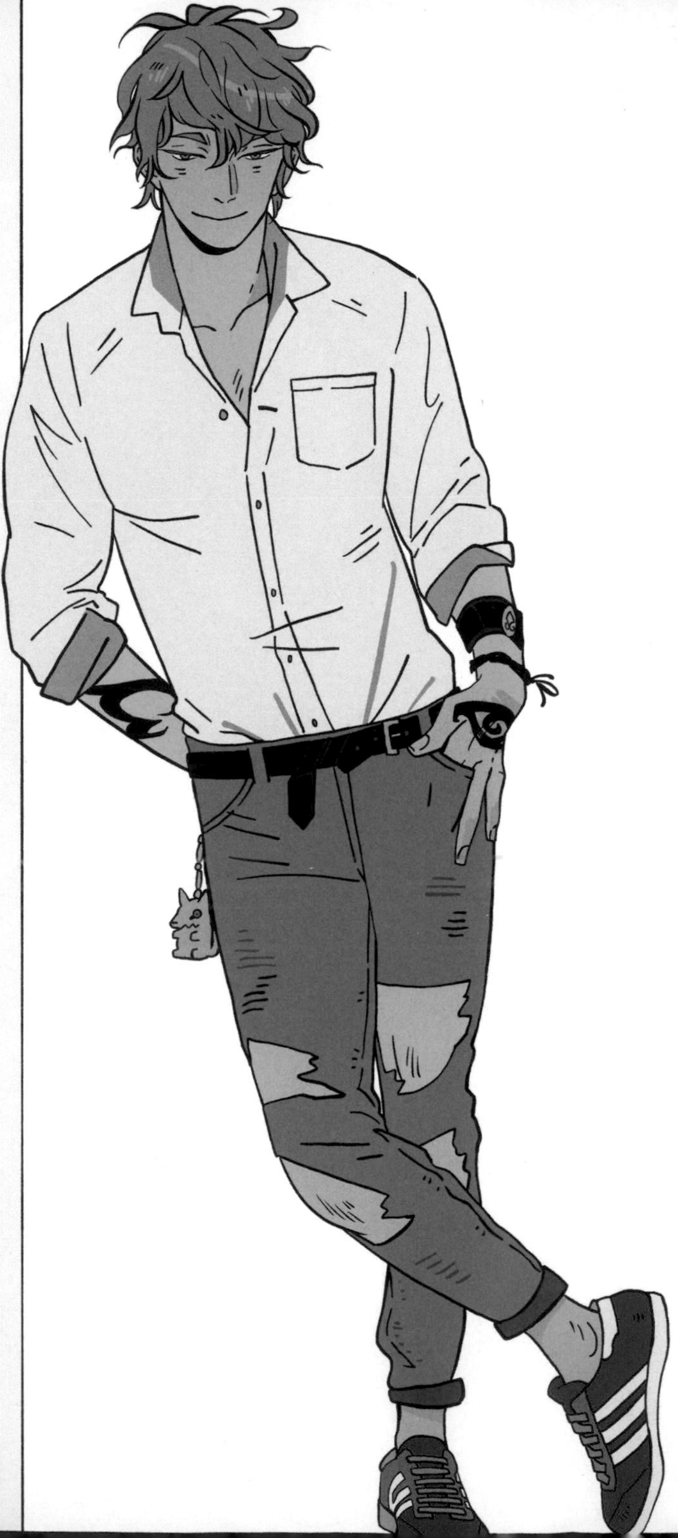

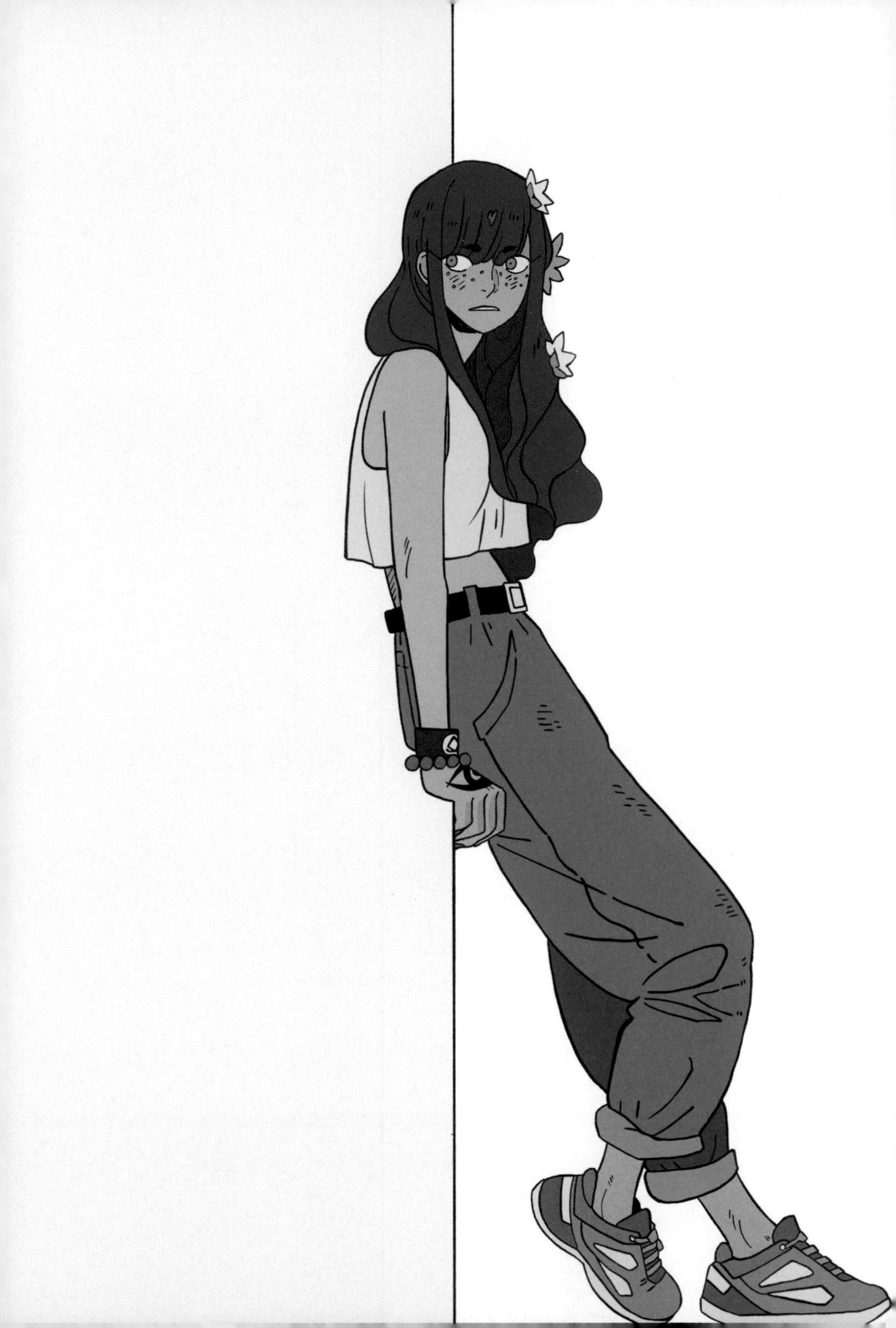

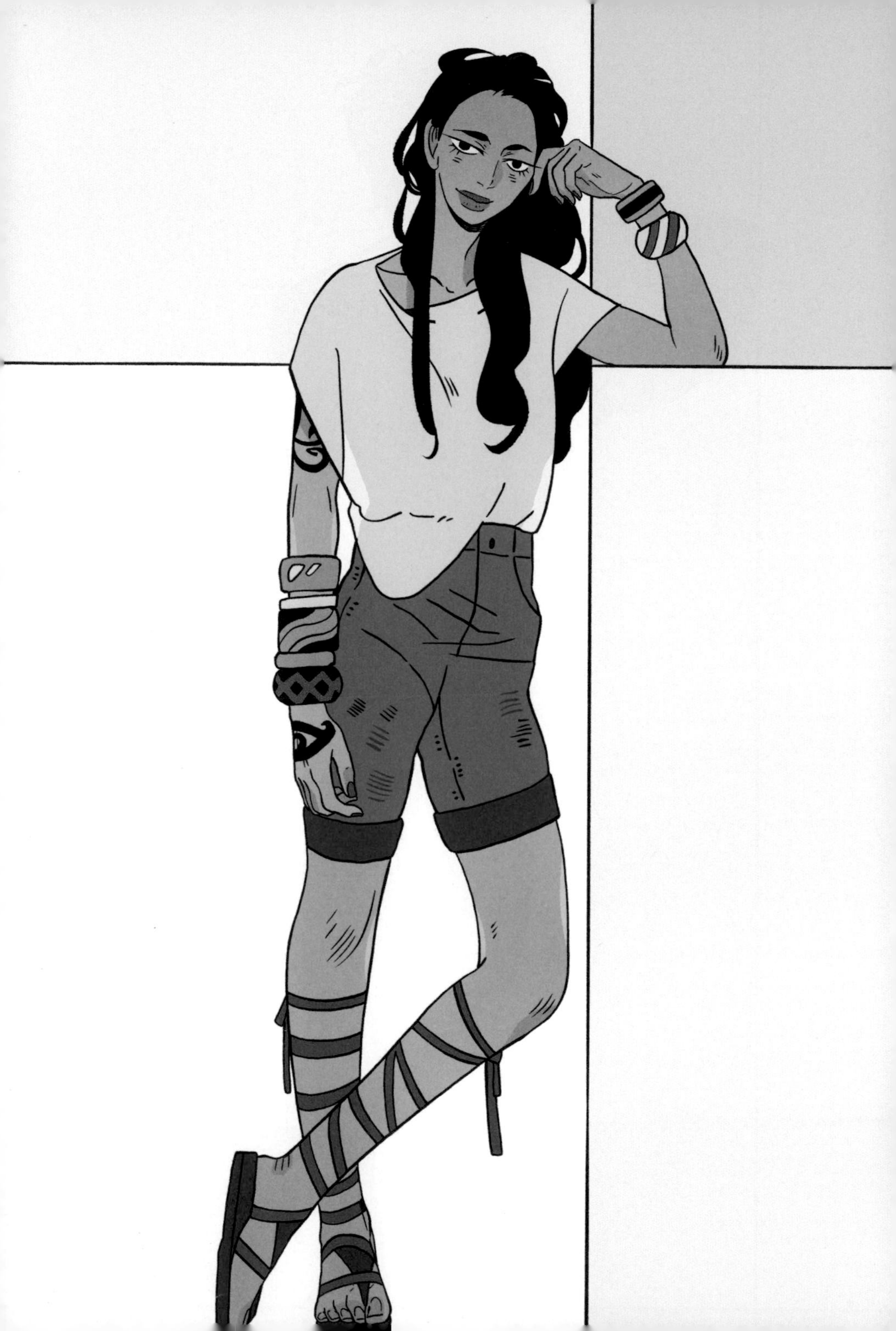

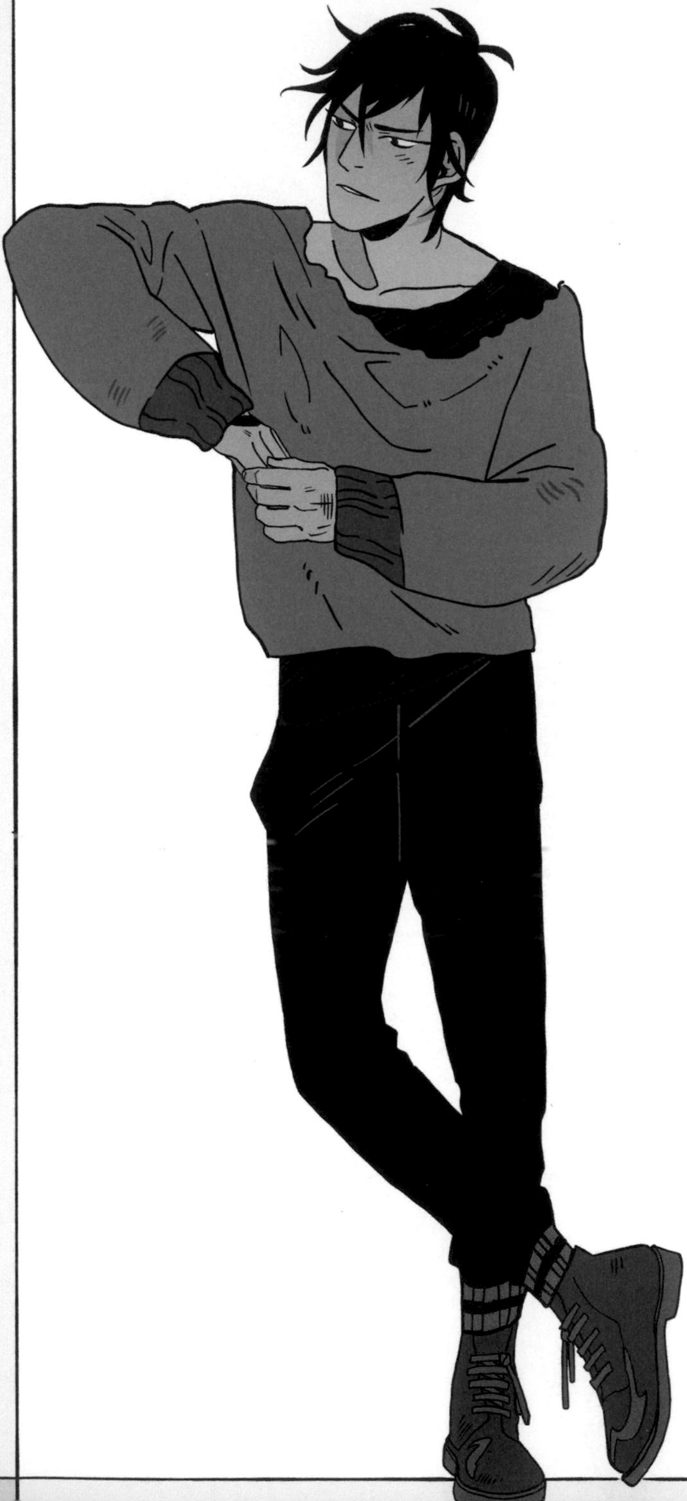

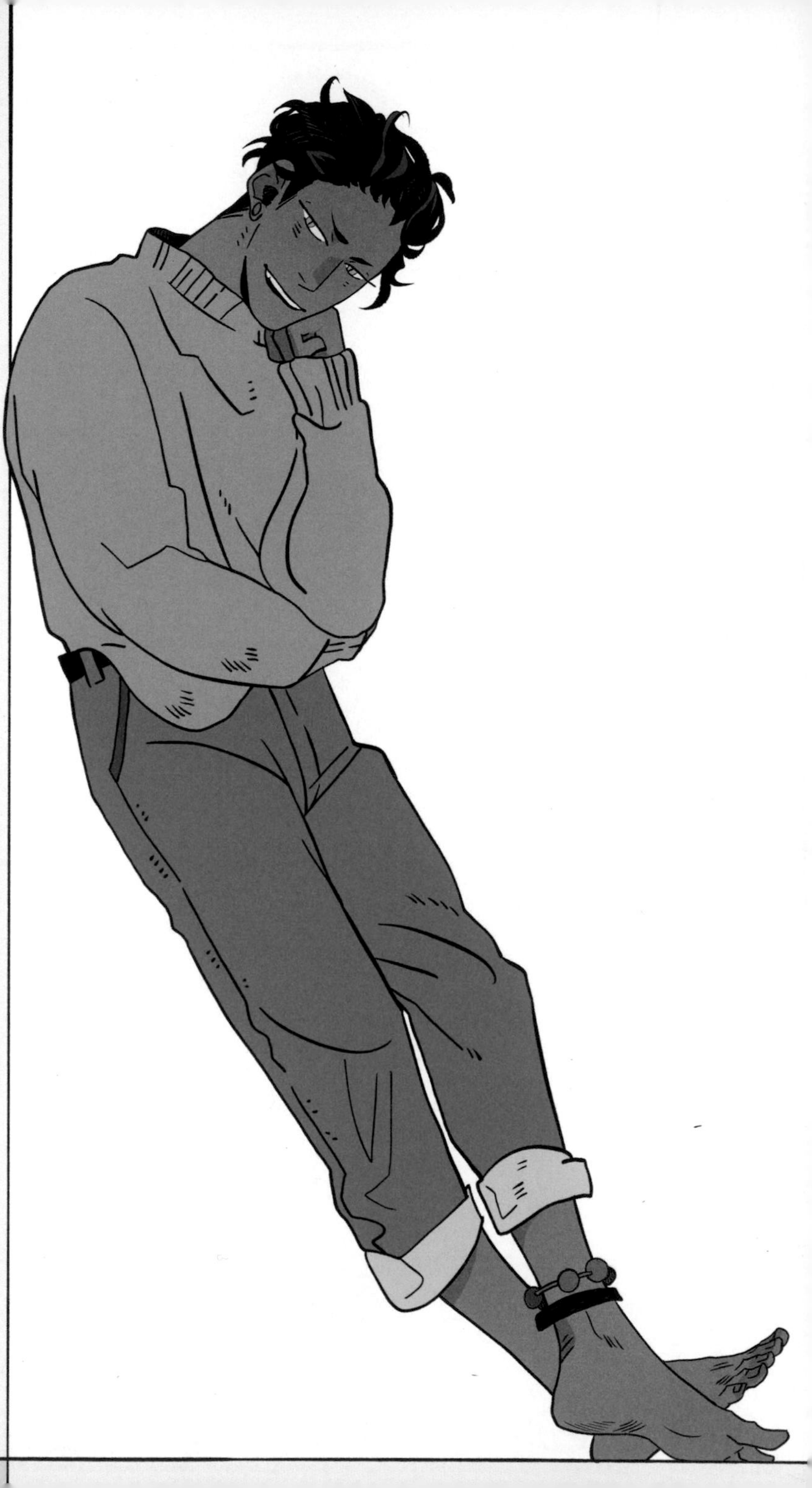

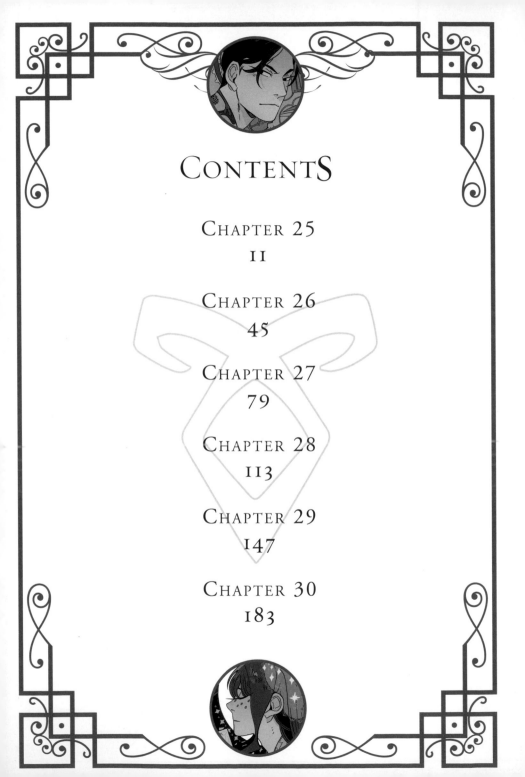

Contents

THE MORTAL INSTRUMENTS

THE GRAPHIC NOVEL

STORY BY
CASSANDRA CLARE

5

ART BY
CASSANDRA JEAN

THE MORTAL INSTRUMENTS
THE GRAPHIC NOVEL

CASSANDRA CLARE
CASSANDRA JEAN

ART AND ADAPTATION: CASSANDRA JEAN
LETTERING: ABIGAIL BLACKMAN

Text copyright © 2009 by Cassandra Clare, LLC

Illustrations © 2022 by Yen Press, LLC

Yen Press
150 West 30th Street, 19th Floor
New York, NY 10001

Visit us at yenpress.com
facebook.com/yenpress
twitter.com/yenpress
yenpress.tumblr.com
instagram.com/yenpress

First Yen Press Edition: February 2022

Yen Press is an imprint of Yen Press, LLC.
The Yen Press name and logo are trademarks of Yen Press, LLC.

The publisher is not responsible for websites (or their content) that are not owned by the publisher.

Library of Congress Control Number: 2017945496

ISBNs: 978-1-9753-4126-8 (paperback)
978-1-9753-4127-5 (ebook)

10 9 8 7 6 5 4 3 2 1

WOR

Printed in the United States of America

Chapter 25

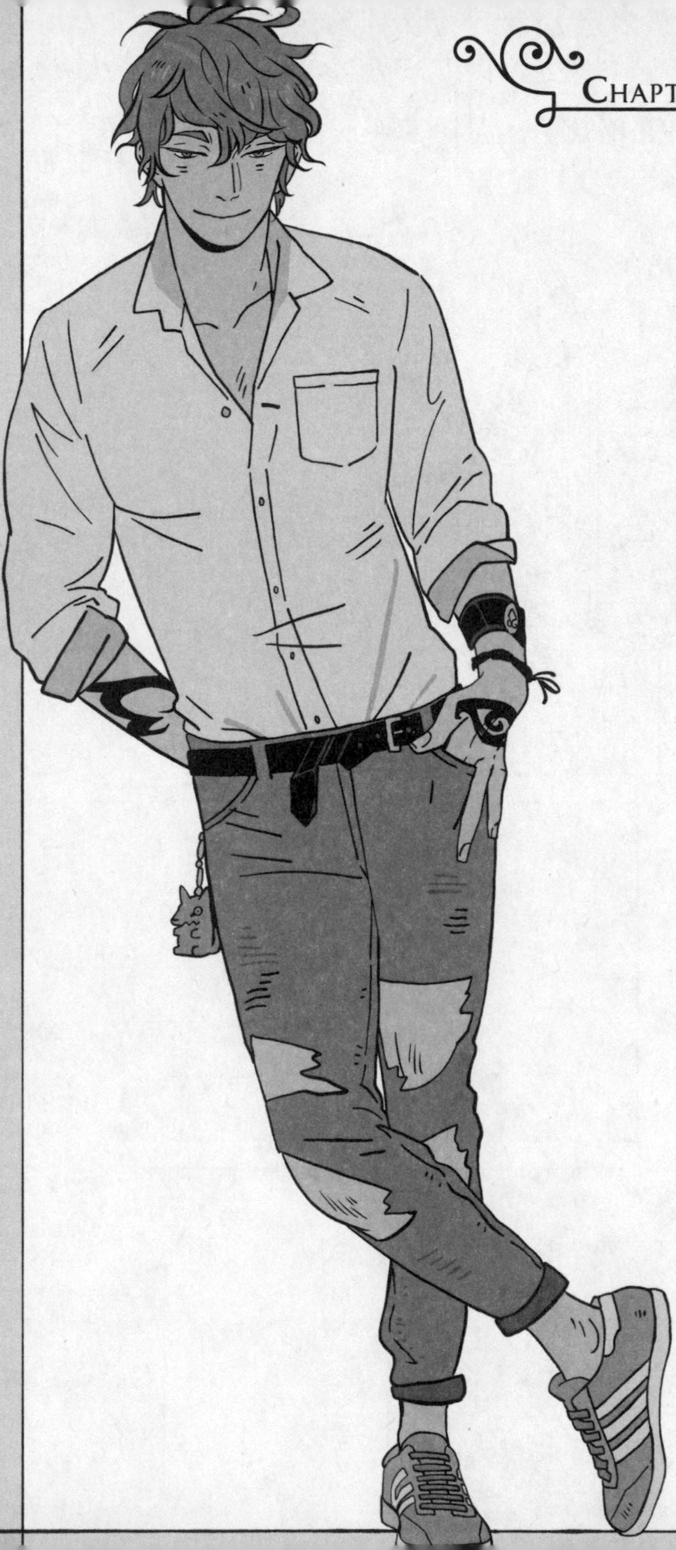

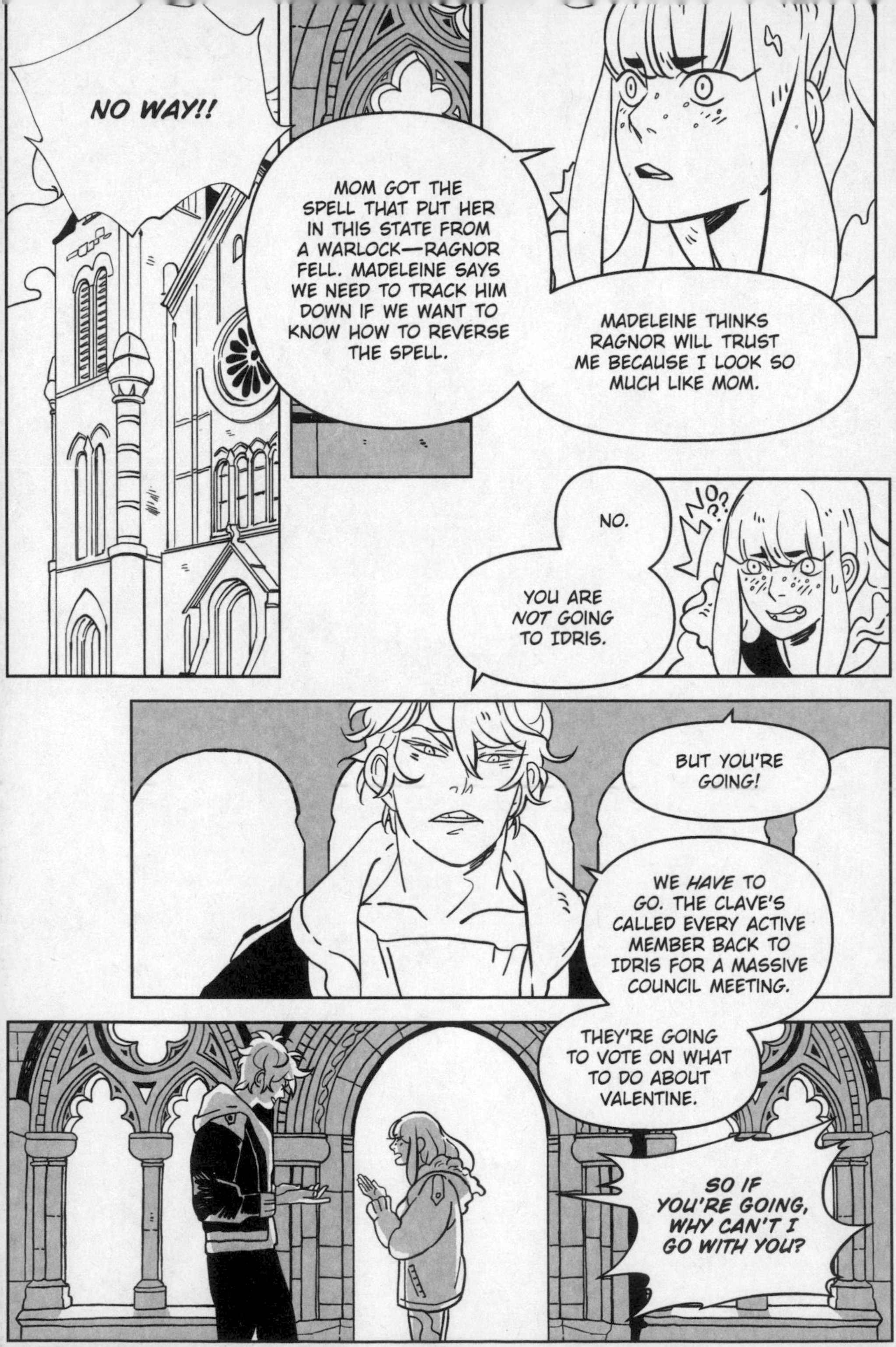
NO WAY!!
MOM GOT THE SPELL THAT PUT HER IN THIS STATE FROM A WARLOCK—RAGNOR FELL. MADELEINE SAYS WE NEED TO TRACK HIM DOWN IF WE WANT TO KNOW HOW TO REVERSE THE SPELL.
MADELEINE THINKS RAGNOR WILL TRUST ME BECAUSE I LOOK SO MUCH LIKE MOM.
NO.
YOU ARE *NOT* GOING TO IDRIS.
NO??
BUT YOU'RE *GOING!*
WE *HAVE* TO GO. THE CLAVE'S CALLED EVERY ACTIVE MEMBER BACK TO IDRIS FOR A MASSIVE COUNCIL MEETING.
THEY'RE GOING TO VOTE ON WHAT TO DO ABOUT VALENTINE.
SO IF YOU'RE GOING, WHY CAN'T I GO WITH YOU?

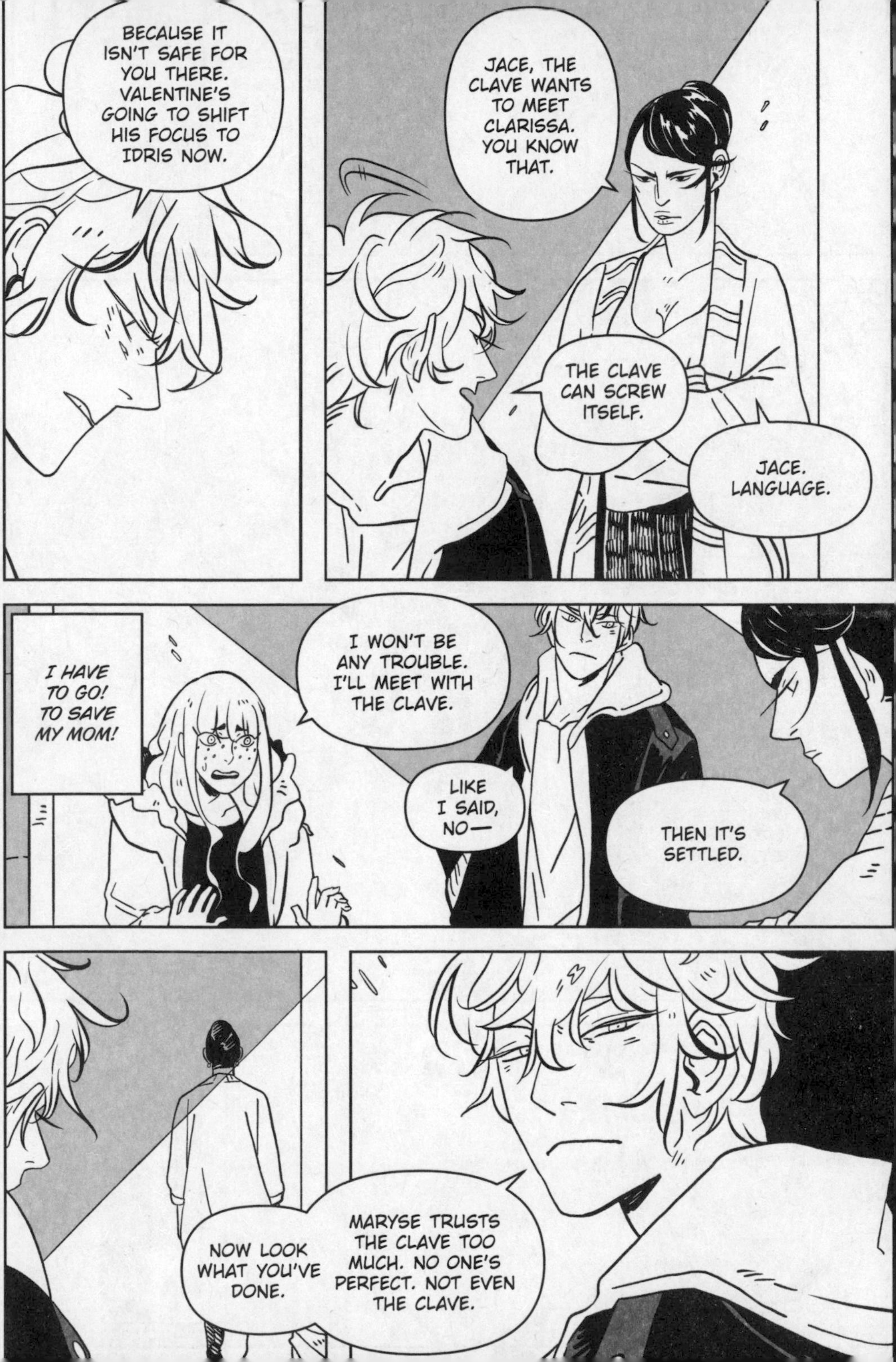
BECAUSE IT ISN'T SAFE FOR YOU THERE. VALENTINE'S GOING TO SHIFT HIS FOCUS TO IDRIS NOW.
JACE, THE CLAVE WANTS TO MEET CLARISSA. YOU KNOW THAT.
THE CLAVE CAN SCREW ITSELF.
JACE. LANGUAGE.
I HAVE TO GO! TO SAVE MY MOM!
I WON'T BE ANY TROUBLE. I'LL MEET WITH THE CLAVE.
LIKE I SAID, NO—
THEN IT'S SETTLED.
NOW LOOK WHAT YOU'VE DONE.
MARYSE TRUSTS THE CLAVE TOO MUCH. NO ONE'S PERFECT. NOT EVEN THE CLAVE.

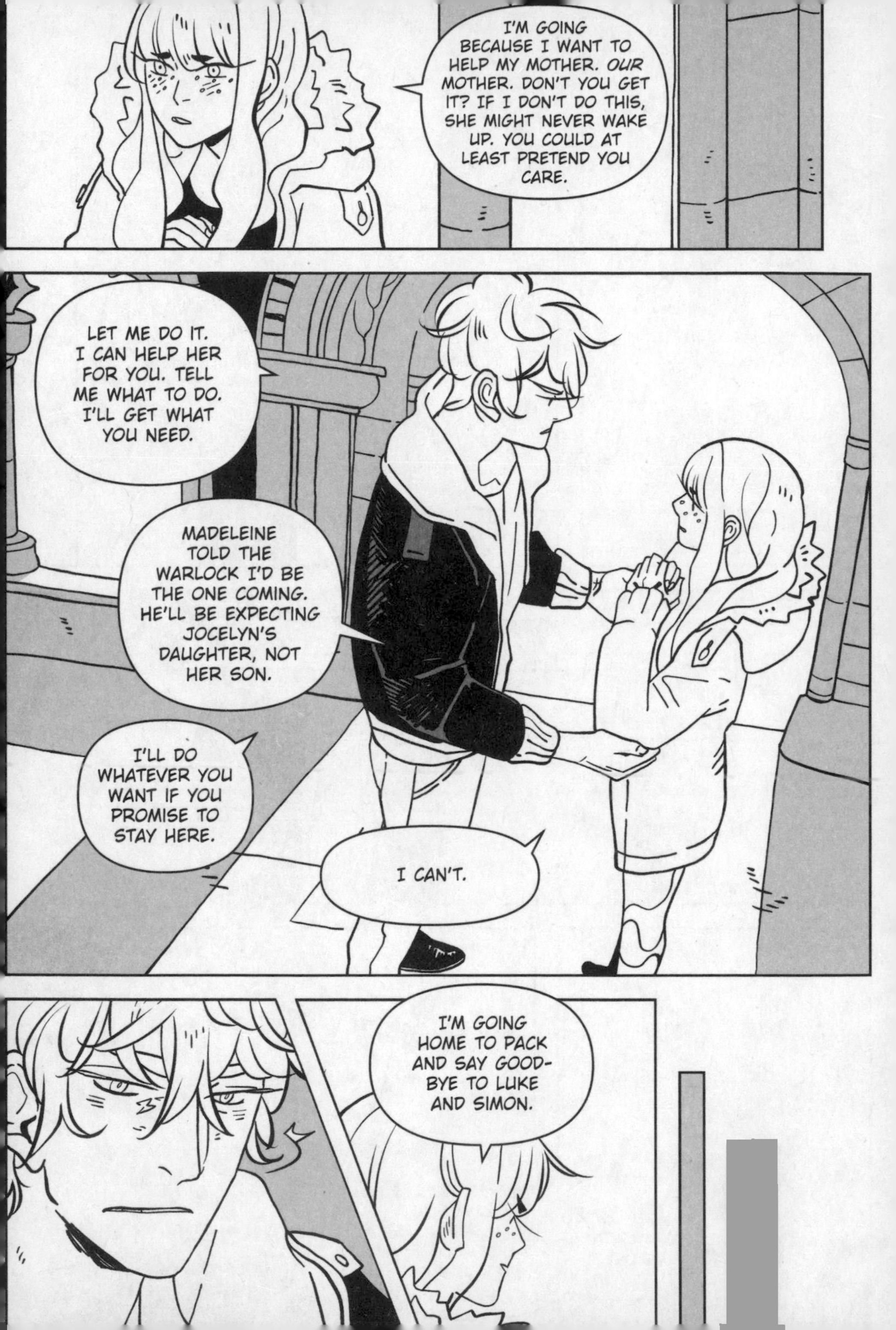
I'M GOING BECAUSE I WANT TO HELP MY MOTHER. *OUR* MOTHER. DON'T YOU GET IT? IF I DON'T DO THIS, SHE MIGHT NEVER WAKE UP. YOU COULD AT LEAST PRETEND YOU CARE.
LET ME DO IT. I CAN HELP HER FOR YOU. TELL ME WHAT TO DO. I'LL GET WHAT YOU NEED.
MADELEINE TOLD THE WARLOCK I'D BE THE ONE COMING. HE'LL BE EXPECTING JOCELYN'S DAUGHTER, NOT HER SON.
I'LL DO WHATEVER YOU WANT IF YOU PROMISE TO STAY HERE.
I CAN'T.
I'M GOING HOME TO PACK AND SAY GOOD-BYE TO LUKE AND SIMON.

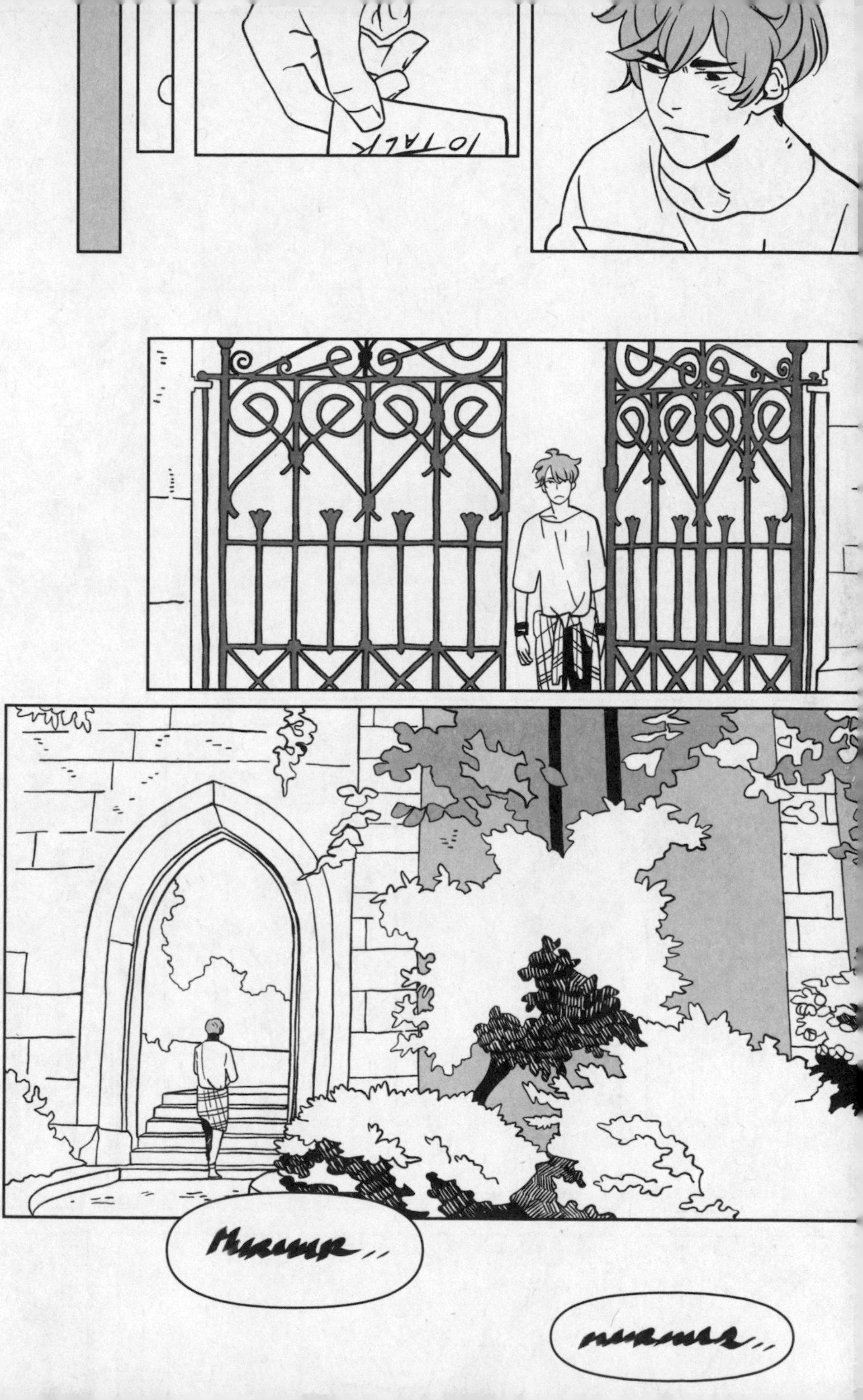

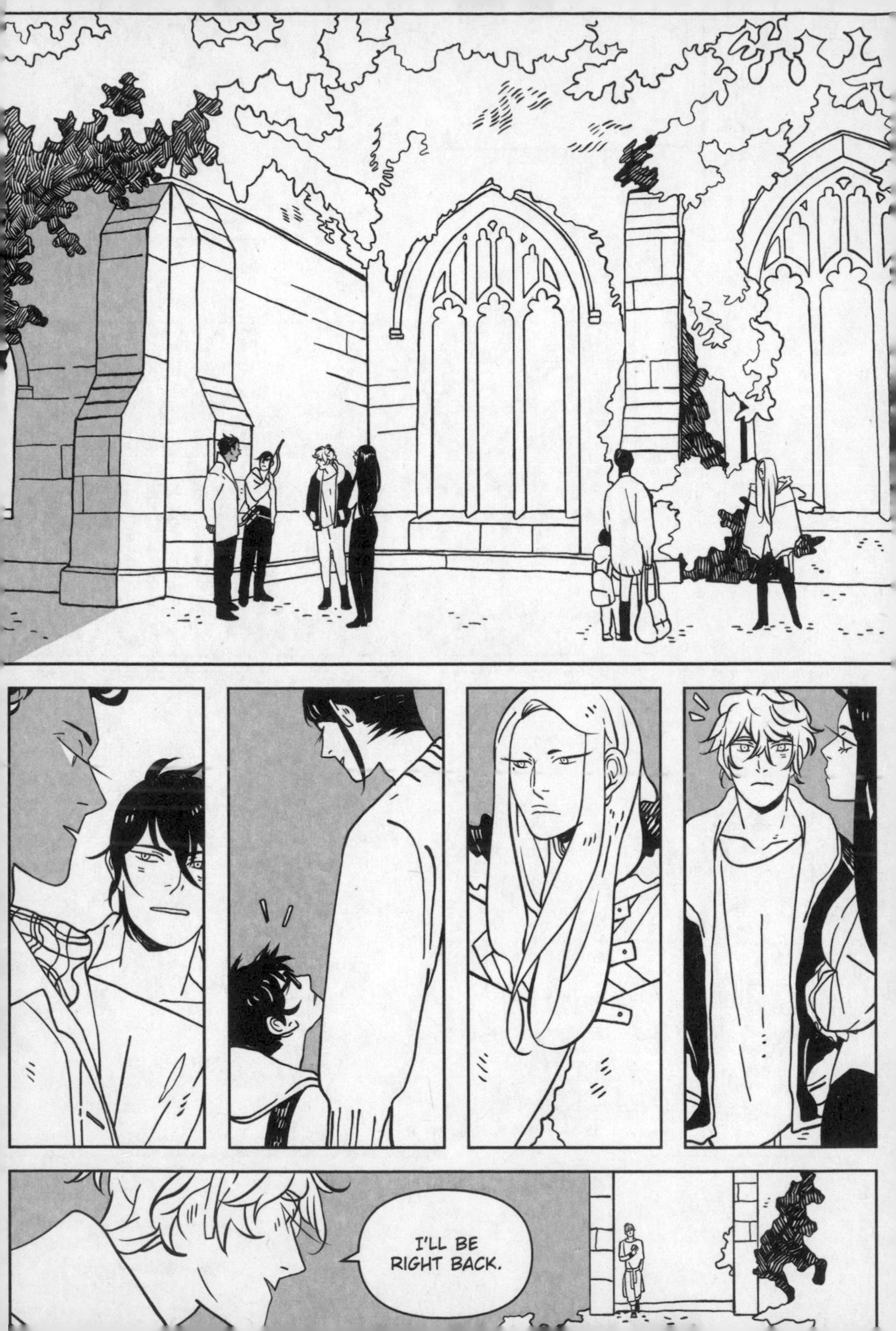
I'LL BE RIGHT BACK.

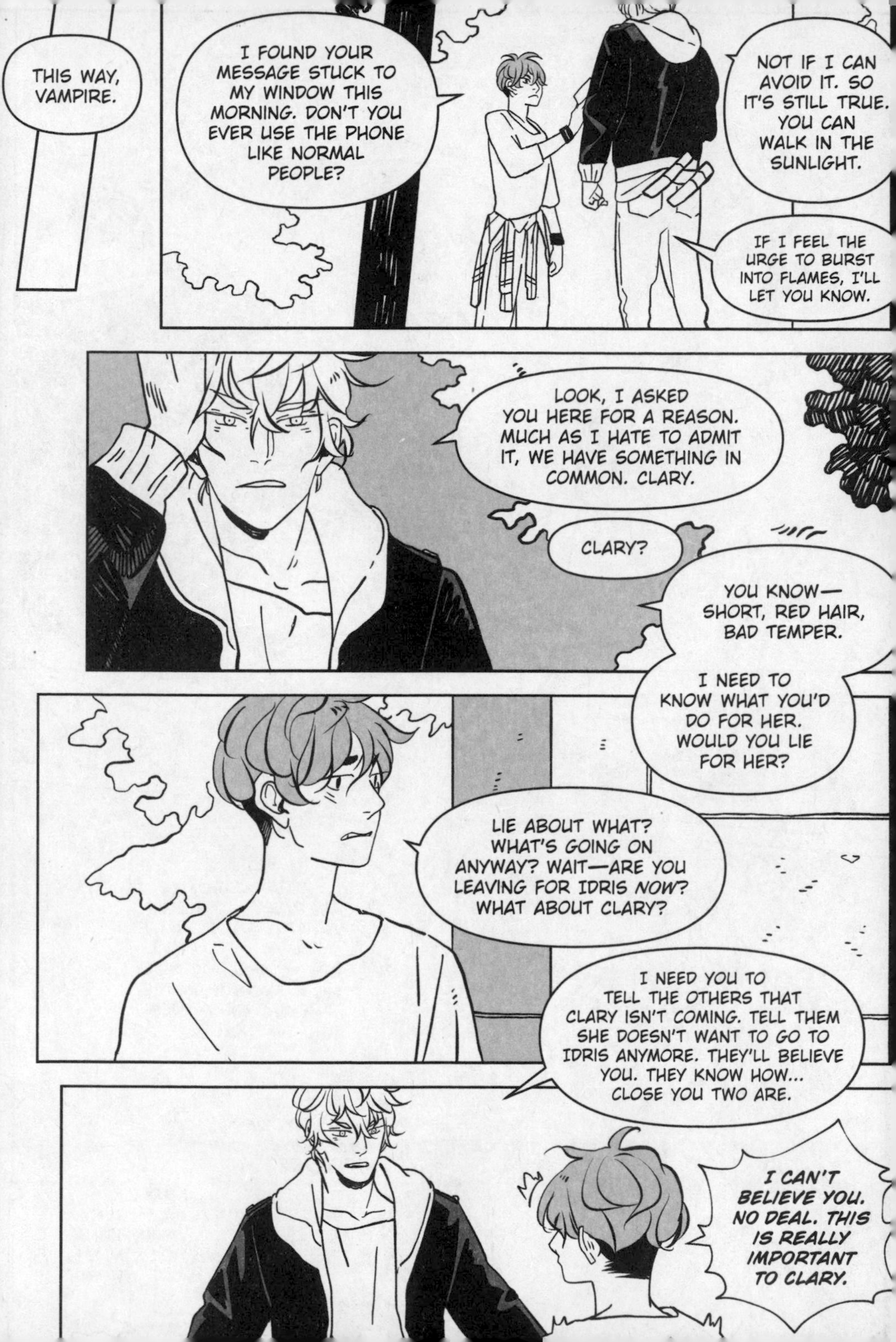
THIS WAY, VAMPIRE.
I FOUND YOUR MESSAGE STUCK TO MY WINDOW THIS MORNING. DON'T YOU EVER USE THE PHONE LIKE NORMAL PEOPLE?
NOT IF I CAN AVOID IT. SO IT'S STILL TRUE. YOU CAN WALK IN THE SUNLIGHT.
IF I FEEL THE URGE TO BURST INTO FLAMES, I'LL LET YOU KNOW.
LOOK, I ASKED YOU HERE FOR A REASON. MUCH AS I HATE TO ADMIT IT, WE HAVE SOMETHING IN COMMON. CLARY.
CLARY?
YOU KNOW— SHORT, RED HAIR, BAD TEMPER.
I NEED TO KNOW WHAT YOU'D DO FOR HER. WOULD YOU LIE FOR HER?
LIE ABOUT WHAT? WHAT'S GOING ON ANYWAY? WAIT—ARE YOU LEAVING FOR IDRIS *NOW*? WHAT ABOUT CLARY?
I NEED YOU TO TELL THE OTHERS THAT CLARY ISN'T COMING. TELL THEM SHE DOESN'T WANT TO GO TO IDRIS ANYMORE. THEY'LL BELIEVE YOU. THEY KNOW HOW... CLOSE YOU TWO ARE.
I CAN'T BELIEVE YOU. NO DEAL. THIS IS REALLY IMPORTANT TO CLARY.

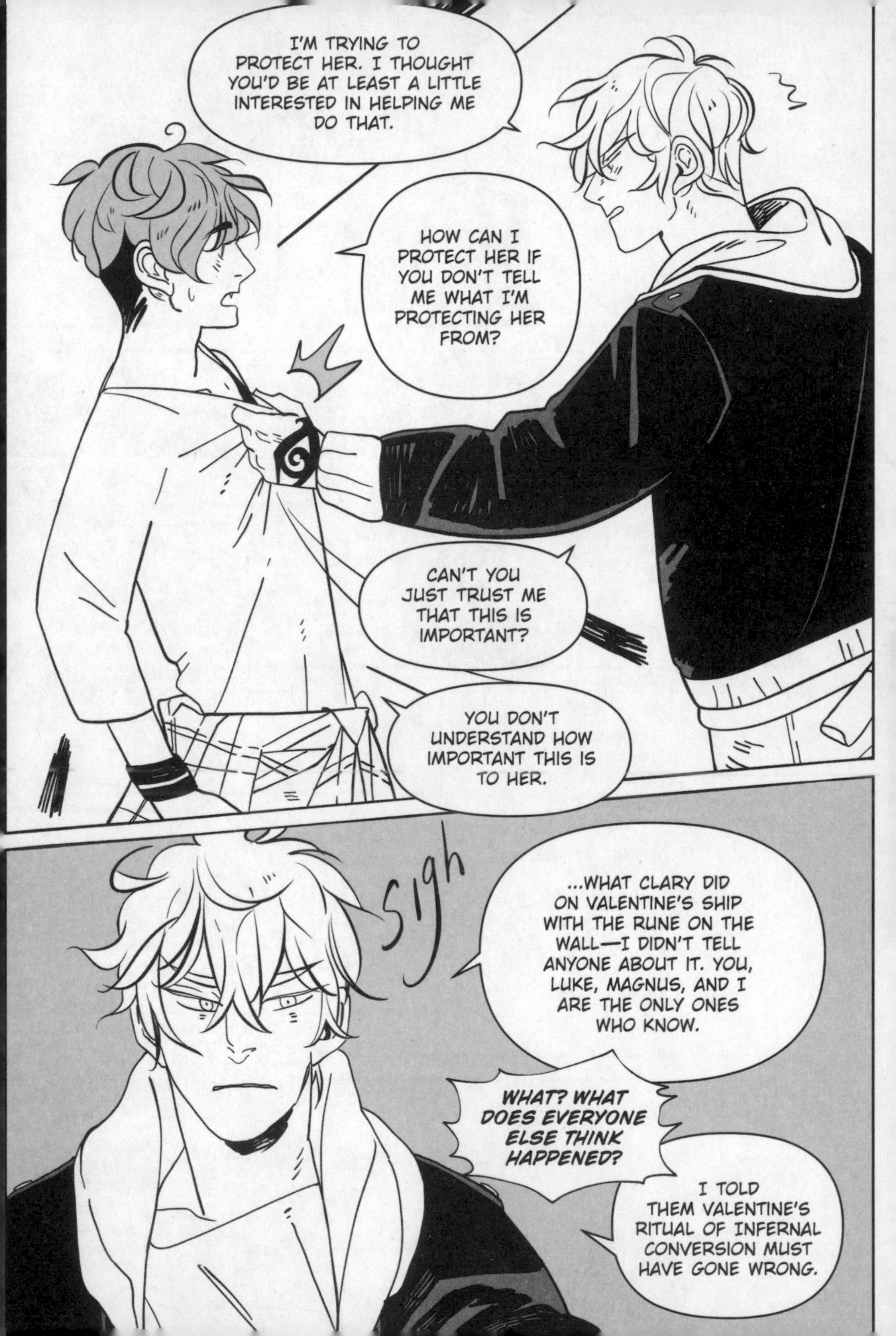
I'M TRYING TO PROTECT HER. I THOUGHT YOU'D BE AT LEAST A LITTLE INTERESTED IN HELPING ME DO THAT.
HOW CAN I PROTECT HER IF YOU DON'T TELL ME WHAT I'M PROTECTING HER FROM?
CAN'T YOU JUST TRUST ME THAT THIS IS IMPORTANT?
YOU DON'T UNDERSTAND HOW IMPORTANT THIS IS TO HER.
SIGH
...WHAT CLARY DID ON VALENTINE'S SHIP WITH THE RUNE ON THE WALL—I DIDN'T TELL ANYONE ABOUT IT. YOU, LUKE, MAGNUS, AND I ARE THE ONLY ONES WHO KNOW.
WHAT? WHAT DOES EVERYONE ELSE THINK HAPPENED?
I TOLD THEM VALENTINE'S RITUAL OF INFERNAL CONVERSION MUST HAVE GONE WRONG.

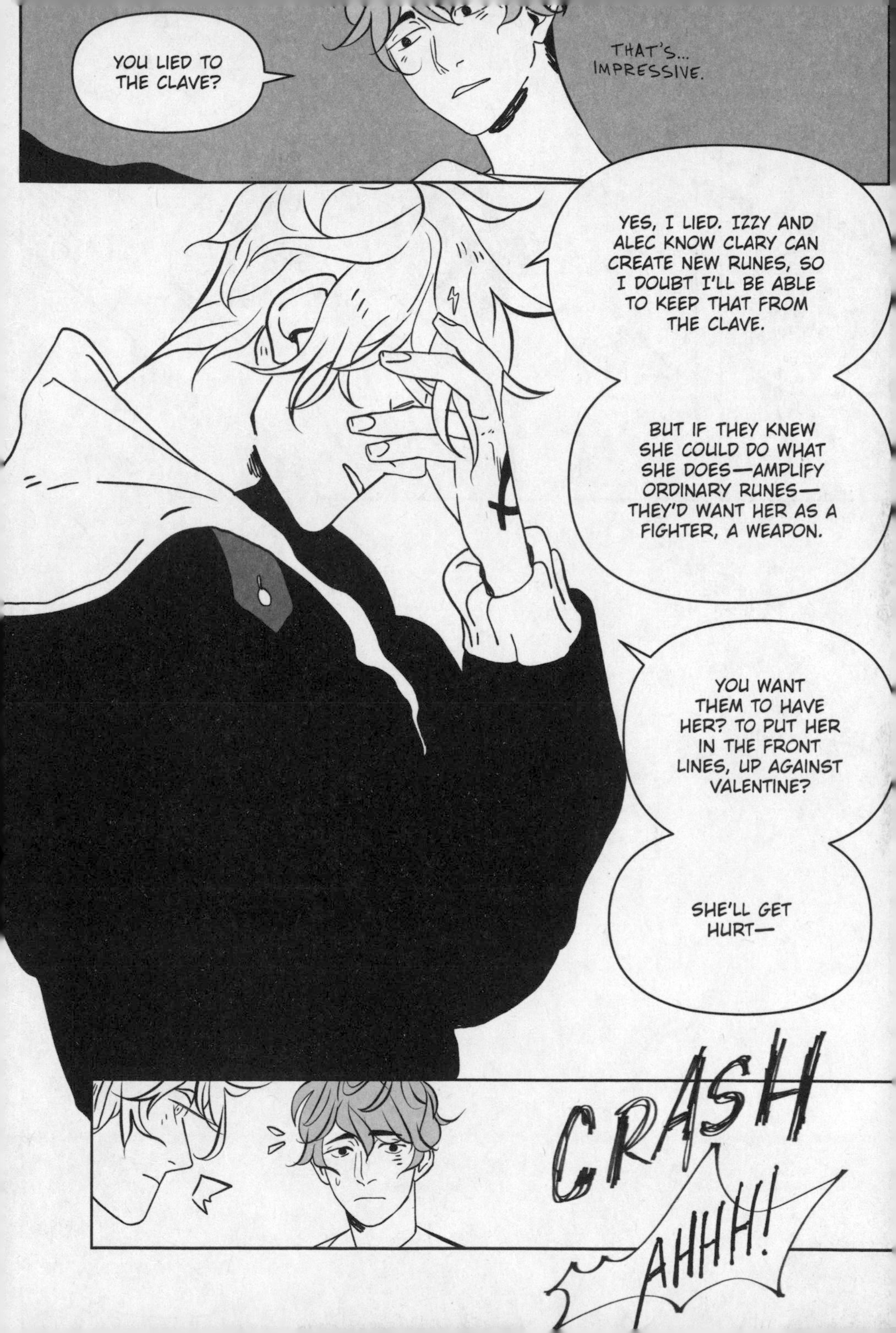

YOU LIED TO THE CLAVE?
THAT'S... IMPRESSIVE.
YES, I LIED. IZZY AND ALEC KNOW CLARY CAN CREATE NEW RUNES, SO I DOUBT I'LL BE ABLE TO KEEP THAT FROM THE CLAVE.
BUT IF THEY KNEW SHE COULD DO WHAT SHE DOES—AMPLIFY ORDINARY RUNES—THEY'D WANT HER AS A FIGHTER, A WEAPON.
YOU WANT THEM TO HAVE HER? TO PUT HER IN THE FRONT LINES, UP AGAINST VALENTINE?
SHE'LL GET HURT—
CRASH
AHHH!

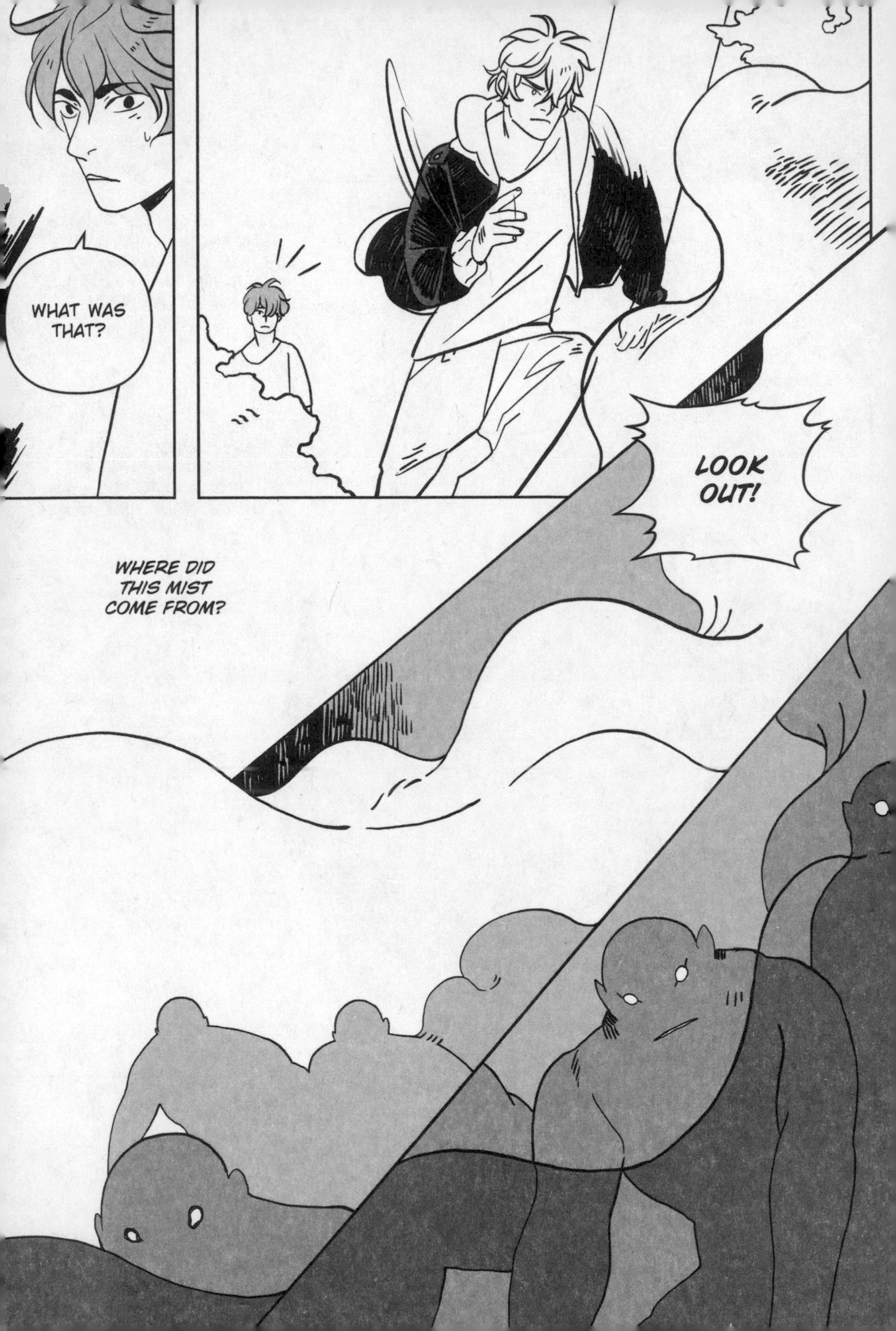
WHAT WAS THAT?
LOOK OUT!
WHERE DID THIS MIST COME FROM?

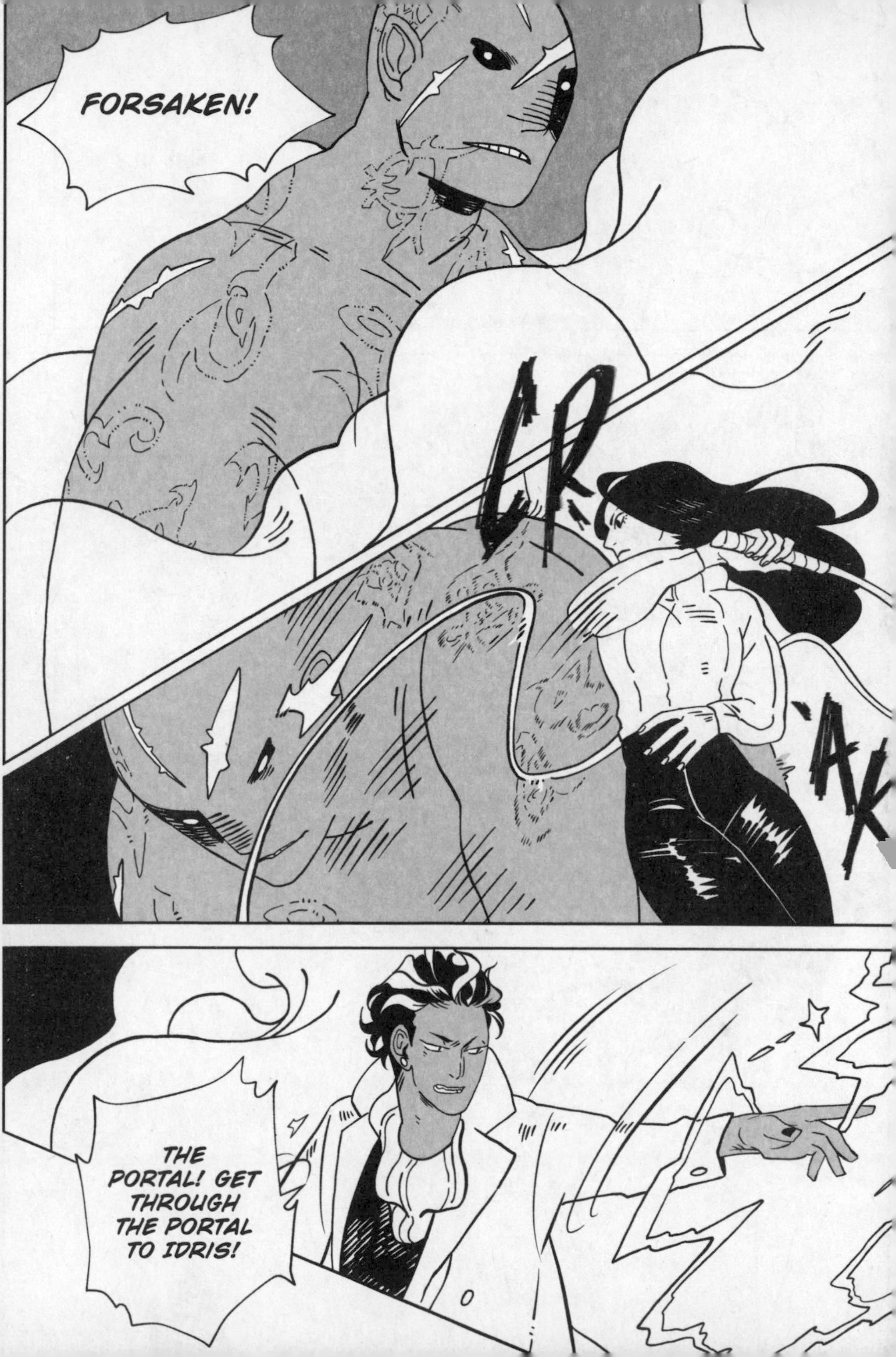
FORSAKEN!
CR
'AK
THE PORTAL! GET THROUGH THE PORTAL TO IDRIS!

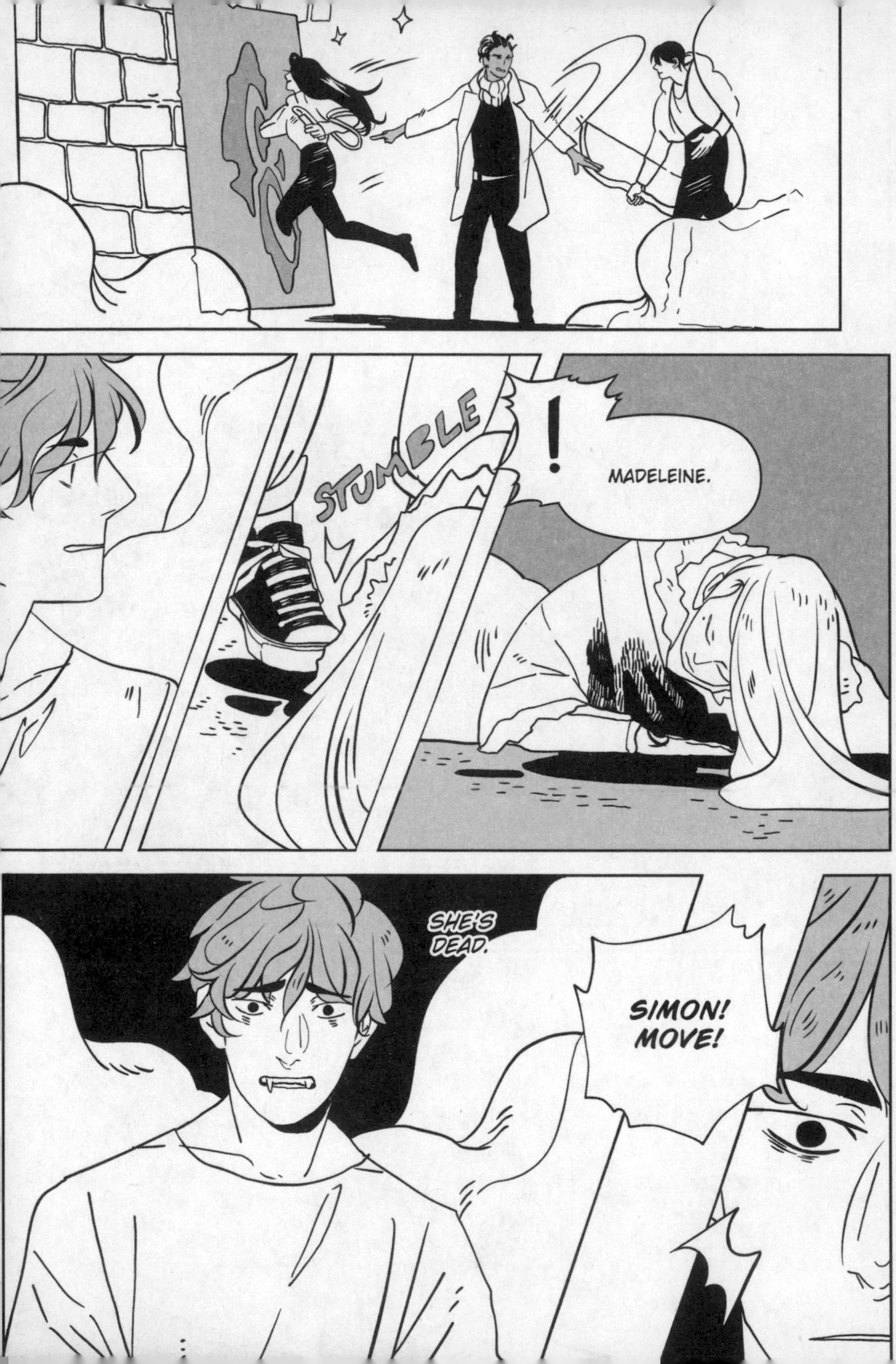
STUMBLE
!
MADELEINE.
SHE'S DEAD.
SIMON! MOVE!

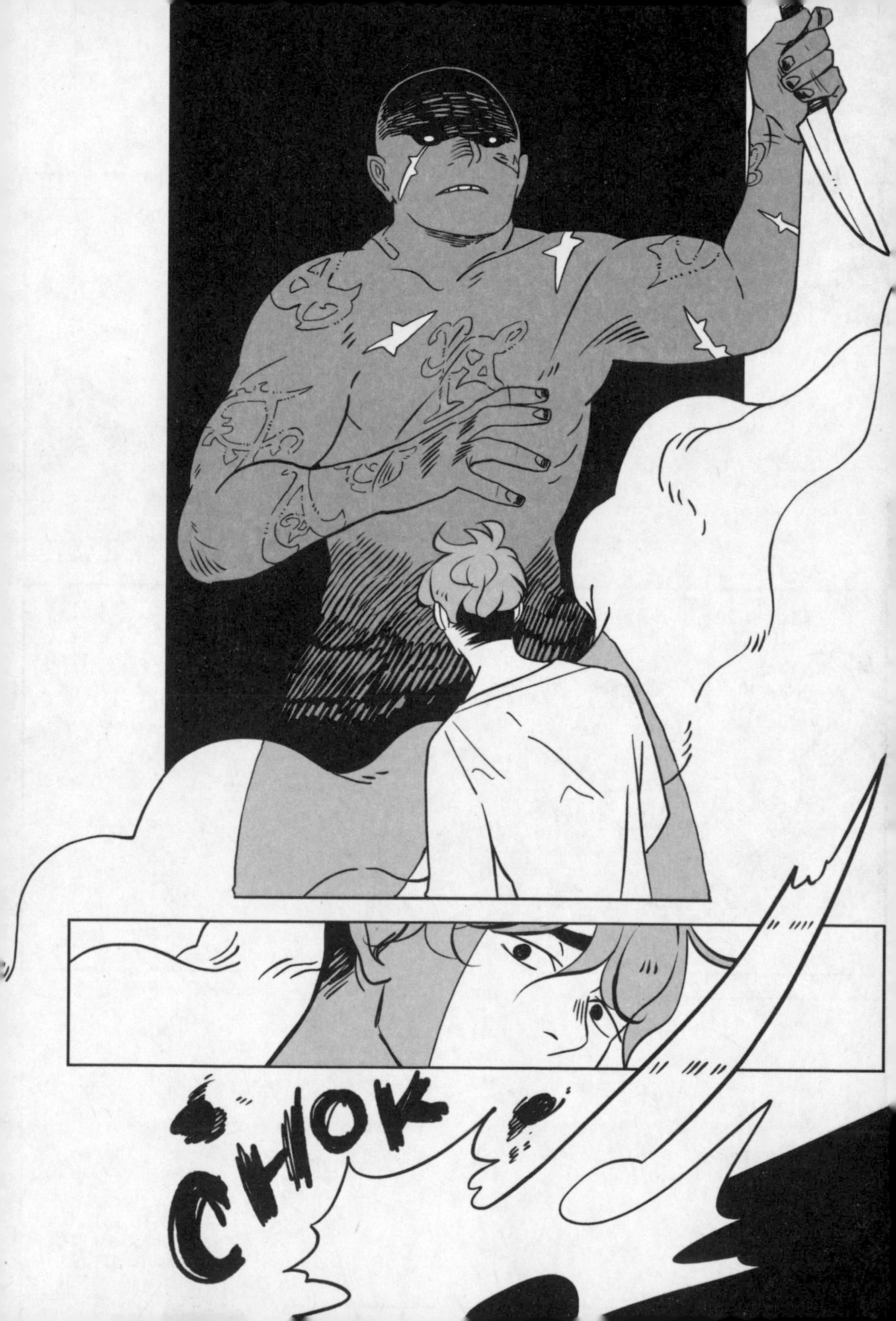
CHOK

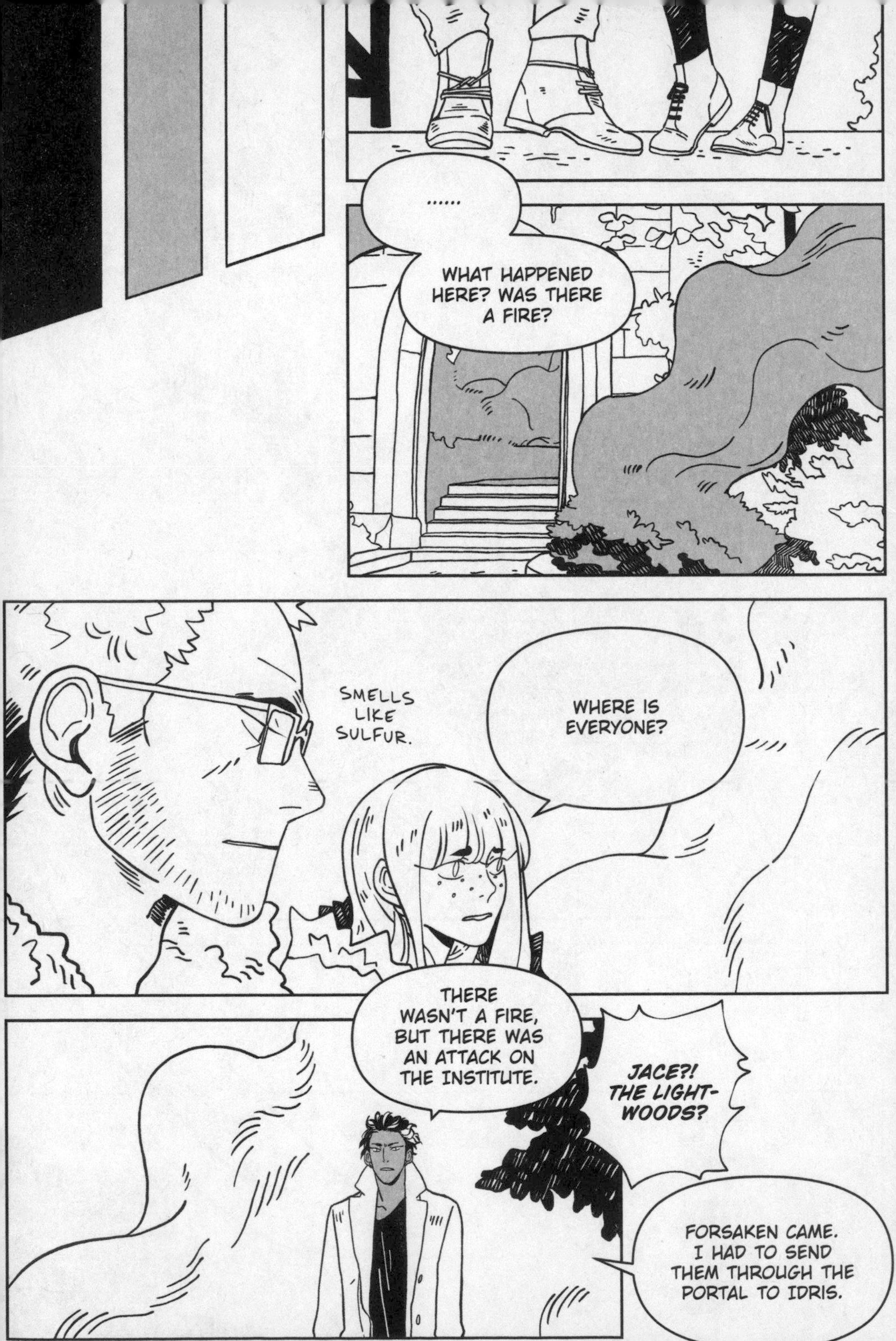
......
WHAT HAPPENED HERE? WAS THERE A FIRE?
SMELLS LIKE SULFUR.
WHERE IS EVERYONE?
THERE WASN'T A FIRE, BUT THERE WAS AN ATTACK ON THE INSTITUTE.
JACE?! THE LIGHT-WOODS?
FORSAKEN CAME. I HAD TO SEND THEM THROUGH THE PORTAL TO IDRIS.

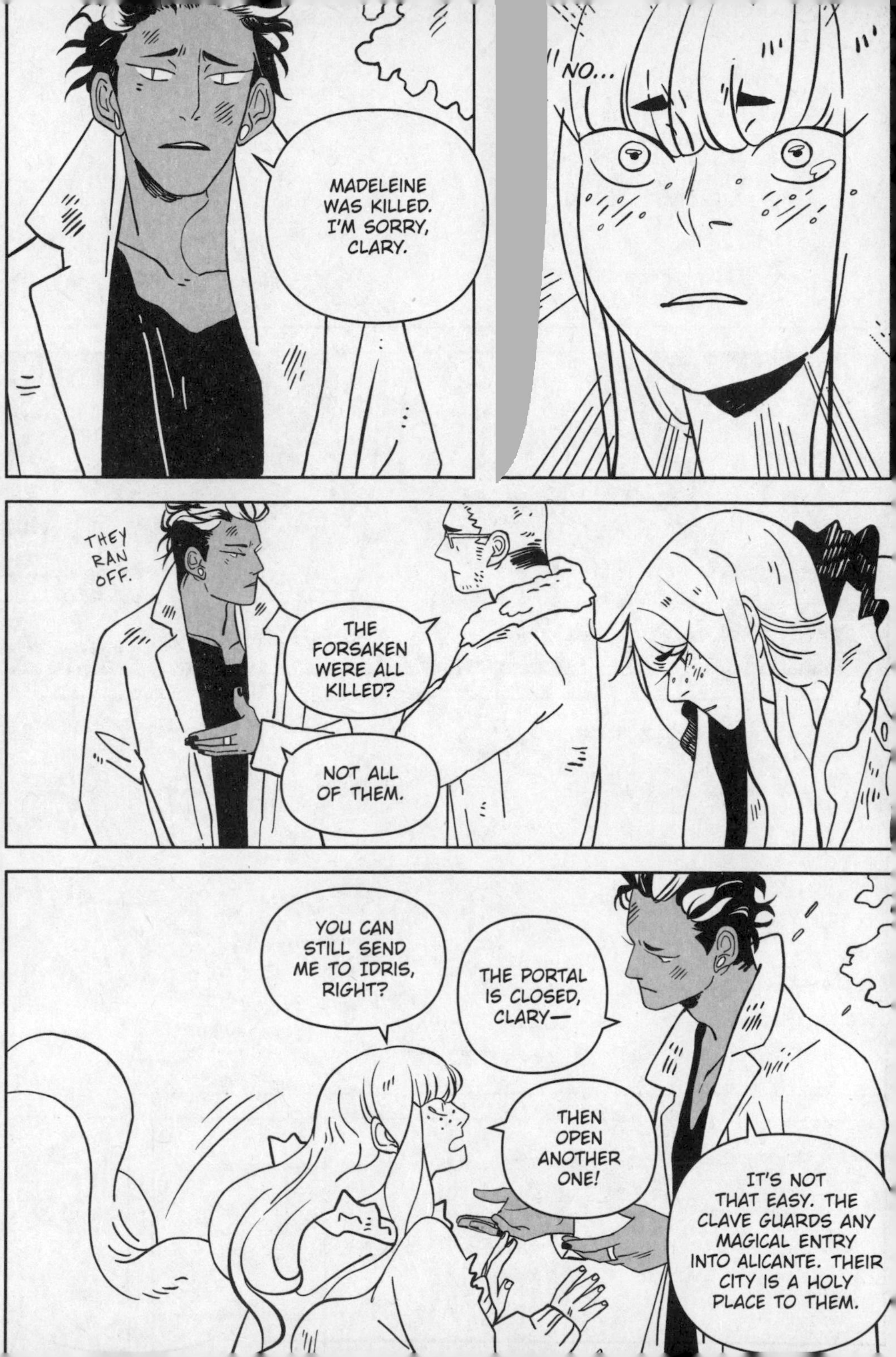
MADELEINE WAS KILLED. I'M SORRY, CLARY.
NO...
THEY RAN OFF.
THE FORSAKEN WERE ALL KILLED?
NOT ALL OF THEM.
YOU CAN STILL SEND ME TO IDRIS, RIGHT?
THE PORTAL IS CLOSED, CLARY—
THEN OPEN ANOTHER ONE!
IT'S NOT THAT EASY. THE CLAVE GUARDS ANY MAGICAL ENTRY INTO ALICANTE. THEIR CITY IS A HOLY PLACE TO THEM.

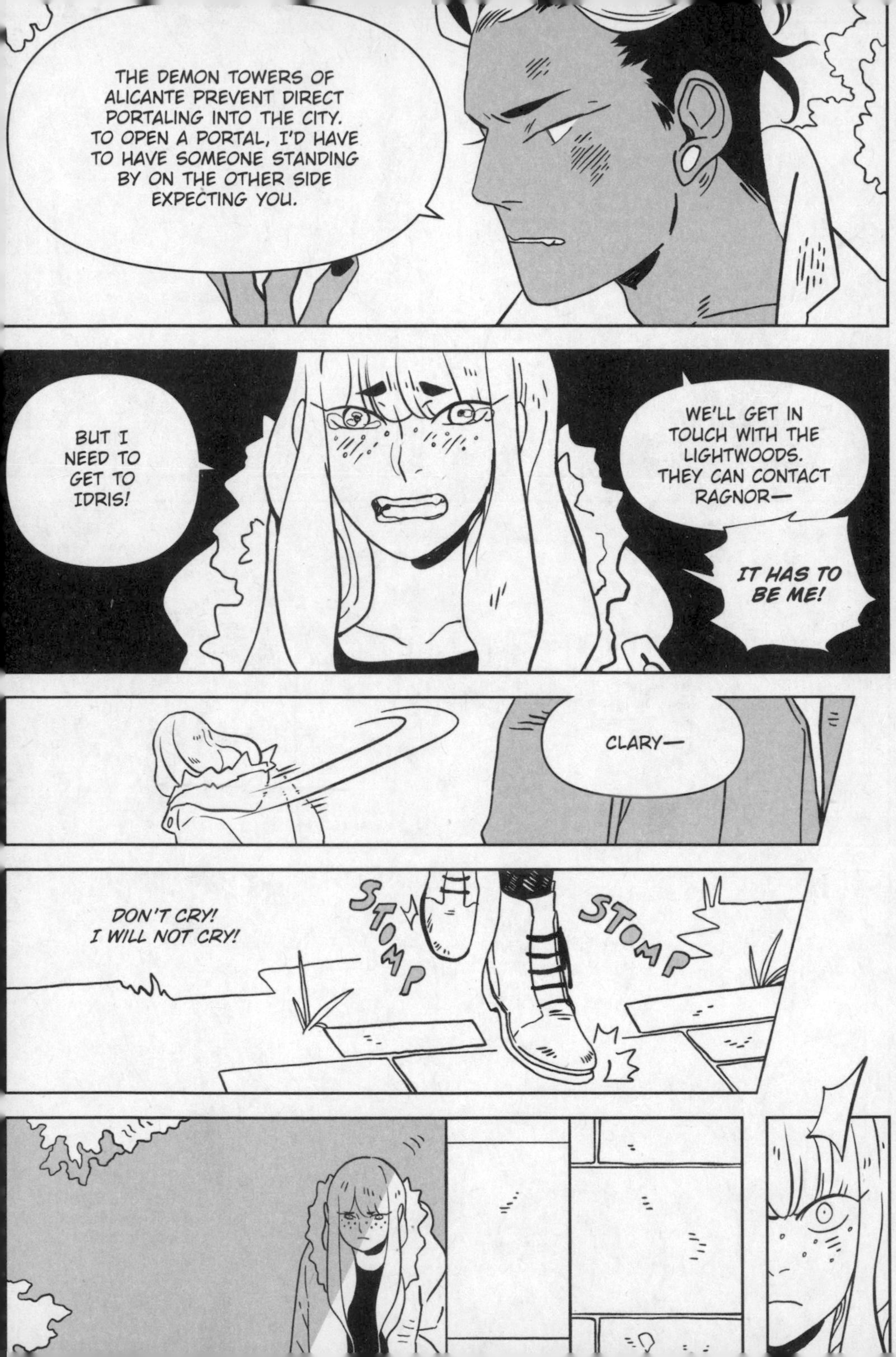
THE DEMON TOWERS OF ALICANTE PREVENT DIRECT PORTALING INTO THE CITY. TO OPEN A PORTAL, I'D HAVE TO HAVE SOMEONE STANDING BY ON THE OTHER SIDE EXPECTING YOU.
BUT I NEED TO GET TO IDRIS!
WE'LL GET IN TOUCH WITH THE LIGHTWOODS. THEY CAN CONTACT RAGNOR—
IT HAS TO BE ME!
CLARY—
DON'T CRY! I WILL NOT CRY!
STOMP
STOMP

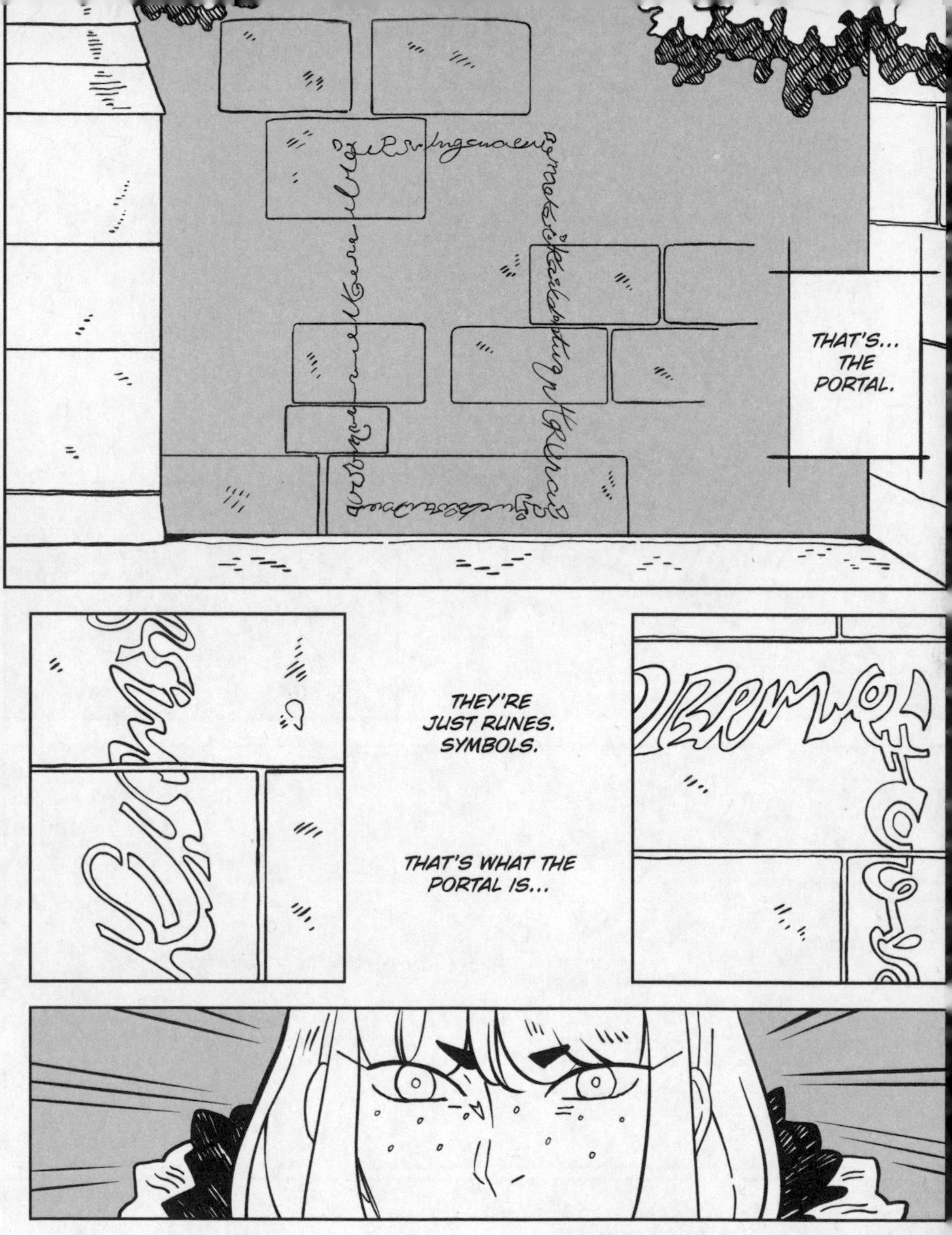
THAT'S...
THE
PORTAL.
THEY'RE
JUST RUNES.
SYMBOLS.
THAT'S WHAT THE
PORTAL IS...

IF MY MOTHER CAN TRAP THE ESSENCE OF
THE MORTAL CUP INSIDE A PIECE OF PAPER,
THEN I CAN MAKE A PORTAL.

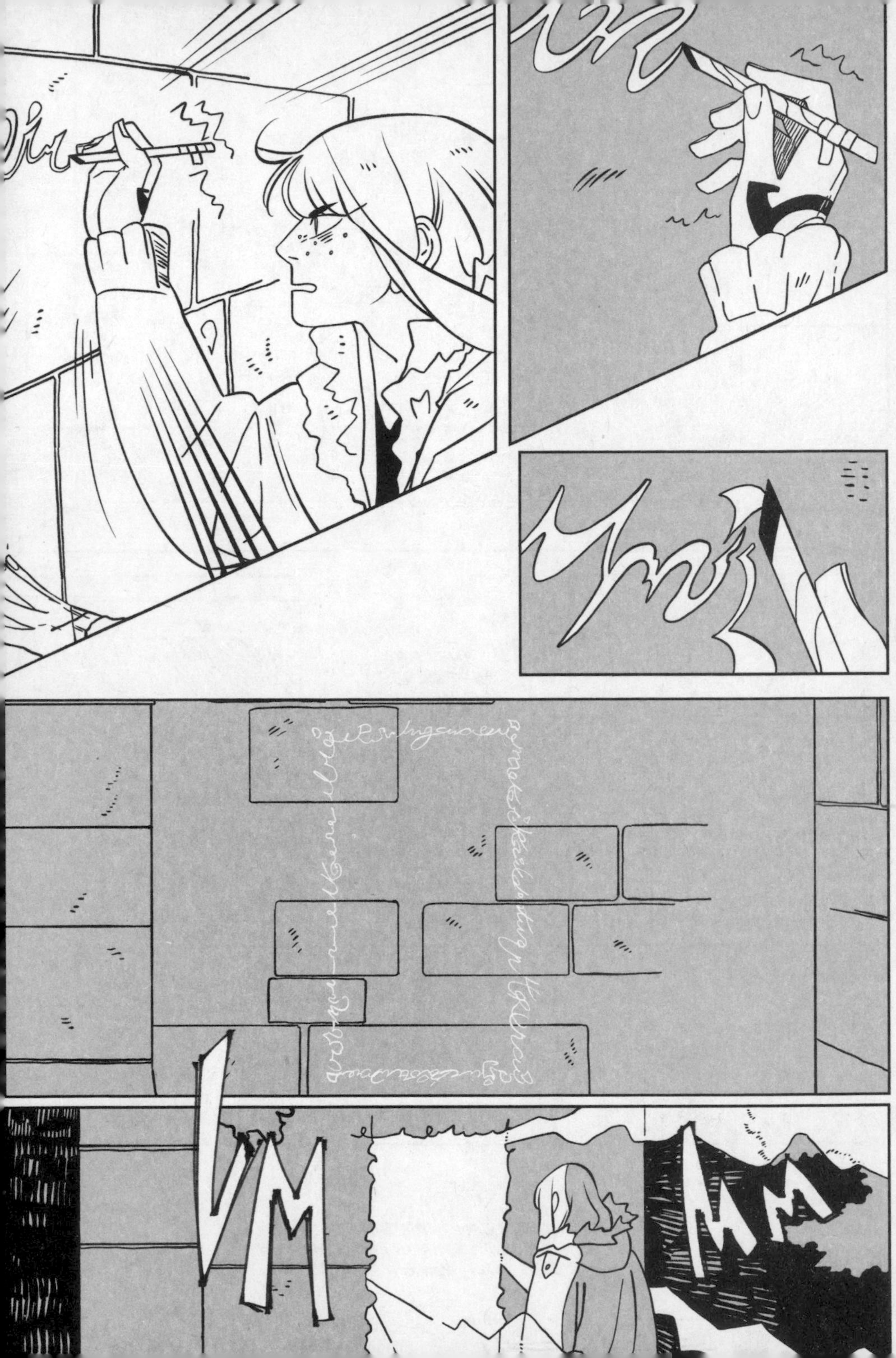

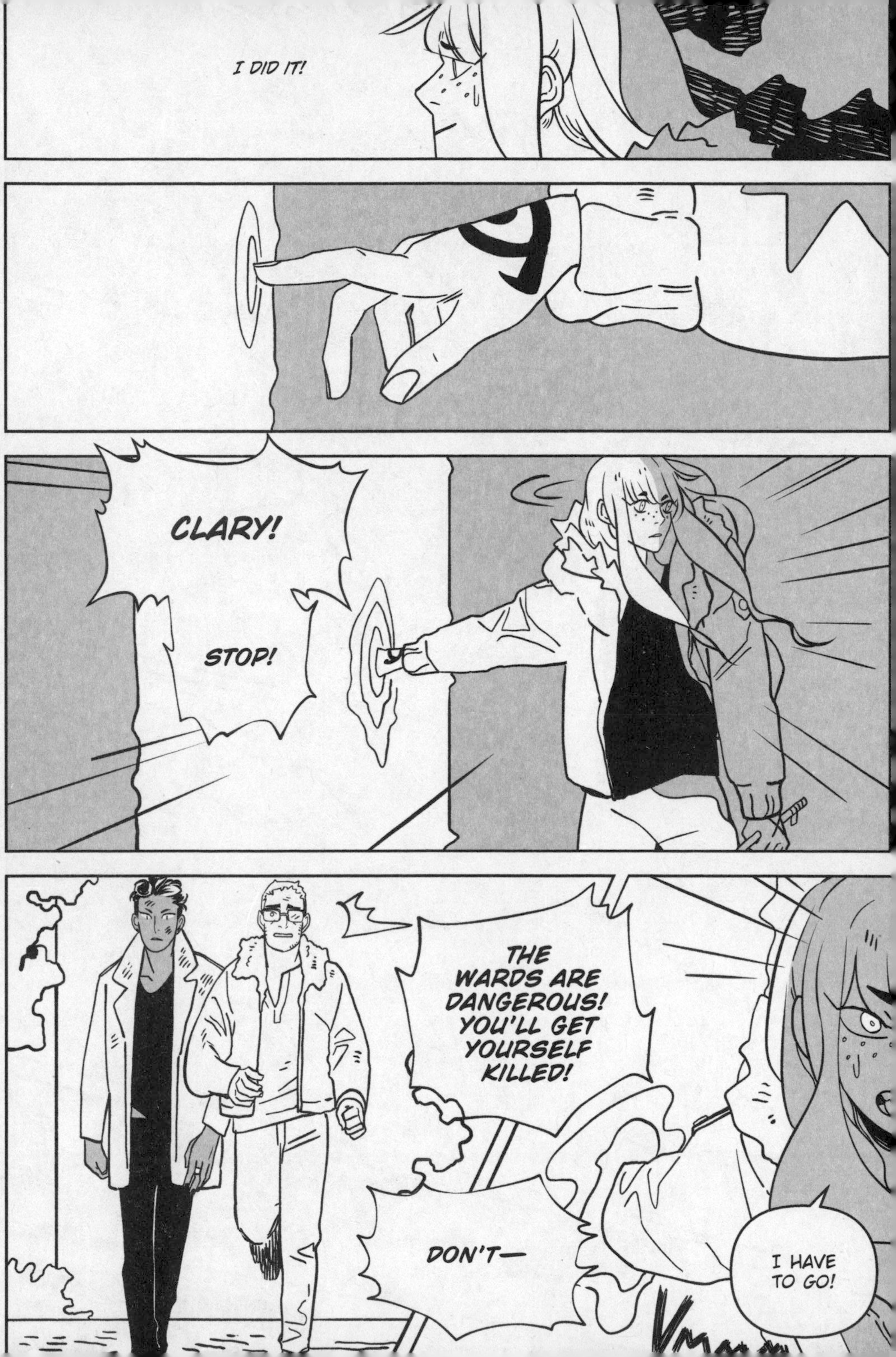
I DID IT!
CLARY!
STOP!
THE WARDS ARE DANGEROUS! YOU'LL GET YOURSELF KILLED!
DON'T—
I HAVE TO GO!

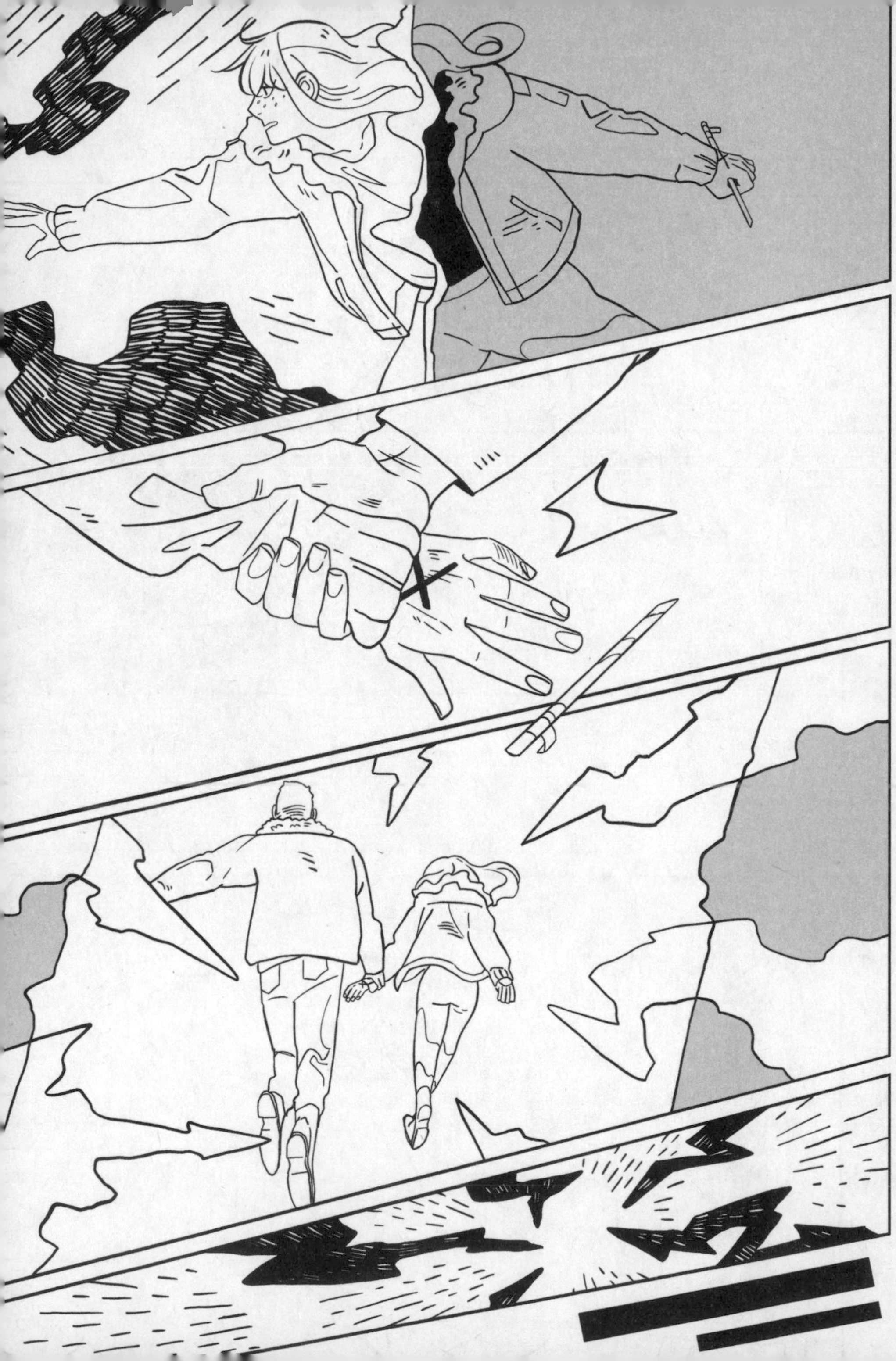

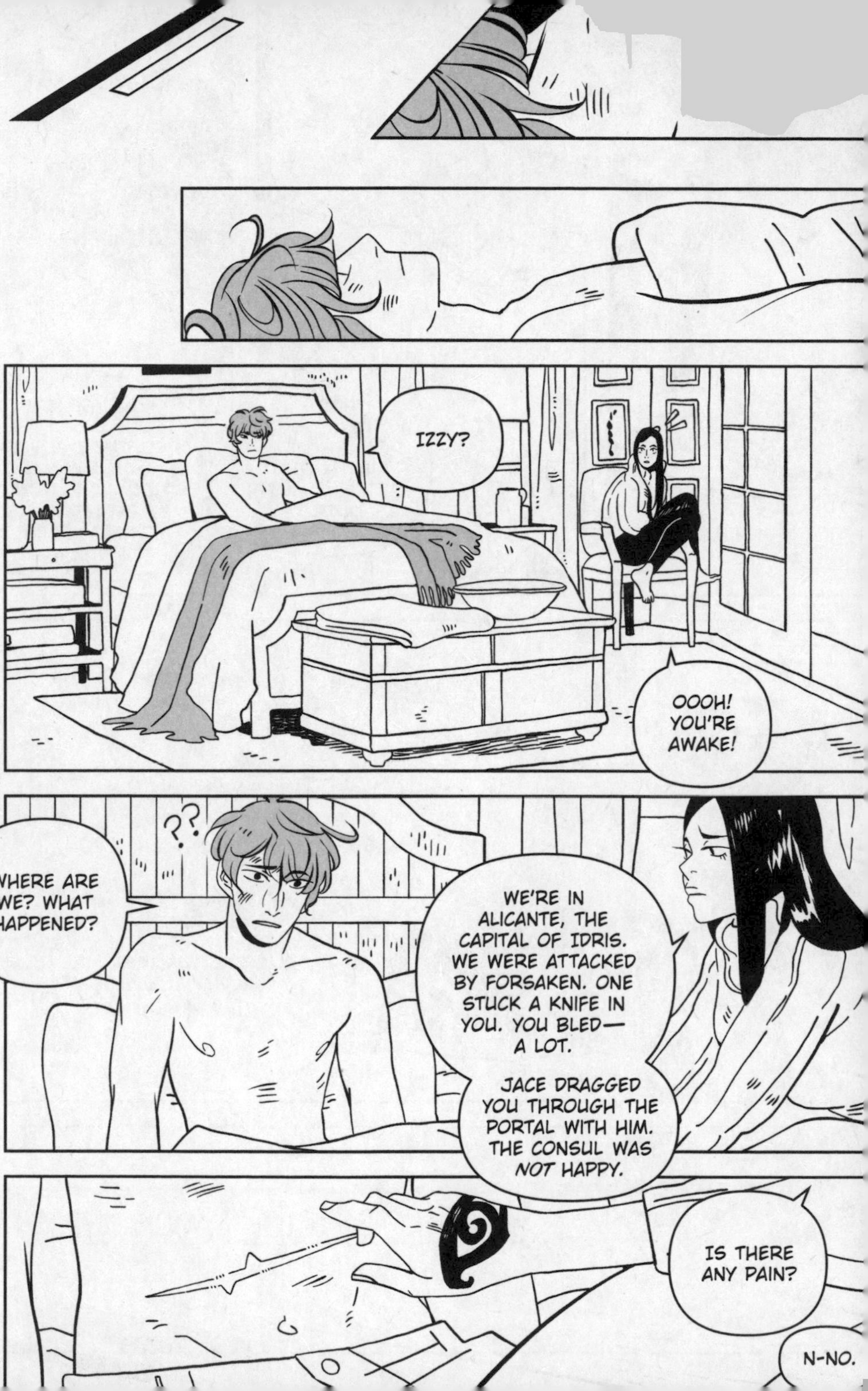
IZZY?
OOOH! YOU'RE AWAKE!
WHERE ARE WE? WHAT HAPPENED?
WE'RE IN ALICANTE, THE CAPITAL OF IDRIS. WE WERE ATTACKED BY FORSAKEN. ONE STUCK A KNIFE IN YOU. YOU BLED— A LOT.
JACE DRAGGED YOU THROUGH THE PORTAL WITH HIM. THE CONSUL WAS *NOT* HAPPY.
IS THERE ANY PAIN?
N-NO.

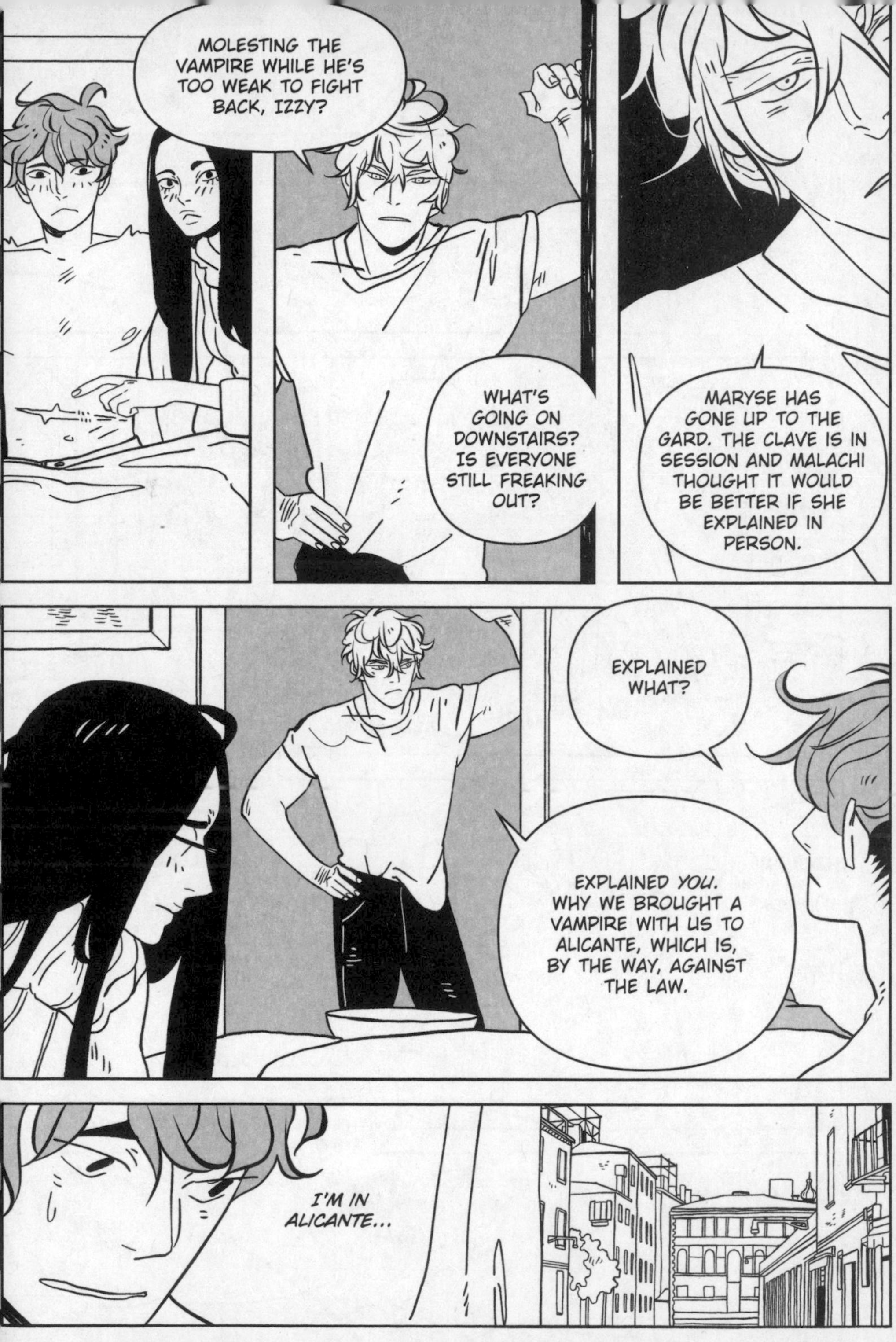
MOLESTING THE VAMPIRE WHILE HE'S TOO WEAK TO FIGHT BACK, IZZY?
WHAT'S GOING ON DOWNSTAIRS? IS EVERYONE STILL FREAKING OUT?
MARYSE HAS GONE UP TO THE GARD. THE CLAVE IS IN SESSION AND MALACHI THOUGHT IT WOULD BE BETTER IF SHE EXPLAINED IN PERSON.
EXPLAINED WHAT?
EXPLAINED *YOU*. WHY WE BROUGHT A VAMPIRE WITH US TO ALICANTE, WHICH IS, BY THE WAY, AGAINST THE LAW.
I'M IN ALICANTE...

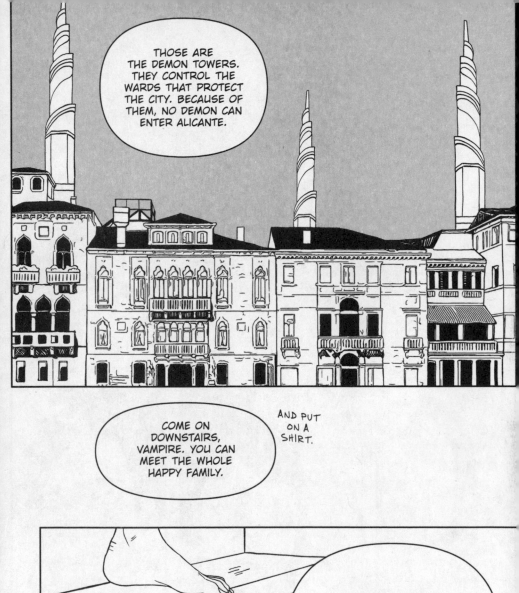

THOSE ARE THE DEMON TOWERS. THEY CONTROL THE WARDS THAT PROTECT THE CITY. BECAUSE OF THEM, NO DEMON CAN ENTER ALICANTE.

COME ON DOWNSTAIRS, VAMPIRE. YOU CAN MEET THE WHOLE HAPPY FAMILY.

AND PUT ON A SHIRT.

THIS IS THE PENHALLOW'S HOUSE. JIA AND PATRICK PENHALLOW USED TO RUN THE BEIJING INSTITUTE. WE'RE STAYING WITH THEM, SINCE WE DON'T HAVE A HOUSE WITHIN ALICANTE.

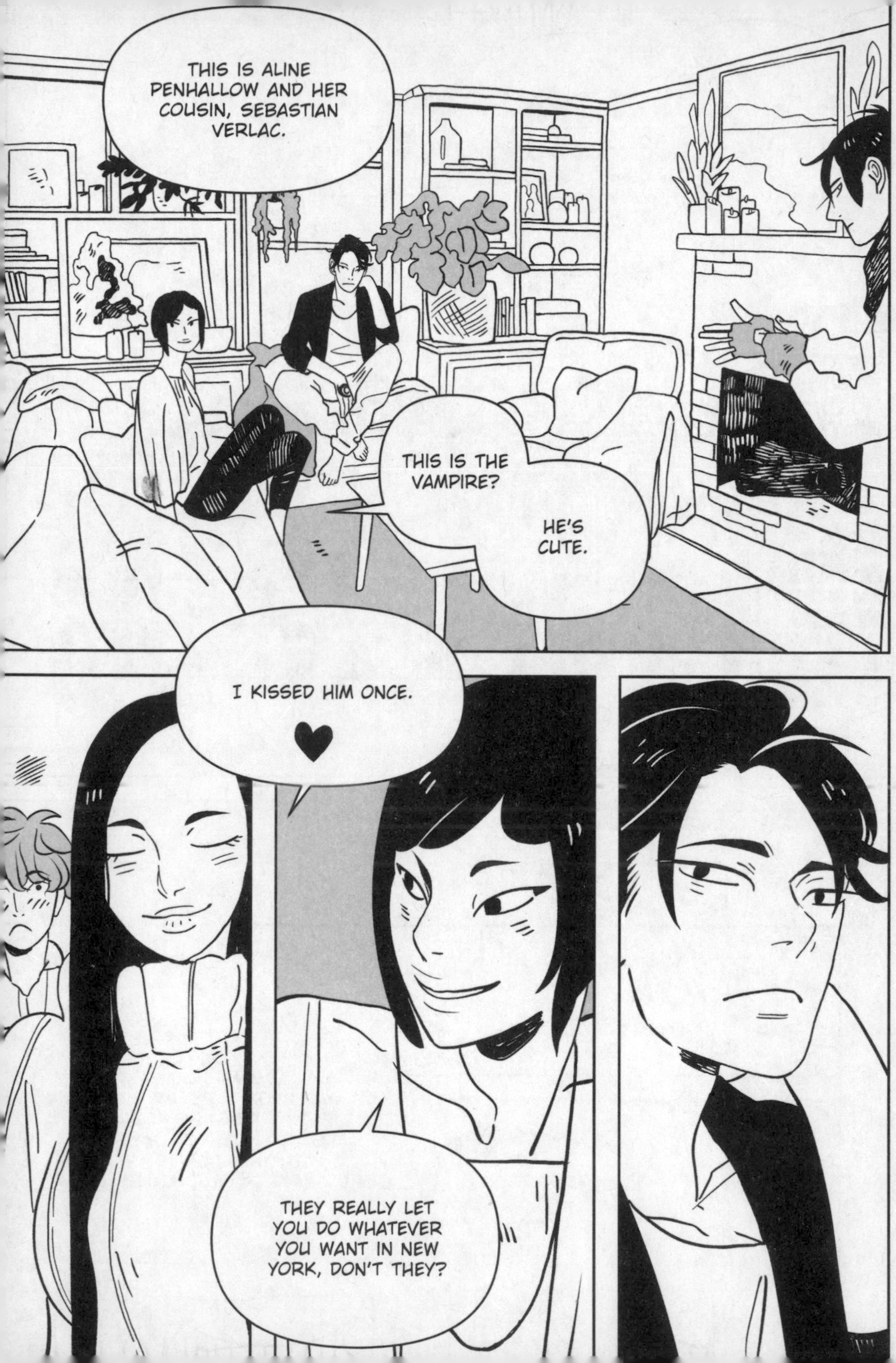
THIS IS ALINE PENHALLOW AND HER COUSIN, SEBASTIAN VERLAC.
THIS IS THE VAMPIRE?
HE'S CUTE.
I KISSED HIM ONCE.
THEY REALLY LET YOU DO WHATEVER YOU WANT IN NEW YORK, DON'T THEY?

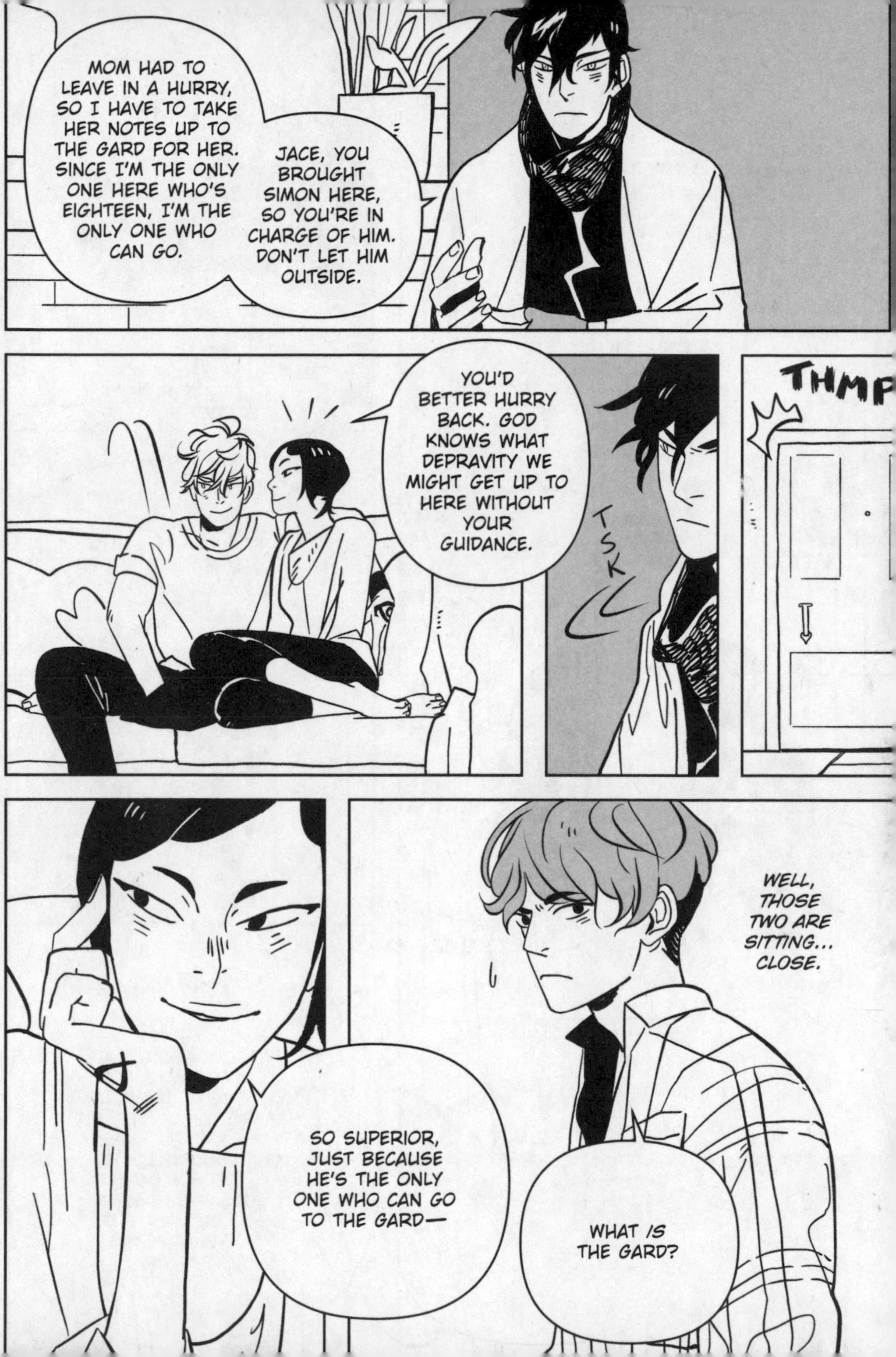
MOM HAD TO LEAVE IN A HURRY, SO I HAVE TO TAKE HER NOTES UP TO THE GARD FOR HER. SINCE I'M THE ONLY ONE HERE WHO'S EIGHTEEN, I'M THE ONLY ONE WHO CAN GO.
JACE, YOU BROUGHT SIMON HERE, SO YOU'RE IN CHARGE OF HIM. DON'T LET HIM OUTSIDE.
YOU'D BETTER HURRY BACK. GOD KNOWS WHAT DEPRAVITY WE MIGHT GET UP TO HERE WITHOUT YOUR GUIDANCE.
TSK
THMP
SO SUPERIOR, JUST BECAUSE HE'S THE ONLY ONE WHO CAN GO TO THE GARD—
WELL, THOSE TWO ARE SITTING... CLOSE.
WHAT *IS* THE GARD?

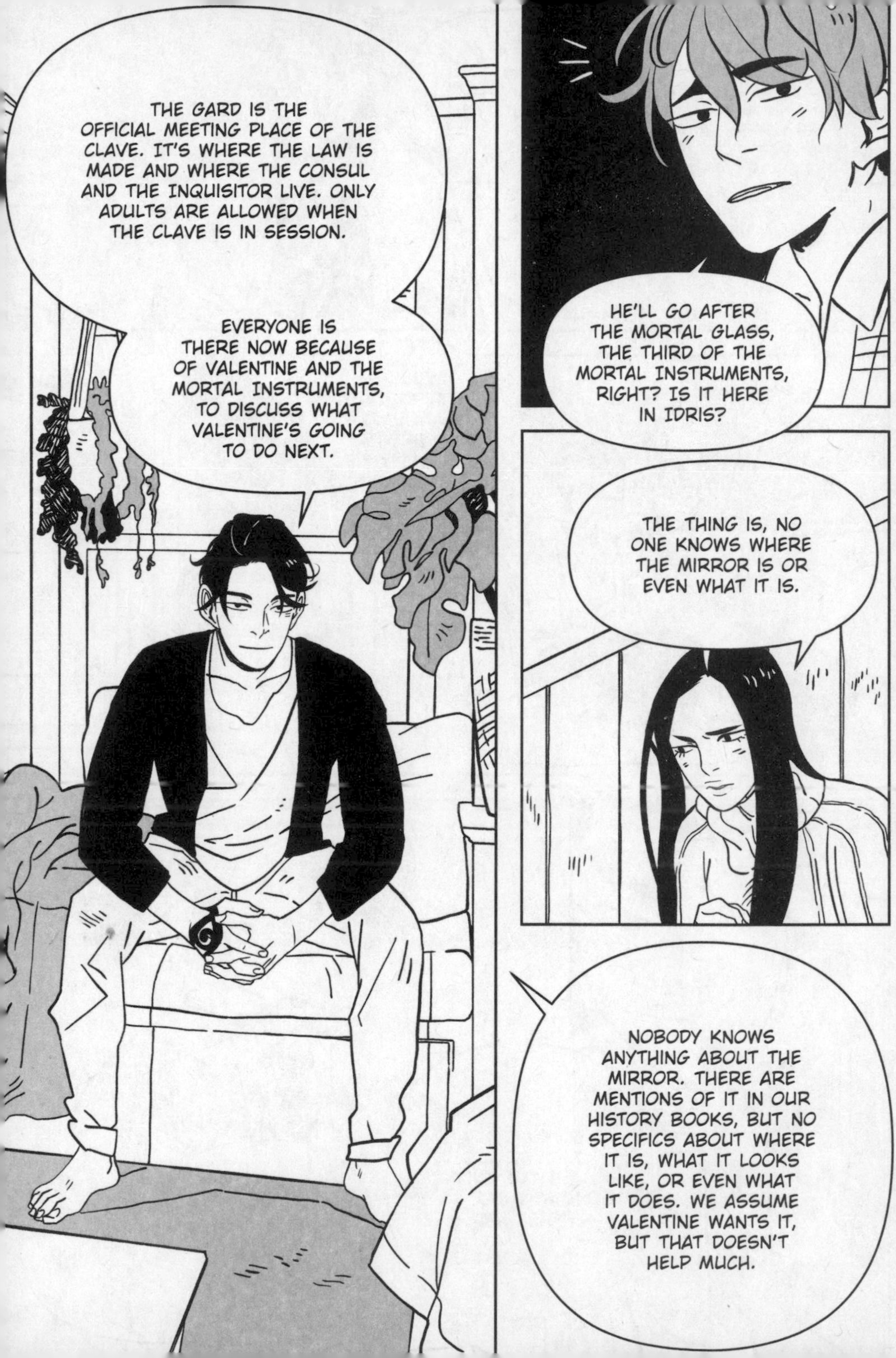
THE GARD IS THE OFFICIAL MEETING PLACE OF THE CLAVE. IT'S WHERE THE LAW IS MADE AND WHERE THE CONSUL AND THE INQUISITOR LIVE. ONLY ADULTS ARE ALLOWED WHEN THE CLAVE IS IN SESSION.
EVERYONE IS THERE NOW BECAUSE OF VALENTINE AND THE MORTAL INSTRUMENTS, TO DISCUSS WHAT VALENTINE'S GOING TO DO NEXT.
HE'LL GO AFTER THE MORTAL GLASS, THE THIRD OF THE MORTAL INSTRUMENTS, RIGHT? IS IT HERE IN IDRIS?
THE THING IS, NO ONE KNOWS WHERE THE MIRROR IS OR EVEN WHAT IT IS.
NOBODY KNOWS ANYTHING ABOUT THE MIRROR. THERE ARE MENTIONS OF IT IN OUR HISTORY BOOKS, BUT NO SPECIFICS ABOUT WHERE IT IS, WHAT IT LOOKS LIKE, OR EVEN WHAT IT DOES. WE ASSUME VALENTINE WANTS IT, BUT THAT DOESN'T HELP MUCH.

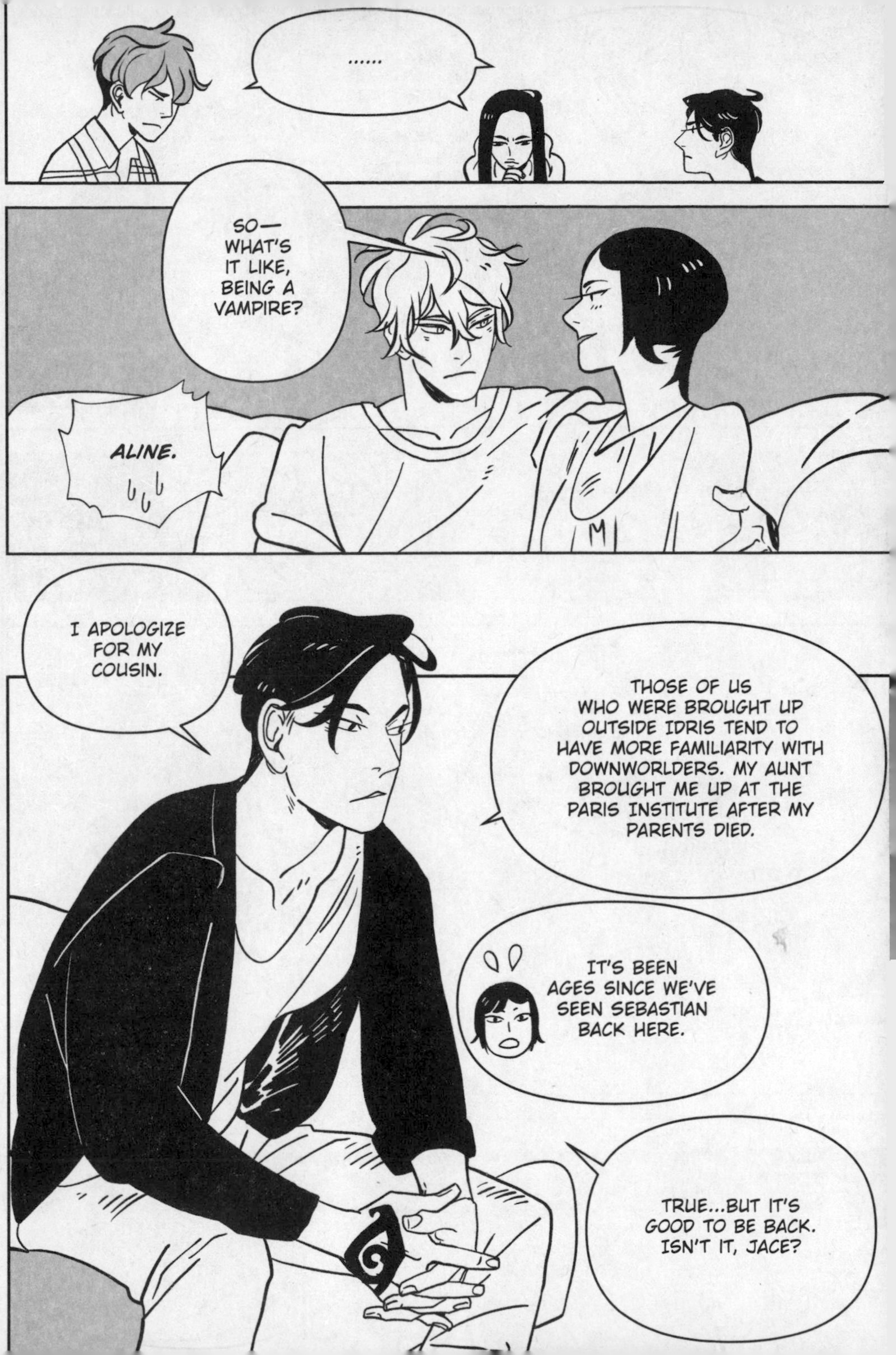
......
SO— WHAT'S IT LIKE, BEING A VAMPIRE?
ALINE.
I APOLOGIZE FOR MY COUSIN.
THOSE OF US WHO WERE BROUGHT UP OUTSIDE IDRIS TEND TO HAVE MORE FAMILIARITY WITH DOWNWORLDERS. MY AUNT BROUGHT ME UP AT THE PARIS INSTITUTE AFTER MY PARENTS DIED.
IT'S BEEN AGES SINCE WE'VE SEEN SEBASTIAN BACK HERE.
TRUE...BUT IT'S GOOD TO BE BACK. ISN'T IT, JACE?

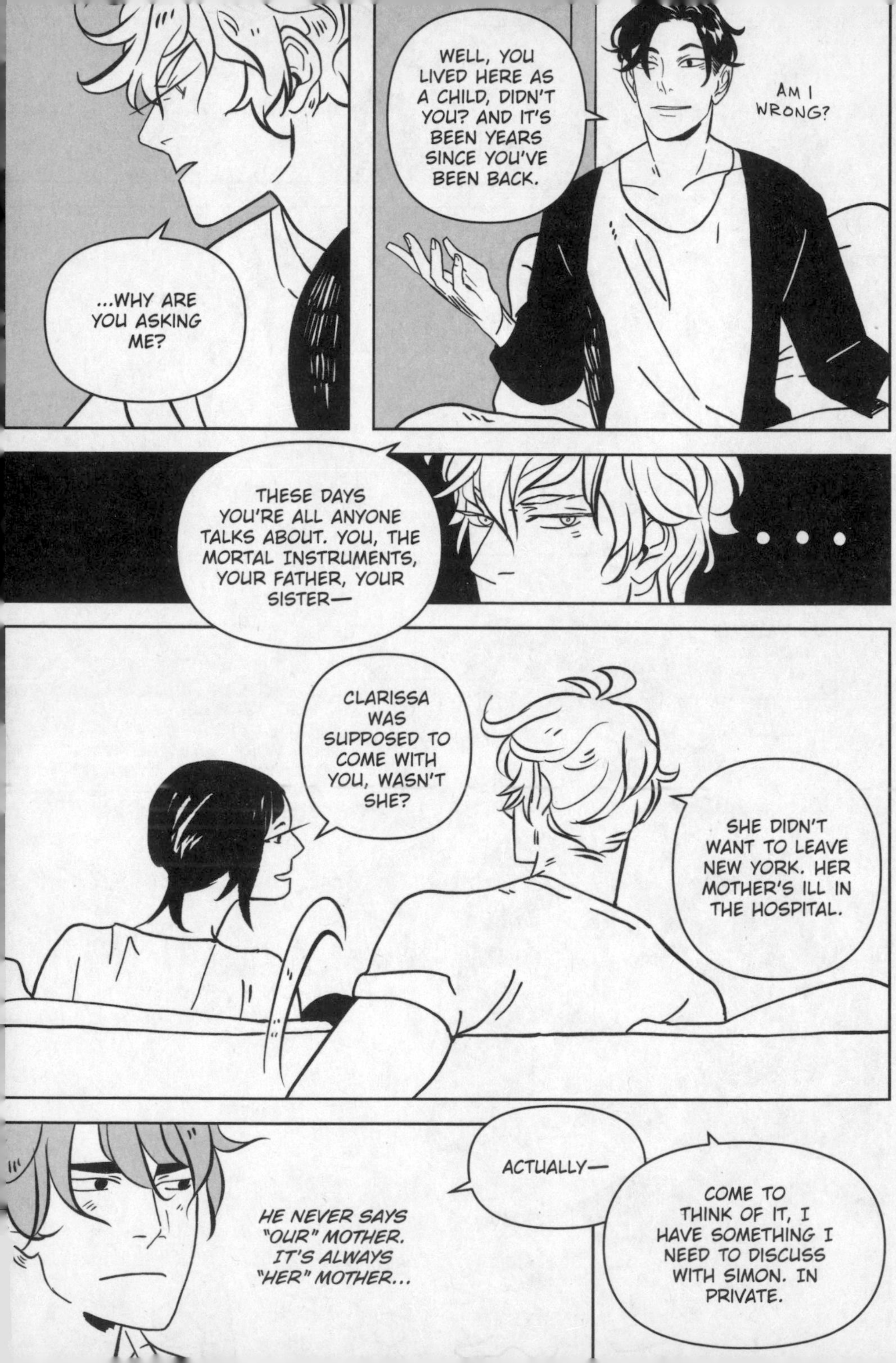
...WHY ARE YOU ASKING ME?
WELL, YOU LIVED HERE AS A CHILD, DIDN'T YOU? AND IT'S BEEN YEARS SINCE YOU'VE BEEN BACK.
AM I WRONG?
THESE DAYS YOU'RE ALL ANYONE TALKS ABOUT. YOU, THE MORTAL INSTRUMENTS, YOUR FATHER, YOUR SISTER—
...
CLARISSA WAS SUPPOSED TO COME WITH YOU, WASN'T SHE?
SHE DIDN'T WANT TO LEAVE NEW YORK. HER MOTHER'S ILL IN THE HOSPITAL.
HE NEVER SAYS "OUR" MOTHER. IT'S ALWAYS "HER" MOTHER...
ACTUALLY—
COME TO THINK OF IT, I HAVE SOMETHING I NEED TO DISCUSS WITH SIMON. IN PRIVATE.

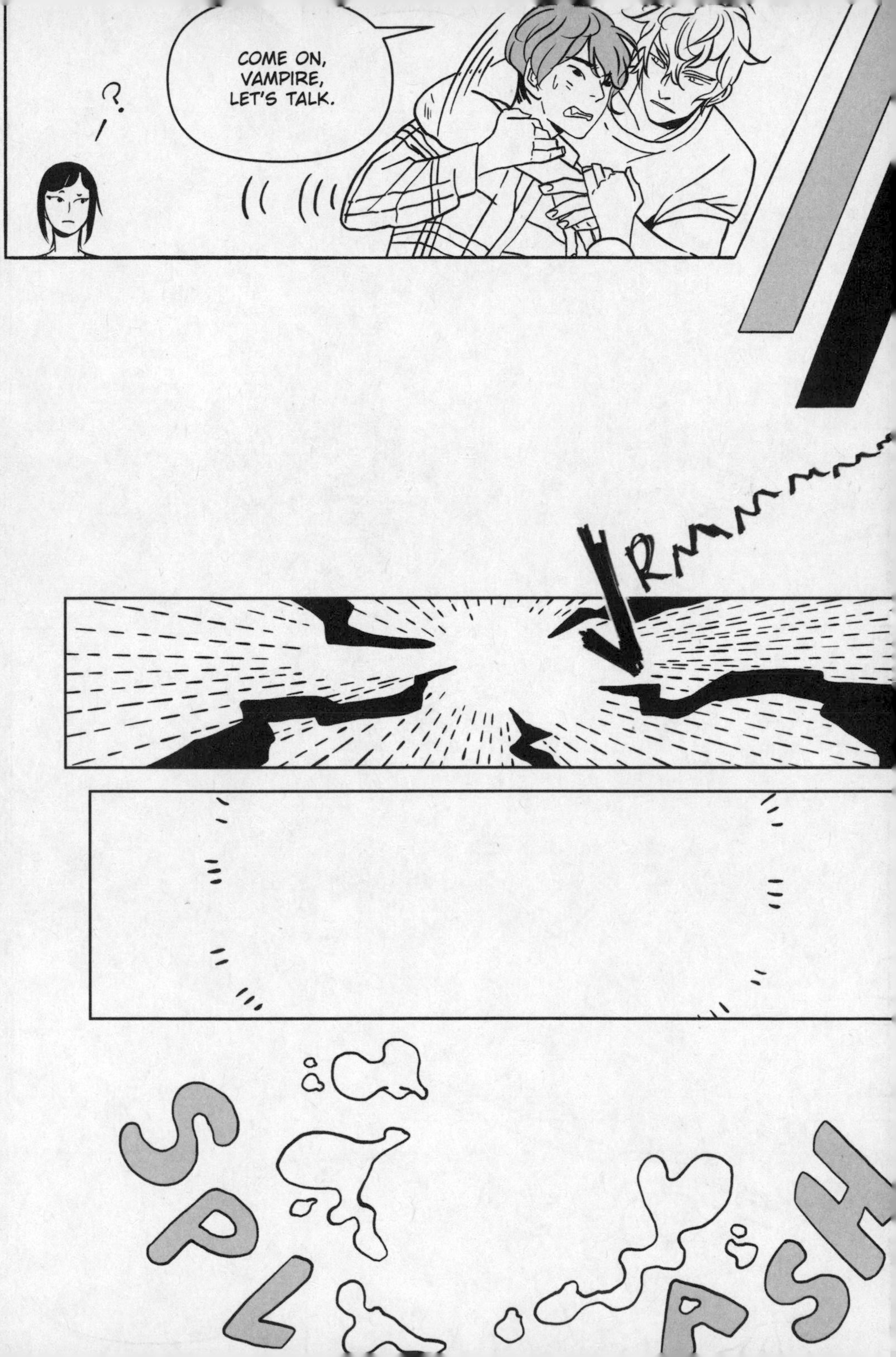

?
COME ON, VAMPIRE, LET'S TALK.
VRMMMMMM
SPLASH

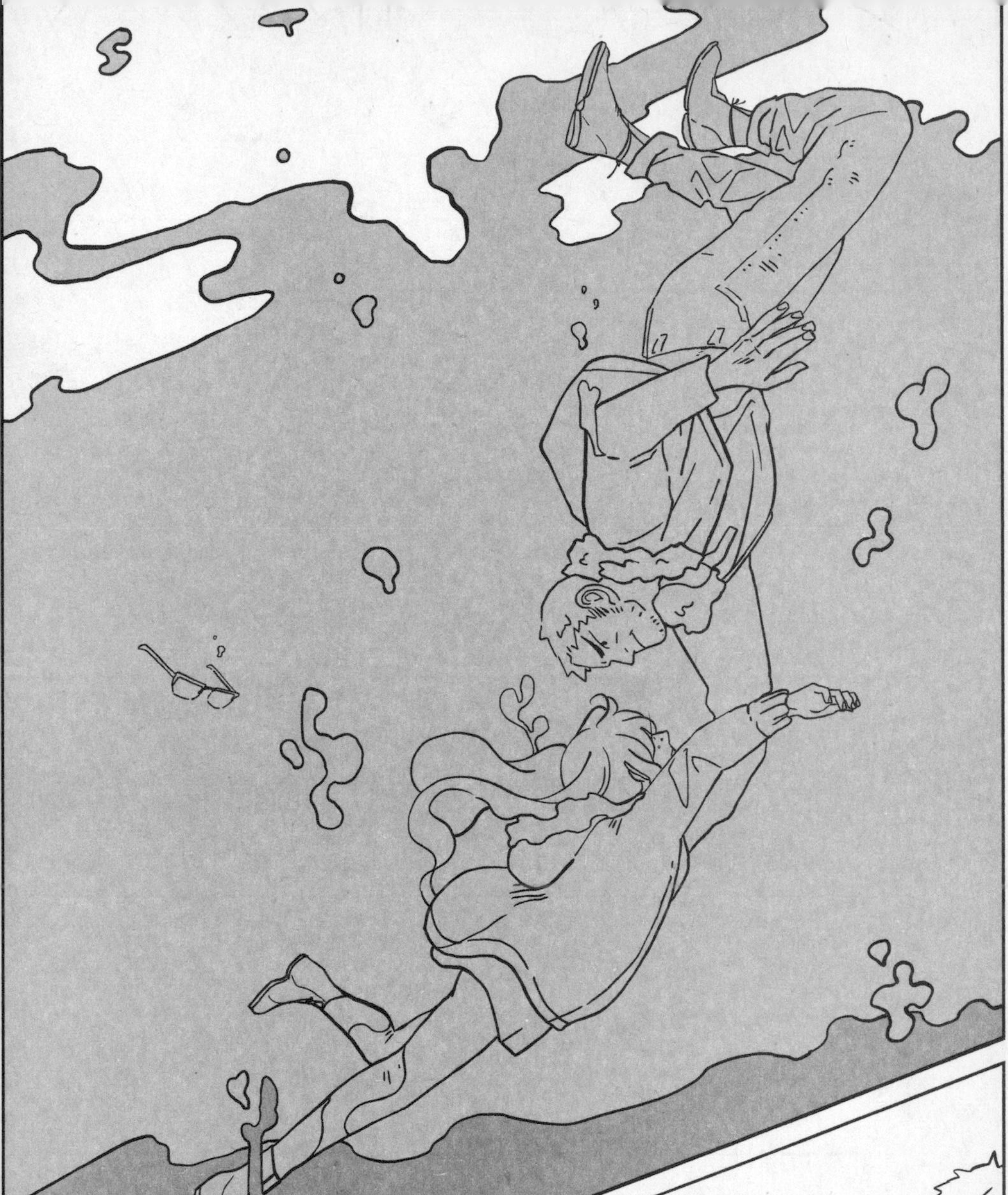

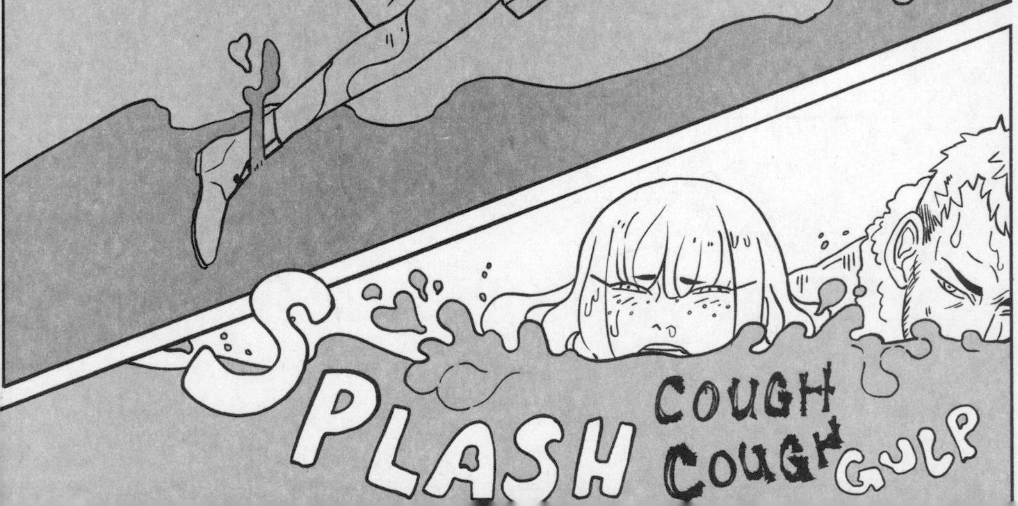
SPLASH
COUGH
COUGH
GULP

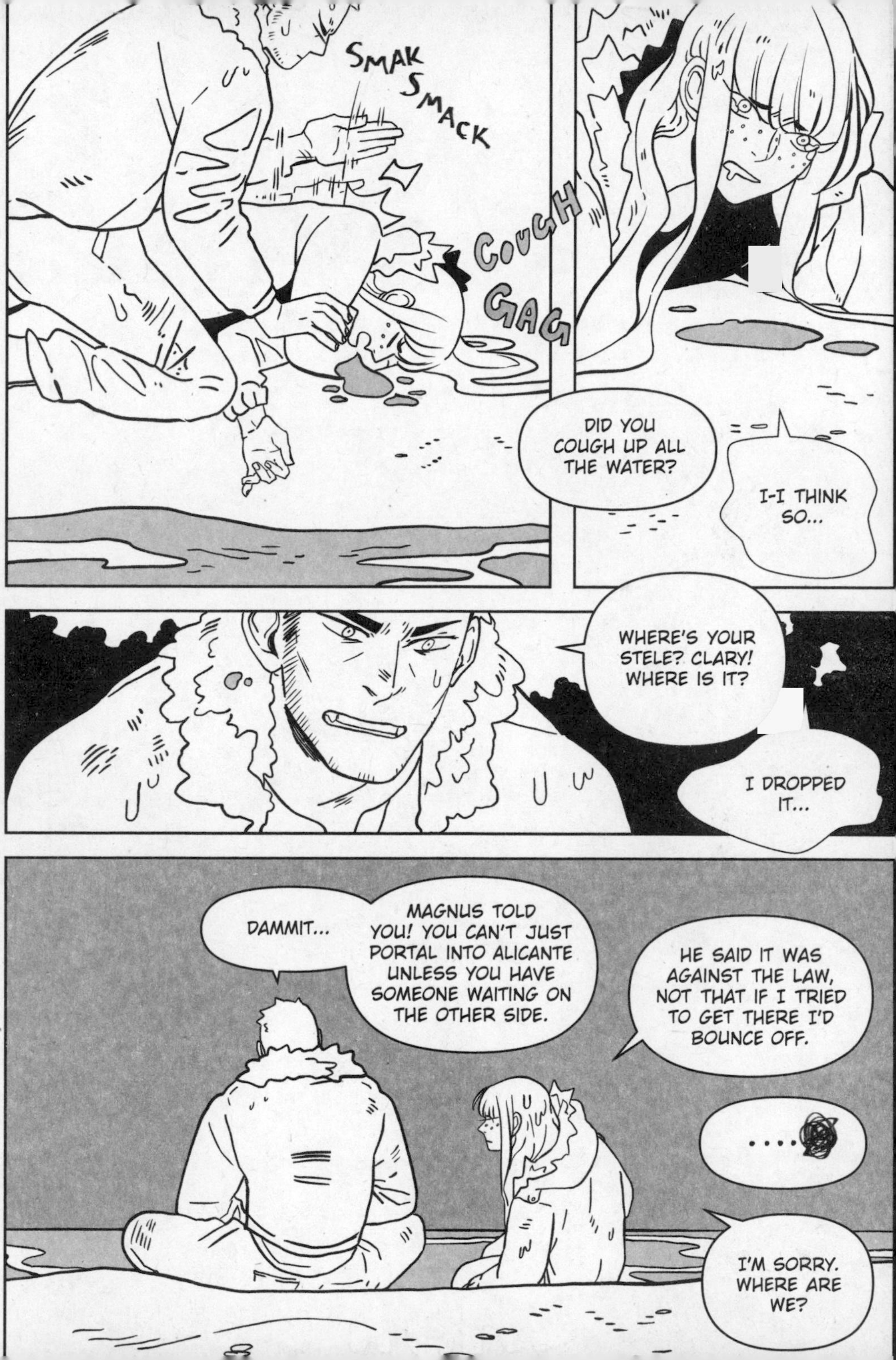
SMAK
SMACK
COUGH
GAG
DID YOU COUGH UP ALL THE WATER?
I-I THINK SO...
WHERE'S YOUR STELE? CLARY! WHERE IS IT?
I DROPPED IT...
DAMMIT...
MAGNUS TOLD YOU! YOU CAN'T JUST PORTAL INTO ALICANTE UNLESS YOU HAVE SOMEONE WAITING ON THE OTHER SIDE.
HE SAID IT WAS AGAINST THE LAW, NOT THAT IF I TRIED TO GET THERE I'D BOUNCE OFF.
....
I'M SORRY. WHERE ARE WE?

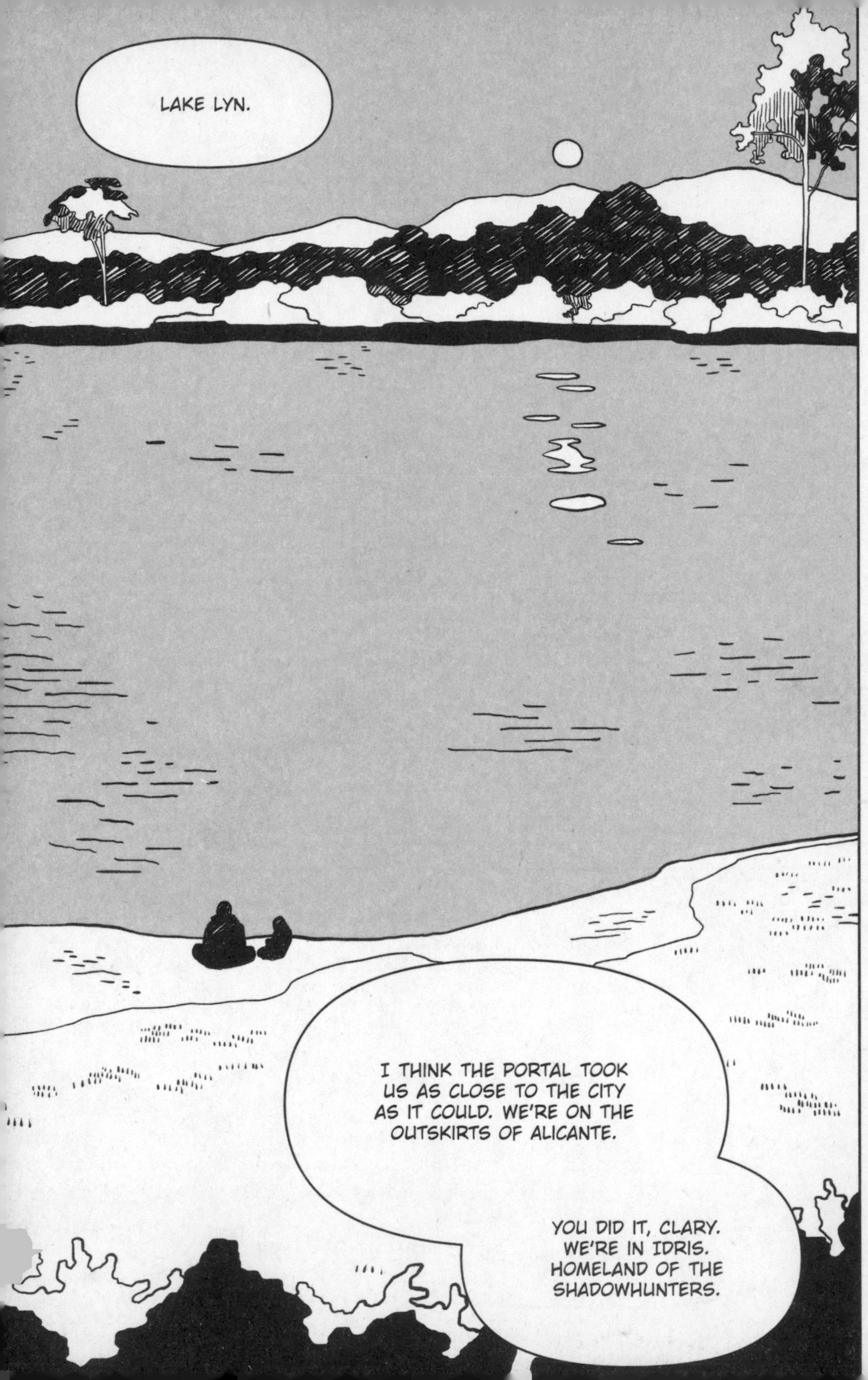
LAKE LYN.
I THINK THE PORTAL TOOK US AS CLOSE TO THE CITY AS IT COULD. WE'RE ON THE OUTSKIRTS OF ALICANTE.
YOU DID IT, CLARY. WE'RE IN IDRIS. HOMELAND OF THE SHADOWHUNTERS.

THE MORTAL INSTRUMENTS

THE GRAPHIC NOVEL

THE MORTAL INSTRUMENTS

THE GRAPHIC NOVEL

Chapter 26

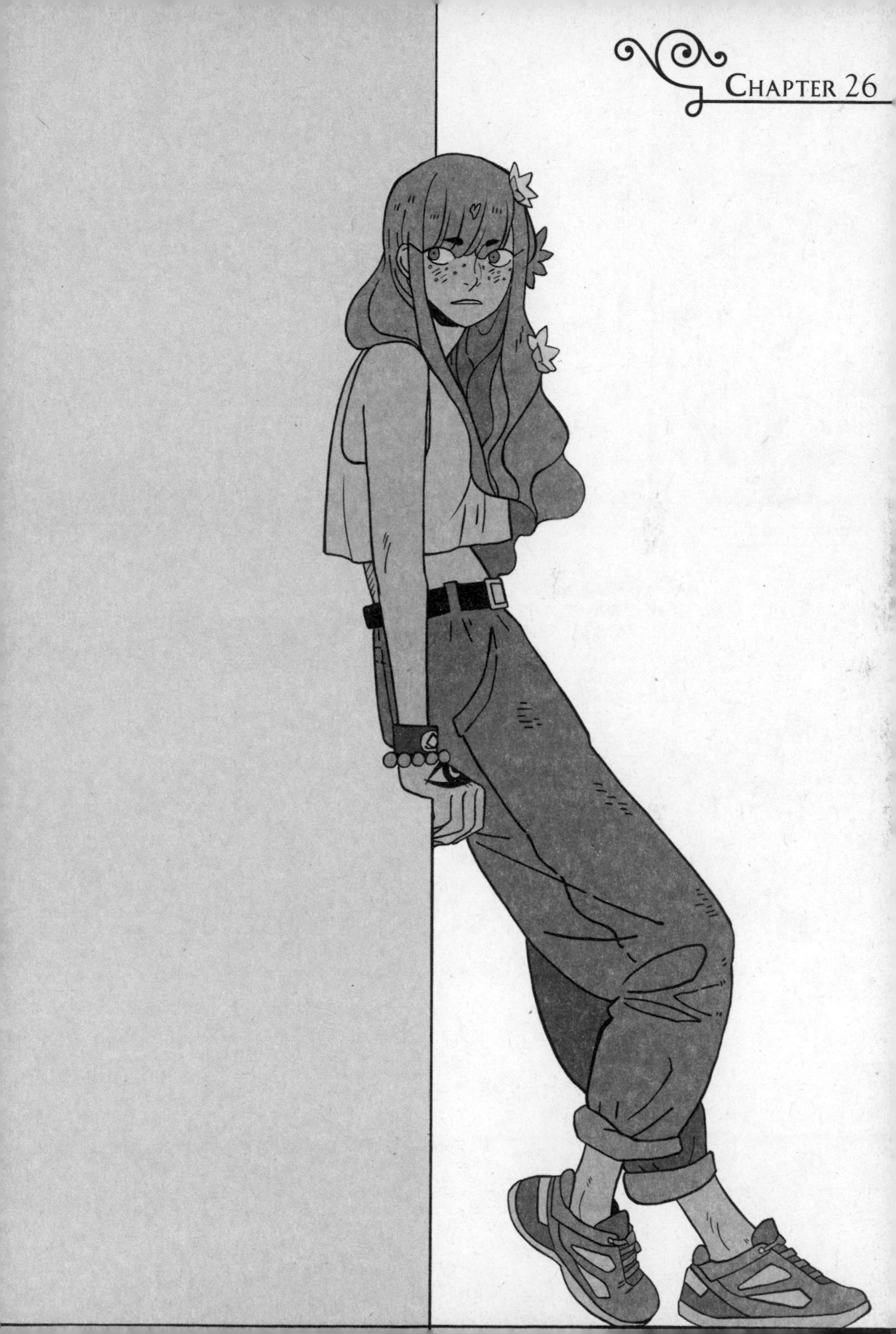

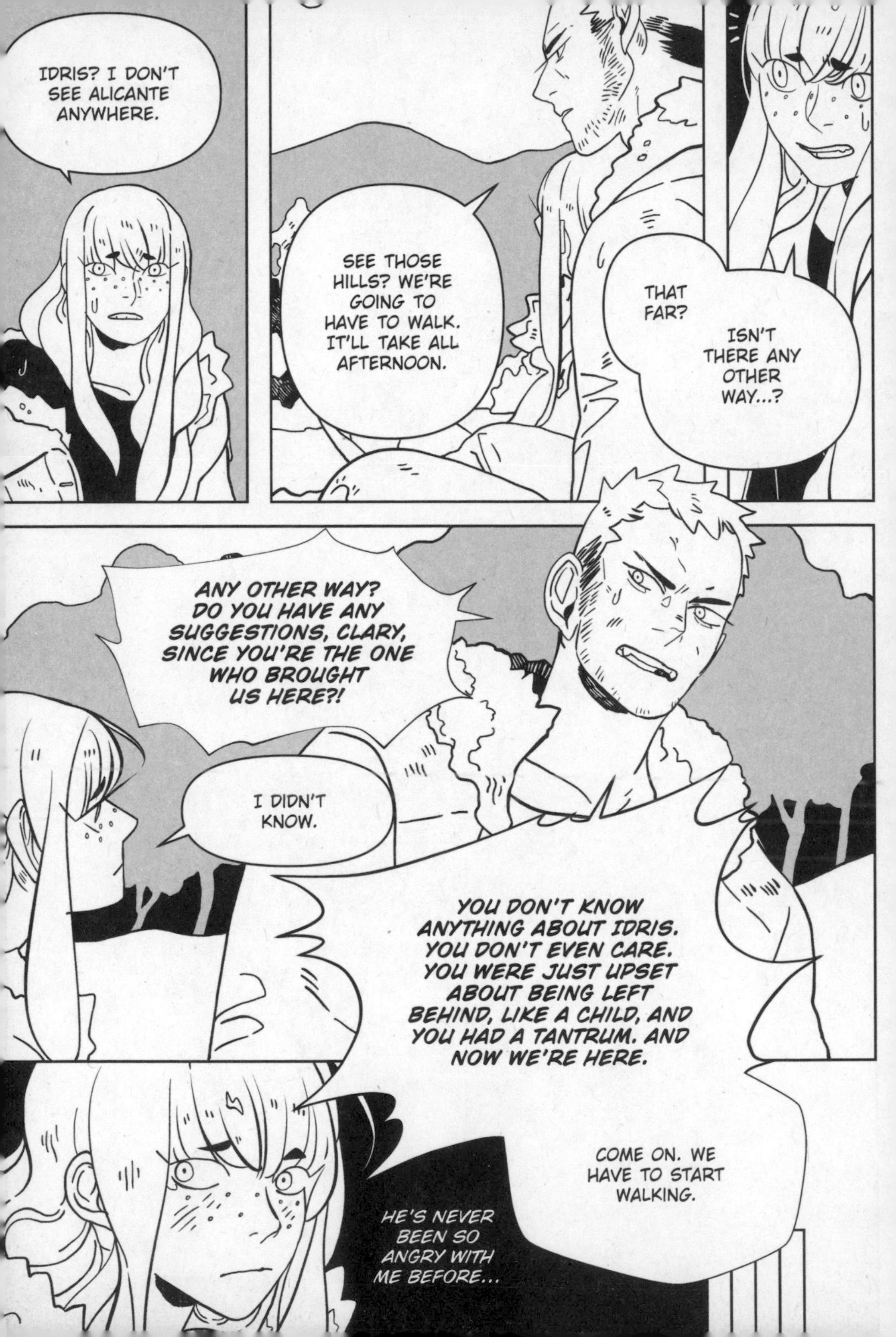
IDRIS? I DON'T SEE ALICANTE ANYWHERE.
SEE THOSE HILLS? WE'RE GOING TO HAVE TO WALK. IT'LL TAKE ALL AFTERNOON.
THAT FAR?
ISN'T THERE ANY OTHER WAY...?
ANY OTHER WAY? DO YOU HAVE ANY SUGGESTIONS, CLARY, SINCE YOU'RE THE ONE WHO BROUGHT US HERE?!
I DIDN'T KNOW.
YOU DON'T KNOW ANYTHING ABOUT IDRIS. YOU DON'T EVEN CARE. YOU WERE JUST UPSET ABOUT BEING LEFT BEHIND, LIKE A CHILD, AND YOU HAD A TANTRUM. AND NOW WE'RE HERE.
COME ON. WE HAVE TO START WALKING.
HE'S NEVER BEEN SO ANGRY WITH ME BEFORE...

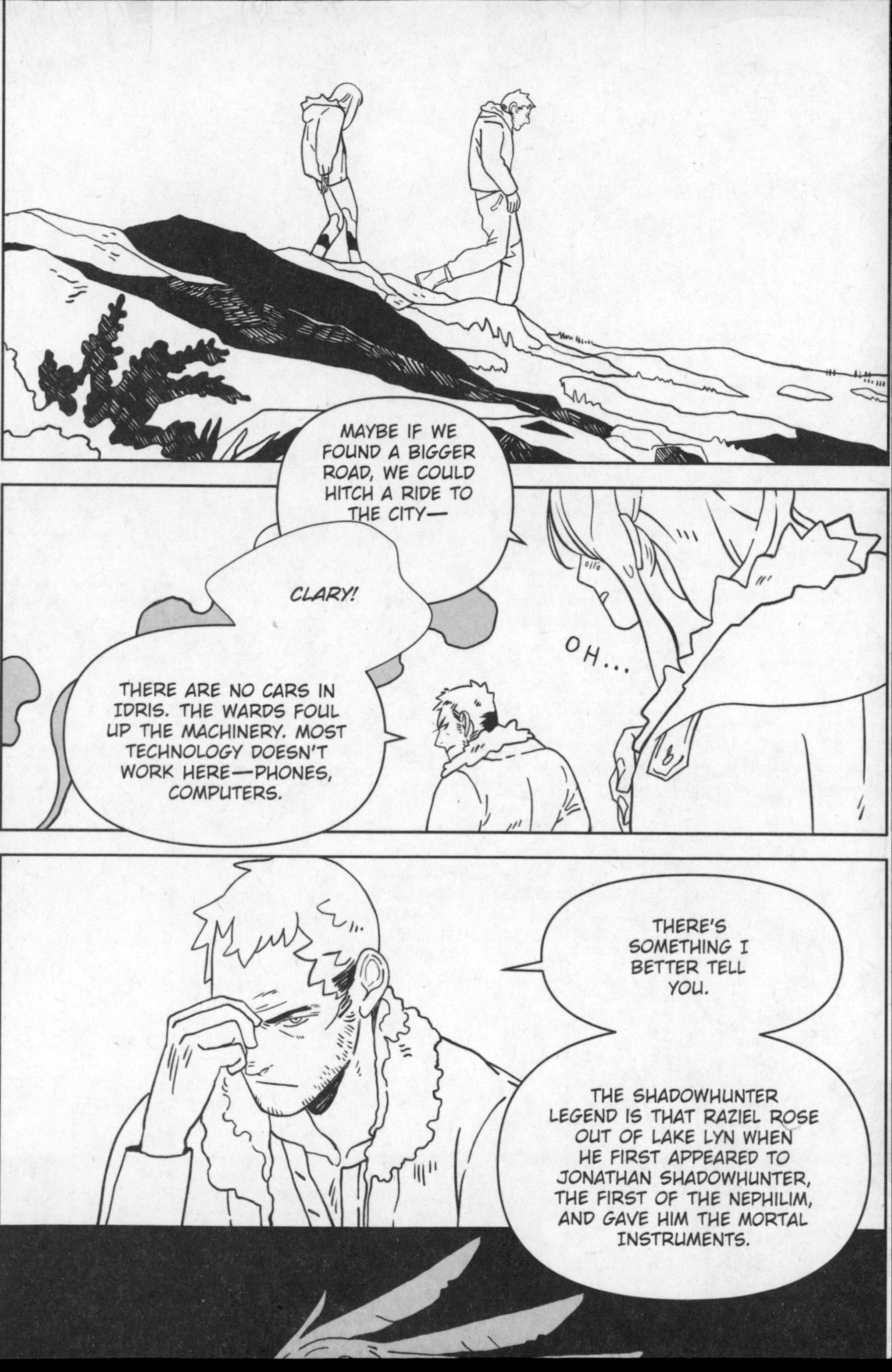
MAYBE IF WE FOUND A BIGGER ROAD, WE COULD HITCH A RIDE TO THE CITY—
CLARY!
THERE ARE NO CARS IN IDRIS. THE WARDS FOUL UP THE MACHINERY. MOST TECHNOLOGY DOESN'T WORK HERE—PHONES, COMPUTERS.
OH...
THERE'S SOMETHING I BETTER TELL YOU.
THE SHADOWHUNTER LEGEND IS THAT RAZIEL ROSE OUT OF LAKE LYN WHEN HE FIRST APPEARED TO JONATHAN SHADOWHUNTER, THE FIRST OF THE NEPHILIM, AND GAVE HIM THE MORTAL INSTRUMENTS.

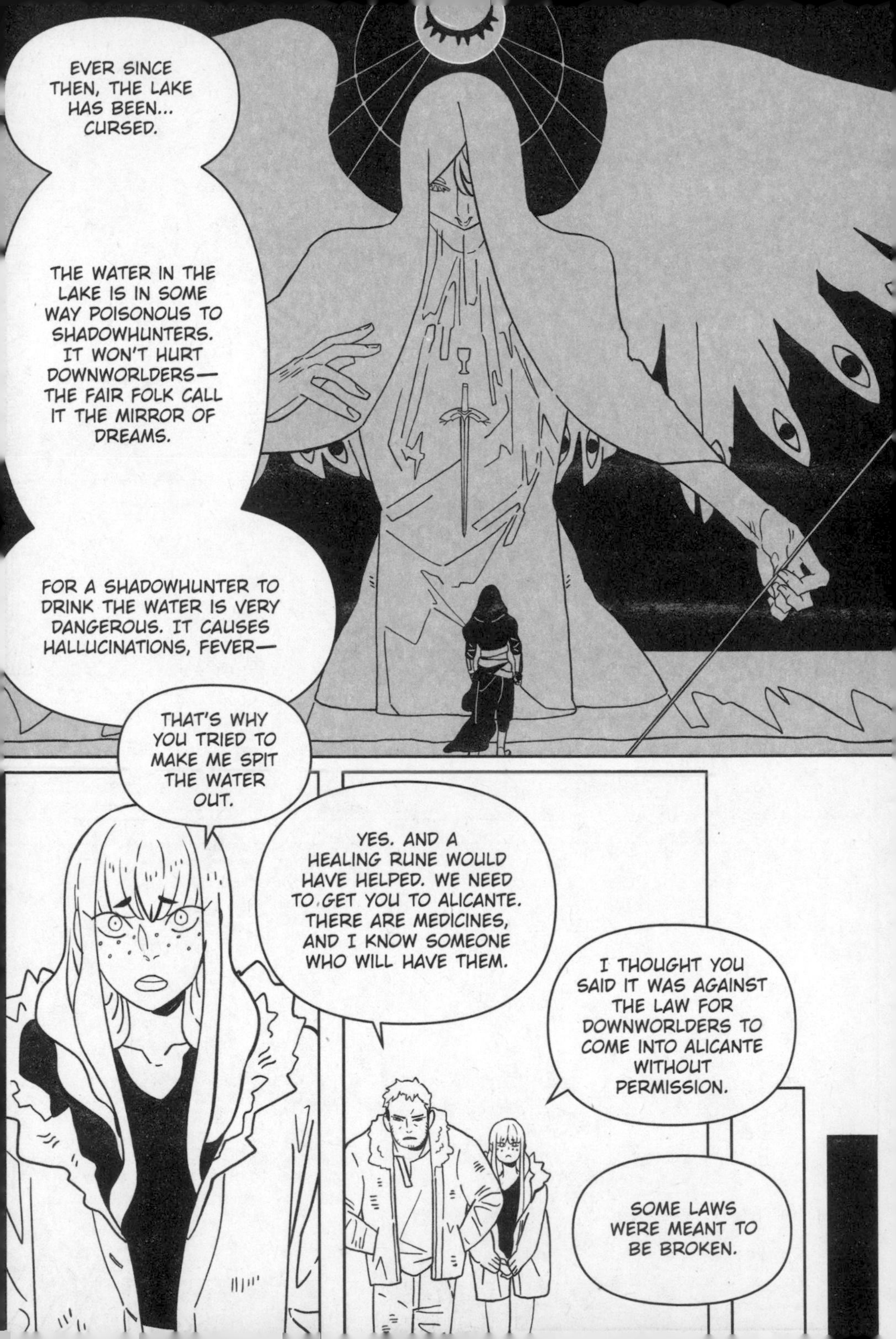
EVER SINCE THEN, THE LAKE HAS BEEN... CURSED.
THE WATER IN THE LAKE IS IN SOME WAY POISONOUS TO SHADOWHUNTERS. IT WON'T HURT DOWNWORLDERS—THE FAIR FOLK CALL IT THE MIRROR OF DREAMS.
FOR A SHADOWHUNTER TO DRINK THE WATER IS VERY DANGEROUS. IT CAUSES HALLUCINATIONS, FEVER—
THAT'S WHY YOU TRIED TO MAKE ME SPIT THE WATER OUT.
YES. AND A HEALING RUNE WOULD HAVE HELPED. WE NEED TO GET YOU TO ALICANTE. THERE ARE MEDICINES, AND I KNOW SOMEONE WHO WILL HAVE THEM.
I THOUGHT YOU SAID IT WAS AGAINST THE LAW FOR DOWNWORLDERS TO COME INTO ALICANTE WITHOUT PERMISSION.
SOME LAWS WERE MEANT TO BE BROKEN.

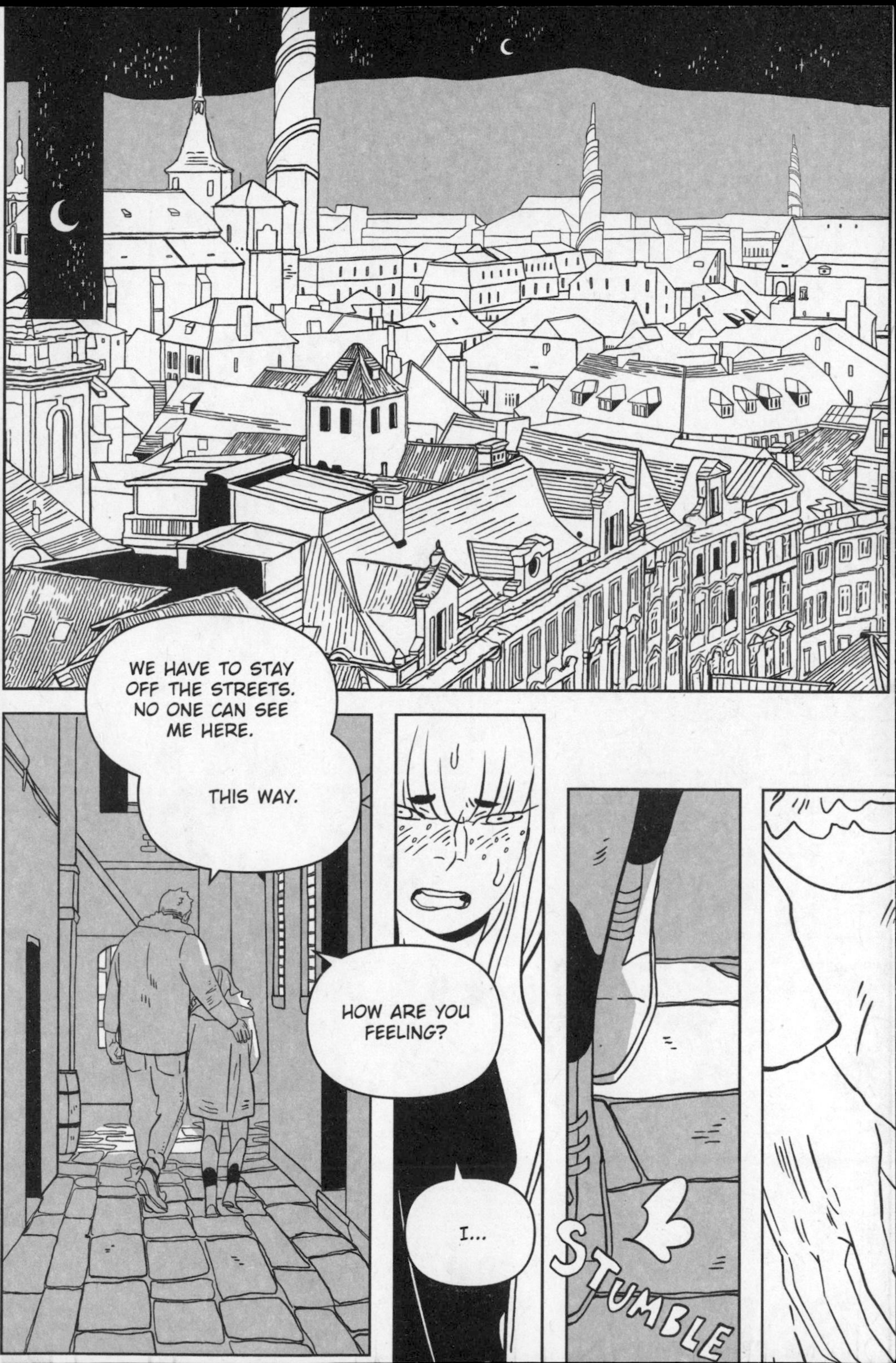

WE HAVE TO STAY OFF THE STREETS. NO ONE CAN SEE ME HERE.
THIS WAY.
HOW ARE YOU FEELING?
I...
STUMBLE

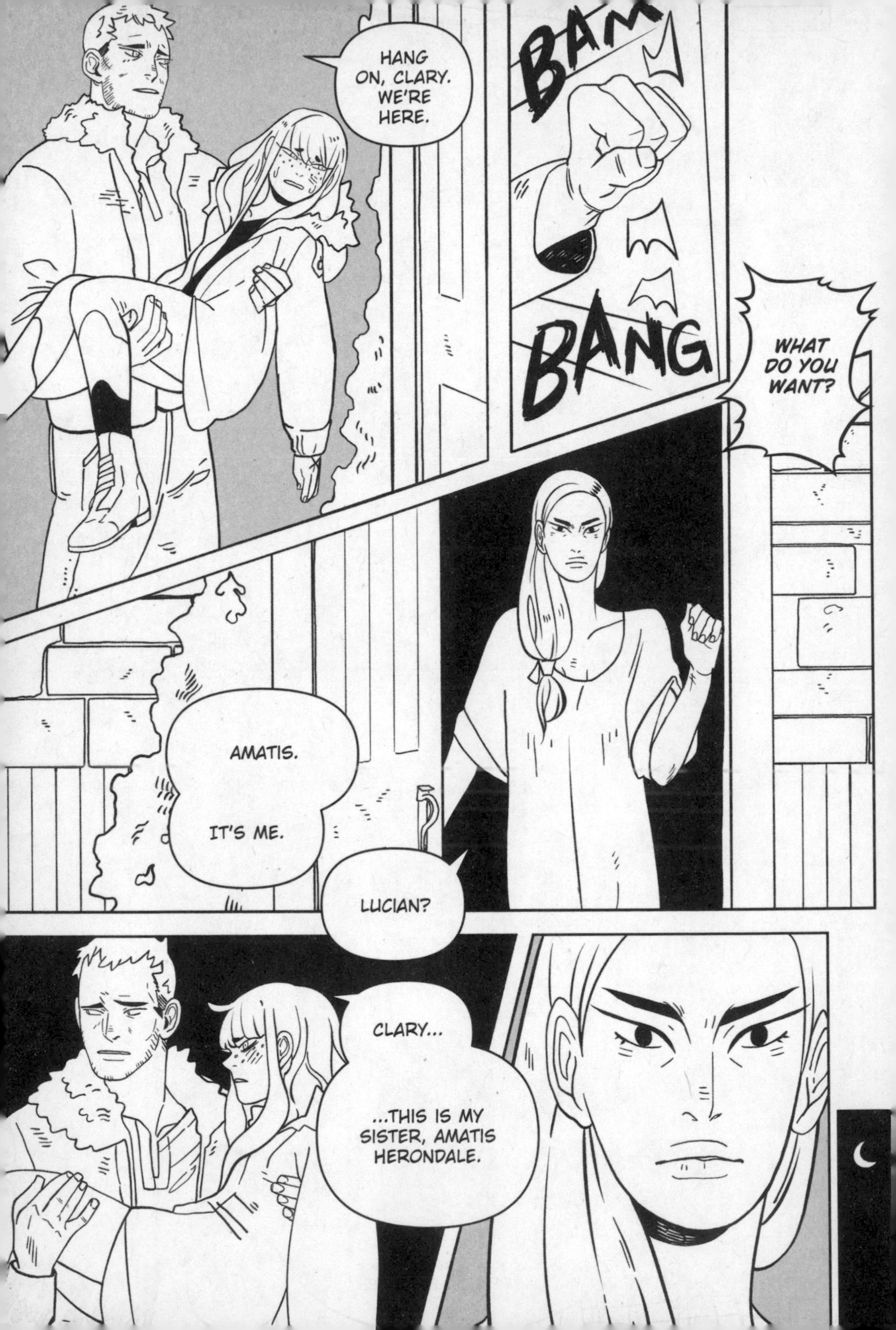
HANG ON, CLARY. WE'RE HERE.
BAM
BANG
WHAT DO YOU WANT?
AMATIS.
IT'S ME.
LUCIAN?
CLARY...
...THIS IS MY SISTER, AMATIS HERONDALE.

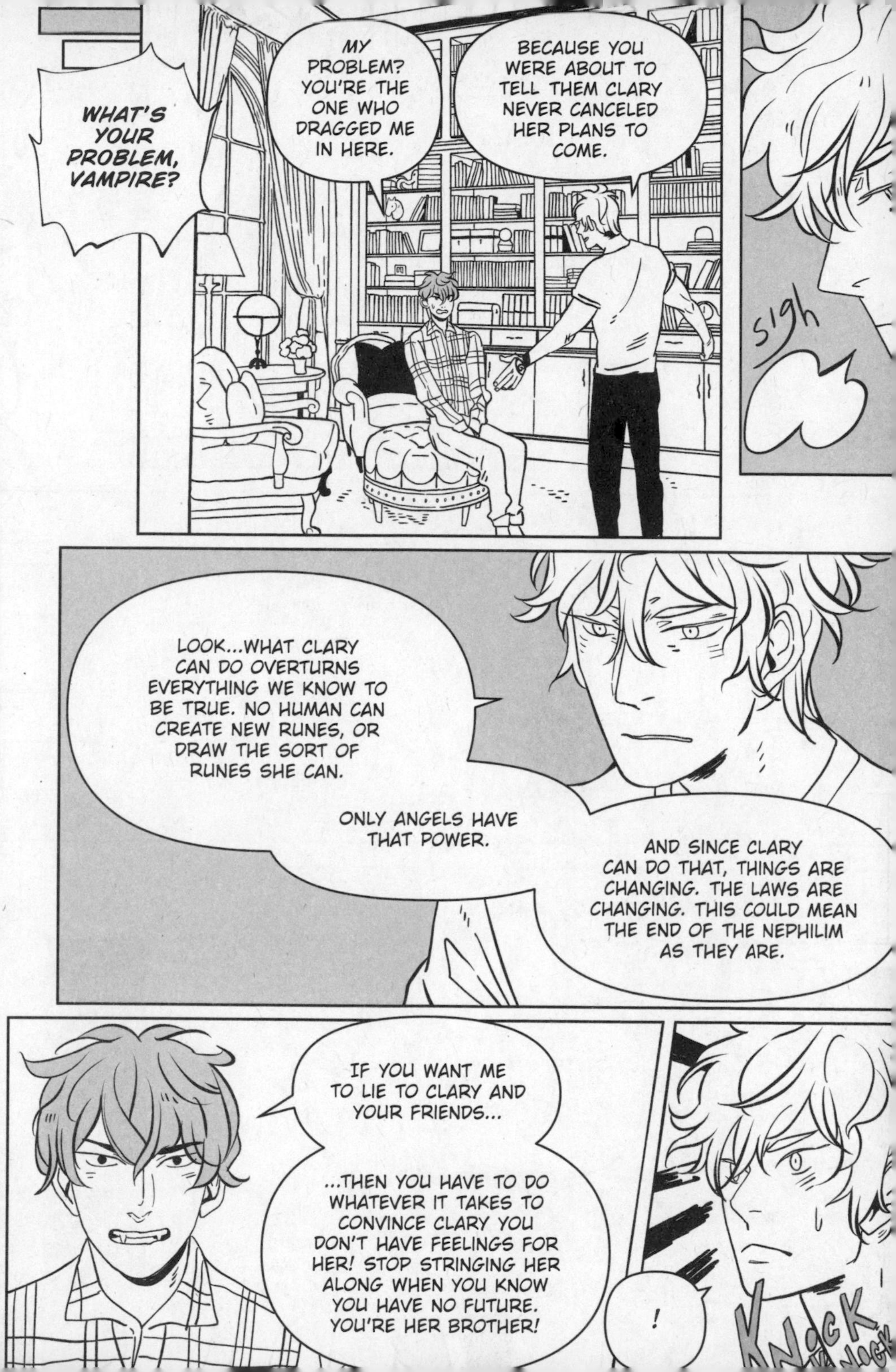
WHAT'S YOUR PROBLEM, VAMPIRE?
MY PROBLEM? YOU'RE THE ONE WHO DRAGGED ME IN HERE.
BECAUSE YOU WERE ABOUT TO TELL THEM CLARY NEVER CANCELED HER PLANS TO COME.
sigh
LOOK...WHAT CLARY CAN DO OVERTURNS EVERYTHING WE KNOW TO BE TRUE. NO HUMAN CAN CREATE NEW RUNES, OR DRAW THE SORT OF RUNES SHE CAN.
ONLY ANGELS HAVE THAT POWER.
AND SINCE CLARY CAN DO THAT, THINGS ARE CHANGING. THE LAWS ARE CHANGING. THIS COULD MEAN THE END OF THE NEPHILIM AS THEY ARE.
IF YOU WANT ME TO LIE TO CLARY AND YOUR FRIENDS...
...THEN YOU HAVE TO DO WHATEVER IT TAKES TO CONVINCE CLARY YOU DON'T HAVE FEELINGS FOR HER! STOP STRINGING HER ALONG WHEN YOU KNOW YOU HAVE NO FUTURE. YOU'RE HER BROTHER!
!
KNOCK
KNOCK

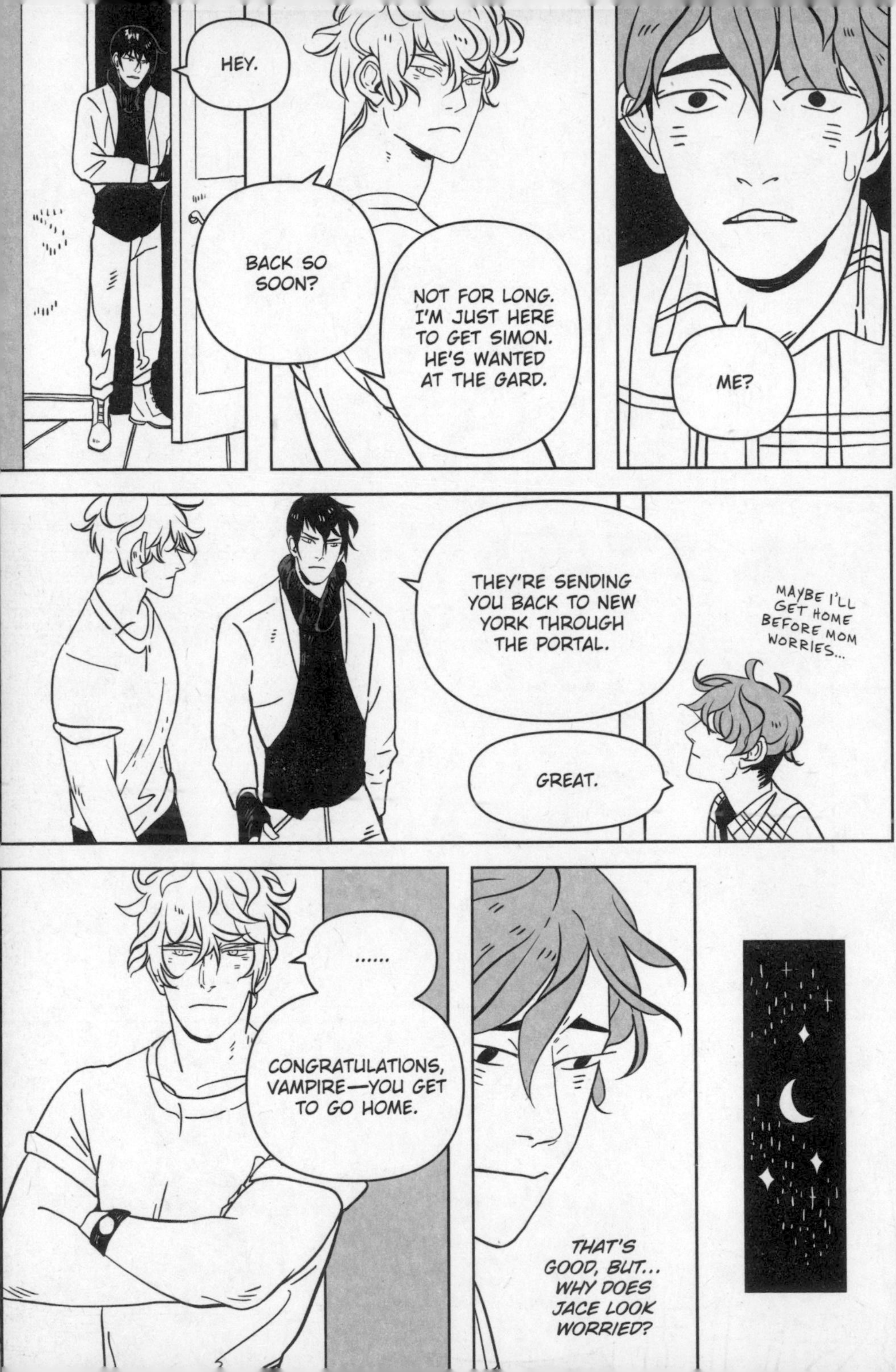
HEY.
BACK SO SOON?
NOT FOR LONG. I'M JUST HERE TO GET SIMON. HE'S WANTED AT THE GARD.
ME?
THEY'RE SENDING YOU BACK TO NEW YORK THROUGH THE PORTAL.
MAYBE I'LL GET HOME BEFORE MOM WORRIES...
GREAT.
......
CONGRATULATIONS, VAMPIRE—YOU GET TO GO HOME.
THAT'S GOOD, BUT... WHY DOES JACE LOOK WORRIED?

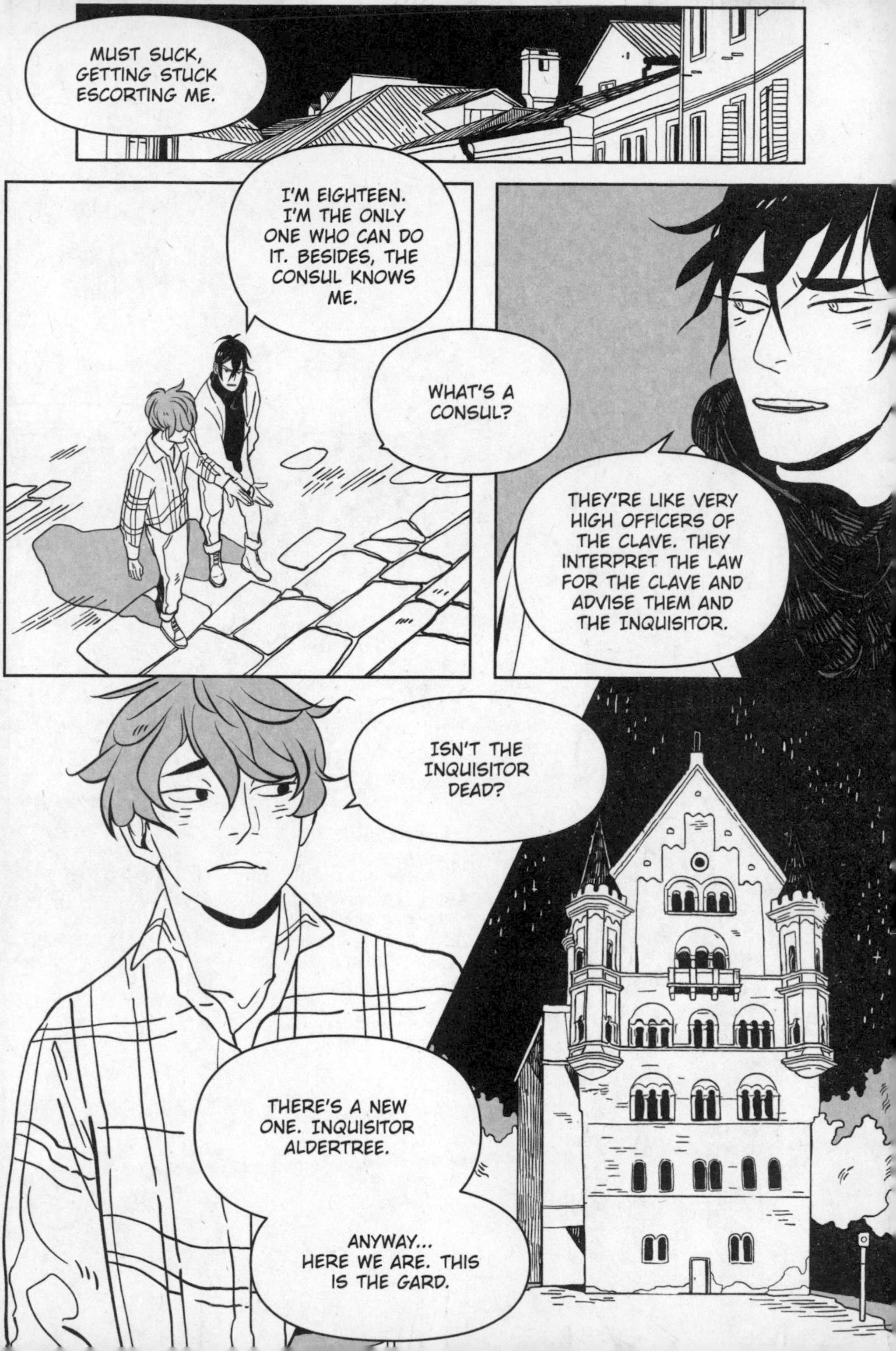
MUST SUCK, GETTING STUCK ESCORTING ME.
I'M EIGHTEEN. I'M THE ONLY ONE WHO CAN DO IT. BESIDES, THE CONSUL KNOWS ME.
WHAT'S A CONSUL?
THEY'RE LIKE VERY HIGH OFFICERS OF THE CLAVE. THEY INTERPRET THE LAW FOR THE CLAVE AND ADVISE THEM AND THE INQUISITOR.
ISN'T THE INQUISITOR DEAD?
THERE'S A NEW ONE. INQUISITOR ALDERTREE.
ANYWAY... HERE WE ARE. THIS IS THE GARD.

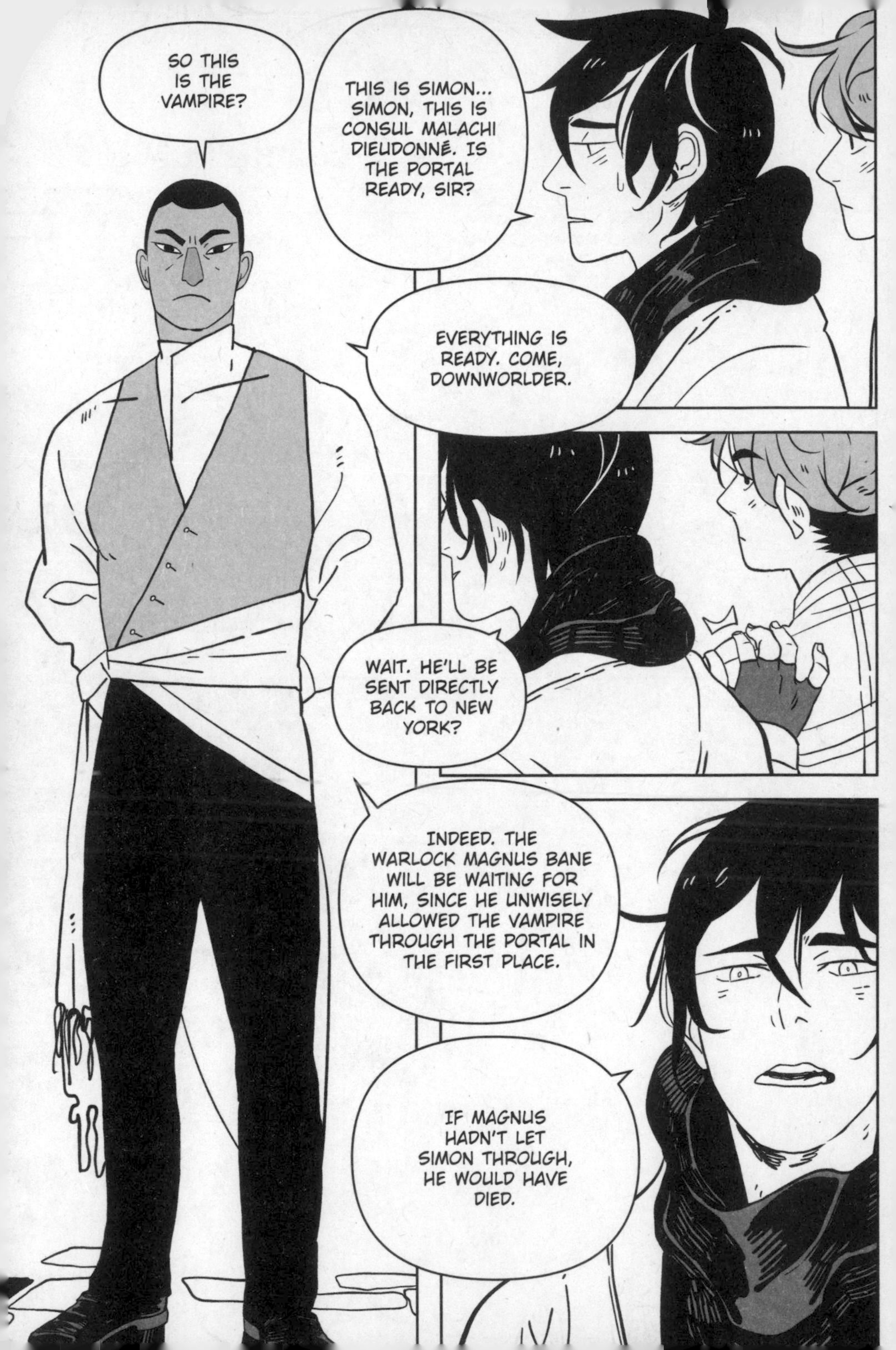
SO THIS IS THE VAMPIRE?
THIS IS SIMON... SIMON, THIS IS CONSUL MALACHI DIEUDONNÉ. IS THE PORTAL READY, SIR?
EVERYTHING IS READY. COME, DOWNWORLDER.
WAIT. HE'LL BE SENT DIRECTLY BACK TO NEW YORK?
INDEED. THE WARLOCK MAGNUS BANE WILL BE WAITING FOR HIM, SINCE HE UNWISELY ALLOWED THE VAMPIRE THROUGH THE PORTAL IN THE FIRST PLACE.
IF MAGNUS HADN'T LET SIMON THROUGH, HE WOULD HAVE DIED.

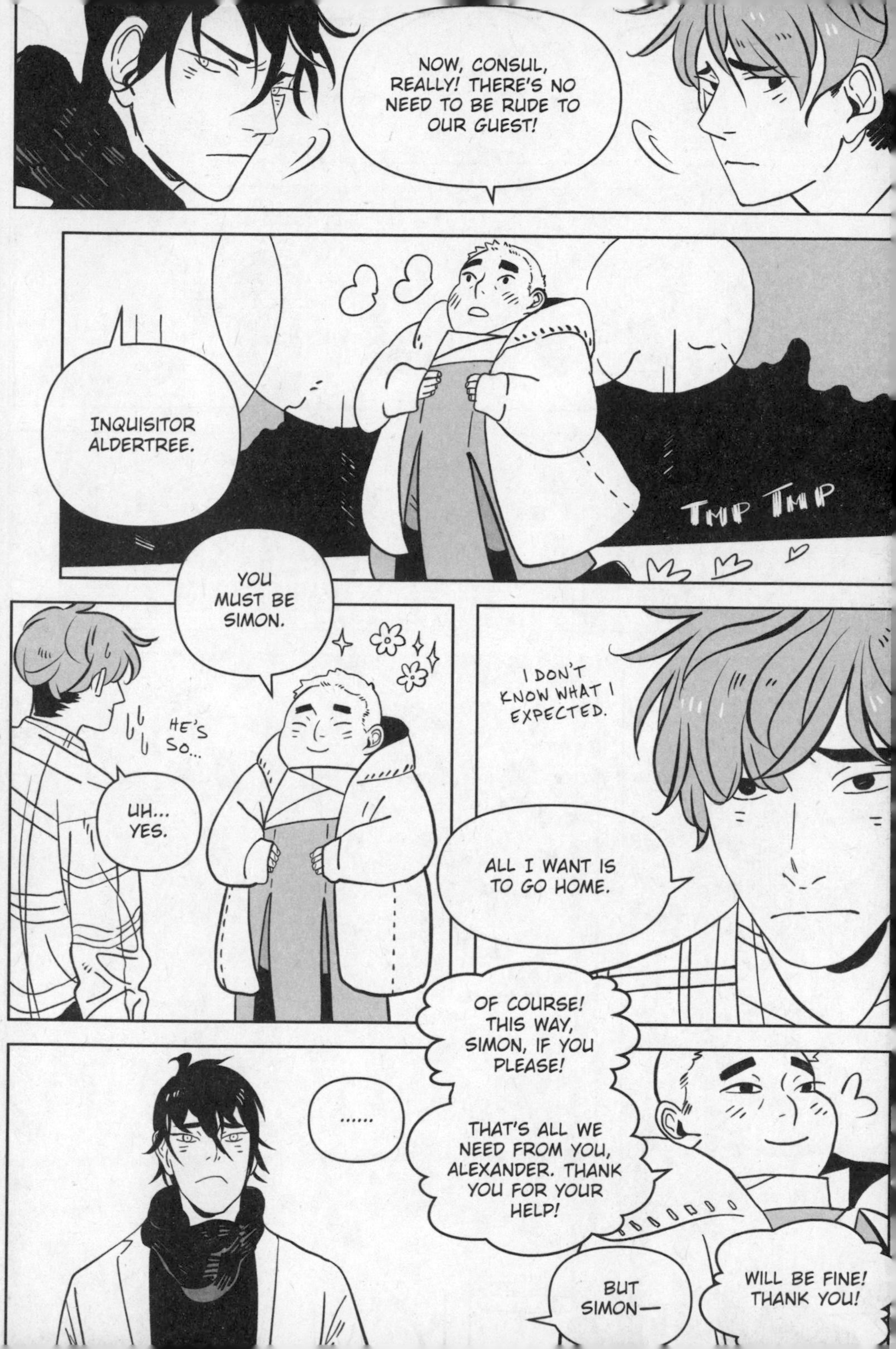
NOW, CONSUL, REALLY! THERE'S NO NEED TO BE RUDE TO OUR GUEST!
INQUISITOR ALDERTREE.
TMP TMP
YOU MUST BE SIMON.
HE'S SO...
UH... YES.
I DON'T KNOW WHAT I EXPECTED.
ALL I WANT IS TO GO HOME.
......
OF COURSE! THIS WAY, SIMON, IF YOU PLEASE!
THAT'S ALL WE NEED FROM YOU, ALEXANDER. THANK YOU FOR YOUR HELP!
BUT SIMON—
WILL BE FINE! THANK YOU!

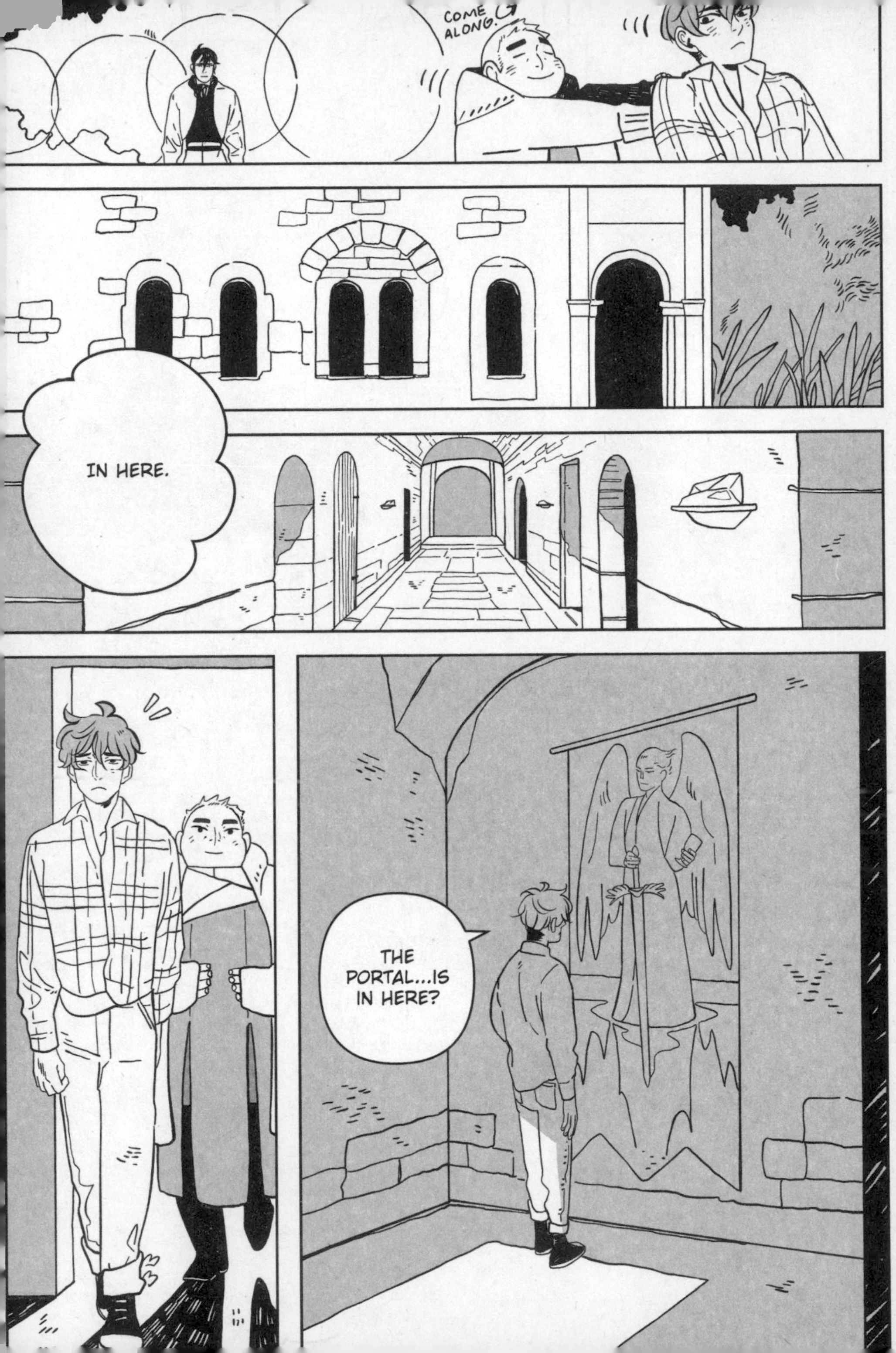
COME ALONG.
IN HERE.
THE PORTAL...IS IN HERE?

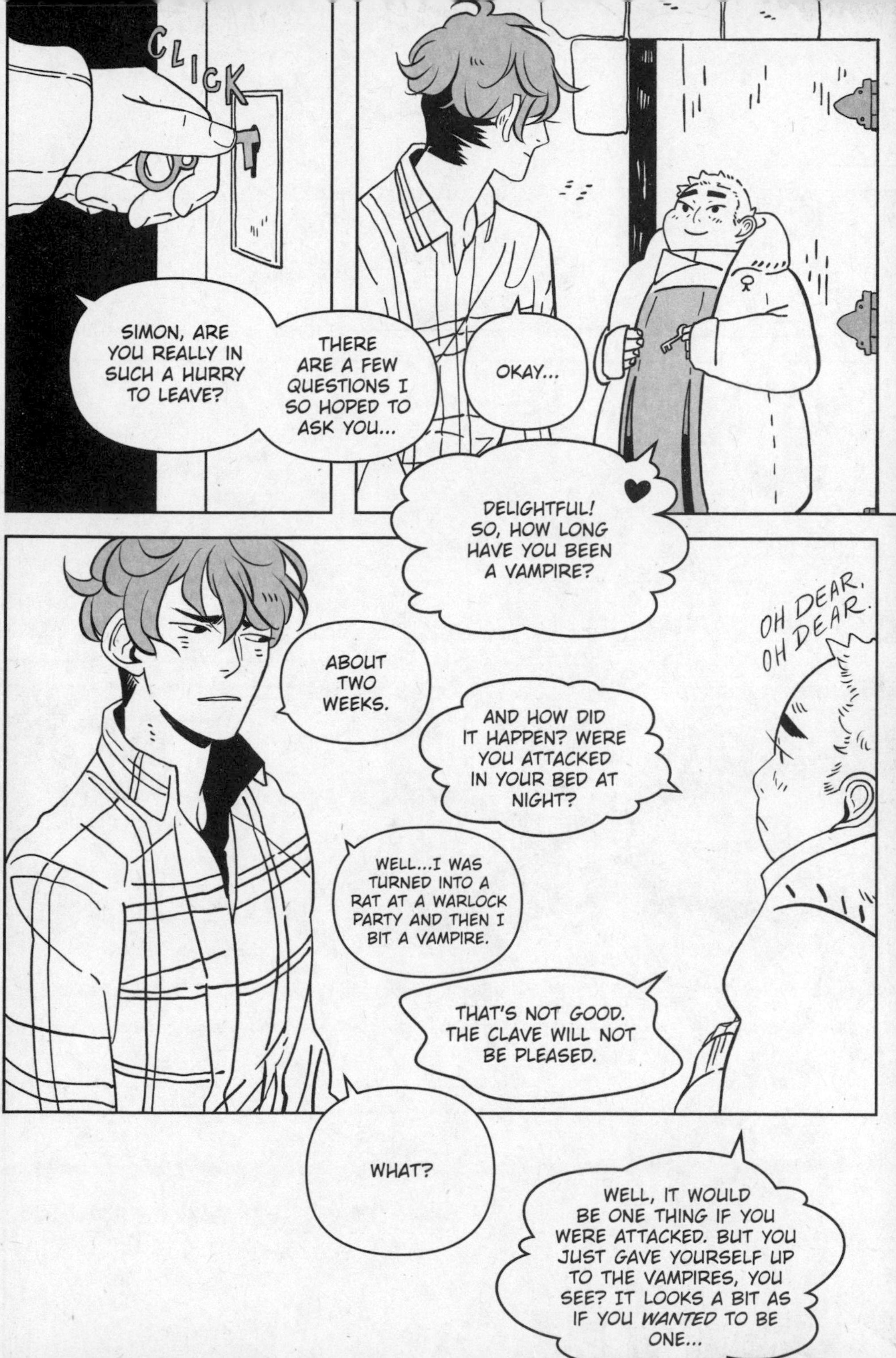
CLICK
SIMON, ARE YOU REALLY IN SUCH A HURRY TO LEAVE?
THERE ARE A FEW QUESTIONS I SO HOPED TO ASK YOU...
OKAY...
DELIGHTFUL! SO, HOW LONG HAVE YOU BEEN A VAMPIRE?
ABOUT TWO WEEKS.
AND HOW DID IT HAPPEN? WERE YOU ATTACKED IN YOUR BED AT NIGHT?
WELL...I WAS TURNED INTO A RAT AT A WARLOCK PARTY AND THEN I BIT A VAMPIRE.
OH DEAR. OH DEAR.
THAT'S NOT GOOD. THE CLAVE WILL NOT BE PLEASED.
WHAT?
WELL, IT WOULD BE ONE THING IF YOU WERE ATTACKED. BUT YOU JUST GAVE YOURSELF UP TO THE VAMPIRES, YOU SEE? IT LOOKS A BIT AS IF YOU *WANTED* TO BE ONE...

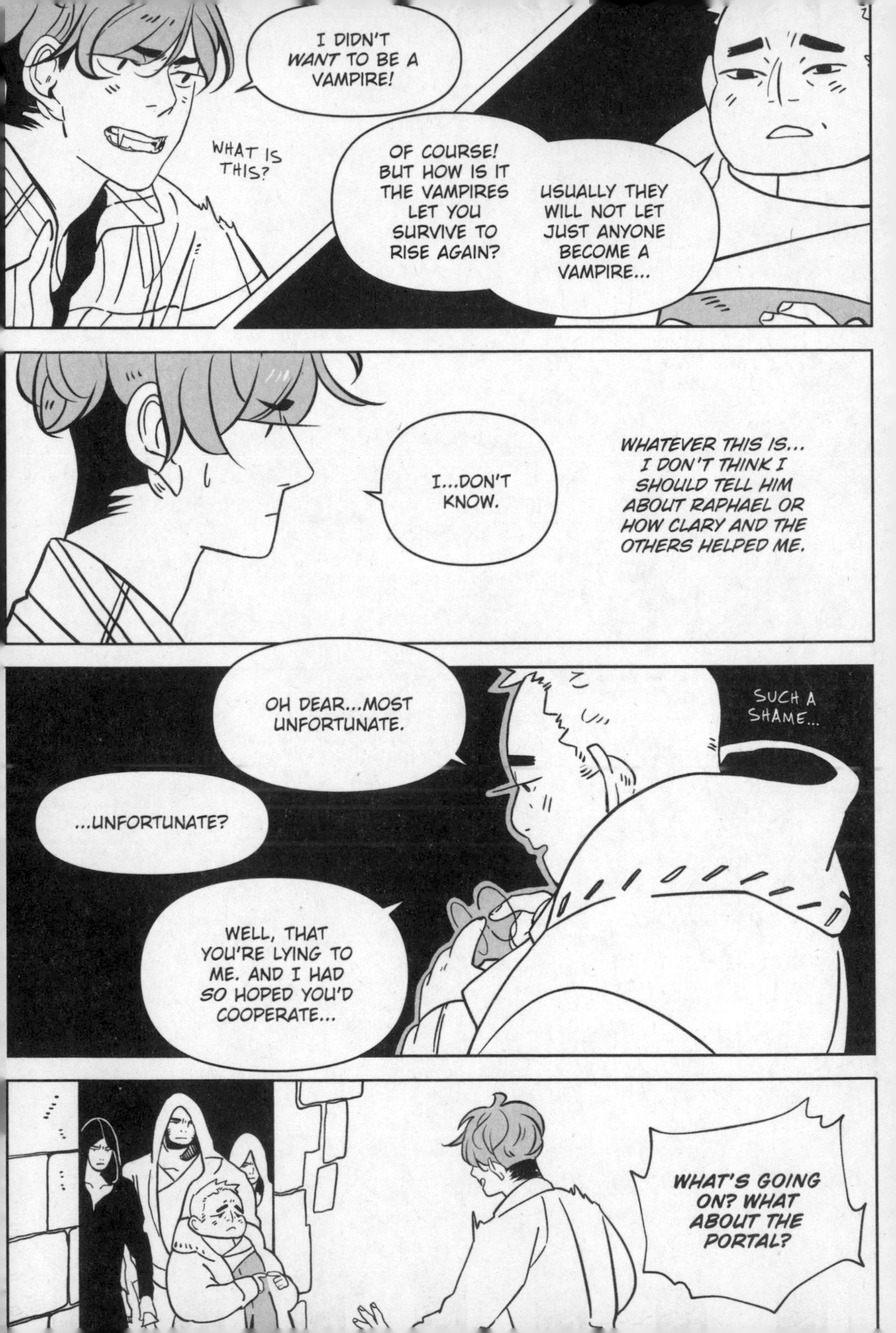
I DIDN'T *WANT* TO BE A VAMPIRE!
WHAT IS THIS?
OF COURSE! BUT HOW IS IT THE VAMPIRES LET YOU SURVIVE TO RISE AGAIN?
USUALLY THEY WILL NOT LET JUST ANYONE BECOME A VAMPIRE...
I...DON'T KNOW.
WHATEVER THIS IS... I DON'T THINK I SHOULD TELL HIM ABOUT RAPHAEL OR HOW CLARY AND THE OTHERS HELPED ME.
OH DEAR...MOST UNFORTUNATE.
SUCH A SHAME...
...UNFORTUNATE?
WELL, THAT YOU'RE LYING TO ME. AND I HAD SO HOPED YOU'D COOPERATE...
WHAT'S GOING ON? WHAT ABOUT THE PORTAL?

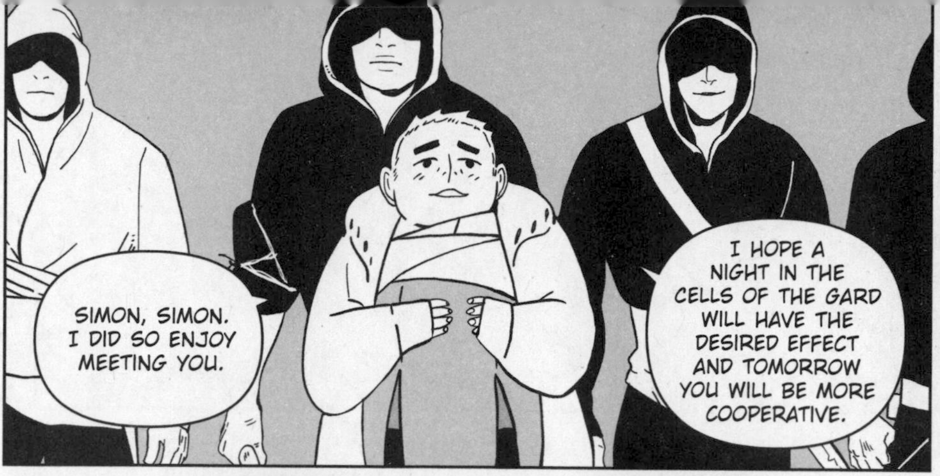
SIMON, SIMON. I DID SO ENJOY MEETING YOU.
I HOPE A NIGHT IN THE CELLS OF THE GARD WILL HAVE THE DESIRED EFFECT AND TOMORROW YOU WILL BE MORE COOPERATIVE.

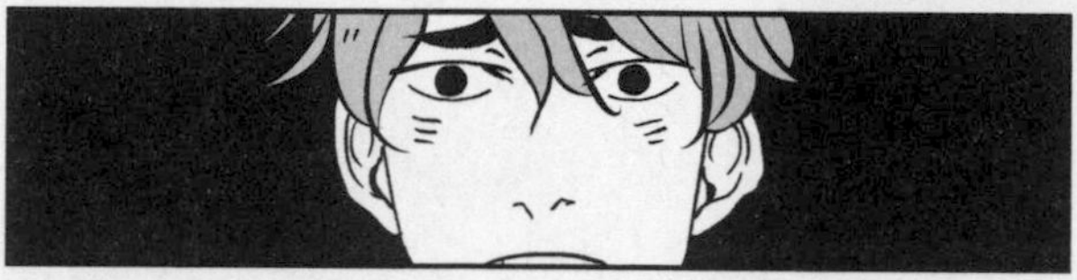

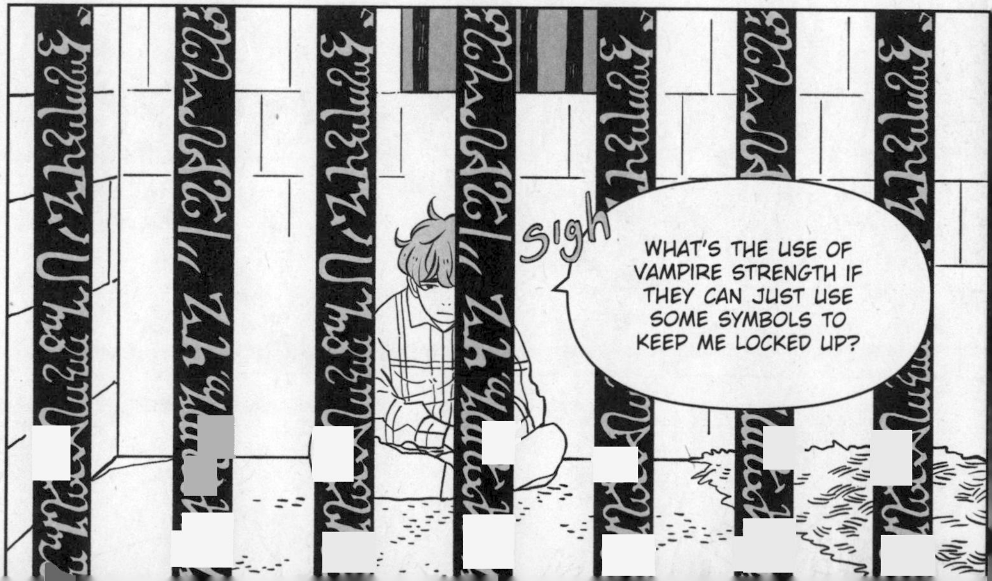
Sigh
WHAT'S THE USE OF VAMPIRE STRENGTH IF THEY CAN JUST USE SOME SYMBOLS TO KEEP ME LOCKED UP?

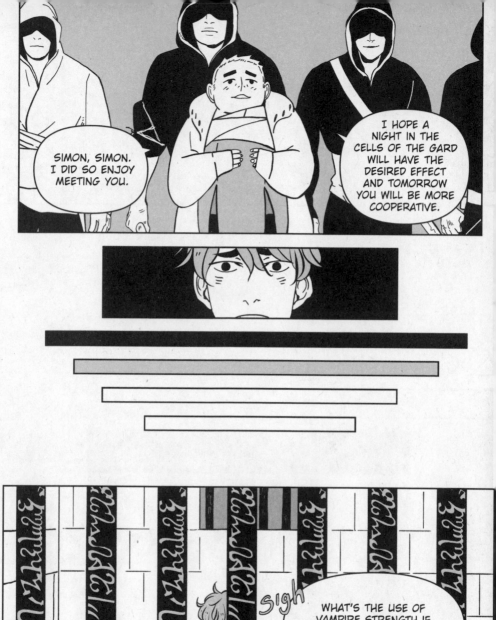

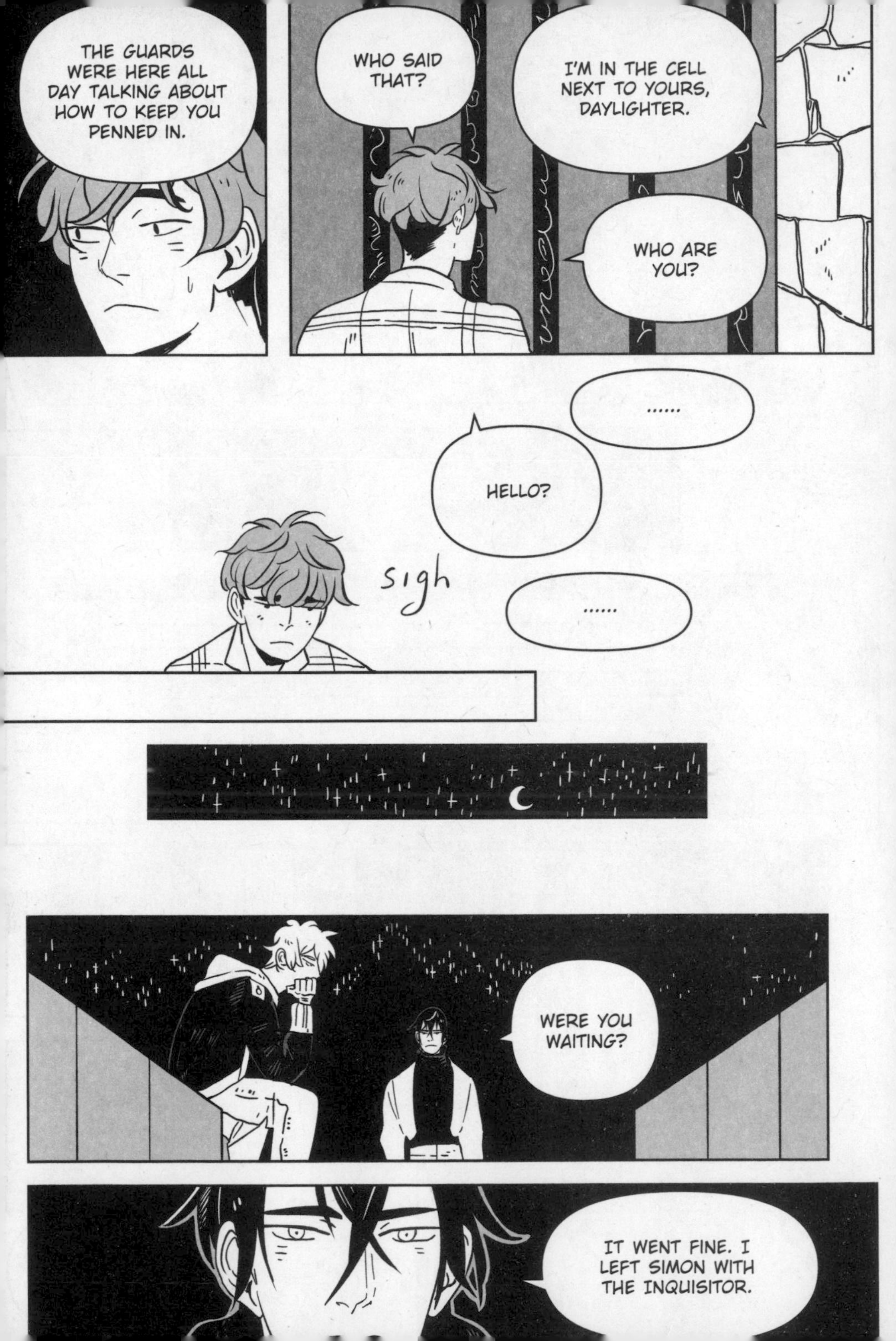
THE GUARDS WERE HERE ALL DAY TALKING ABOUT HOW TO KEEP YOU PENNED IN.
WHO SAID THAT?
I'M IN THE CELL NEXT TO YOURS, DAYLIGHTER.
WHO ARE YOU?
......
HELLO?
sigh
......
WERE YOU WAITING?
IT WENT FINE. I LEFT SIMON WITH THE INQUISITOR.

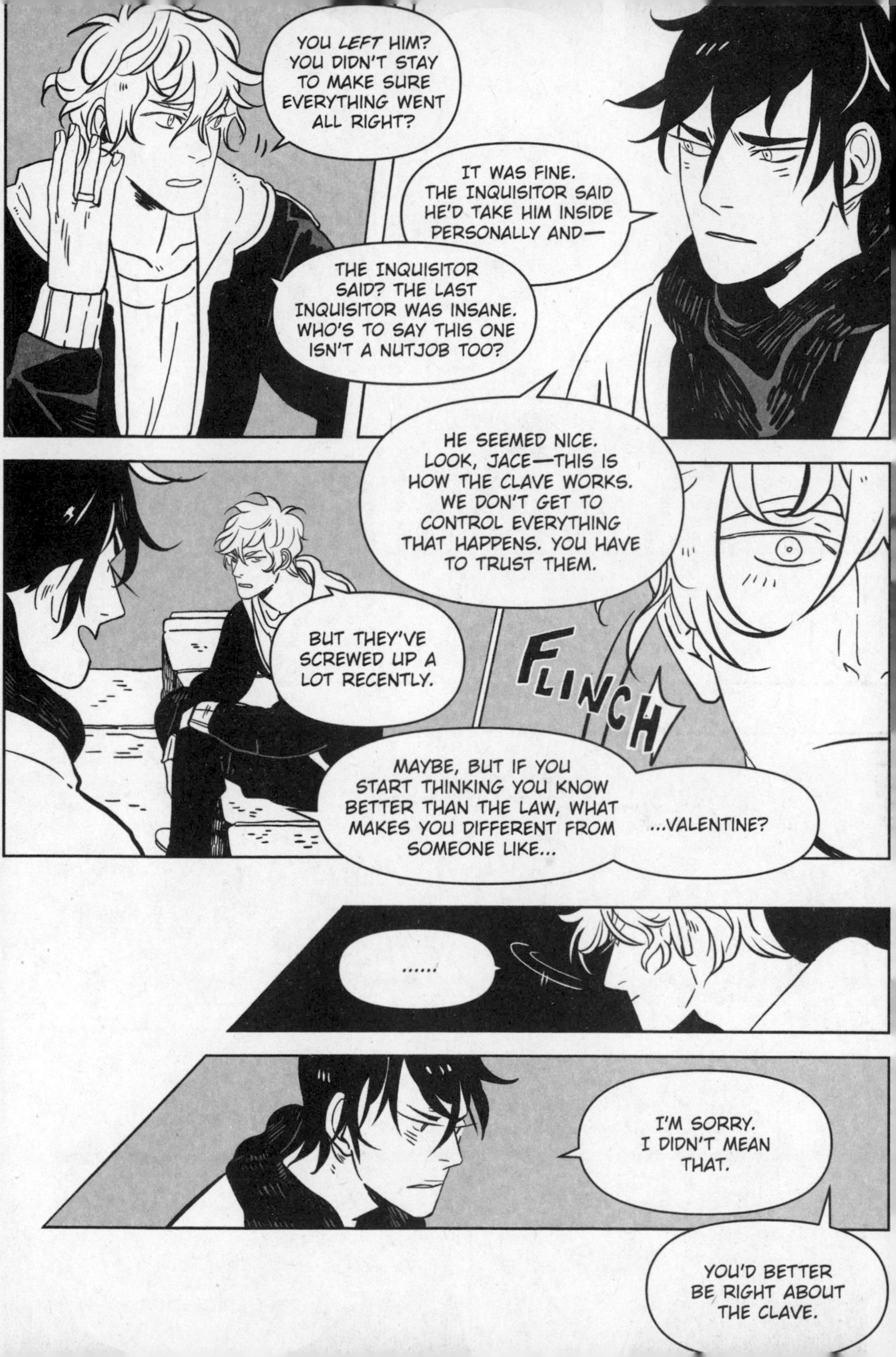
YOU *LEFT* HIM? YOU DIDN'T STAY TO MAKE SURE EVERYTHING WENT ALL RIGHT?
IT WAS FINE. THE INQUISITOR SAID HE'D TAKE HIM INSIDE PERSONALLY AND—
THE INQUISITOR SAID? THE LAST INQUISITOR WAS INSANE. WHO'S TO SAY THIS ONE ISN'T A NUTJOB TOO?
HE SEEMED NICE. LOOK, JACE—THIS IS HOW THE CLAVE WORKS. WE DON'T GET TO CONTROL EVERYTHING THAT HAPPENS. YOU HAVE TO TRUST THEM.
BUT THEY'VE SCREWED UP A LOT RECENTLY.
MAYBE, BUT IF YOU START THINKING YOU KNOW BETTER THAN THE LAW, WHAT MAKES YOU DIFFERENT FROM SOMEONE LIKE...
FLINCH
...VALENTINE?
......
I'M SORRY. I DIDN'T MEAN THAT.
YOU'D BETTER BE RIGHT ABOUT THE CLAVE.

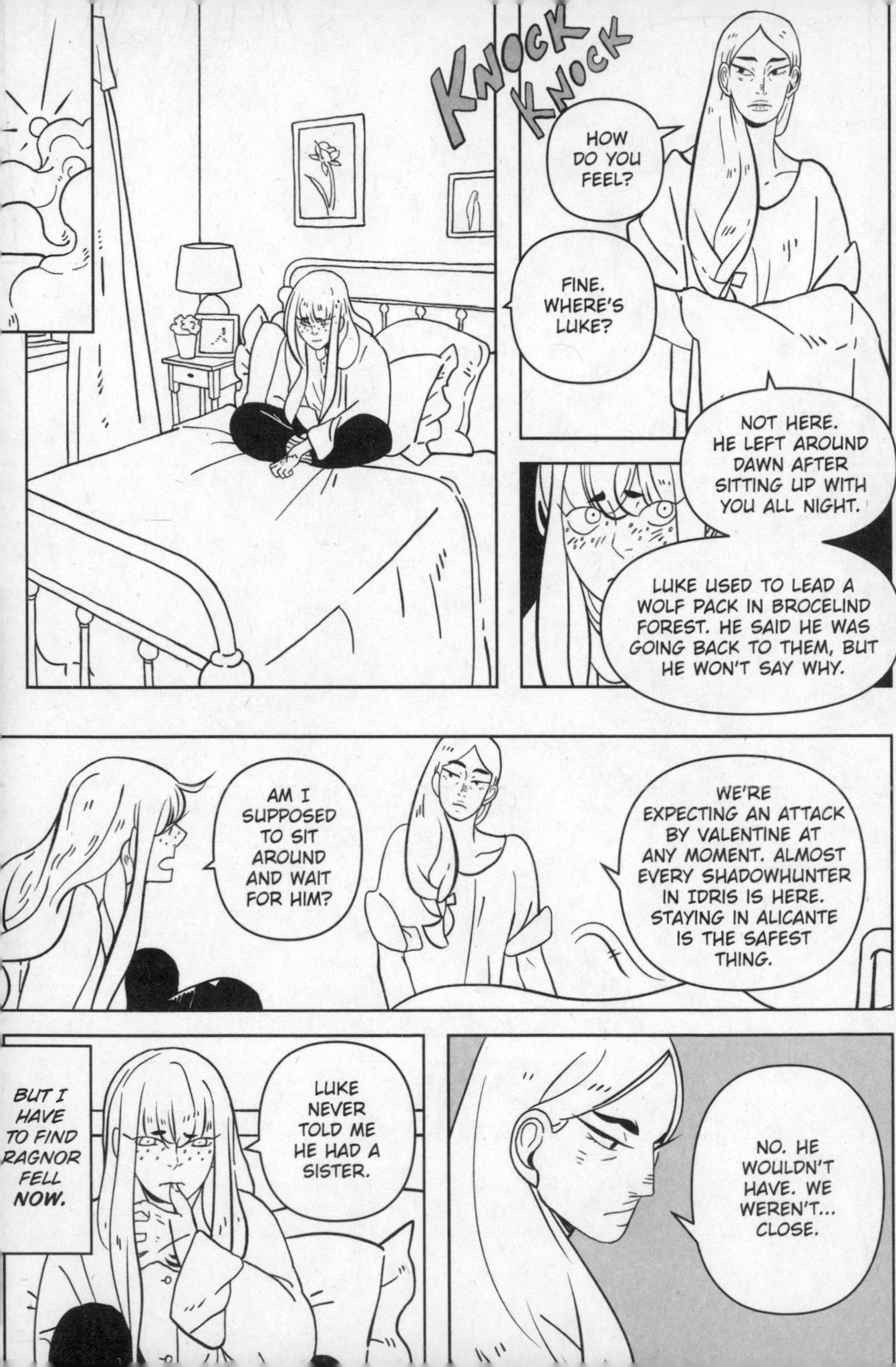
KNOCK KNOCK
HOW DO YOU FEEL?
FINE. WHERE'S LUKE?
NOT HERE. HE LEFT AROUND DAWN AFTER SITTING UP WITH YOU ALL NIGHT.
LUKE USED TO LEAD A WOLF PACK IN BROCELIND FOREST. HE SAID HE WAS GOING BACK TO THEM, BUT HE WON'T SAY WHY.
AM I SUPPOSED TO SIT AROUND AND WAIT FOR HIM?
WE'RE EXPECTING AN ATTACK BY VALENTINE AT ANY MOMENT. ALMOST EVERY SHADOWHUNTER IN IDRIS IS HERE. STAYING IN ALICANTE IS THE SAFEST THING.
BUT I HAVE TO FIND RAGNOR FELL *NOW.*
LUKE NEVER TOLD ME HE HAD A SISTER.
NO. HE WOULDN'T HAVE. WE WEREN'T... CLOSE.

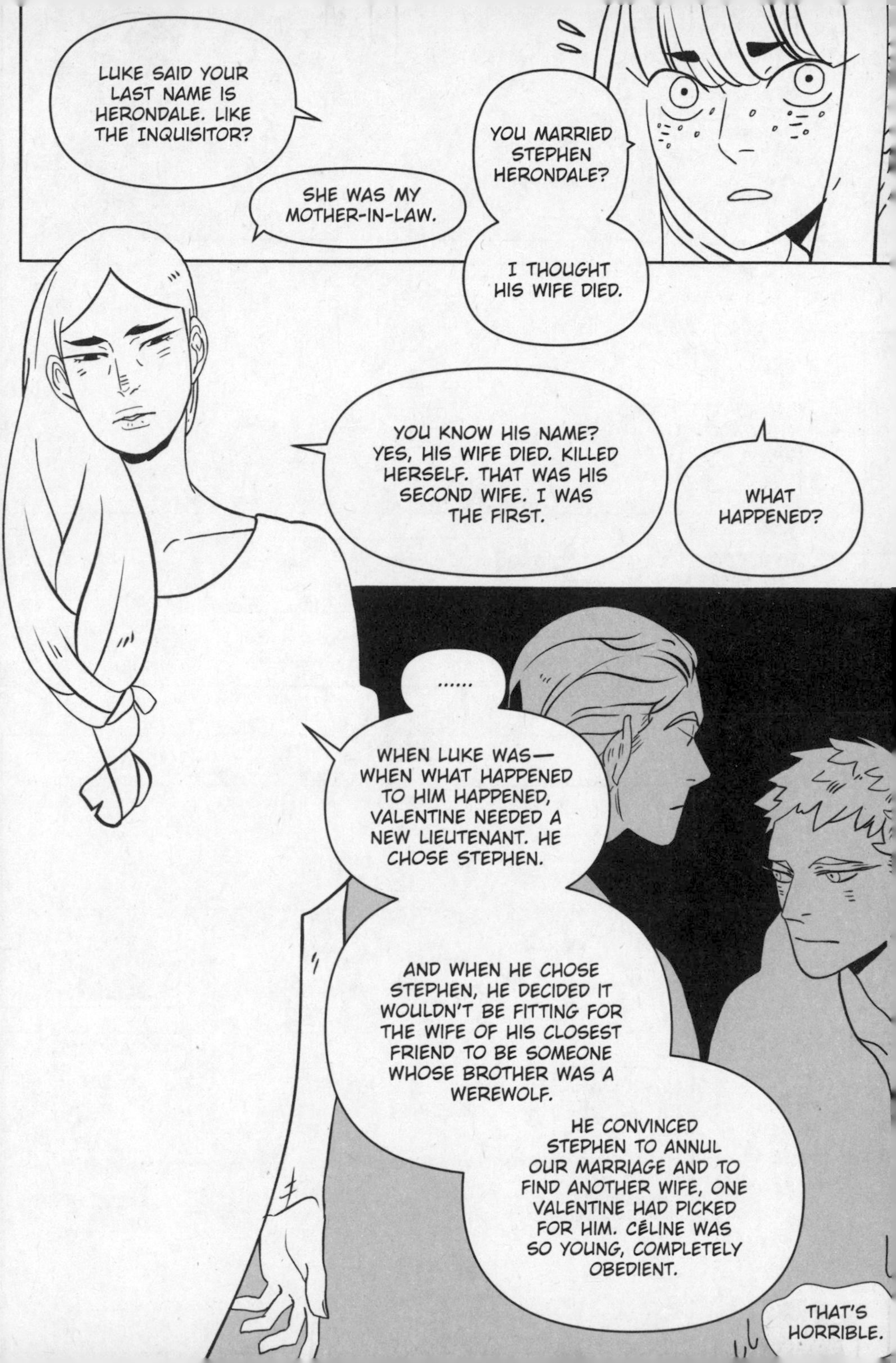
LUKE SAID YOUR LAST NAME IS HERONDALE. LIKE THE INQUISITOR?
SHE WAS MY MOTHER-IN-LAW.
YOU MARRIED STEPHEN HERONDALE?
I THOUGHT HIS WIFE DIED.
YOU KNOW HIS NAME? YES, HIS WIFE DIED. KILLED HERSELF. THAT WAS HIS SECOND WIFE. I WAS THE FIRST.
WHAT HAPPENED?
......
WHEN LUKE WAS— WHEN WHAT HAPPENED TO HIM HAPPENED, VALENTINE NEEDED A NEW LIEUTENANT. HE CHOSE STEPHEN.
AND WHEN HE CHOSE STEPHEN, HE DECIDED IT WOULDN'T BE FITTING FOR THE WIFE OF HIS CLOSEST FRIEND TO BE SOMEONE WHOSE BROTHER WAS A WEREWOLF.
HE CONVINCED STEPHEN TO ANNUL OUR MARRIAGE AND TO FIND ANOTHER WIFE, ONE VALENTINE HAD PICKED FOR HIM. CÉLINE WAS SO YOUNG, COMPLETELY OBEDIENT.
THAT'S HORRIBLE.

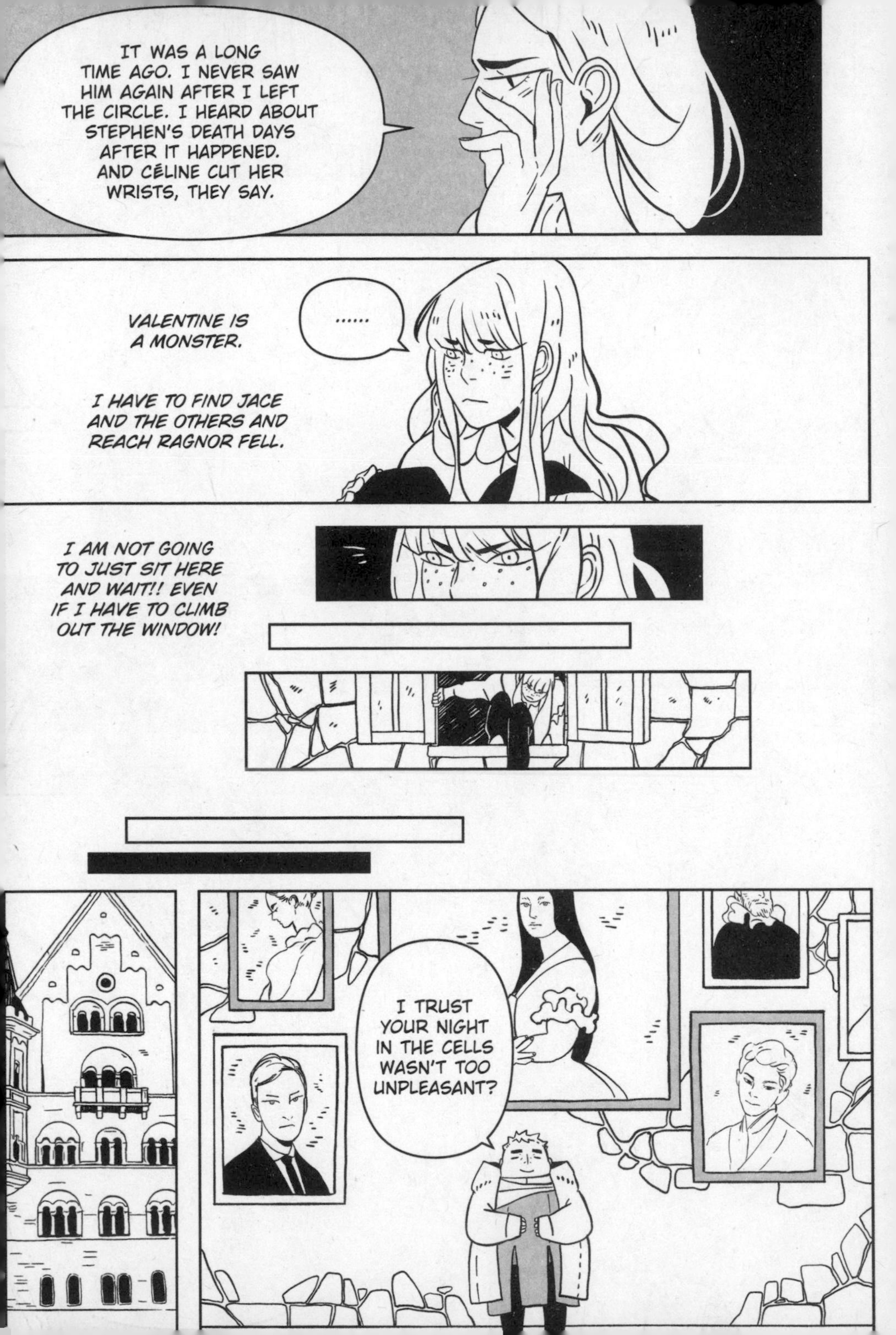
IT WAS A LONG TIME AGO. I NEVER SAW HIM AGAIN AFTER I LEFT THE CIRCLE. I HEARD ABOUT STEPHEN'S DEATH DAYS AFTER IT HAPPENED. AND CÉLINE CUT HER WRISTS, THEY SAY.
VALENTINE IS A MONSTER.
......
I HAVE TO FIND JACE AND THE OTHERS AND REACH RAGNOR FELL.
I AM NOT GOING TO JUST SIT HERE AND WAIT!! EVEN IF I HAVE TO CLIMB OUT THE WINDOW!
I TRUST YOUR NIGHT IN THE CELLS WASN'T TOO UNPLEASANT?

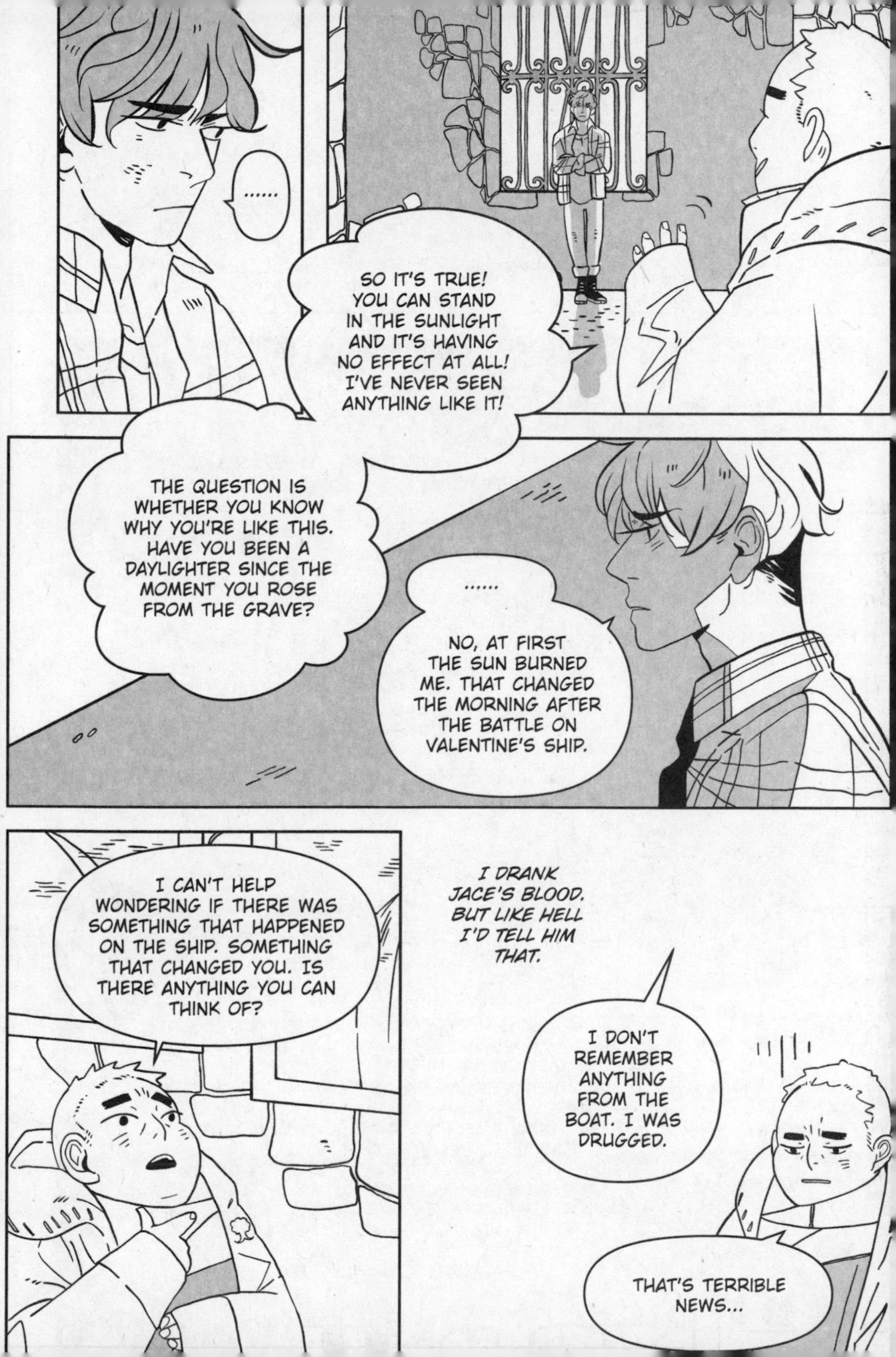
......
SO IT'S TRUE! YOU CAN STAND IN THE SUNLIGHT AND IT'S HAVING NO EFFECT AT ALL! I'VE NEVER SEEN ANYTHING LIKE IT!
THE QUESTION IS WHETHER YOU KNOW WHY YOU'RE LIKE THIS. HAVE YOU BEEN A DAYLIGHTER SINCE THE MOMENT YOU ROSE FROM THE GRAVE?
......
NO, AT FIRST THE SUN BURNED ME. THAT CHANGED THE MORNING AFTER THE BATTLE ON VALENTINE'S SHIP.
I CAN'T HELP WONDERING IF THERE WAS SOMETHING THAT HAPPENED ON THE SHIP. SOMETHING THAT CHANGED YOU. IS THERE ANYTHING YOU CAN THINK OF?
I DRANK JACE'S BLOOD. BUT LIKE HELL I'D TELL HIM THAT.
I DON'T REMEMBER ANYTHING FROM THE BOAT. I WAS DRUGGED.
THAT'S TERRIBLE NEWS...

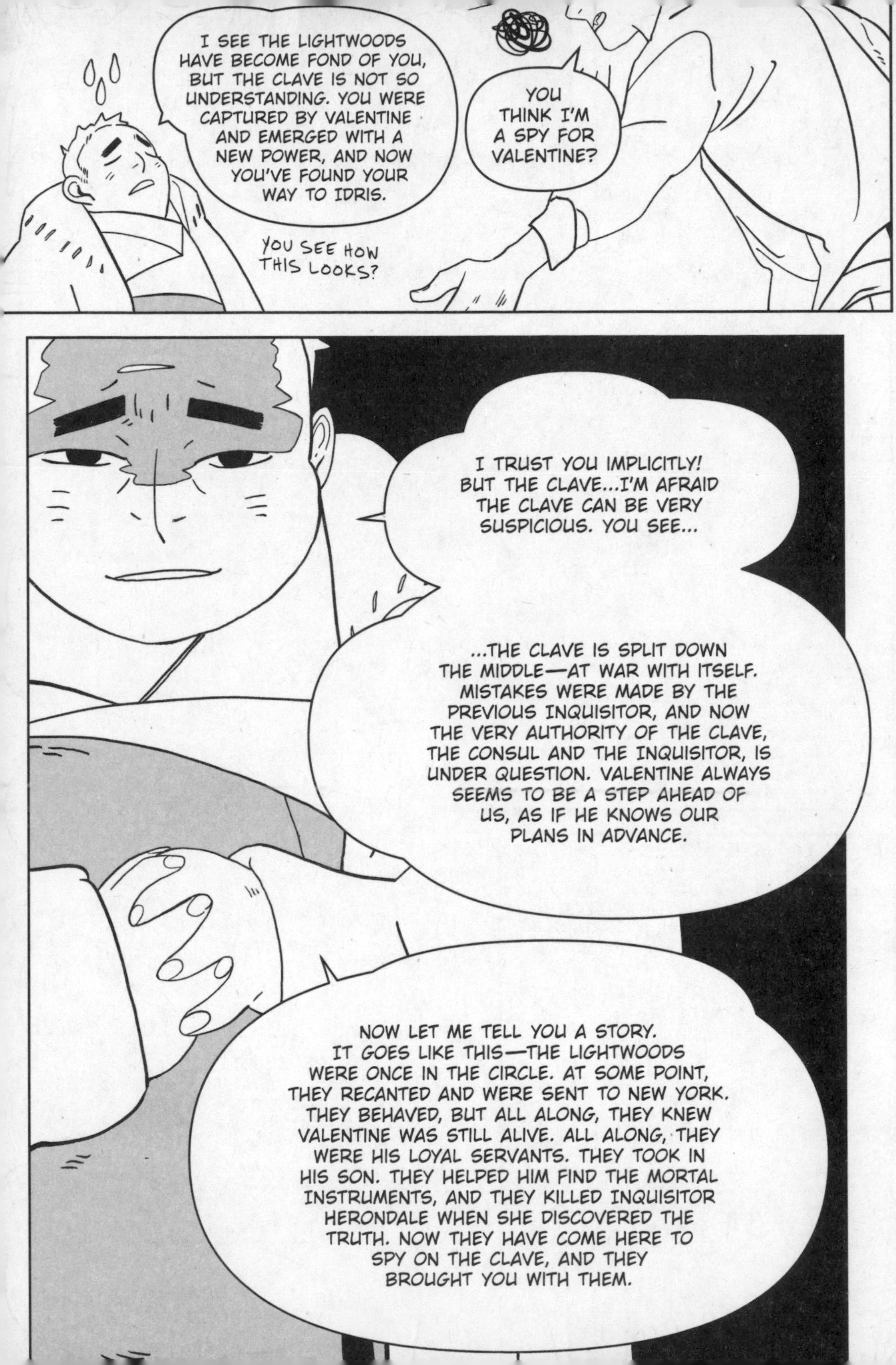
I SEE THE LIGHTWOODS HAVE BECOME FOND OF YOU, BUT THE CLAVE IS NOT SO UNDERSTANDING. YOU WERE CAPTURED BY VALENTINE AND EMERGED WITH A NEW POWER, AND NOW YOU'VE FOUND YOUR WAY TO IDRIS.
YOU SEE HOW THIS LOOKS?
YOU THINK I'M A SPY FOR VALENTINE?
I TRUST YOU IMPLICITLY! BUT THE CLAVE...I'M AFRAID THE CLAVE CAN BE VERY SUSPICIOUS. YOU SEE...
...THE CLAVE IS SPLIT DOWN THE MIDDLE—AT WAR WITH ITSELF. MISTAKES WERE MADE BY THE PREVIOUS INQUISITOR, AND NOW THE VERY AUTHORITY OF THE CLAVE, THE CONSUL AND THE INQUISITOR, IS UNDER QUESTION. VALENTINE ALWAYS SEEMS TO BE A STEP AHEAD OF US, AS IF HE KNOWS OUR PLANS IN ADVANCE.
NOW LET ME TELL YOU A STORY. IT GOES LIKE THIS—THE LIGHTWOODS WERE ONCE IN THE CIRCLE. AT SOME POINT, THEY RECANTED AND WERE SENT TO NEW YORK. THEY BEHAVED, BUT ALL ALONG, THEY KNEW VALENTINE WAS STILL ALIVE. ALL ALONG, THEY WERE HIS LOYAL SERVANTS. THEY TOOK IN HIS SON. THEY HELPED HIM FIND THE MORTAL INSTRUMENTS, AND THEY KILLED INQUISITOR HERONDALE WHEN SHE DISCOVERED THE TRUTH. NOW THEY HAVE COME HERE TO SPY ON THE CLAVE, AND THEY BROUGHT YOU WITH THEM.

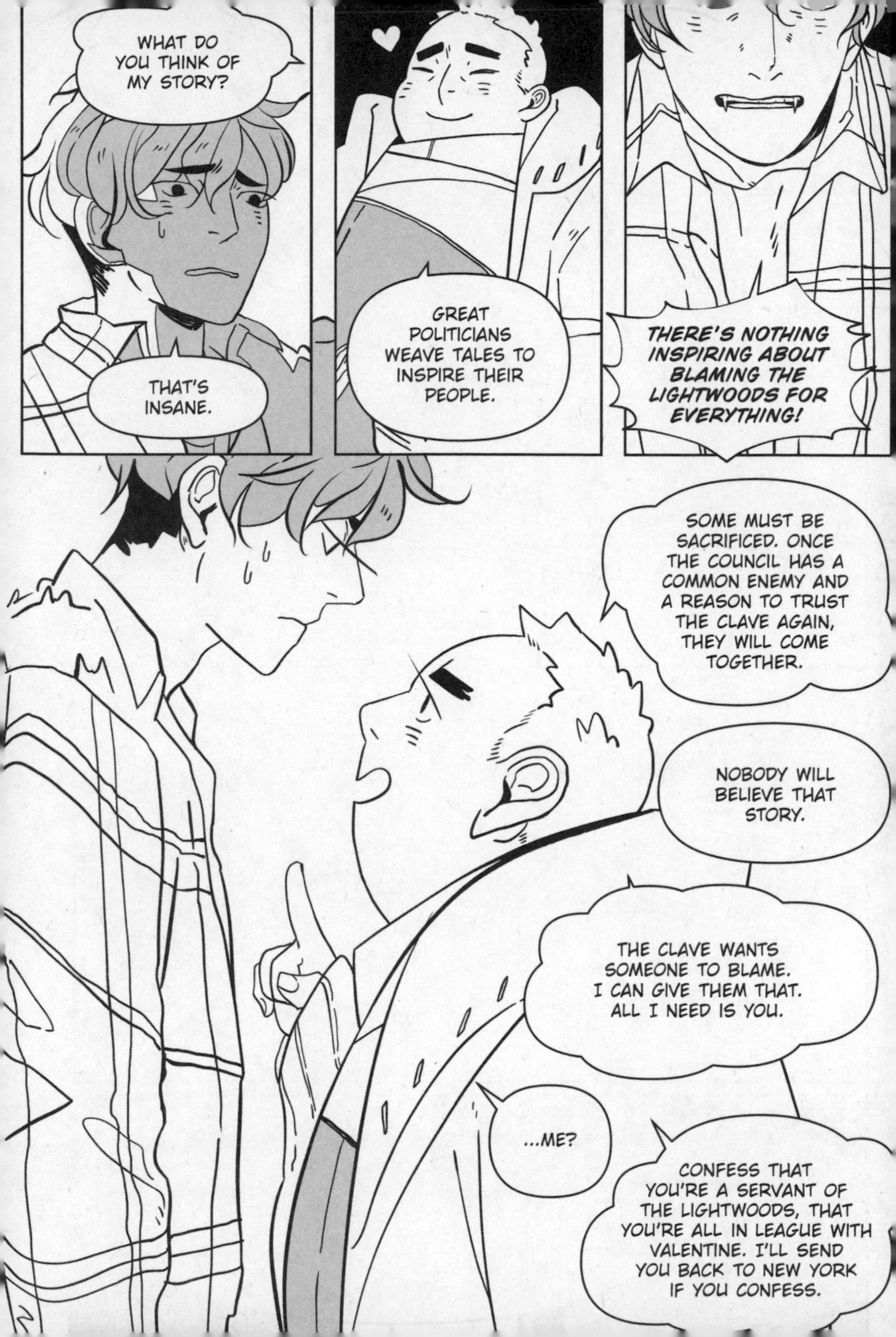
WHAT DO YOU THINK OF MY STORY?
THAT'S INSANE.
GREAT POLITICIANS WEAVE TALES TO INSPIRE THEIR PEOPLE.
THERE'S NOTHING INSPIRING ABOUT BLAMING THE LIGHTWOODS FOR EVERYTHING!
SOME MUST BE SACRIFICED. ONCE THE COUNCIL HAS A COMMON ENEMY AND A REASON TO TRUST THE CLAVE AGAIN, THEY WILL COME TOGETHER.
NOBODY WILL BELIEVE THAT STORY.
THE CLAVE WANTS SOMEONE TO BLAME. I CAN GIVE THEM THAT. ALL I NEED IS YOU.
...ME?
CONFESS THAT YOU'RE A SERVANT OF THE LIGHTWOODS, THAT YOU'RE ALL IN LEAGUE WITH VALENTINE. I'LL SEND YOU BACK TO NEW YORK IF YOU CONFESS.

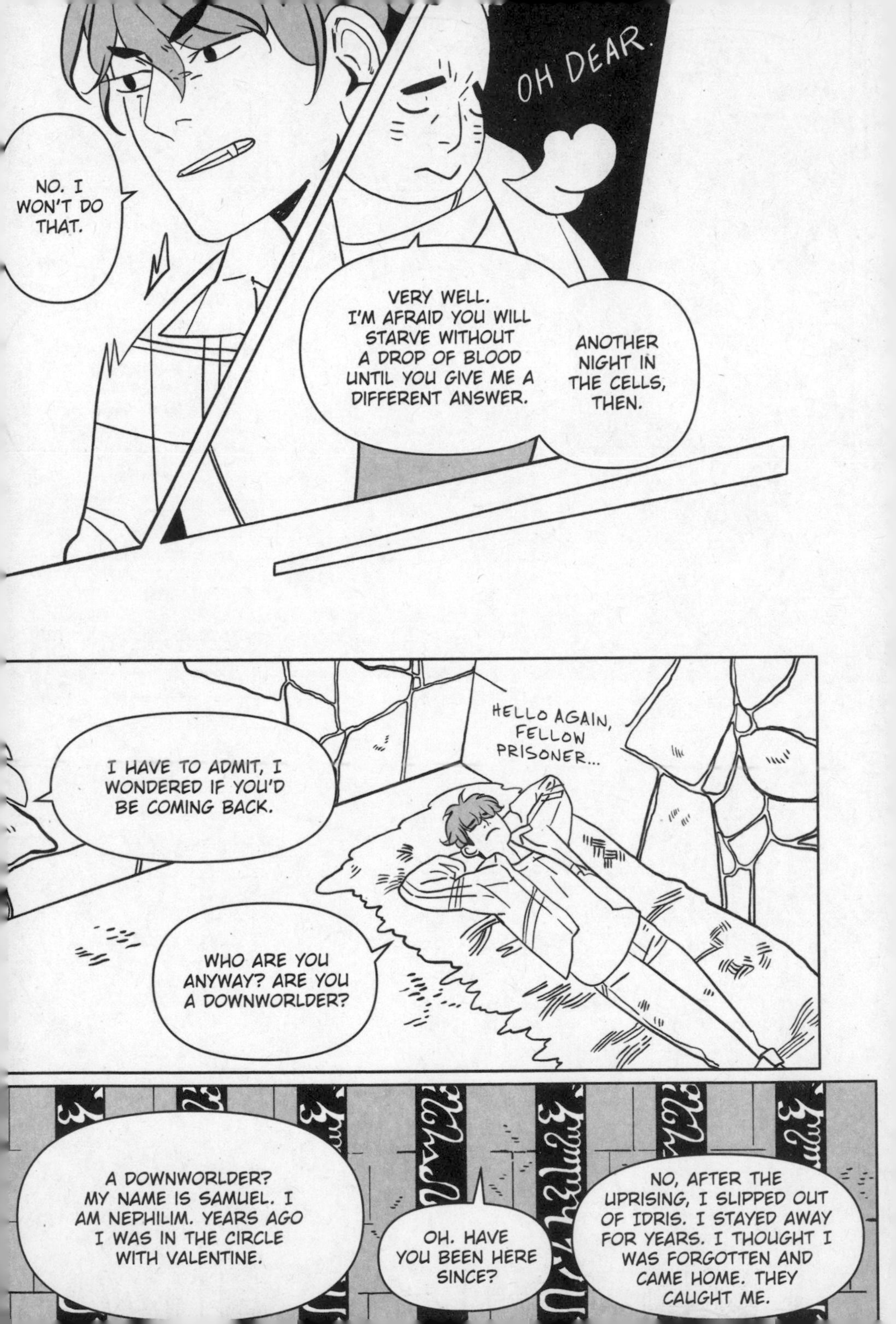
NO. I WON'T DO THAT.
OH DEAR.
VERY WELL. I'M AFRAID YOU WILL STARVE WITHOUT A DROP OF BLOOD UNTIL YOU GIVE ME A DIFFERENT ANSWER.
ANOTHER NIGHT IN THE CELLS, THEN.
I HAVE TO ADMIT, I WONDERED IF YOU'D BE COMING BACK.
HELLO AGAIN, FELLOW PRISONER...
WHO ARE YOU ANYWAY? ARE YOU A DOWNWORLDER?
A DOWNWORLDER? MY NAME IS SAMUEL. I AM NEPHILIM. YEARS AGO I WAS IN THE CIRCLE WITH VALENTINE.
OH. HAVE YOU BEEN HERE SINCE?
NO, AFTER THE UPRISING, I SLIPPED OUT OF IDRIS. I STAYED AWAY FOR YEARS. I THOUGHT I WAS FORGOTTEN AND CAME HOME. THEY CAUGHT ME.

BUT THERE ARE PLENTY OF OTHER SHADOWHUNTERS WHO USED TO BE CIRCLE MEMBERS.

LIKE THE LIGHTWOODS AND PENHALLOWS.

THEY ALL RECANTED, TURNED THEIR BACKS ON VALENTINE. I DIDN'T.

WHY NOT?

I'M MORE AFRAID OF VALENTINE THAN I AM OF THE CLAVE. IF YOU WERE SMART, YOU WOULD BE TOO.

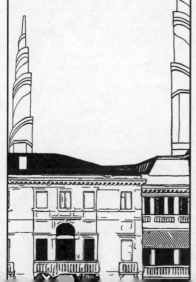

KNOCK KNOCK

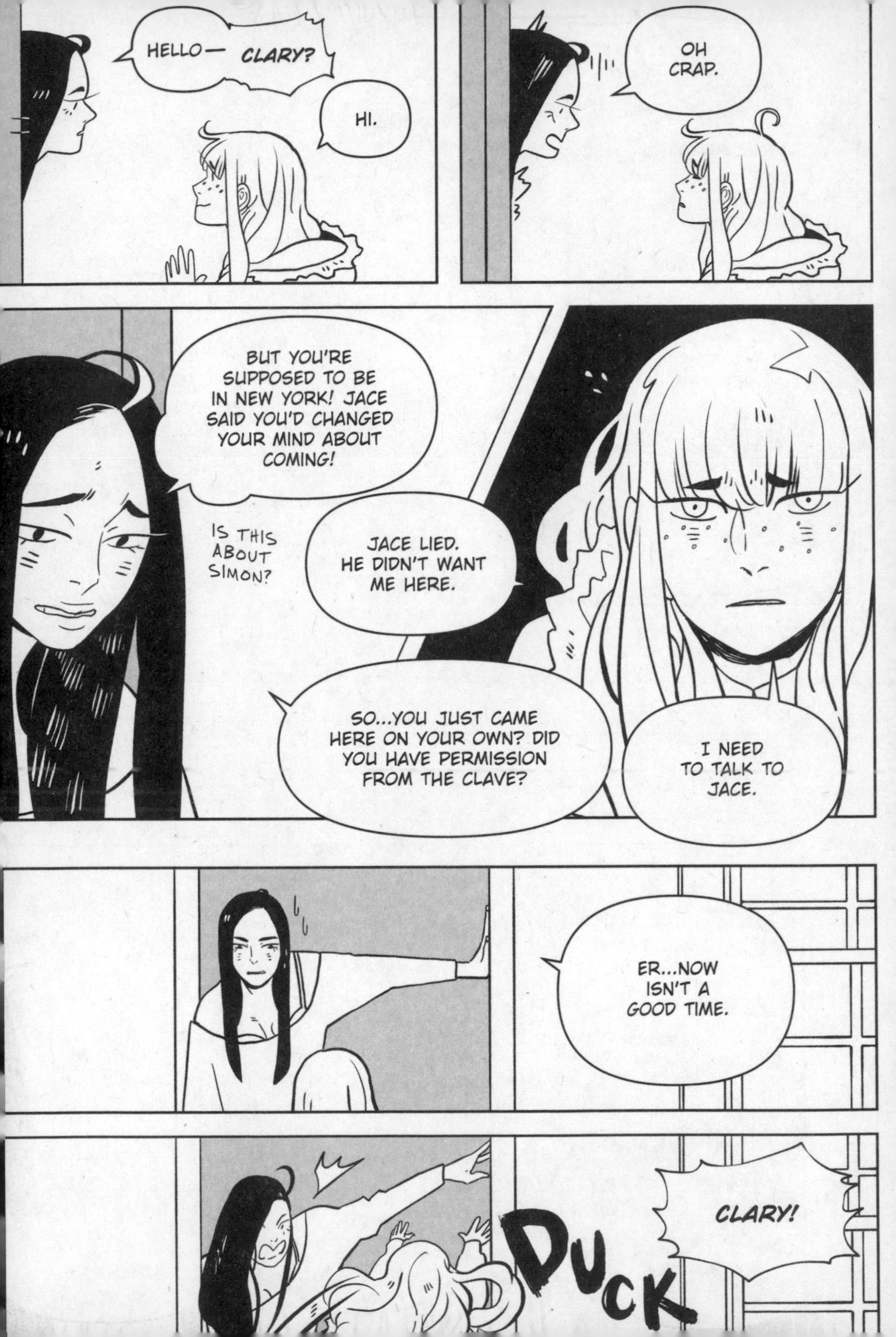
HELLO— CLARY?
HI.
OH CRAP.
BUT YOU'RE SUPPOSED TO BE IN NEW YORK! JACE SAID YOU'D CHANGED YOUR MIND ABOUT COMING!
IS THIS ABOUT SIMON?
JACE LIED. HE DIDN'T WANT ME HERE.
SO...YOU JUST CAME HERE ON YOUR OWN? DID YOU HAVE PERMISSION FROM THE CLAVE?
I NEED TO TALK TO JACE.
ER...NOW ISN'T A GOOD TIME.
DUCK
CLARY!

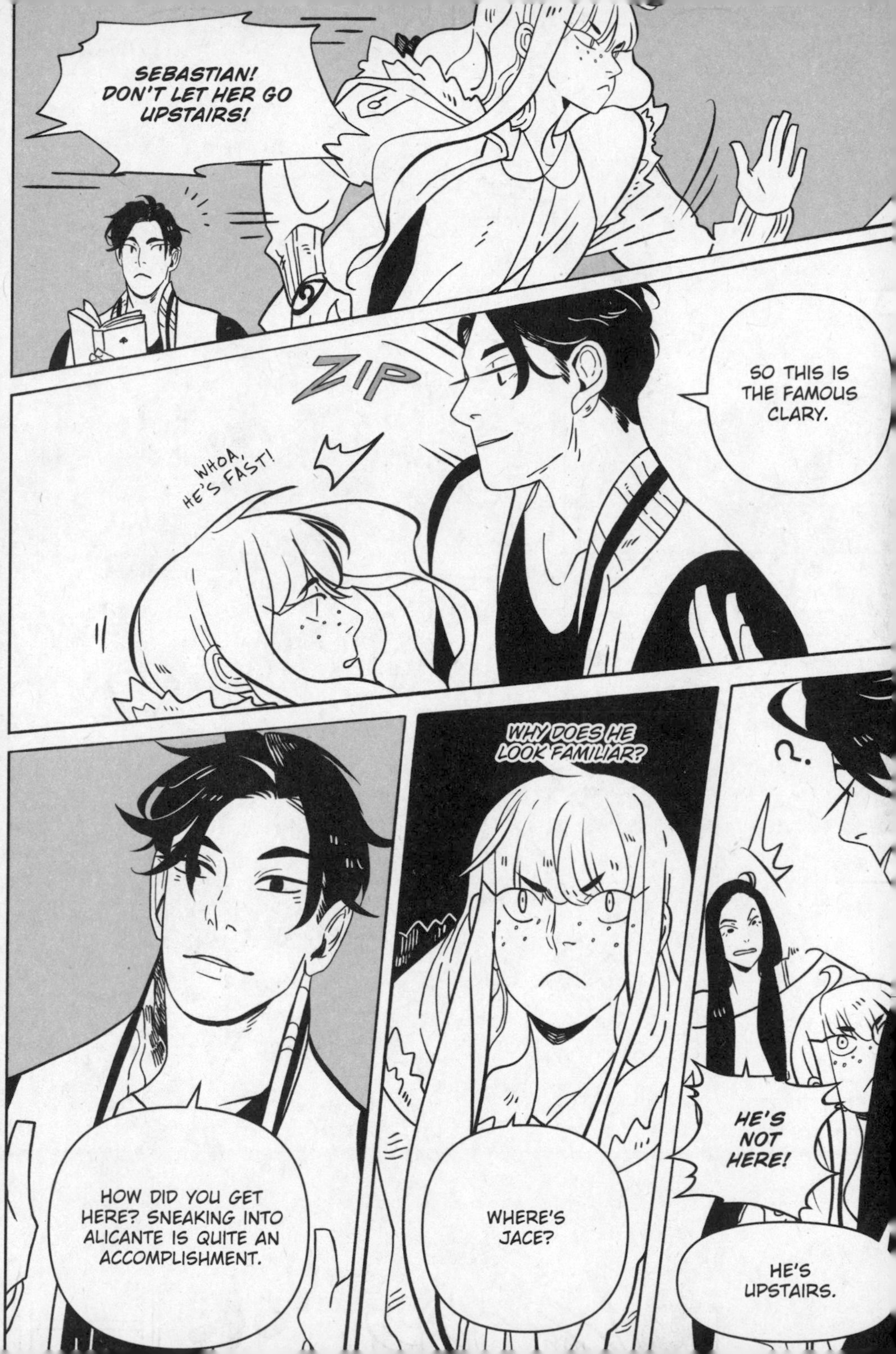
SEBASTIAN! DON'T LET HER GO UPSTAIRS!
ZIP
WHOA, HE'S FAST!
SO THIS IS THE FAMOUS CLARY.
HOW DID YOU GET HERE? SNEAKING INTO ALICANTE IS QUITE AN ACCOMPLISHMENT.
WHY DOES HE LOOK FAMILIAR?
WHERE'S JACE?
?
HE'S NOT HERE!
HE'S UPSTAIRS.

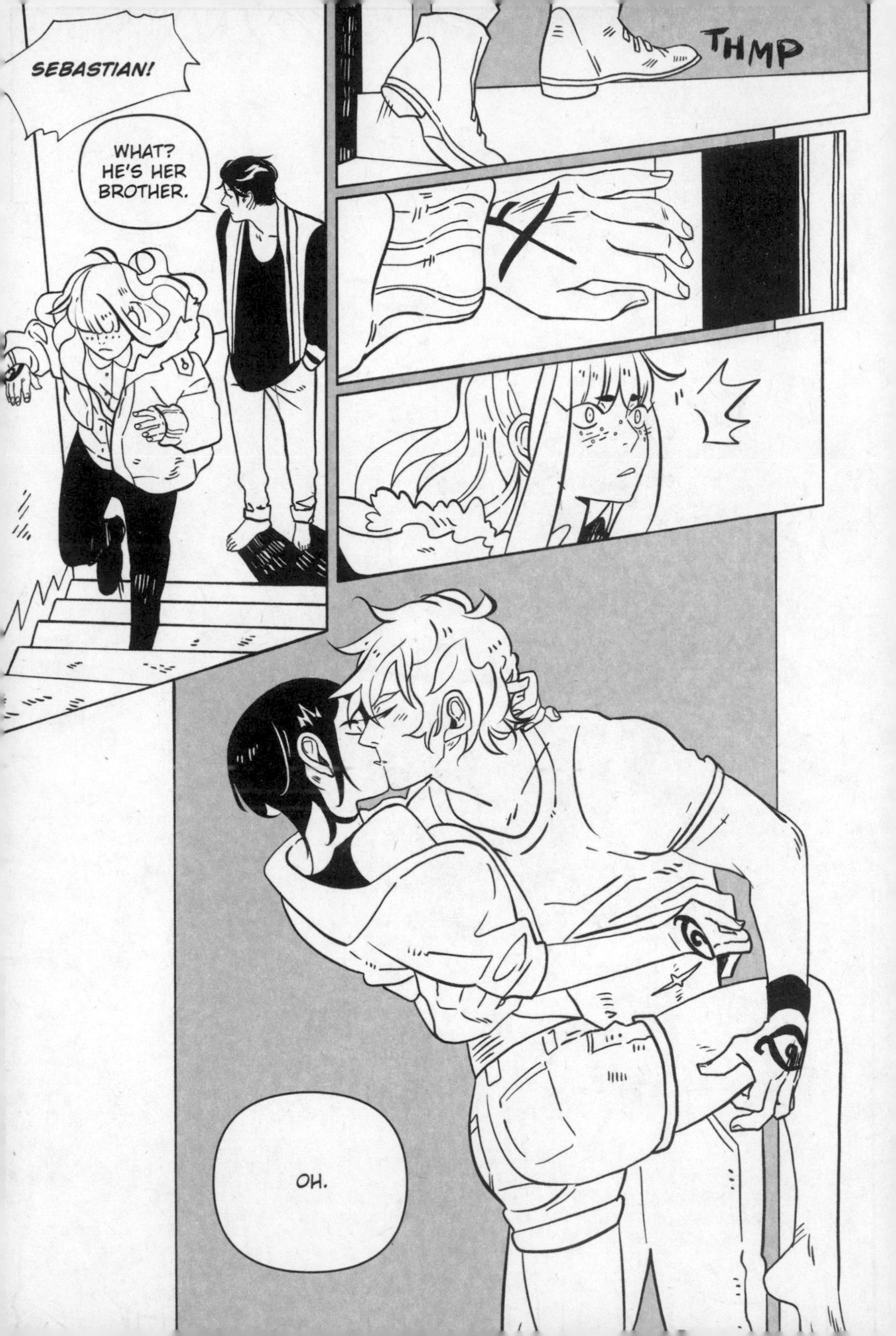
SEBASTIAN!
WHAT? HE'S HER BROTHER.
THMP
OH.

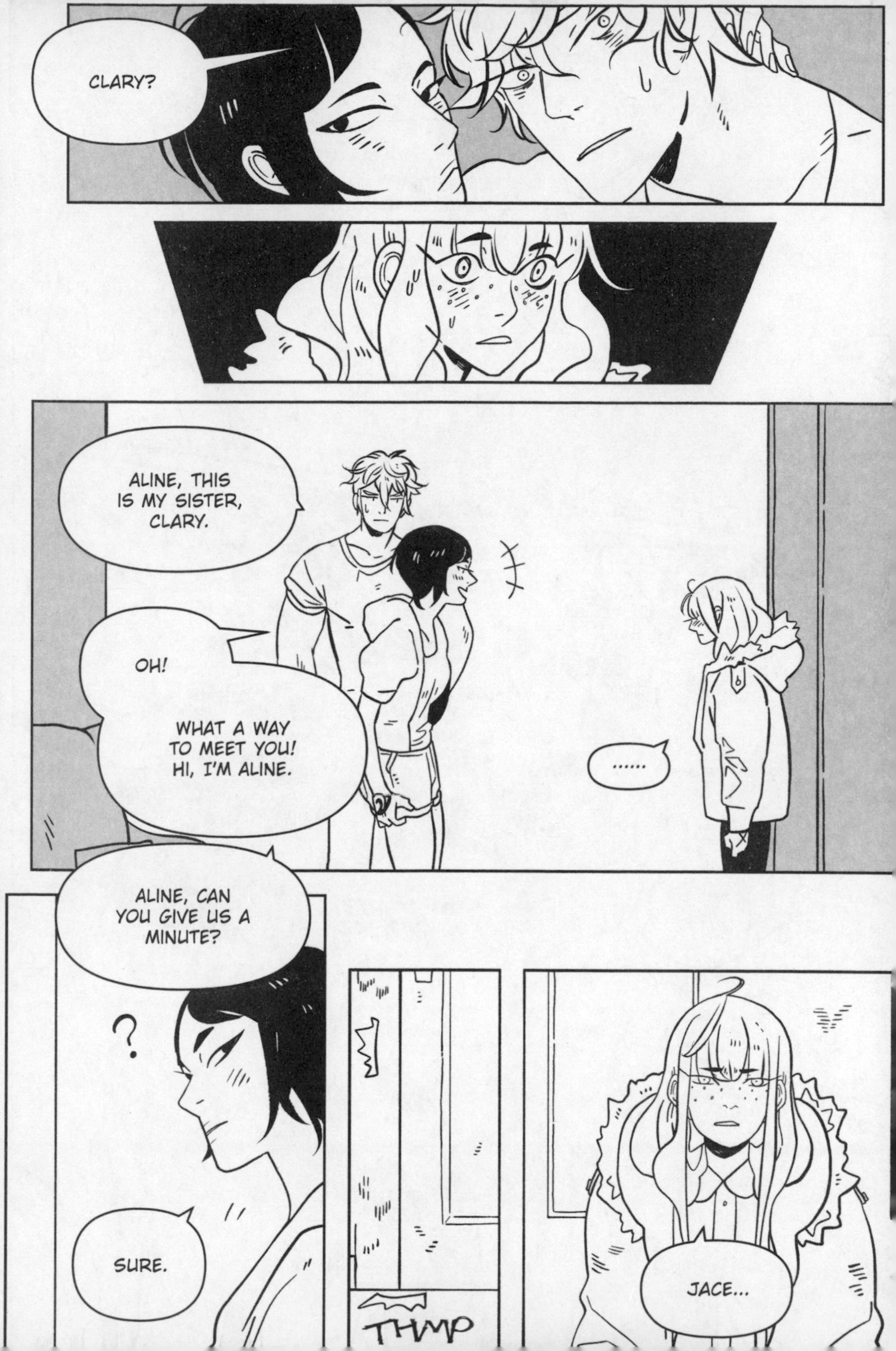
CLARY?
ALINE, THIS IS MY SISTER, CLARY.
OH!
WHAT A WAY TO MEET YOU! HI, I'M ALINE.
......
ALINE, CAN YOU GIVE US A MINUTE?
?
SURE.
THMP
JACE...

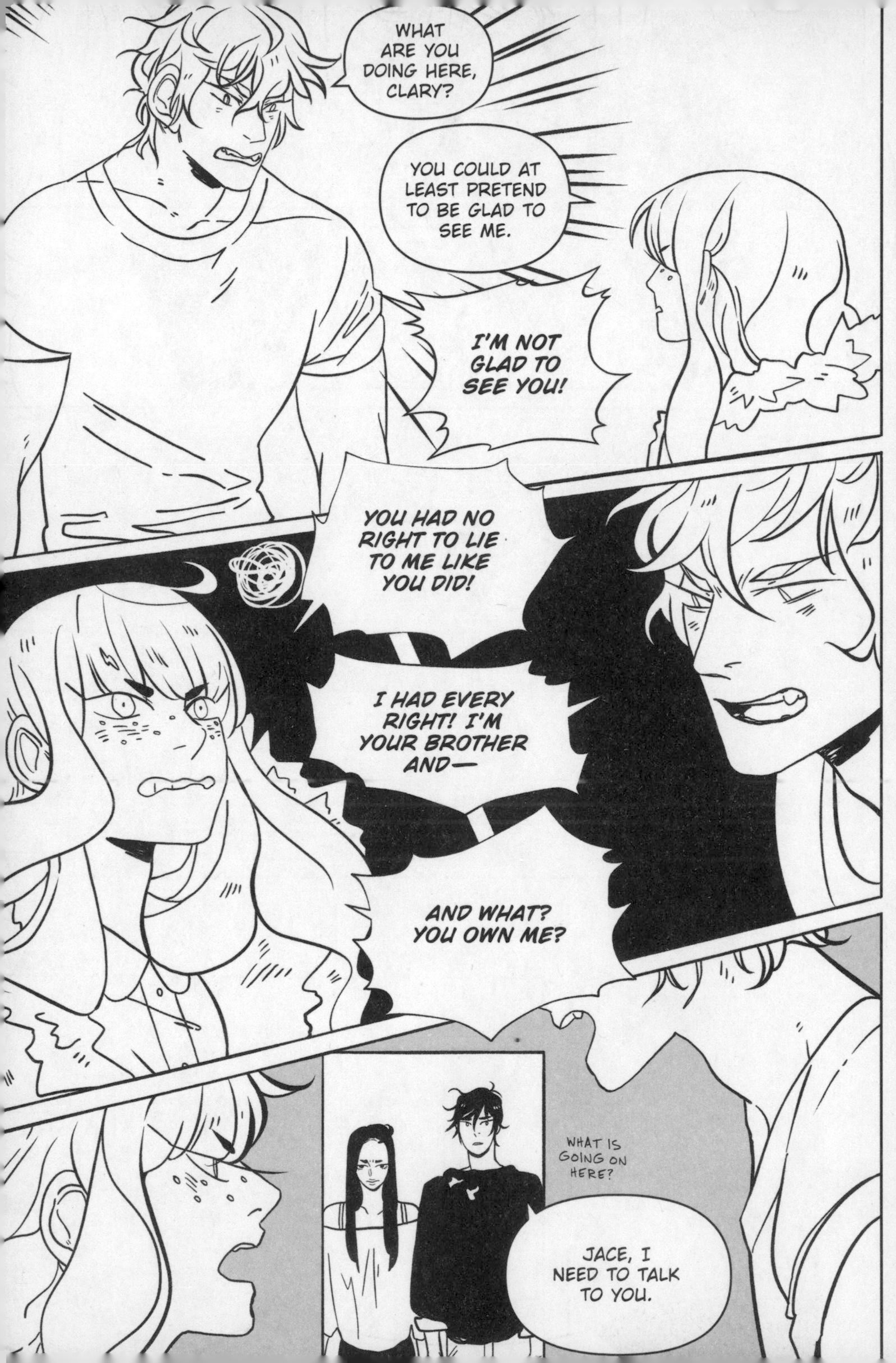
WHAT ARE YOU DOING HERE, CLARY?
YOU COULD AT LEAST PRETEND TO BE GLAD TO SEE ME.
I'M NOT GLAD TO SEE YOU!
YOU HAD NO RIGHT TO LIE TO ME LIKE YOU DID!
I HAD EVERY RIGHT! I'M YOUR BROTHER AND—
AND WHAT? YOU OWN ME?
WHAT IS GOING ON HERE?
JACE, I NEED TO TALK TO YOU.

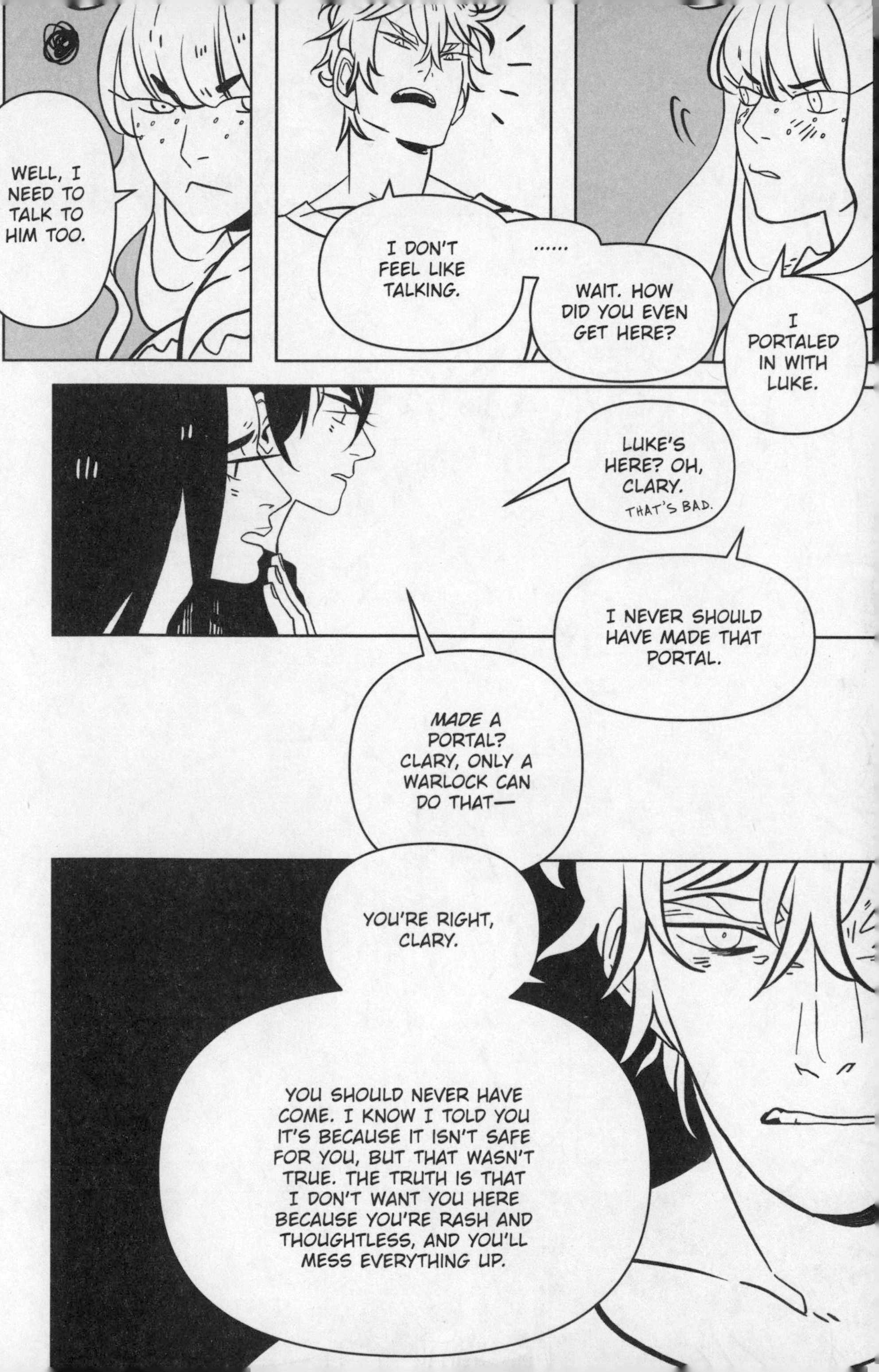
WELL, I NEED TO TALK TO HIM TOO.
I DON'T FEEL LIKE TALKING.
......
WAIT. HOW DID YOU EVEN GET HERE?
I PORTALED IN WITH LUKE.
LUKE'S HERE? OH, CLARY. THAT'S BAD.
I NEVER SHOULD HAVE MADE THAT PORTAL.
MADE A PORTAL? CLARY, ONLY A WARLOCK CAN DO THAT—
YOU'RE RIGHT, CLARY.
YOU SHOULD NEVER HAVE COME. I KNOW I TOLD YOU IT'S BECAUSE IT ISN'T SAFE FOR YOU, BUT THAT WASN'T TRUE. THE TRUTH IS THAT I DON'T WANT YOU HERE BECAUSE YOU'RE RASH AND THOUGHTLESS, AND YOU'LL MESS EVERYTHING UP.

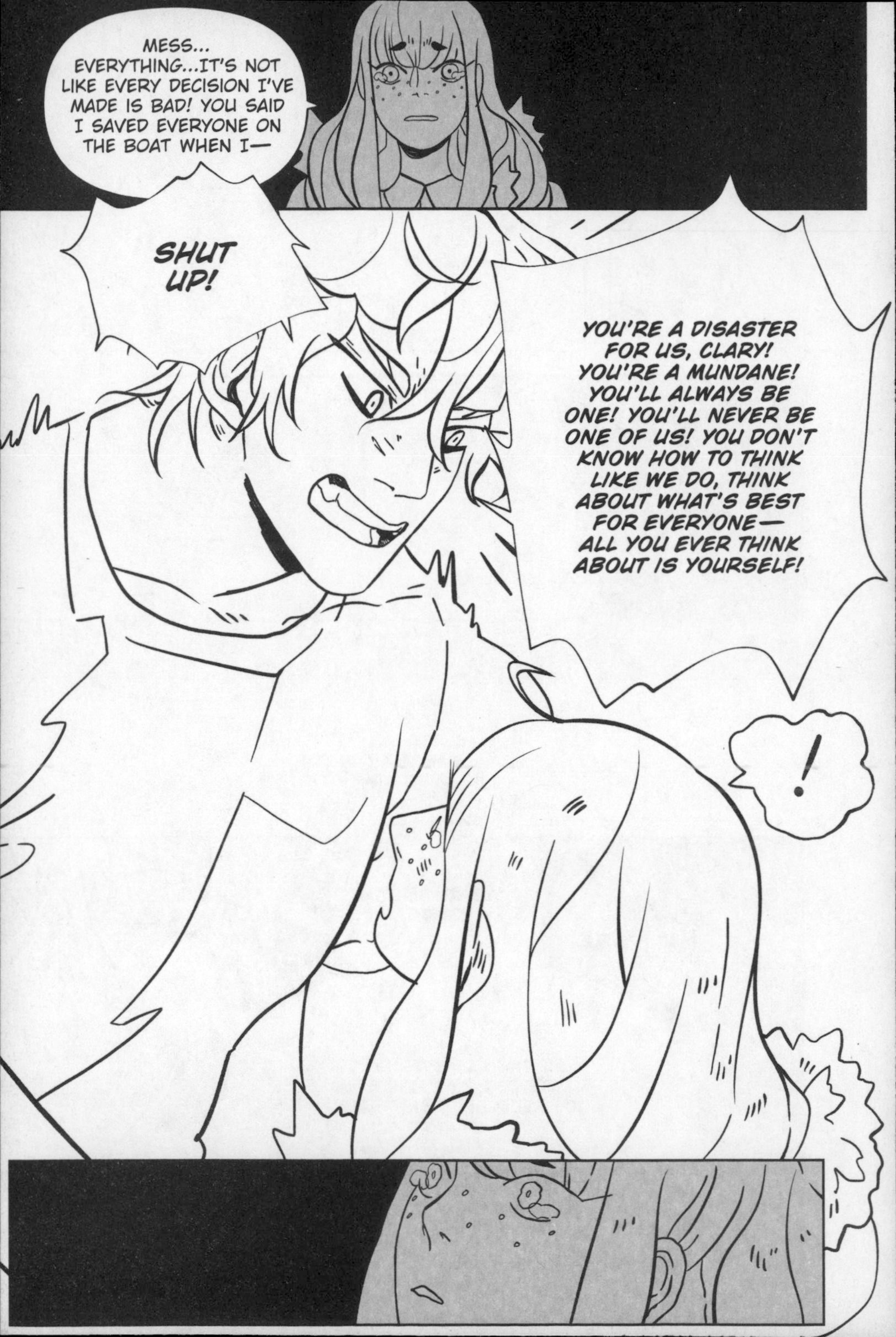
MESS... EVERYTHING...IT'S NOT LIKE EVERY DECISION I'VE MADE IS BAD! YOU SAID I SAVED EVERYONE ON THE BOAT WHEN I—
SHUT UP!
YOU'RE A DISASTER FOR US, CLARY! YOU'RE A MUNDANE! YOU'LL ALWAYS BE ONE! YOU'LL NEVER BE ONE OF US! YOU DON'T KNOW HOW TO THINK LIKE WE DO, THINK ABOUT WHAT'S BEST FOR EVERYONE— ALL YOU EVER THINK ABOUT IS YOURSELF!
!

THE MORTAL INSTRUMENTS

THE GRAPHIC NOVEL

THE MORTAL INSTRUMENTS

THE GRAPHIC NOVEL

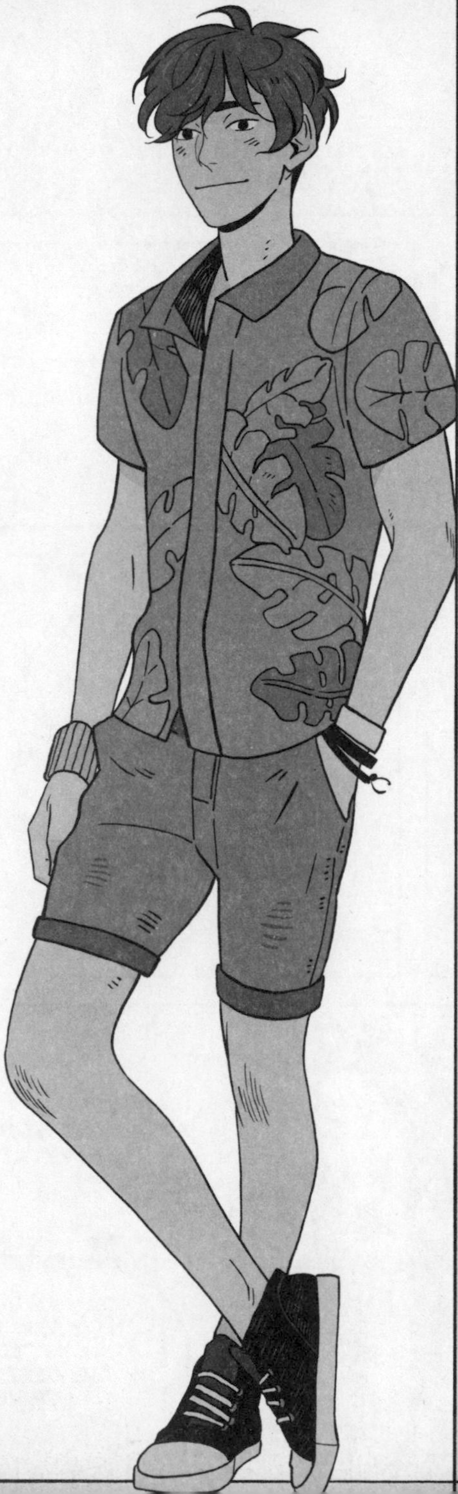

Chapter 27

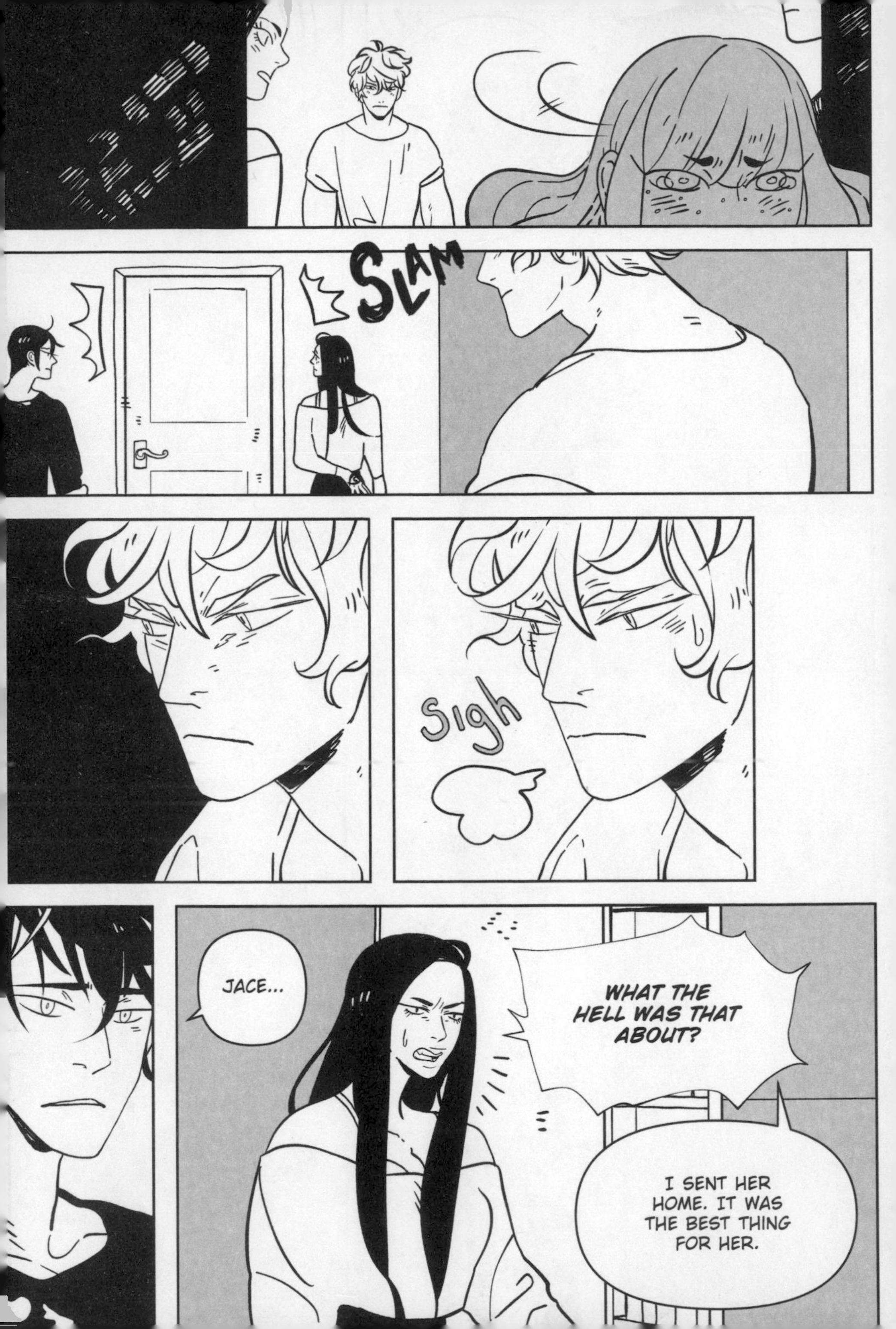
SLAM
Sigh
JACE...
WHAT THE HELL WAS THAT ABOUT?
I SENT HER HOME. IT WAS THE BEST THING FOR HER.

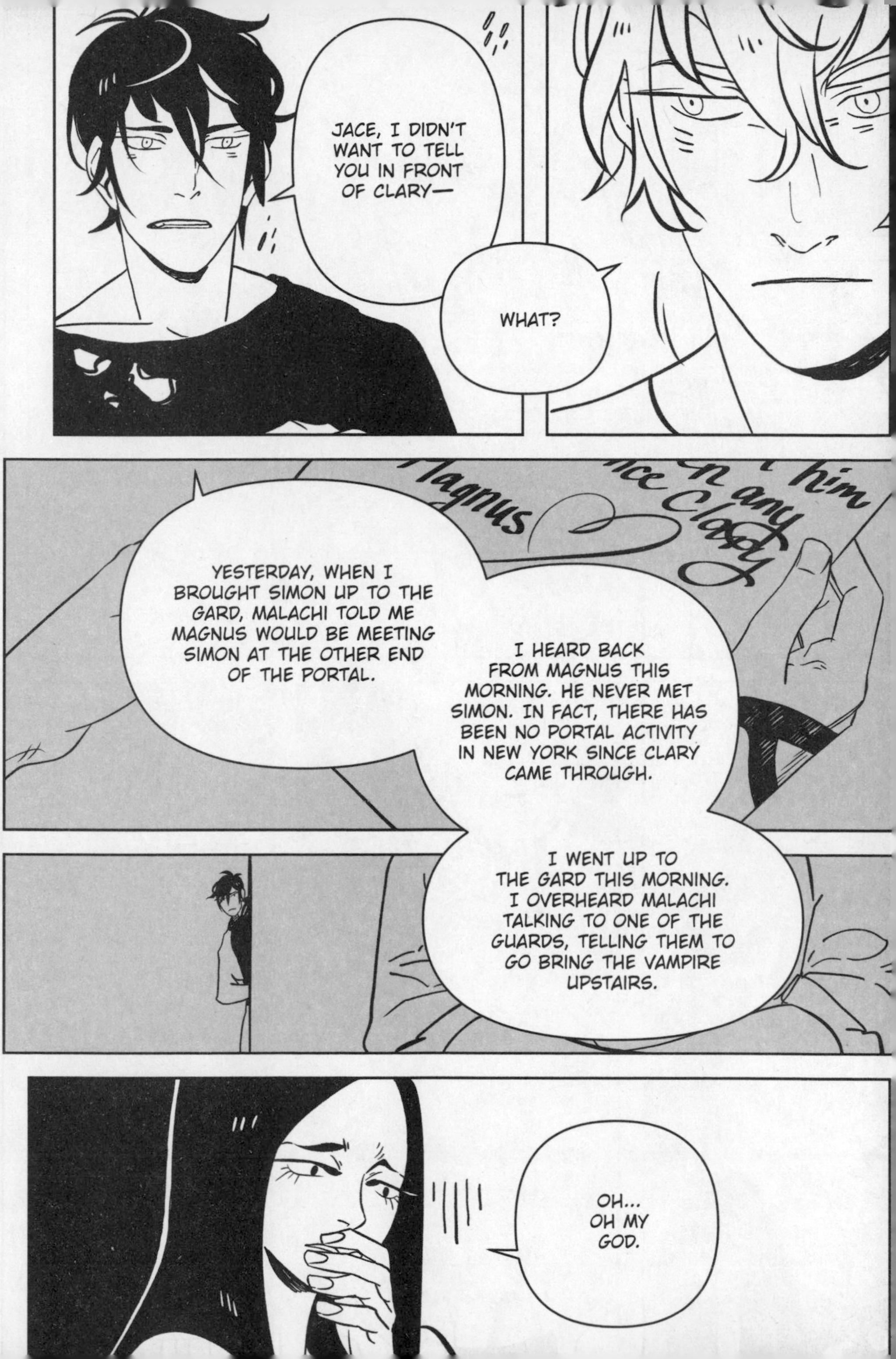
JACE, I DIDN'T WANT TO TELL YOU IN FRONT OF CLARY—
WHAT?
Magnus
Clary
YESTERDAY, WHEN I BROUGHT SIMON UP TO THE GARD, MALACHI TOLD ME MAGNUS WOULD BE MEETING SIMON AT THE OTHER END OF THE PORTAL.
I HEARD BACK FROM MAGNUS THIS MORNING. HE NEVER MET SIMON. IN FACT, THERE HAS BEEN NO PORTAL ACTIVITY IN NEW YORK SINCE CLARY CAME THROUGH.
I WENT UP TO THE GARD THIS MORNING. I OVERHEARD MALACHI TALKING TO ONE OF THE GUARDS, TELLING THEM TO GO BRING THE VAMPIRE UPSTAIRS.
OH... OH MY GOD.

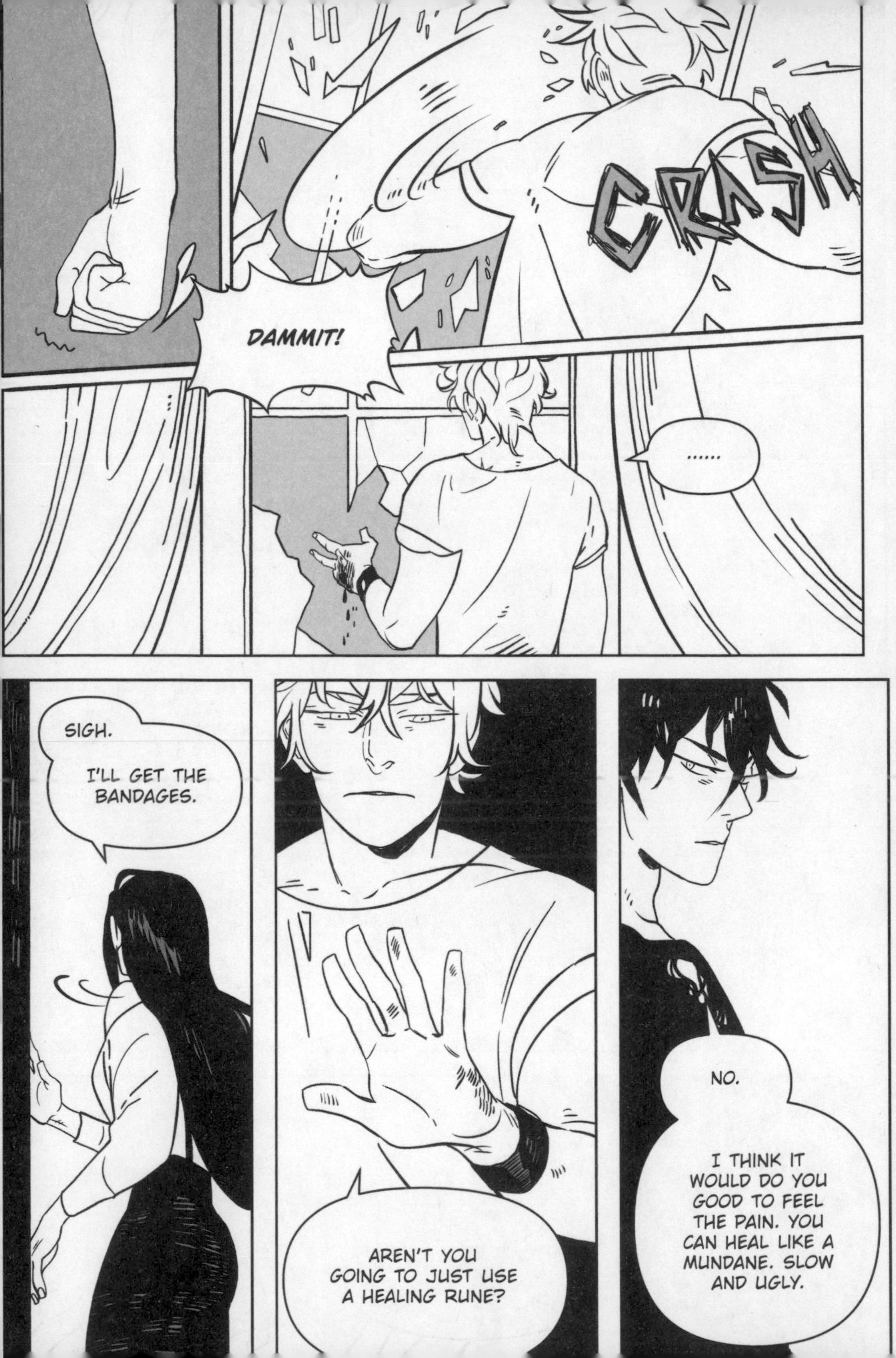
CRASH
DAMMIT!
......
SIGH.
I'LL GET THE BANDAGES.
AREN'T YOU GOING TO JUST USE A HEALING RUNE?
NO.
I THINK IT WOULD DO YOU GOOD TO FEEL THE PAIN. YOU CAN HEAL LIKE A MUNDANE. SLOW AND UGLY.

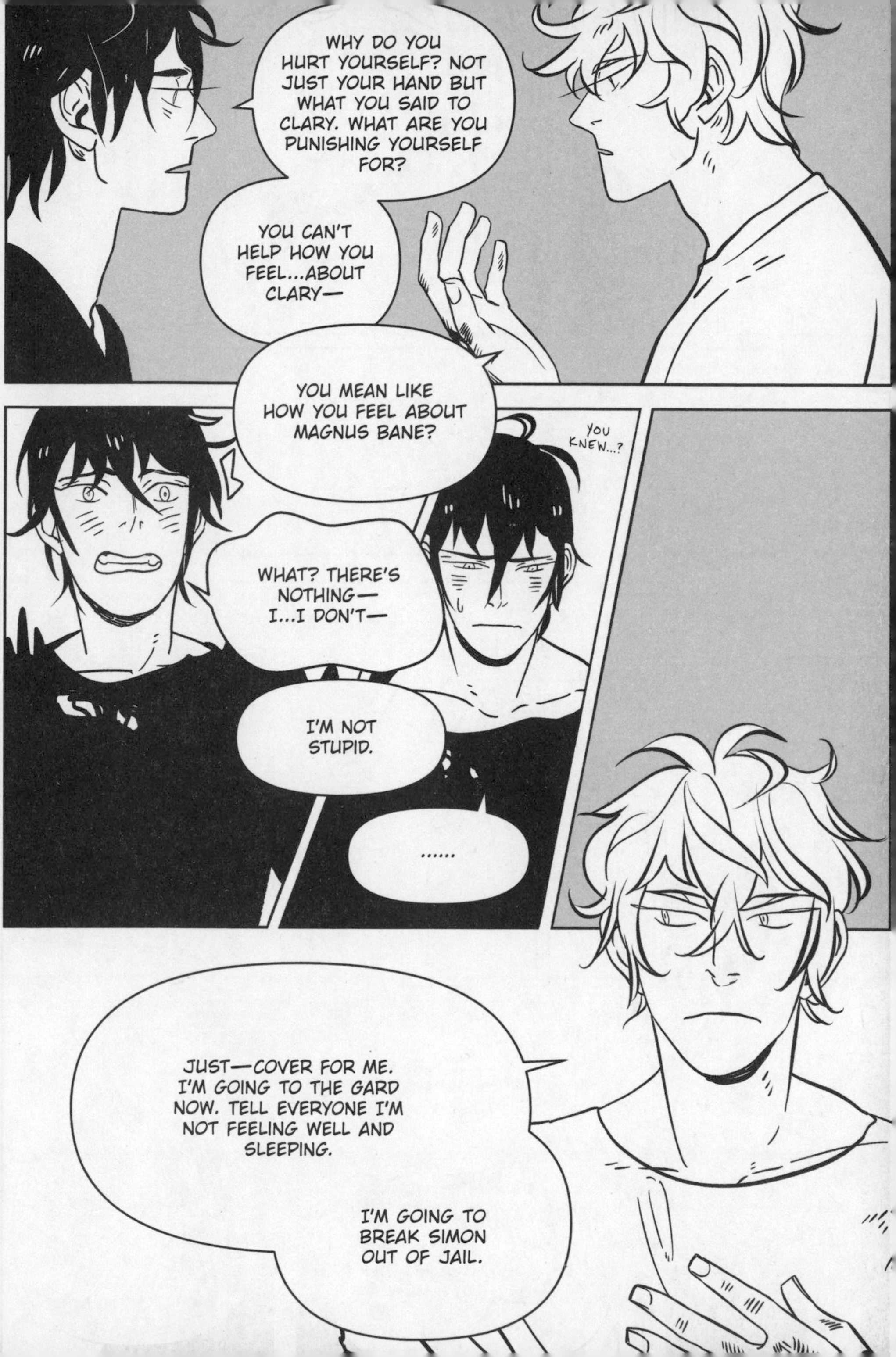
WHY DO YOU HURT YOURSELF? NOT JUST YOUR HAND BUT WHAT YOU SAID TO CLARY. WHAT ARE YOU PUNISHING YOURSELF FOR?
YOU CAN'T HELP HOW YOU FEEL...ABOUT CLARY—
YOU MEAN LIKE HOW YOU FEEL ABOUT MAGNUS BANE?
WHAT? THERE'S NOTHING— I...I DON'T—
I'M NOT STUPID.
YOU KNEW...?
......
JUST—COVER FOR ME. I'M GOING TO THE GARD NOW. TELL EVERYONE I'M NOT FEELING WELL AND SLEEPING.
I'M GOING TO BREAK SIMON OUT OF JAIL.

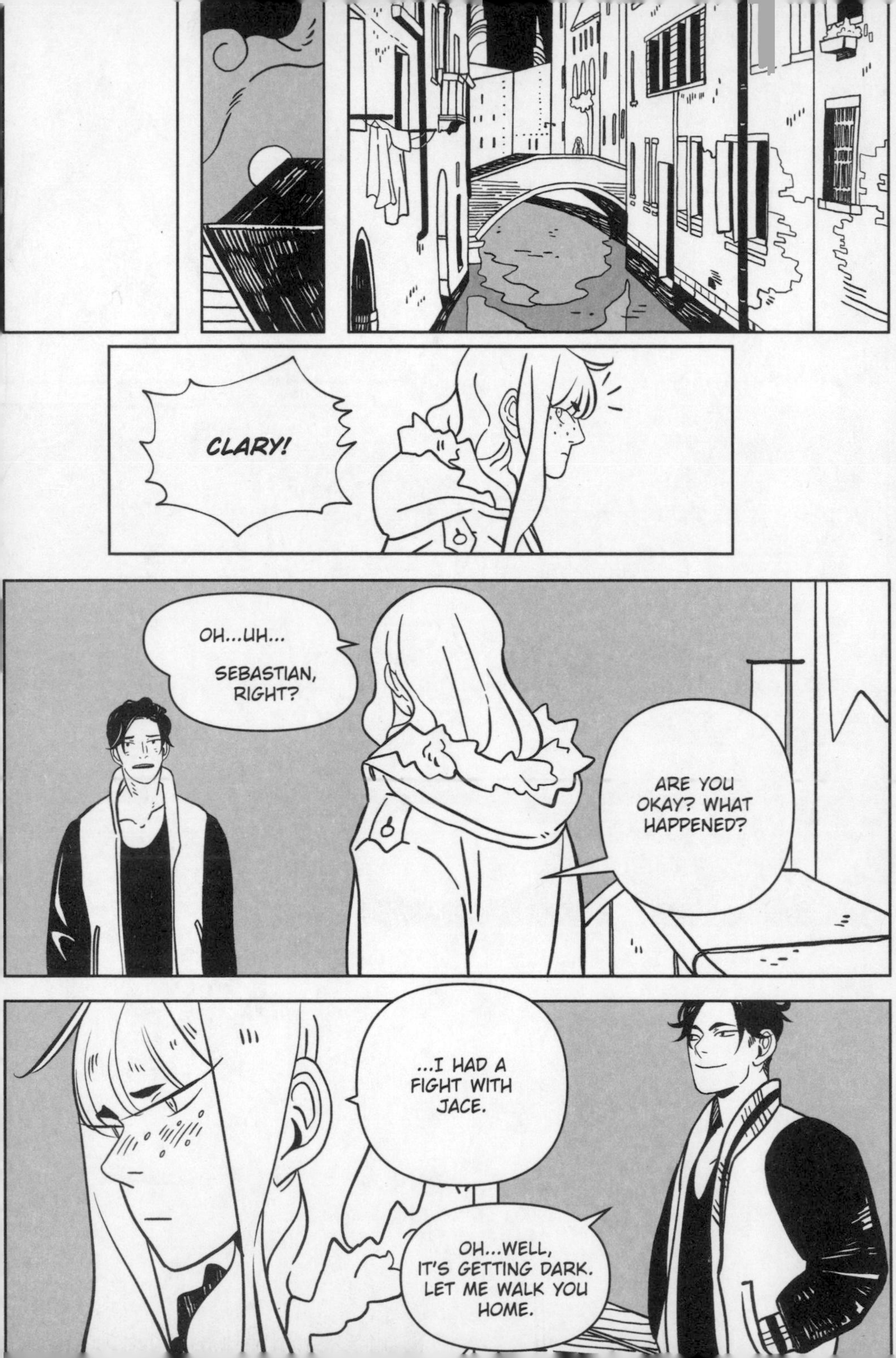
CLARY!
OH...UH... SEBASTIAN, RIGHT?
ARE YOU OKAY? WHAT HAPPENED?
...I HAD A FIGHT WITH JACE.
OH...WELL, IT'S GETTING DARK. LET ME WALK YOU HOME.

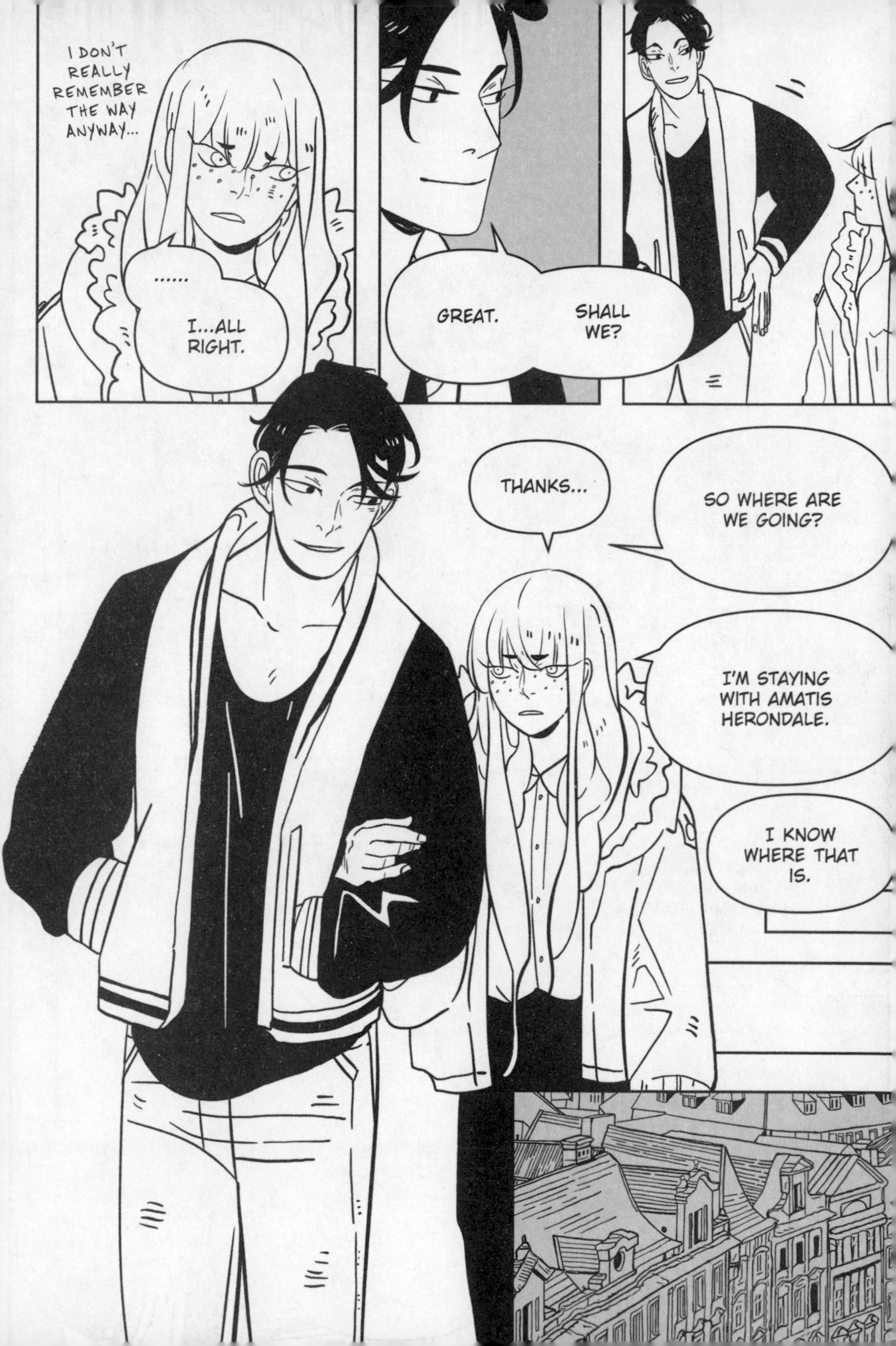
I DON'T REALLY REMEMBER THE WAY ANYWAY...
......
I...ALL RIGHT.
GREAT.
SHALL WE?
THANKS...
SO WHERE ARE WE GOING?
I'M STAYING WITH AMATIS HERONDALE.
I KNOW WHERE THAT IS.

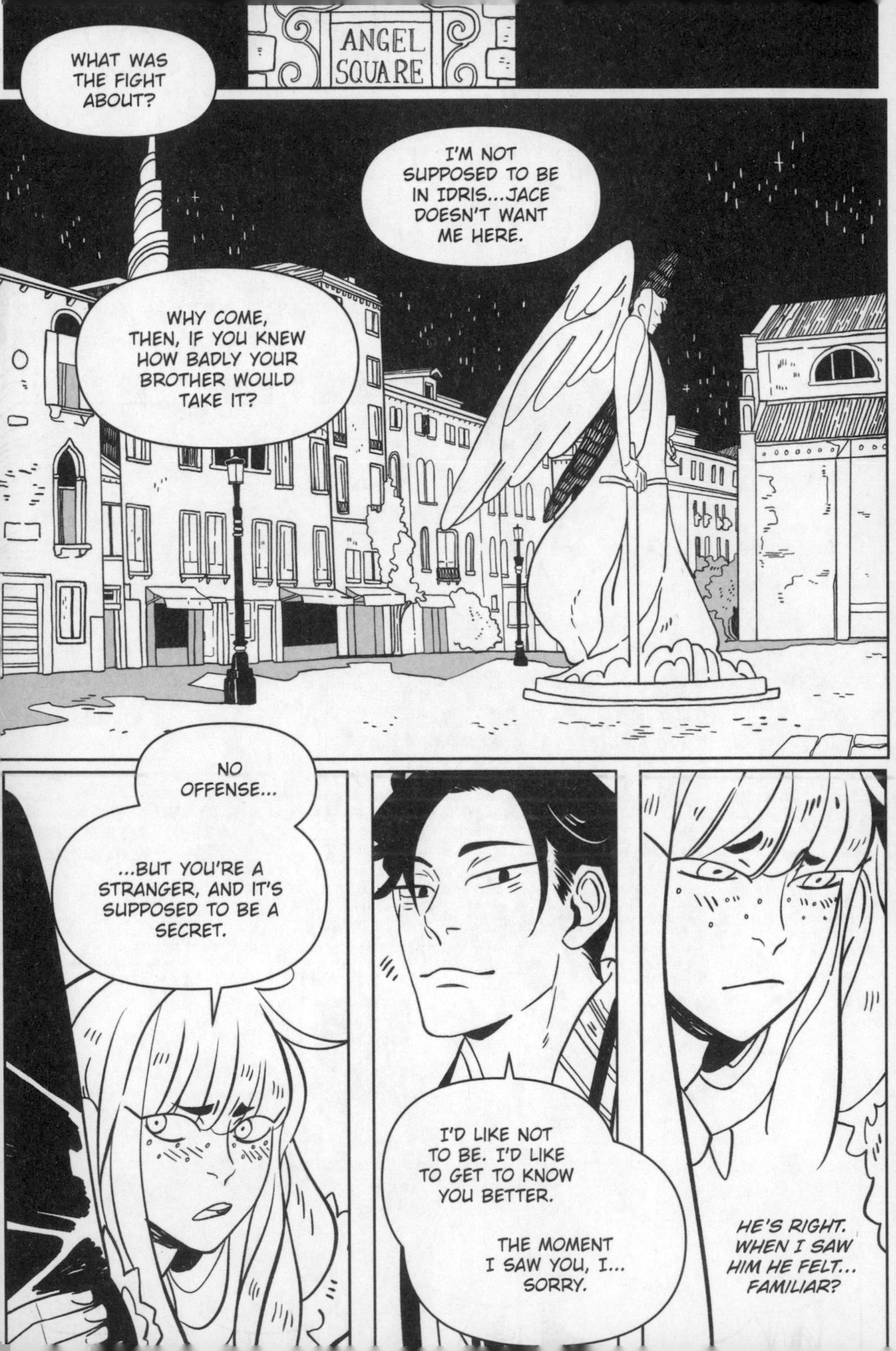
ANGEL SQUARE
WHAT WAS THE FIGHT ABOUT?
I'M NOT SUPPOSED TO BE IN IDRIS...JACE DOESN'T WANT ME HERE.
WHY COME, THEN, IF YOU KNEW HOW BADLY YOUR BROTHER WOULD TAKE IT?
NO OFFENSE...
...BUT YOU'RE A STRANGER, AND IT'S SUPPOSED TO BE A SECRET.
I'D LIKE NOT TO BE. I'D LIKE TO GET TO KNOW YOU BETTER.
THE MOMENT I SAW YOU, I... SORRY.
HE'S RIGHT. WHEN I SAW HIM HE FELT... FAMILIAR?

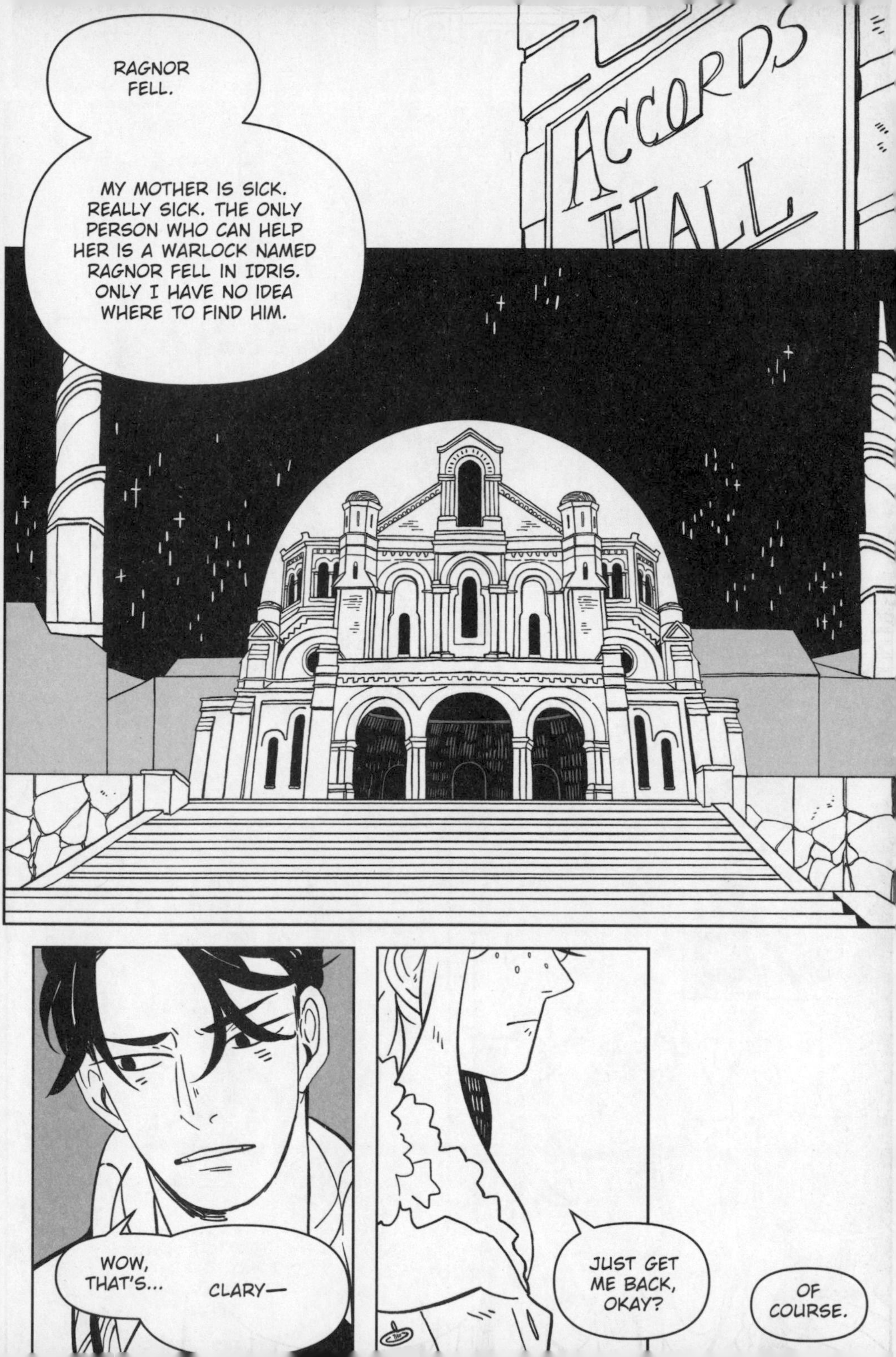
RAGNOR FELL.
MY MOTHER IS SICK. REALLY SICK. THE ONLY PERSON WHO CAN HELP HER IS A WARLOCK NAMED RAGNOR FELL IN IDRIS. ONLY I HAVE NO IDEA WHERE TO FIND HIM.
ACCORDS HALL
WOW, THAT'S...
CLARY—
JUST GET ME BACK, OKAY?
OF COURSE.

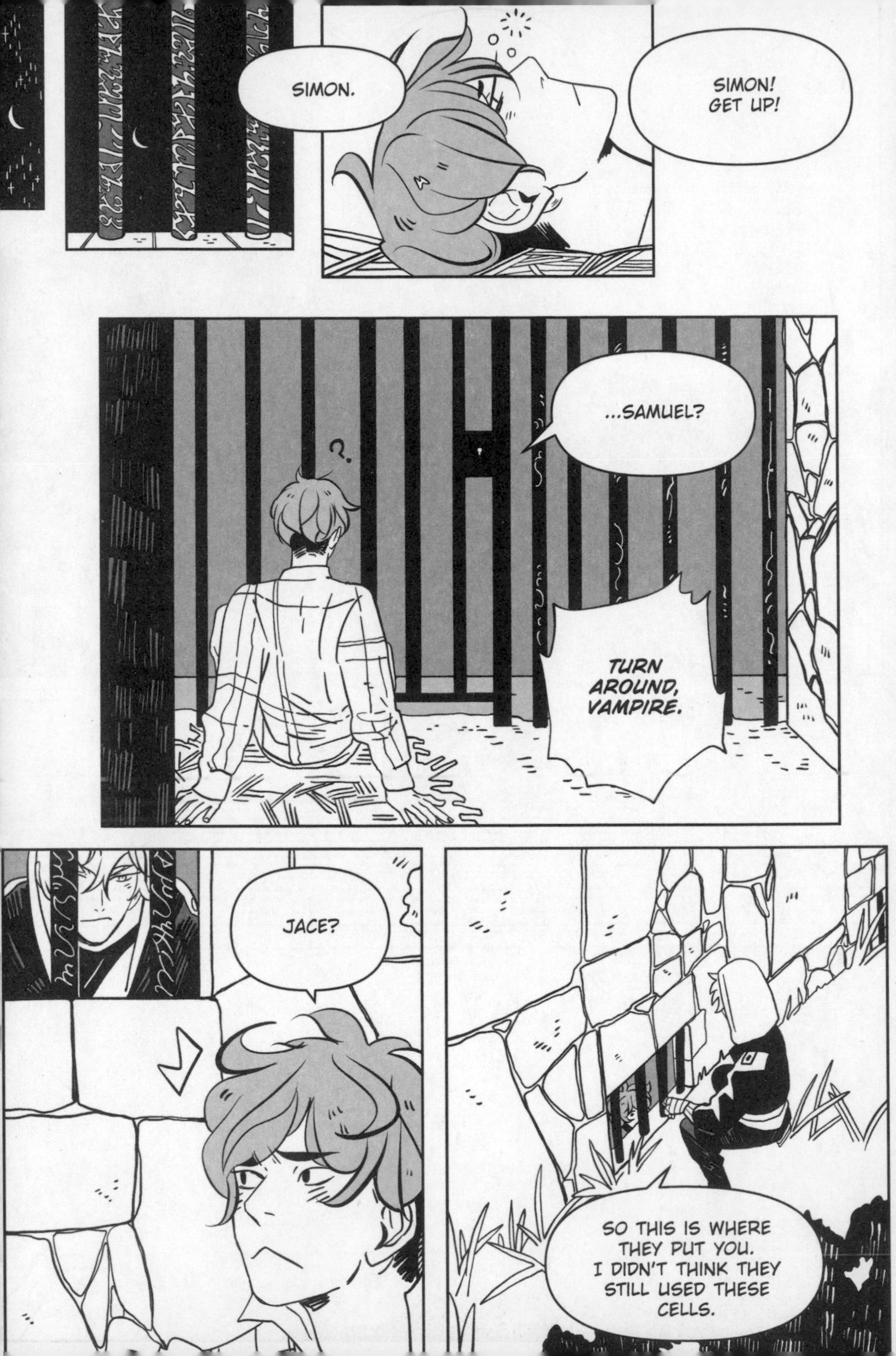
SIMON.
SIMON! GET UP!
...SAMUEL?
TURN AROUND, VAMPIRE.
JACE?
SO THIS IS WHERE THEY PUT YOU. I DIDN'T THINK THEY STILL USED THESE CELLS.

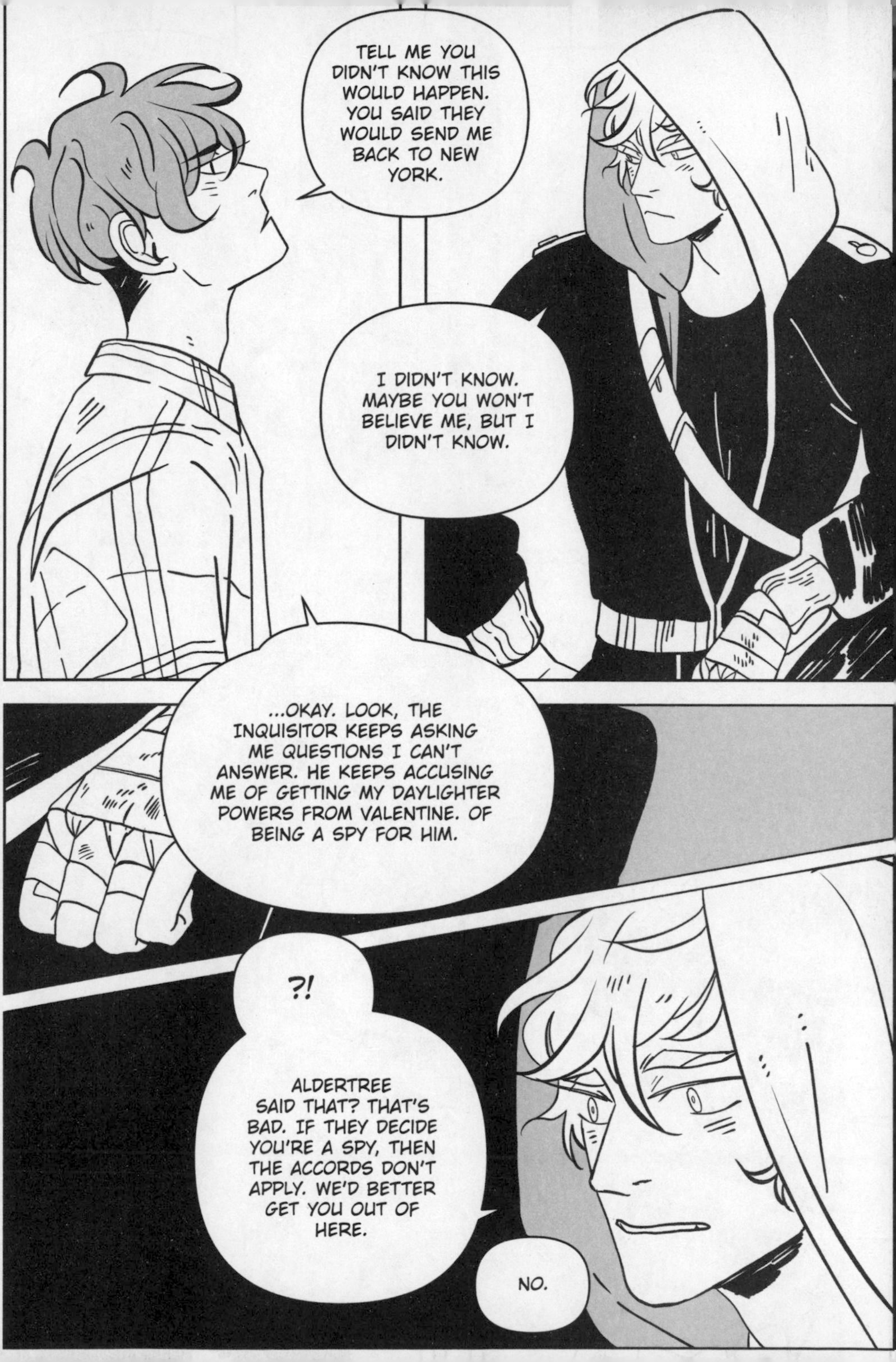
TELL ME YOU DIDN'T KNOW THIS WOULD HAPPEN. YOU SAID THEY WOULD SEND ME BACK TO NEW YORK.
I DIDN'T KNOW. MAYBE YOU WON'T BELIEVE ME, BUT I DIDN'T KNOW.
...OKAY. LOOK, THE INQUISITOR KEEPS ASKING ME QUESTIONS I CAN'T ANSWER. HE KEEPS ACCUSING ME OF GETTING MY DAYLIGHTER POWERS FROM VALENTINE. OF BEING A SPY FOR HIM.
?!
ALDERTREE SAID THAT? THAT'S BAD. IF THEY DECIDE YOU'RE A SPY, THEN THE ACCORDS DON'T APPLY. WE'D BETTER GET YOU OUT OF HERE.
NO.

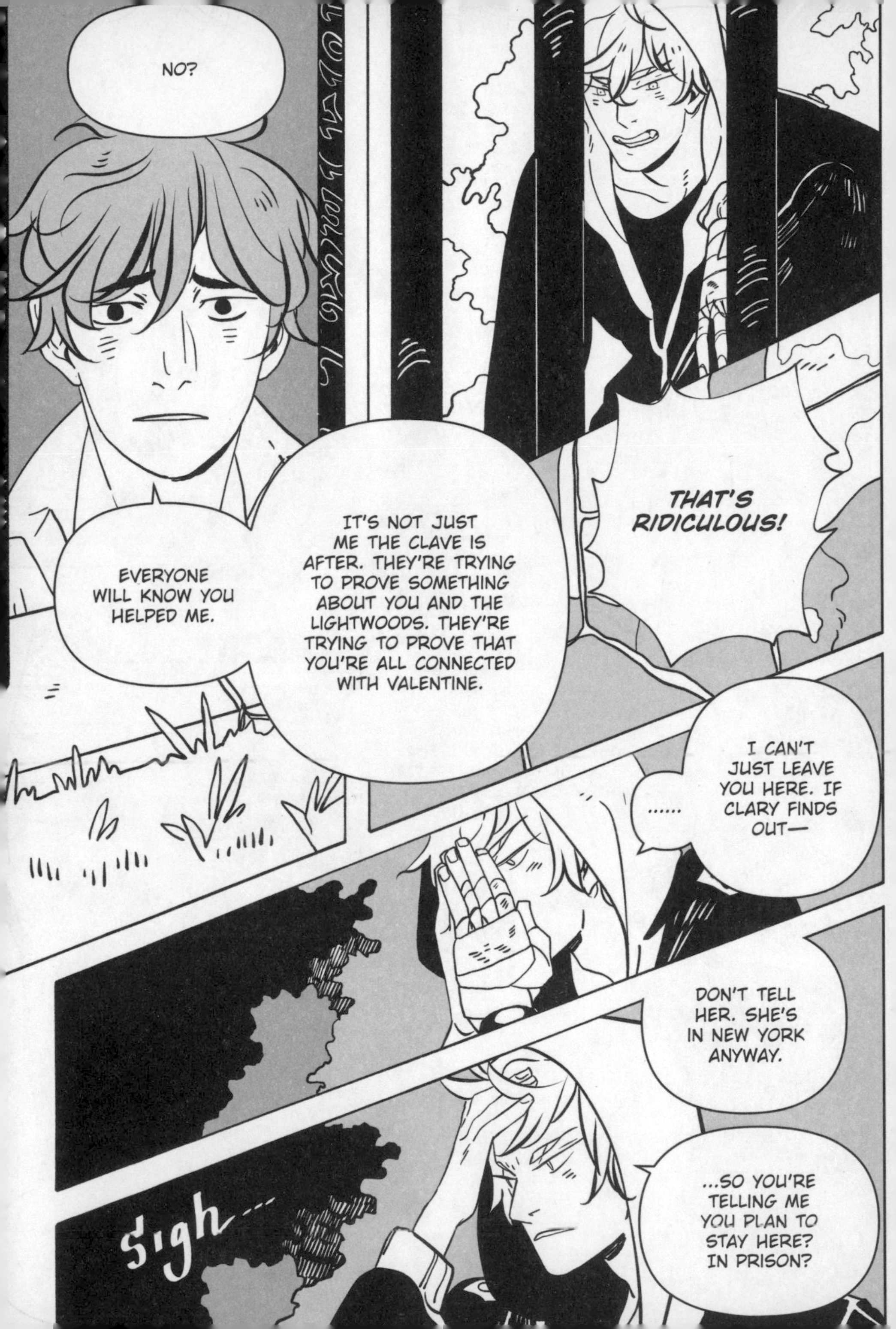

NO?
EVERYONE WILL KNOW YOU HELPED ME.
IT'S NOT JUST ME THE CLAVE IS AFTER. THEY'RE TRYING TO PROVE SOMETHING ABOUT YOU AND THE LIGHTWOODS. THEY'RE TRYING TO PROVE THAT YOU'RE ALL CONNECTED WITH VALENTINE.
THAT'S RIDICULOUS!
......
I CAN'T JUST LEAVE YOU HERE. IF CLARY FINDS OUT—
DON'T TELL HER. SHE'S IN NEW YORK ANYWAY.
Sigh...
...SO YOU'RE TELLING ME YOU PLAN TO STAY HERE? IN PRISON?

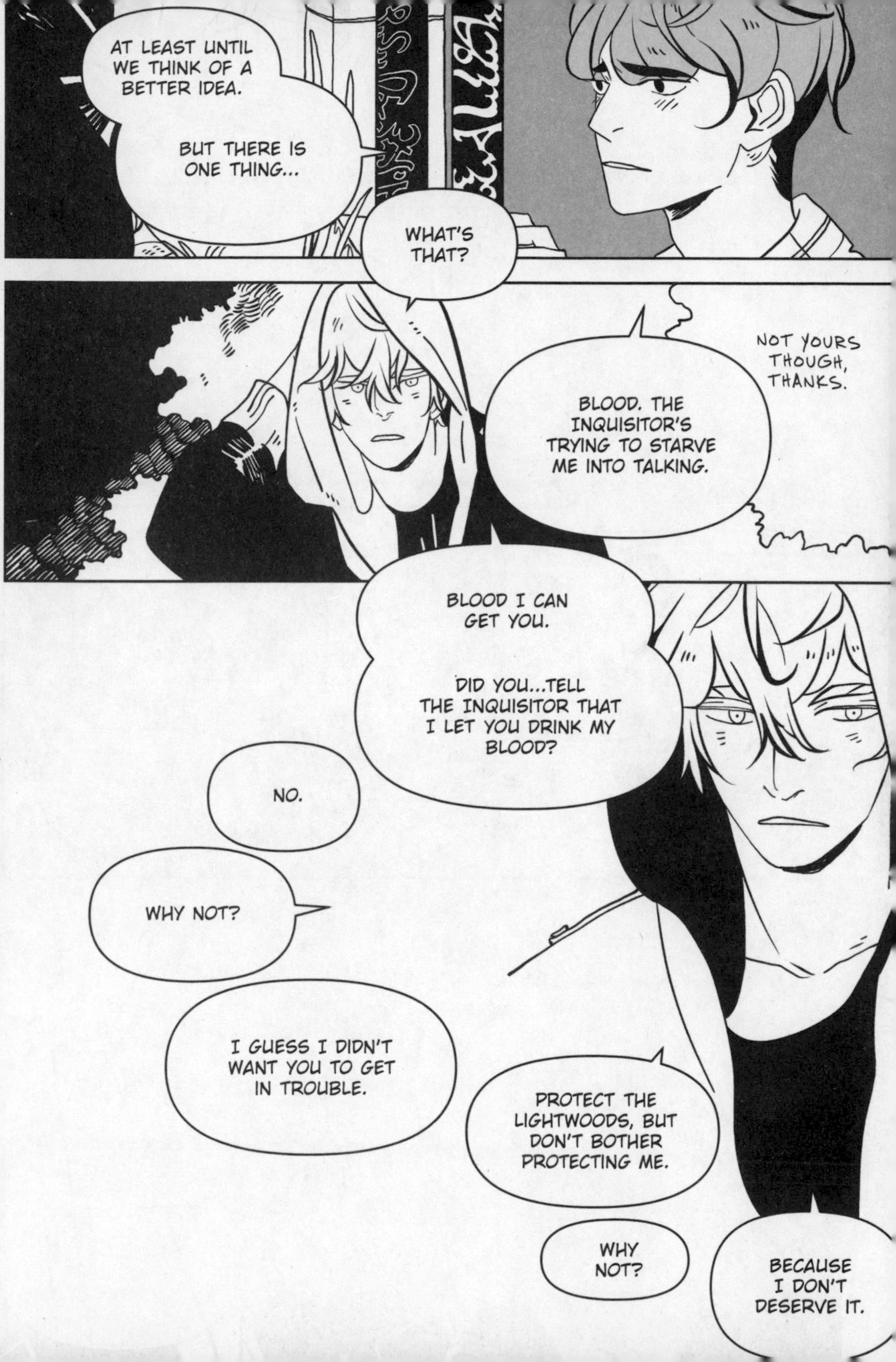
AT LEAST UNTIL WE THINK OF A BETTER IDEA.
BUT THERE IS ONE THING...
WHAT'S THAT?
BLOOD. THE INQUISITOR'S TRYING TO STARVE ME INTO TALKING.
NOT YOURS THOUGH, THANKS.
BLOOD I CAN GET YOU.
DID YOU...TELL THE INQUISITOR THAT I LET YOU DRINK MY BLOOD?
NO.
WHY NOT?
I GUESS I DIDN'T WANT YOU TO GET IN TROUBLE.
PROTECT THE LIGHTWOODS, BUT DON'T BOTHER PROTECTING ME.
WHY NOT?
BECAUSE I DON'T DESERVE IT.

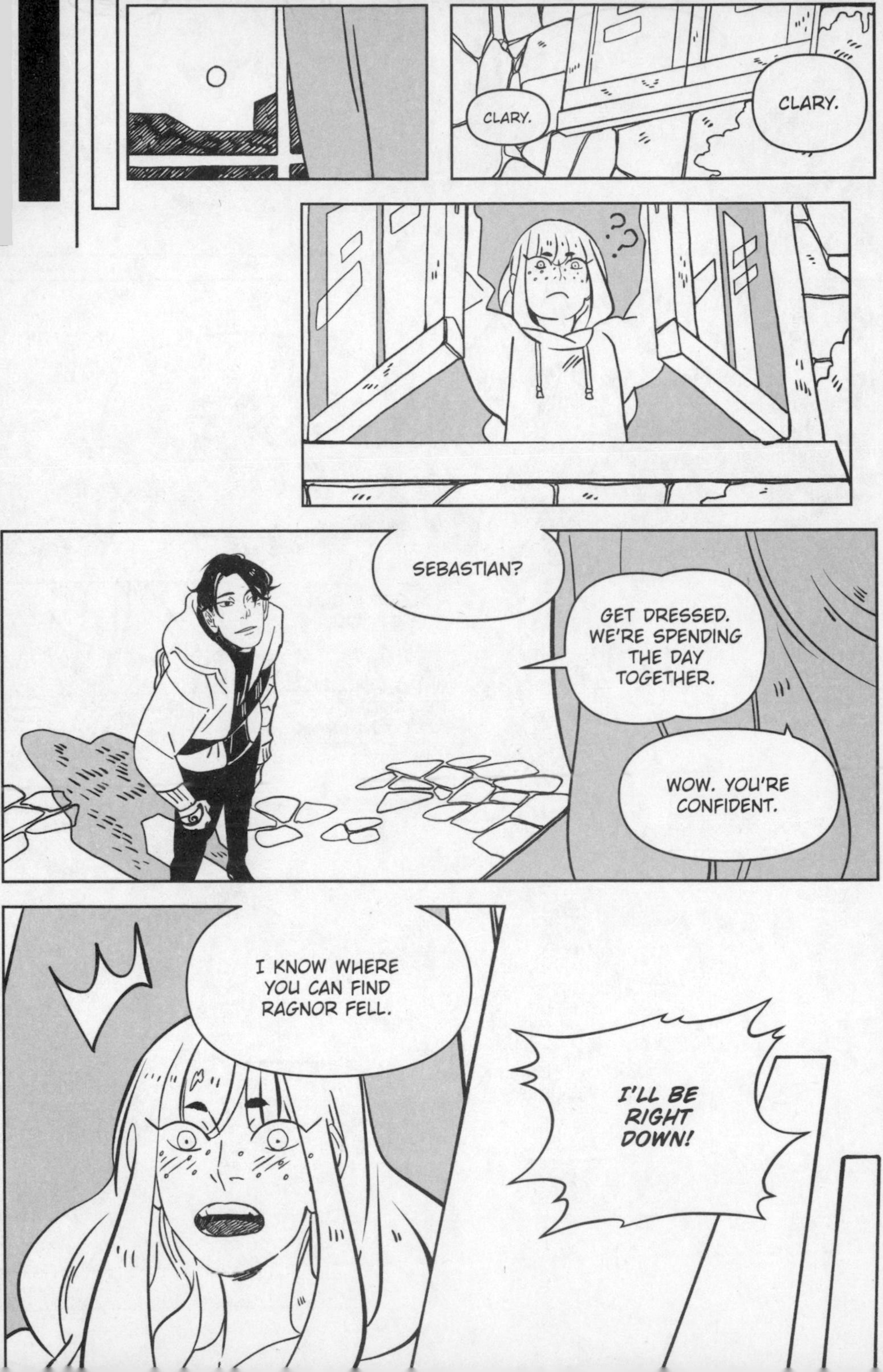
CLARY.
CLARY.
SEBASTIAN?
GET DRESSED. WE'RE SPENDING THE DAY TOGETHER.
WOW. YOU'RE CONFIDENT.
I KNOW WHERE YOU CAN FIND RAGNOR FELL.
I'LL BE RIGHT DOWN!

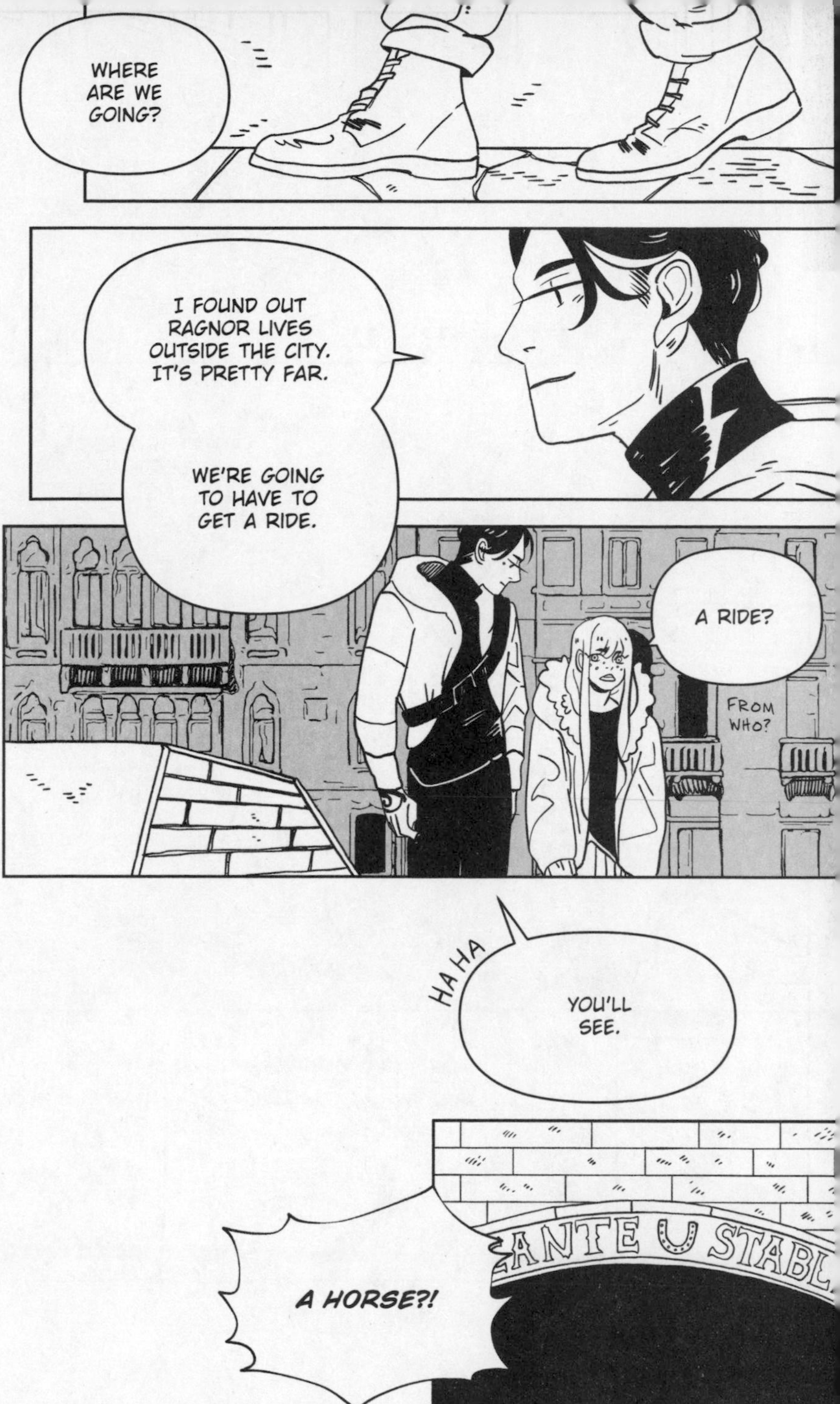
WHERE ARE WE GOING?
I FOUND OUT RAGNOR LIVES OUTSIDE THE CITY. IT'S PRETTY FAR.
WE'RE GOING TO HAVE TO GET A RIDE.
A RIDE?
FROM WHO?
HA HA
YOU'LL SEE.
A HORSE?!
ANTE U STABL

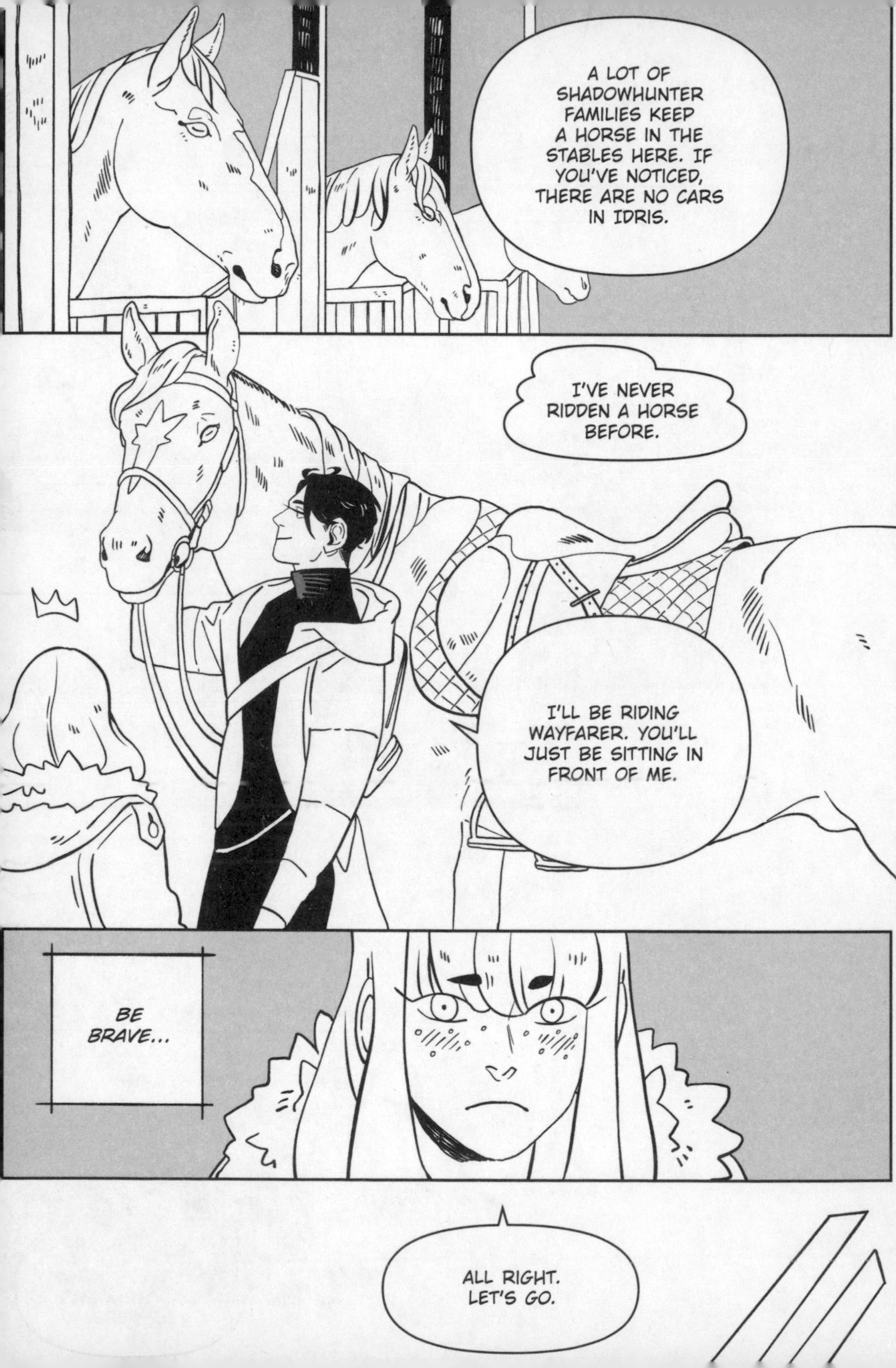
A LOT OF SHADOWHUNTER FAMILIES KEEP A HORSE IN THE STABLES HERE. IF YOU'VE NOTICED, THERE ARE NO CARS IN IDRIS.
I'VE NEVER RIDDEN A HORSE BEFORE.
I'LL BE RIDING WAYFARER. YOU'LL JUST BE SITTING IN FRONT OF ME.
BE BRAVE...
ALL RIGHT. LET'S GO.

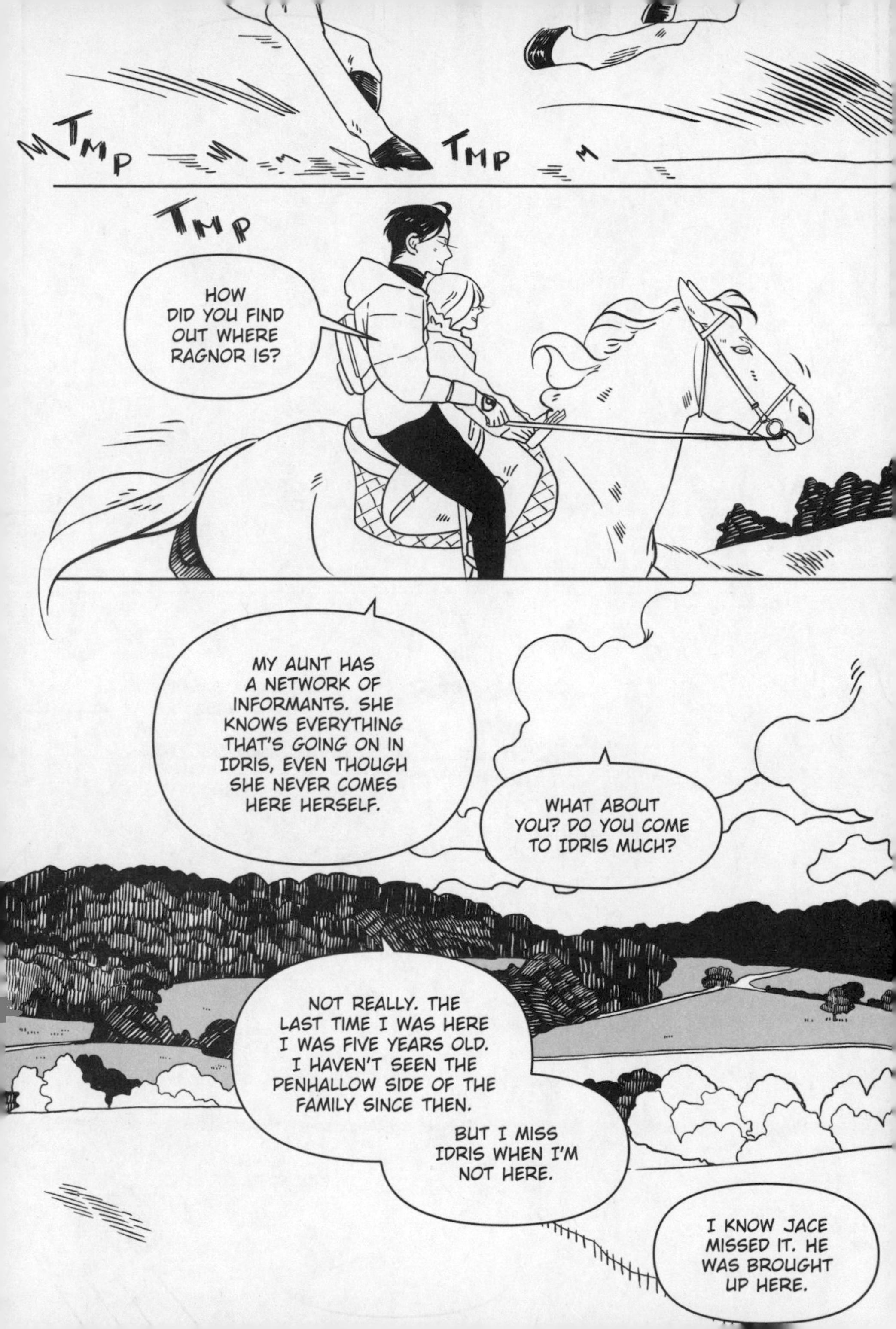
MTMP
TMP
M
TMP
HOW DID YOU FIND OUT WHERE RAGNOR IS?
MY AUNT HAS A NETWORK OF INFORMANTS. SHE KNOWS EVERYTHING THAT'S GOING ON IN IDRIS, EVEN THOUGH SHE NEVER COMES HERE HERSELF.
WHAT ABOUT YOU? DO YOU COME TO IDRIS MUCH?
NOT REALLY. THE LAST TIME I WAS HERE I WAS FIVE YEARS OLD. I HAVEN'T SEEN THE PENHALLOW SIDE OF THE FAMILY SINCE THEN.
BUT I MISS IDRIS WHEN I'M NOT HERE.
I KNOW JACE MISSED IT. HE WAS BROUGHT UP HERE.

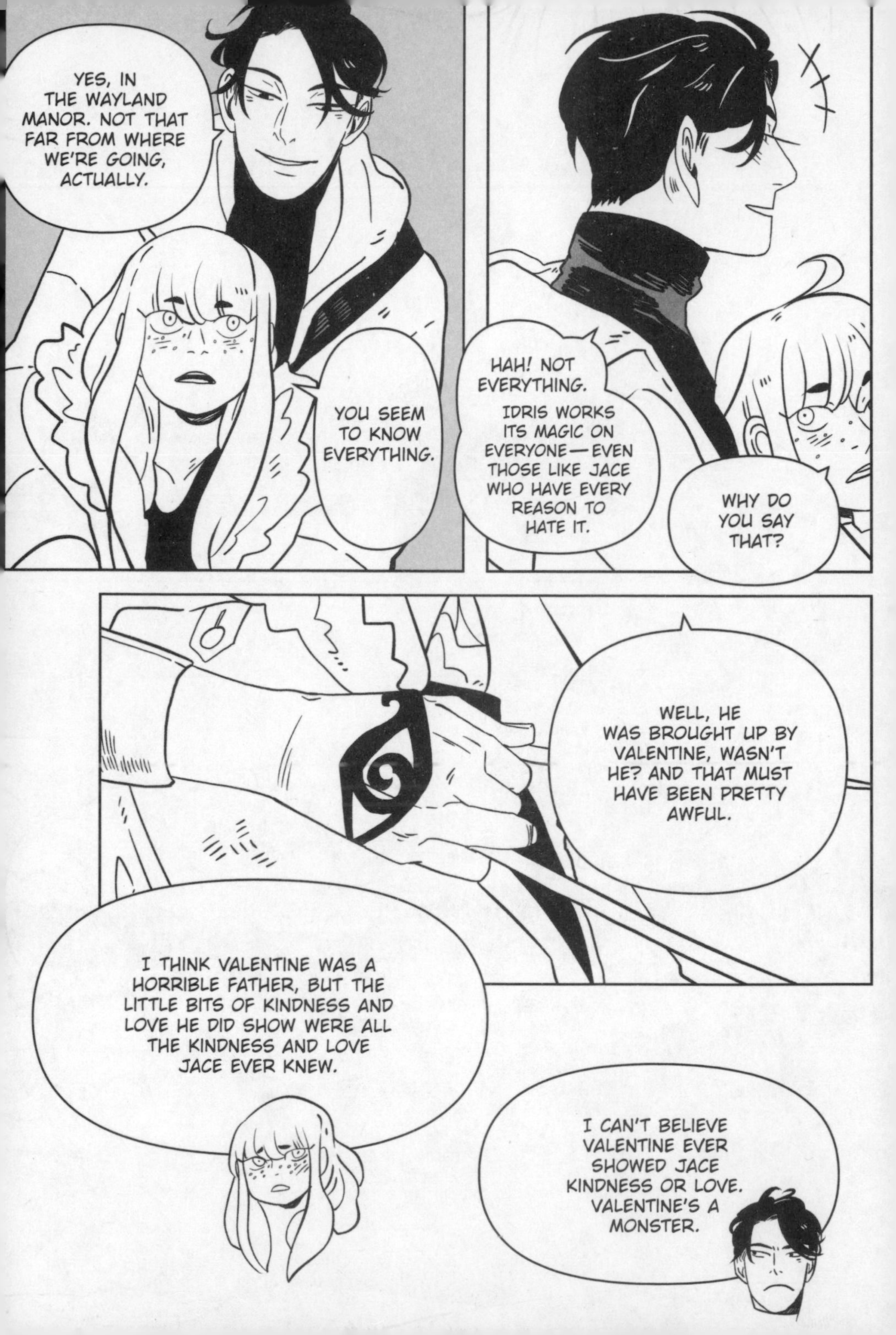
YES, IN THE WAYLAND MANOR. NOT THAT FAR FROM WHERE WE'RE GOING, ACTUALLY.
YOU SEEM TO KNOW EVERYTHING.
HAH! NOT EVERYTHING.
IDRIS WORKS ITS MAGIC ON EVERYONE—EVEN THOSE LIKE JACE WHO HAVE EVERY REASON TO HATE IT.
WHY DO YOU SAY THAT?
WELL, HE WAS BROUGHT UP BY VALENTINE, WASN'T HE? AND THAT MUST HAVE BEEN PRETTY AWFUL.
I THINK VALENTINE WAS A HORRIBLE FATHER, BUT THE LITTLE BITS OF KINDNESS AND LOVE HE DID SHOW WERE ALL THE KINDNESS AND LOVE JACE EVER KNEW.
I CAN'T BELIEVE VALENTINE EVER SHOWED JACE KINDNESS OR LOVE. VALENTINE'S A MONSTER.

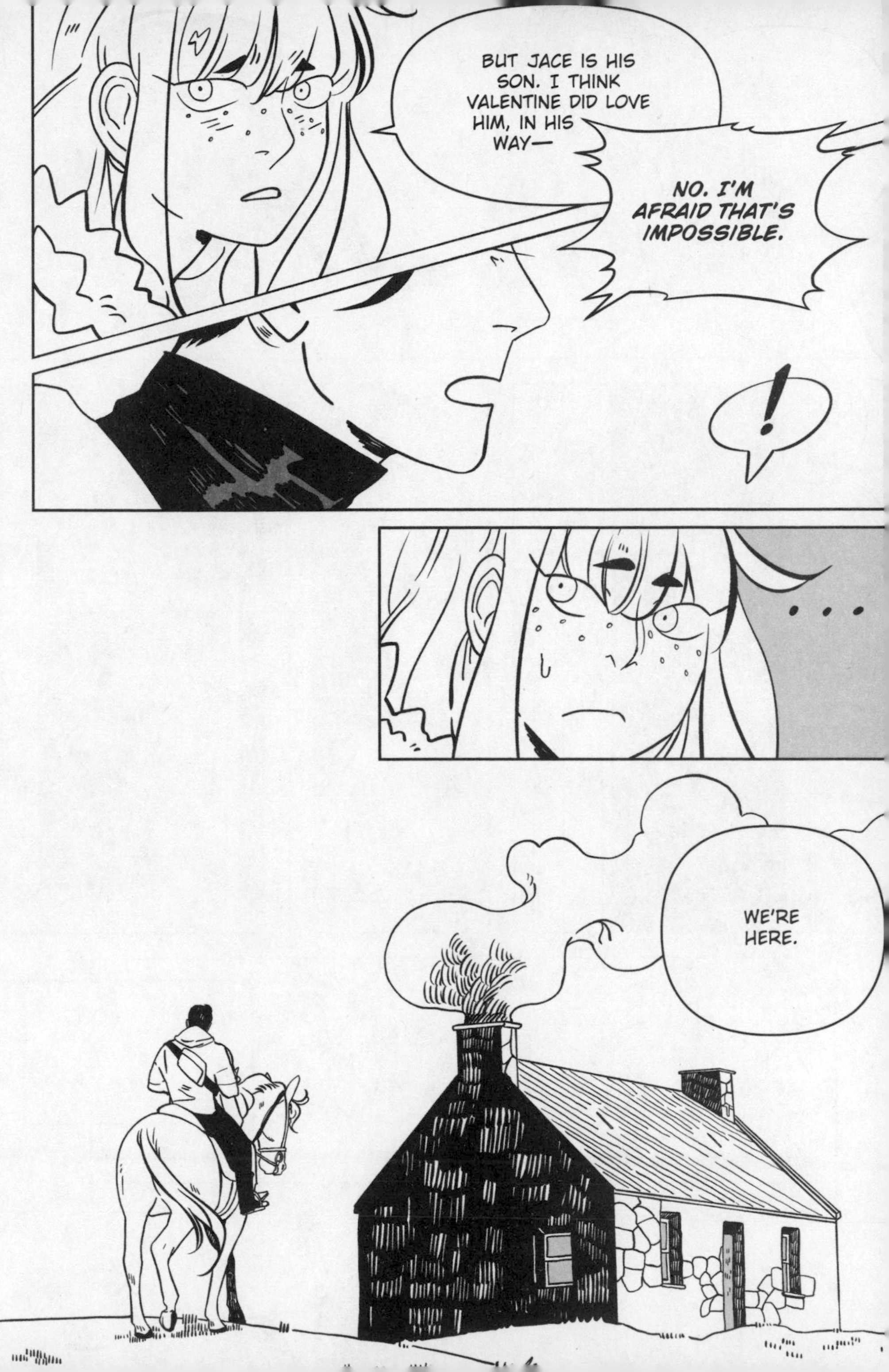
BUT JACE IS HIS SON. I THINK VALENTINE DID LOVE HIM, IN HIS WAY—
NO. I'M AFRAID THAT'S IMPOSSIBLE.
!
...
WE'RE HERE.

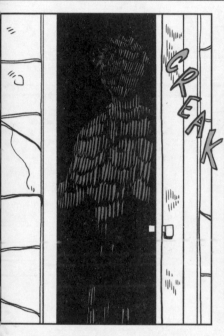

CREAK

!

MAGNUS?!

UH...ARE YOU RAGNOR FELL?

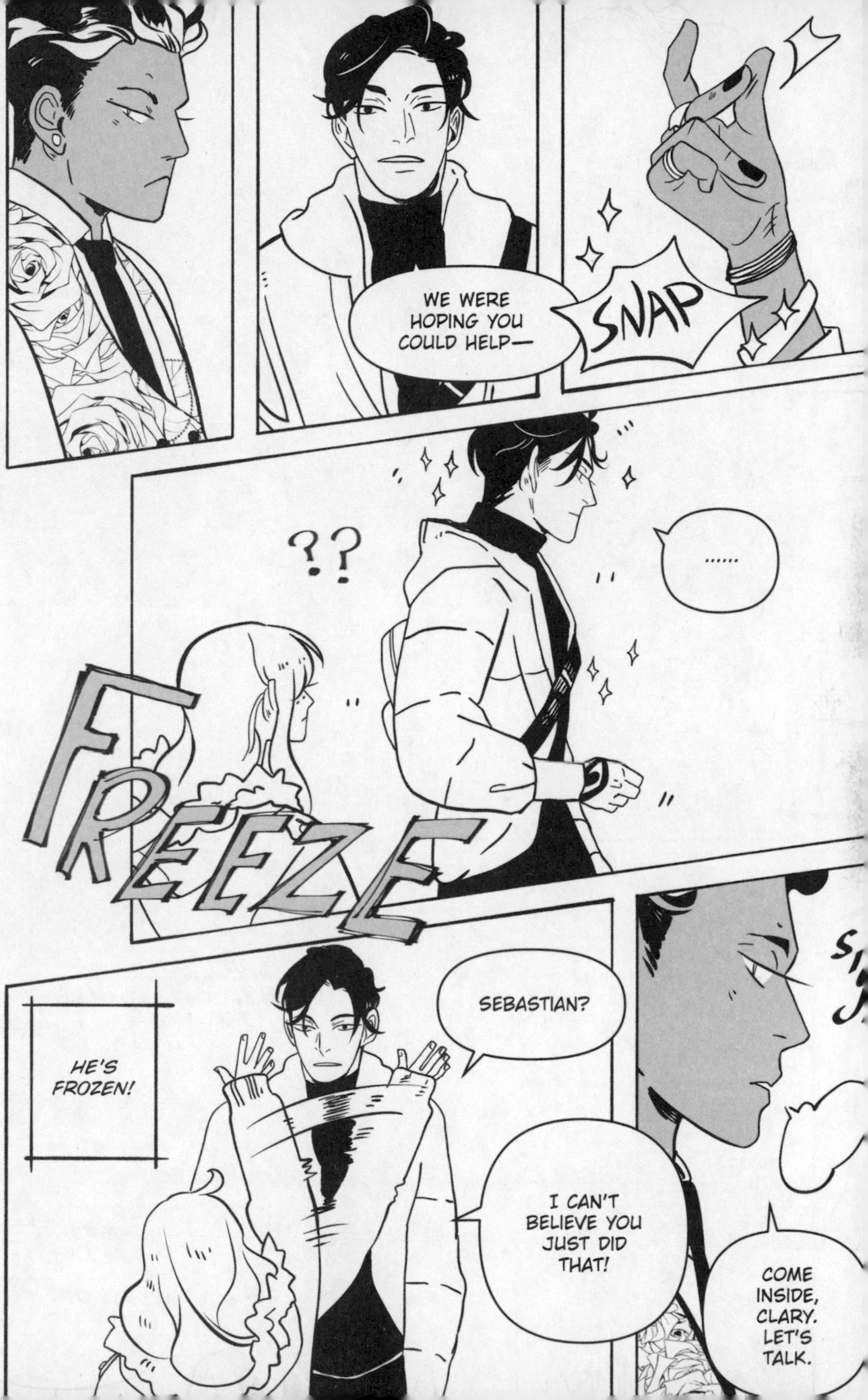
WE WERE HOPING YOU COULD HELP—
SNAP
??
FREEZE
......
HE'S FROZEN!
SEBASTIAN?
I CAN'T BELIEVE YOU JUST DID THAT!
COME INSIDE, CLARY. LET'S TALK.

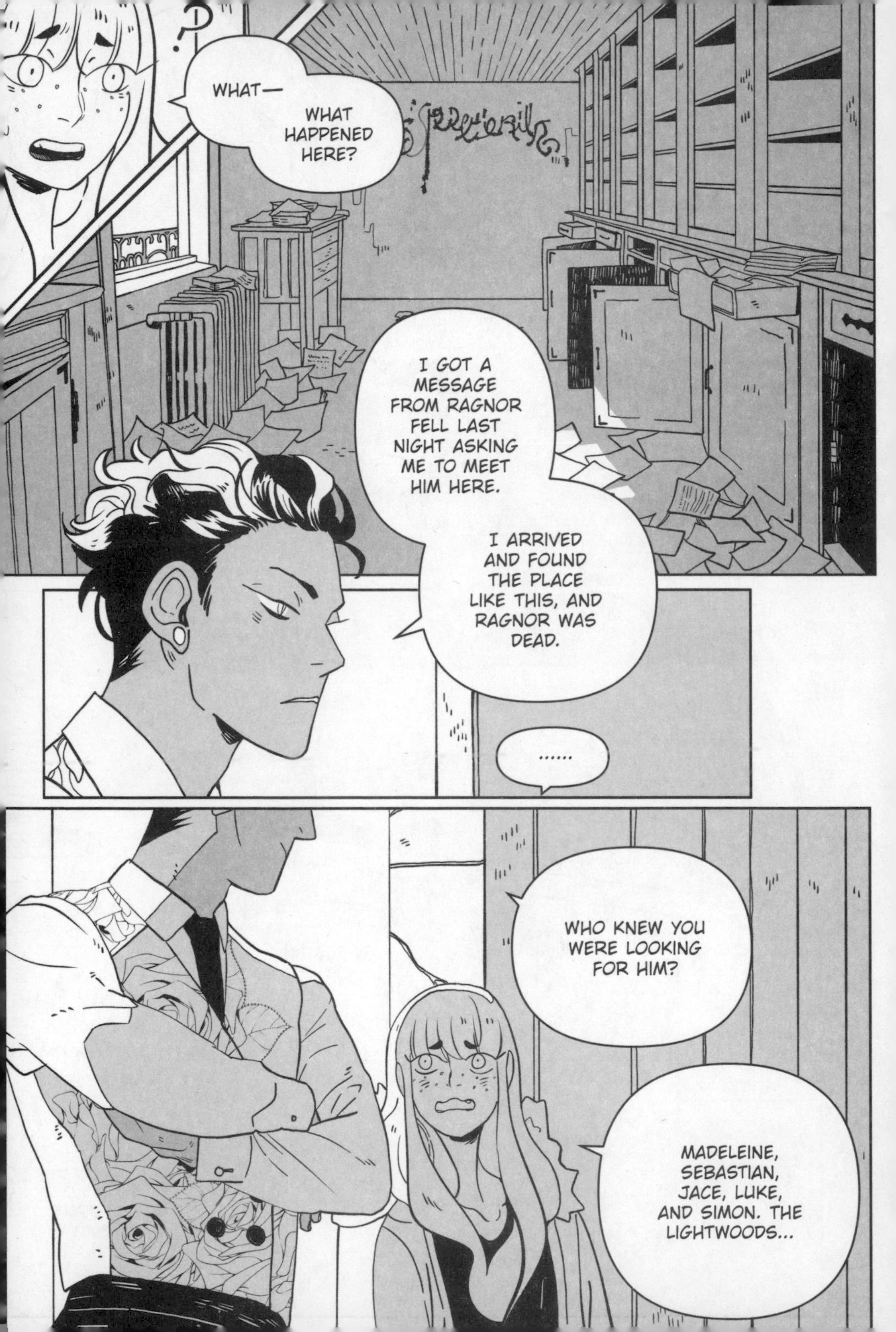
?
WHAT— WHAT HAPPENED HERE?
I GOT A MESSAGE FROM RAGNOR FELL LAST NIGHT ASKING ME TO MEET HIM HERE.
I ARRIVED AND FOUND THE PLACE LIKE THIS, AND RAGNOR WAS DEAD.
......
WHO KNEW YOU WERE LOOKING FOR HIM?
MADELEINE, SEBASTIAN, JACE, LUKE, AND SIMON. THE LIGHTWOODS...

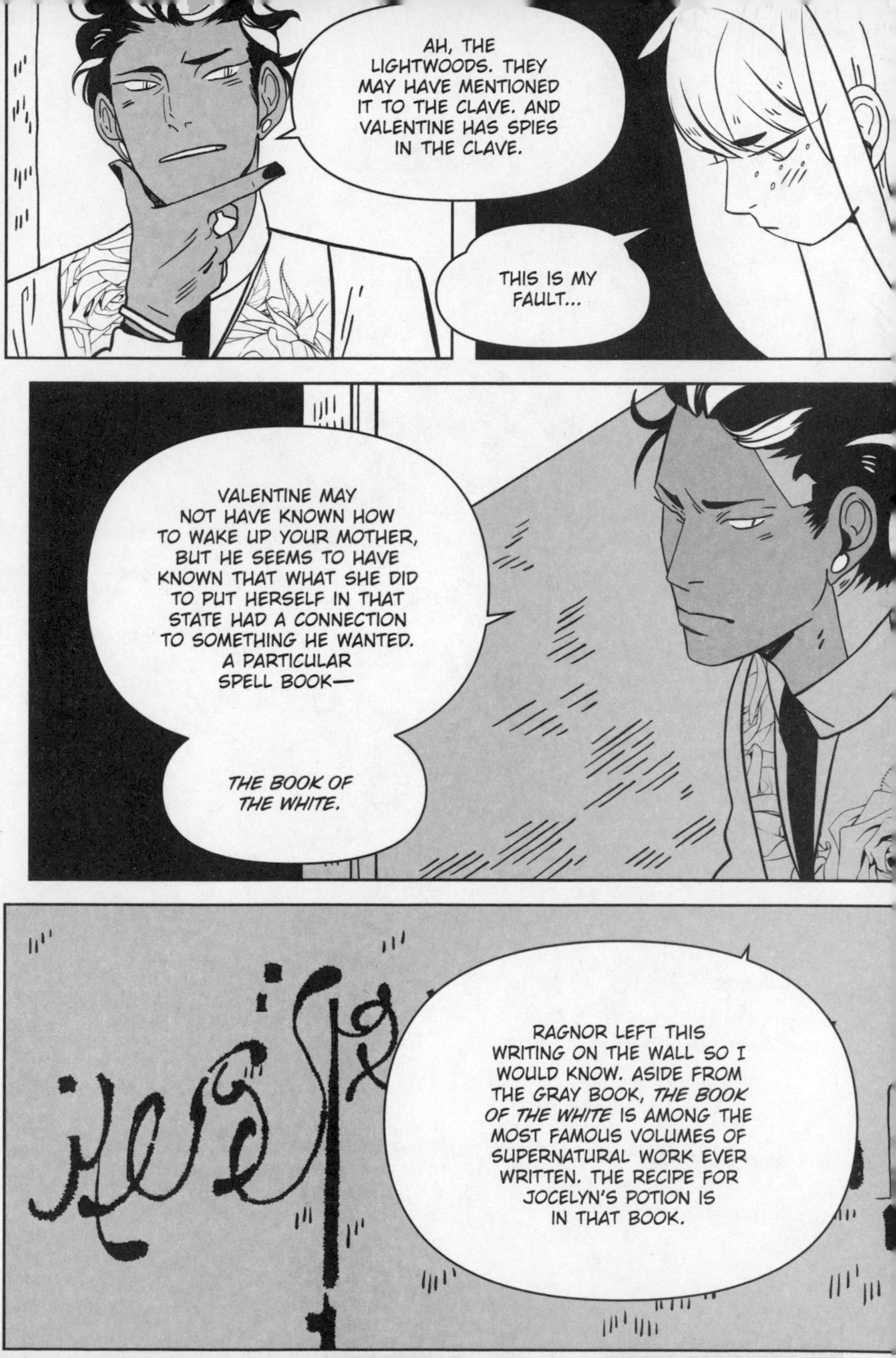
AH, THE LIGHTWOODS. THEY MAY HAVE MENTIONED IT TO THE CLAVE. AND VALENTINE HAS SPIES IN THE CLAVE.
THIS IS MY FAULT...
VALENTINE MAY NOT HAVE KNOWN HOW TO WAKE UP YOUR MOTHER, BUT HE SEEMS TO HAVE KNOWN THAT WHAT SHE DID TO PUT HERSELF IN THAT STATE HAD A CONNECTION TO SOMETHING HE WANTED. A PARTICULAR SPELL BOOK—
THE BOOK OF THE WHITE.
RAGNOR LEFT THIS WRITING ON THE WALL SO I WOULD KNOW. ASIDE FROM THE GRAY BOOK, *THE BOOK OF THE WHITE* IS AMONG THE MOST FAMOUS VOLUMES OF SUPERNATURAL WORK EVER WRITTEN. THE RECIPE FOR JOCELYN'S POTION IS IN THAT BOOK.

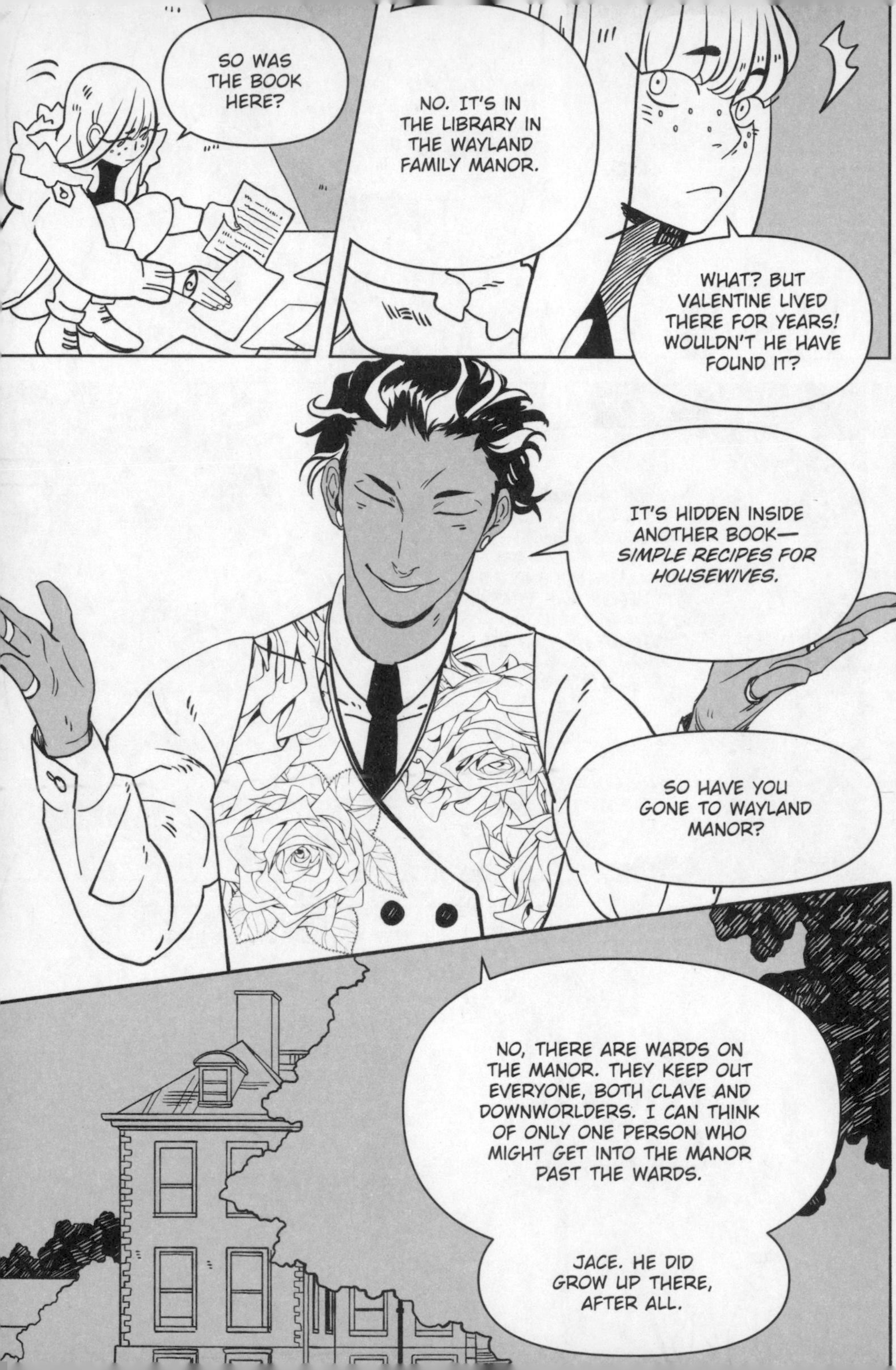
SO WAS THE BOOK HERE?
NO. IT'S IN THE LIBRARY IN THE WAYLAND FAMILY MANOR.
WHAT? BUT VALENTINE LIVED THERE FOR YEARS! WOULDN'T HE HAVE FOUND IT?
IT'S HIDDEN INSIDE ANOTHER BOOK—*SIMPLE RECIPES FOR HOUSEWIVES.*
SO HAVE YOU GONE TO WAYLAND MANOR?
NO, THERE ARE WARDS ON THE MANOR. THEY KEEP OUT EVERYONE, BOTH CLAVE AND DOWNWORLDERS. I CAN THINK OF ONLY ONE PERSON WHO MIGHT GET INTO THE MANOR PAST THE WARDS.
JACE. HE DID GROW UP THERE, AFTER ALL.

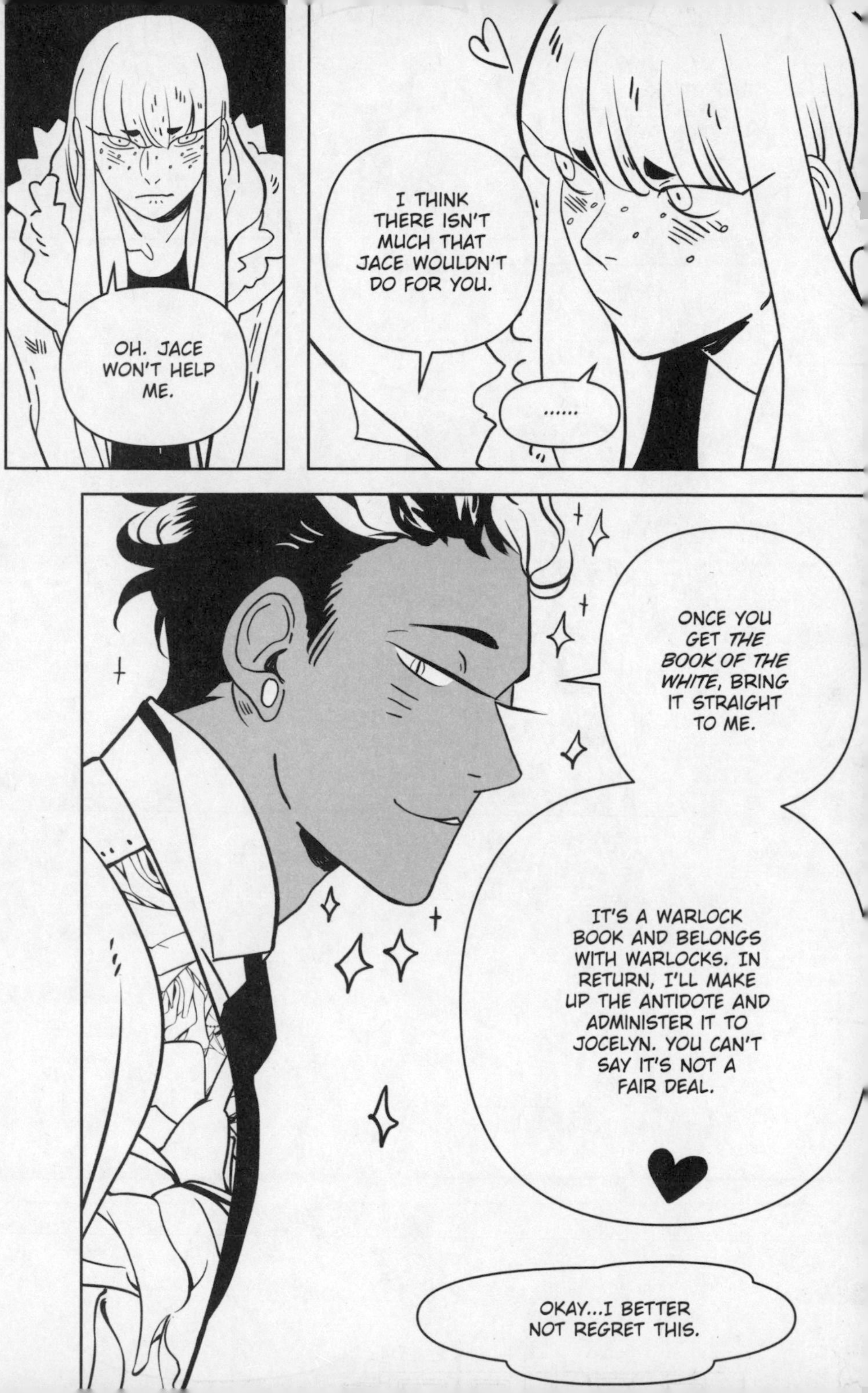
OH. JACE WON'T HELP ME.
I THINK THERE ISN'T MUCH THAT JACE WOULDN'T DO FOR YOU.
......
ONCE YOU GET *THE BOOK OF THE WHITE*, BRING IT STRAIGHT TO ME.
IT'S A WARLOCK BOOK AND BELONGS WITH WARLOCKS. IN RETURN, I'LL MAKE UP THE ANTIDOTE AND ADMINISTER IT TO JOCELYN. YOU CAN'T SAY IT'S NOT A FAIR DEAL.
OKAY...I BETTER NOT REGRET THIS.

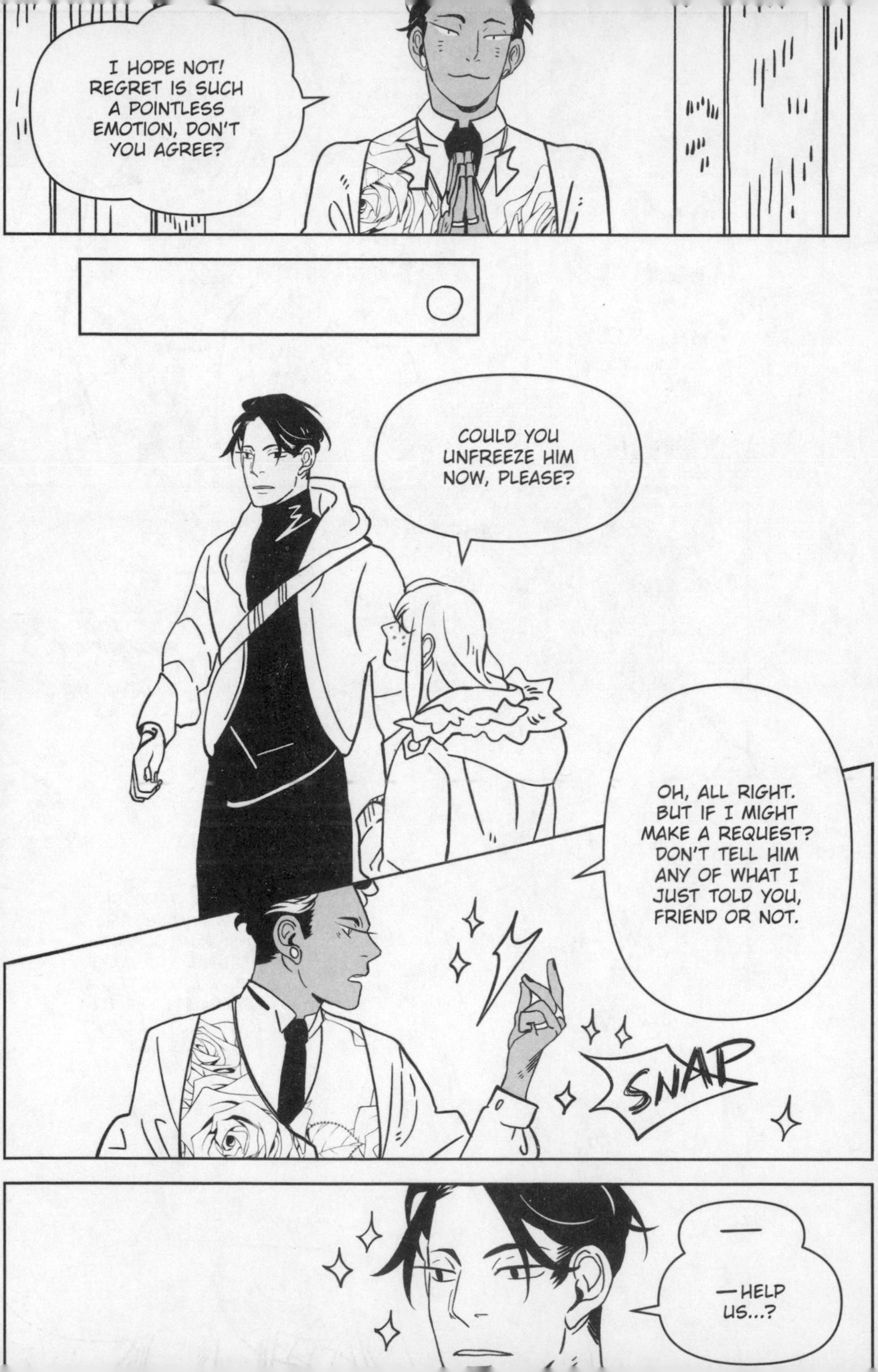
I HOPE NOT! REGRET IS SUCH A POINTLESS EMOTION, DON'T YOU AGREE?
COULD YOU UNFREEZE HIM NOW, PLEASE?
OH, ALL RIGHT. BUT IF I MIGHT MAKE A REQUEST? DON'T TELL HIM ANY OF WHAT I JUST TOLD YOU, FRIEND OR NOT.
SNAP
—
—HELP US...?

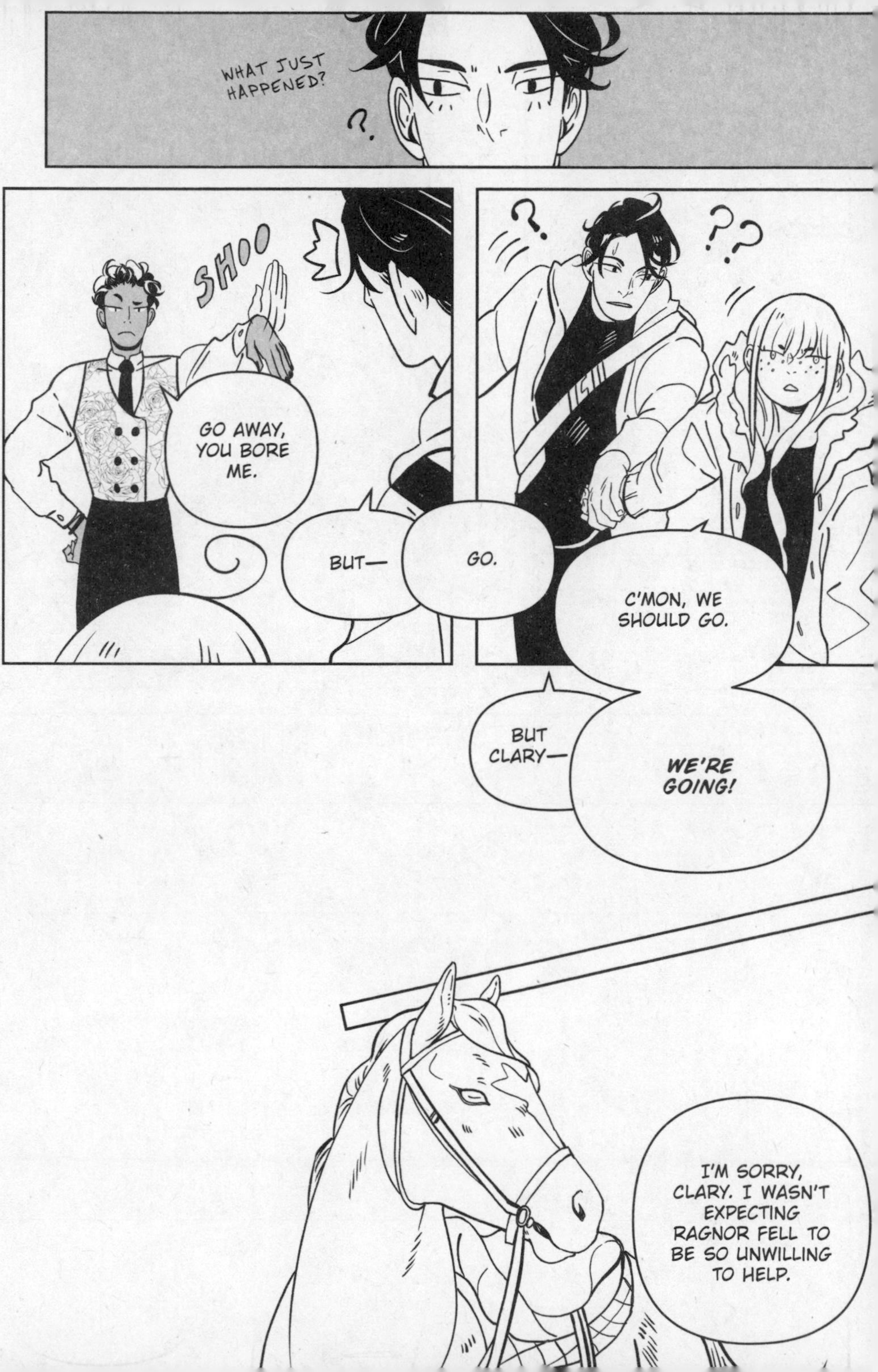
WHAT JUST HAPPENED?
?
SHOO
GO AWAY, YOU BORE ME.
BUT—
GO.
?
??
C'MON, WE SHOULD GO.
BUT CLARY—
WE'RE GOING!
I'M SORRY, CLARY. I WASN'T EXPECTING RAGNOR FELL TO BE SO UNWILLING TO HELP.

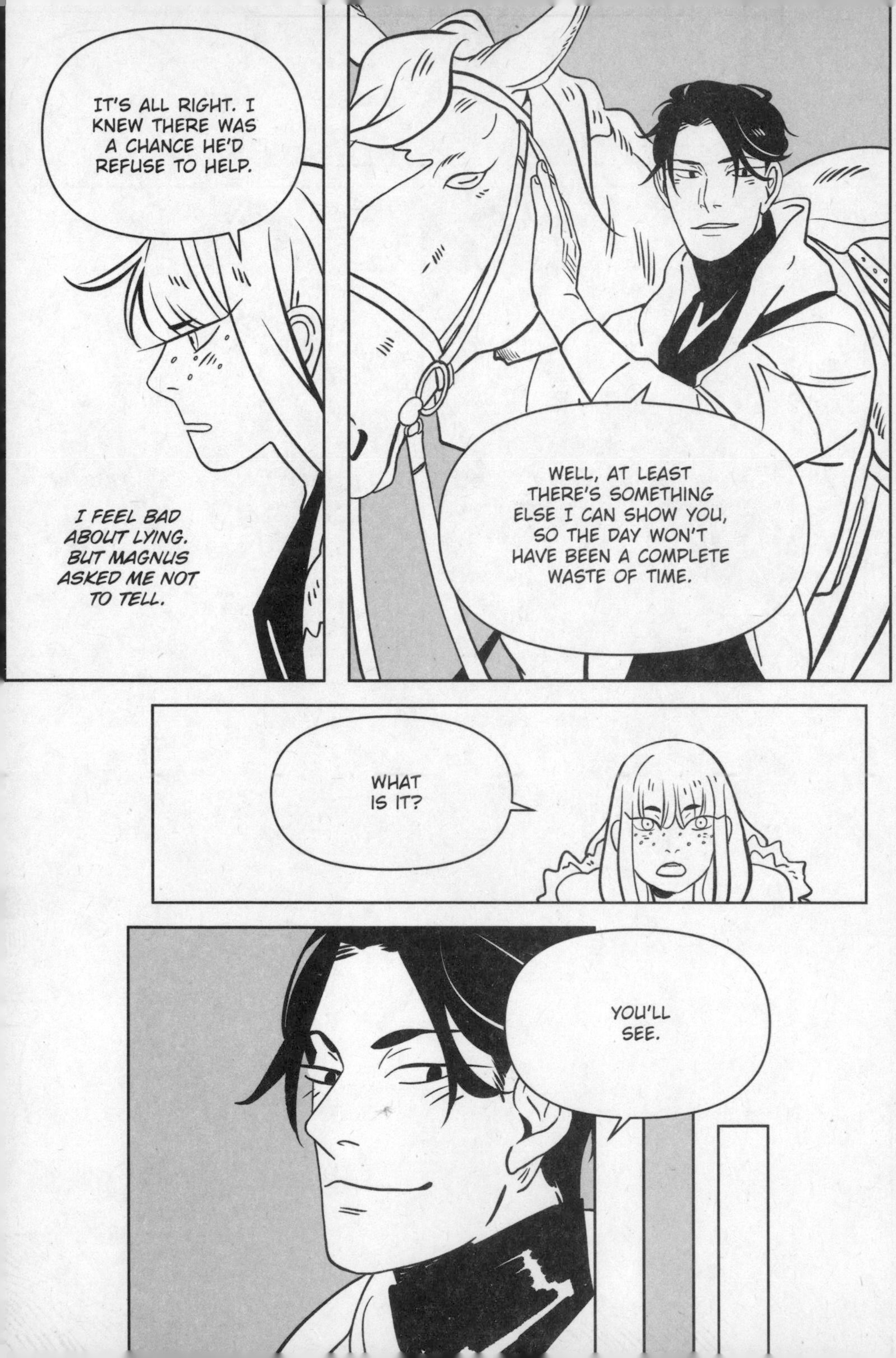
IT'S ALL RIGHT. I KNEW THERE WAS A CHANCE HE'D REFUSE TO HELP.
I FEEL BAD ABOUT LYING. BUT MAGNUS ASKED ME NOT TO TELL.
WELL, AT LEAST THERE'S SOMETHING ELSE I CAN SHOW YOU, SO THE DAY WON'T HAVE BEEN A COMPLETE WASTE OF TIME.
WHAT IS IT?
YOU'LL SEE.

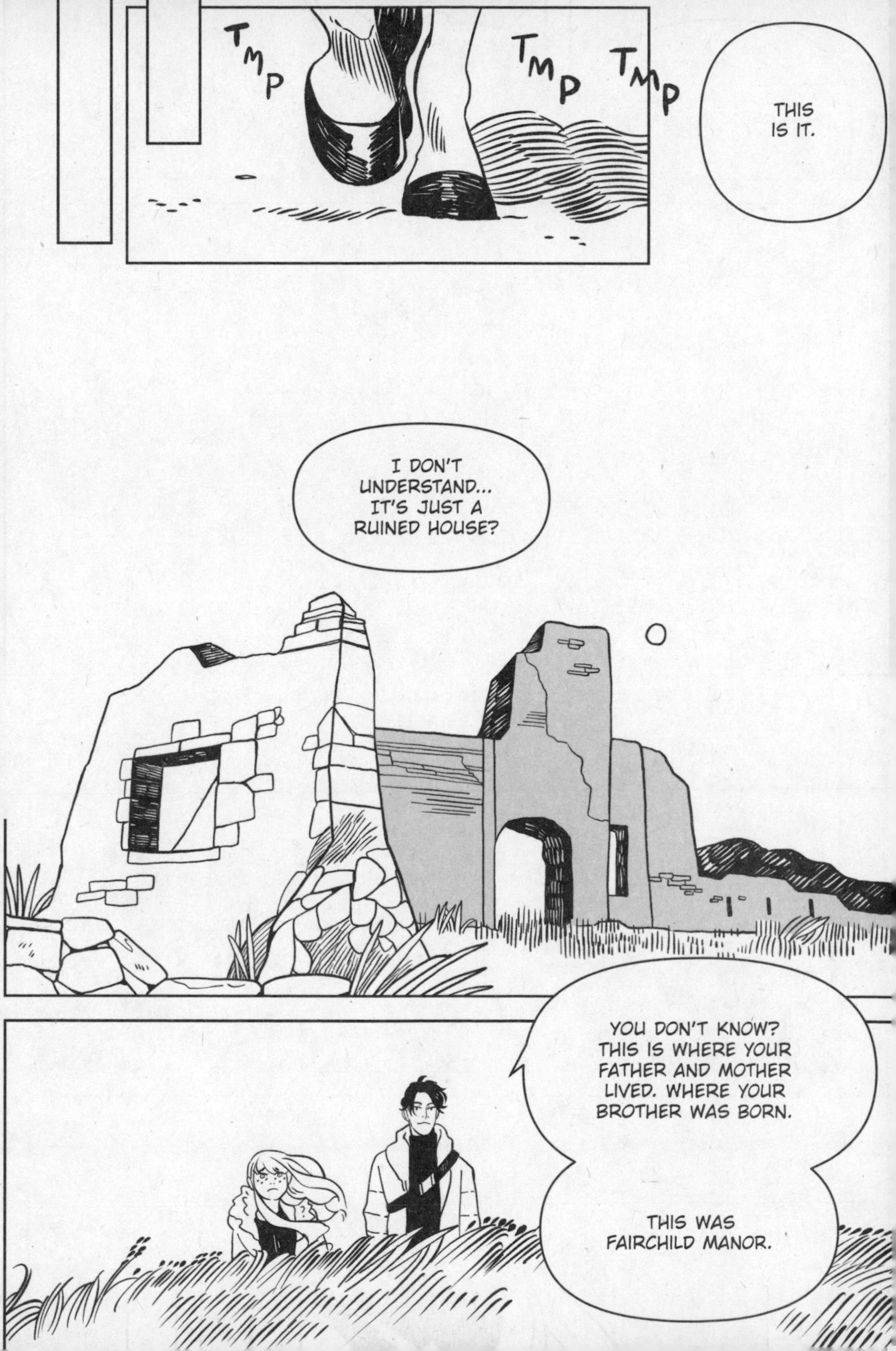
TMP
TMP TMP
THIS IS IT.
I DON'T UNDERSTAND... IT'S JUST A RUINED HOUSE?
YOU DON'T KNOW? THIS IS WHERE YOUR FATHER AND MOTHER LIVED. WHERE YOUR BROTHER WAS BORN.
THIS WAS FAIRCHILD MANOR.

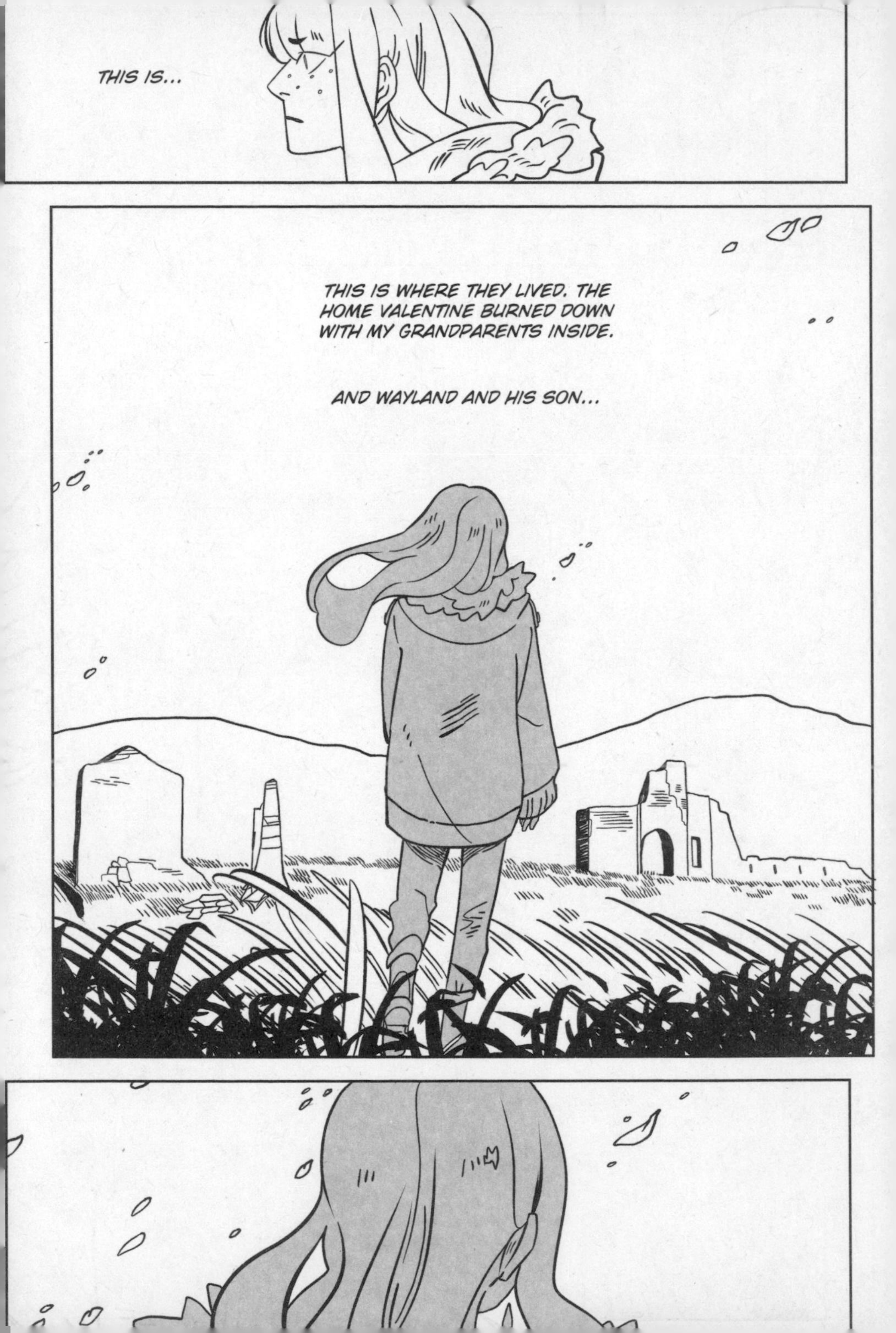
THIS IS...
THIS IS WHERE THEY LIVED. THE HOME VALENTINE BURNED DOWN WITH MY GRANDPARENTS INSIDE.
AND WAYLAND AND HIS SON...

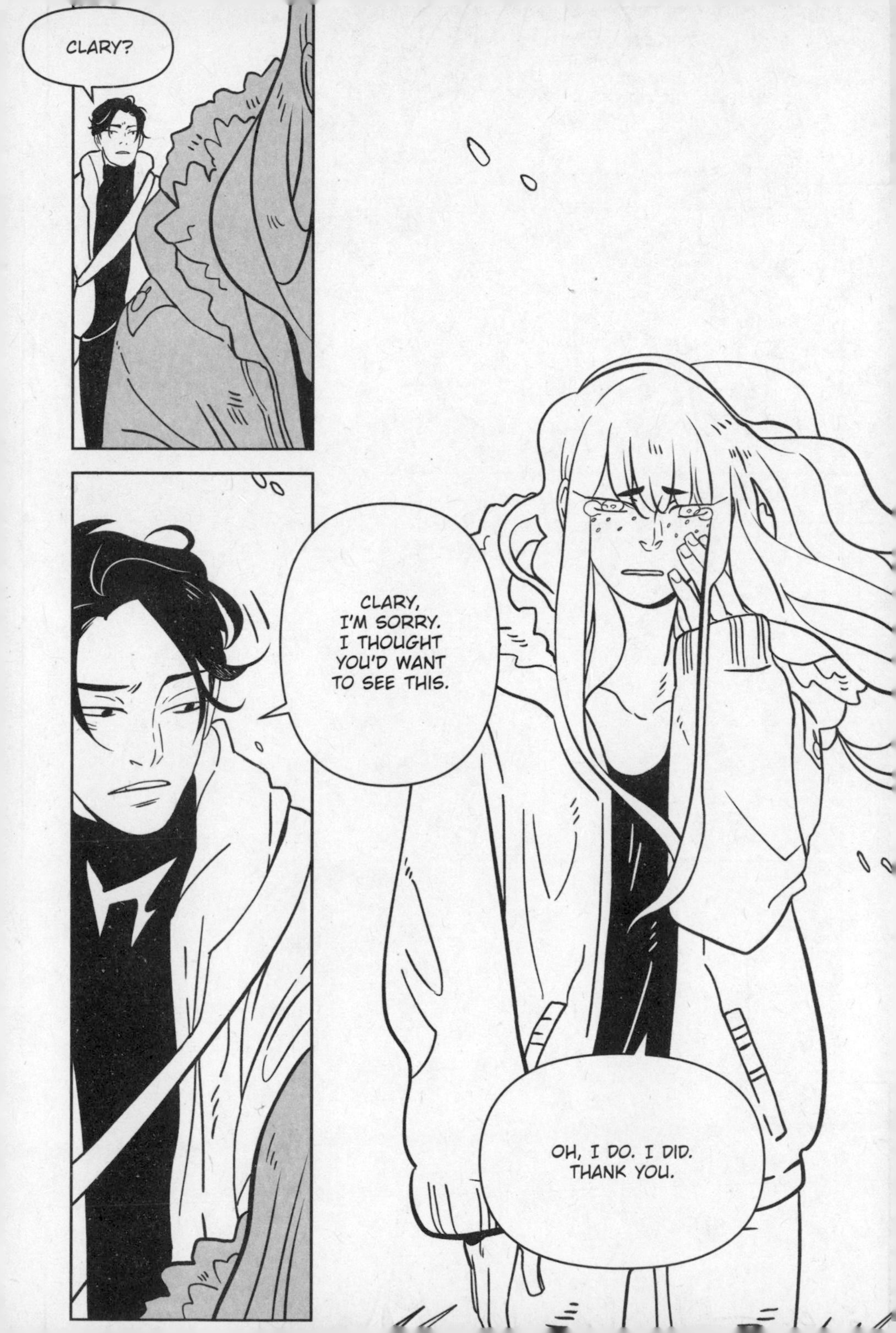
CLARY?
CLARY, I'M SORRY. I THOUGHT YOU'D WANT TO SEE THIS.
OH, I DO. I DID. THANK YOU.

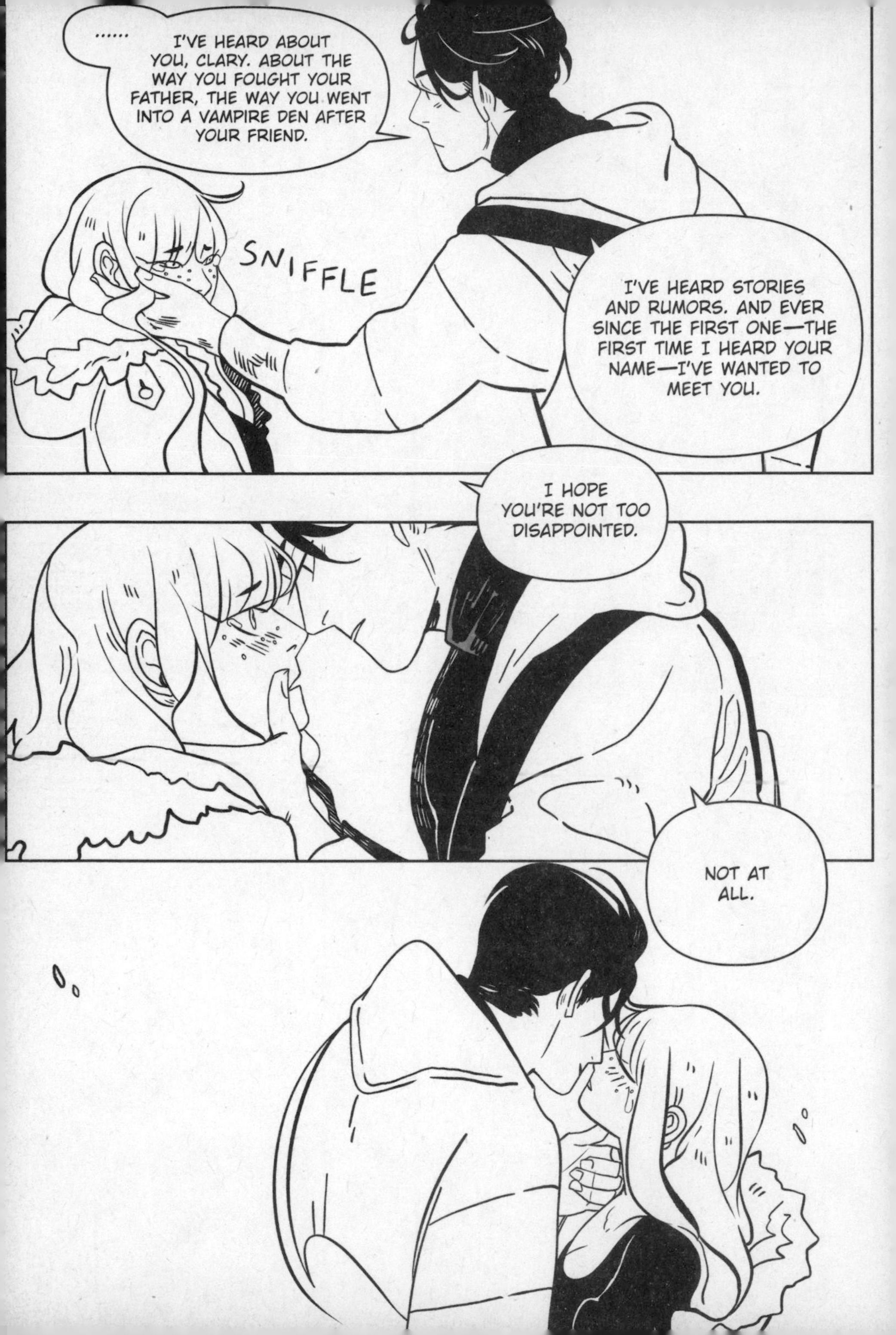
......
I'VE HEARD ABOUT YOU, CLARY. ABOUT THE WAY YOU FOUGHT YOUR FATHER, THE WAY YOU WENT INTO A VAMPIRE DEN AFTER YOUR FRIEND.
SNIFFLE
I'VE HEARD STORIES AND RUMORS. AND EVER SINCE THE FIRST ONE—THE FIRST TIME I HEARD YOUR NAME—I'VE WANTED TO MEET YOU.
I HOPE YOU'RE NOT TOO DISAPPOINTED.
NOT AT ALL.

THE MORTAL INSTRUMENTS

THE GRAPHIC NOVEL

THE MORTAL INSTRUMENTS

THE GRAPHIC NOVEL

Chapter 28

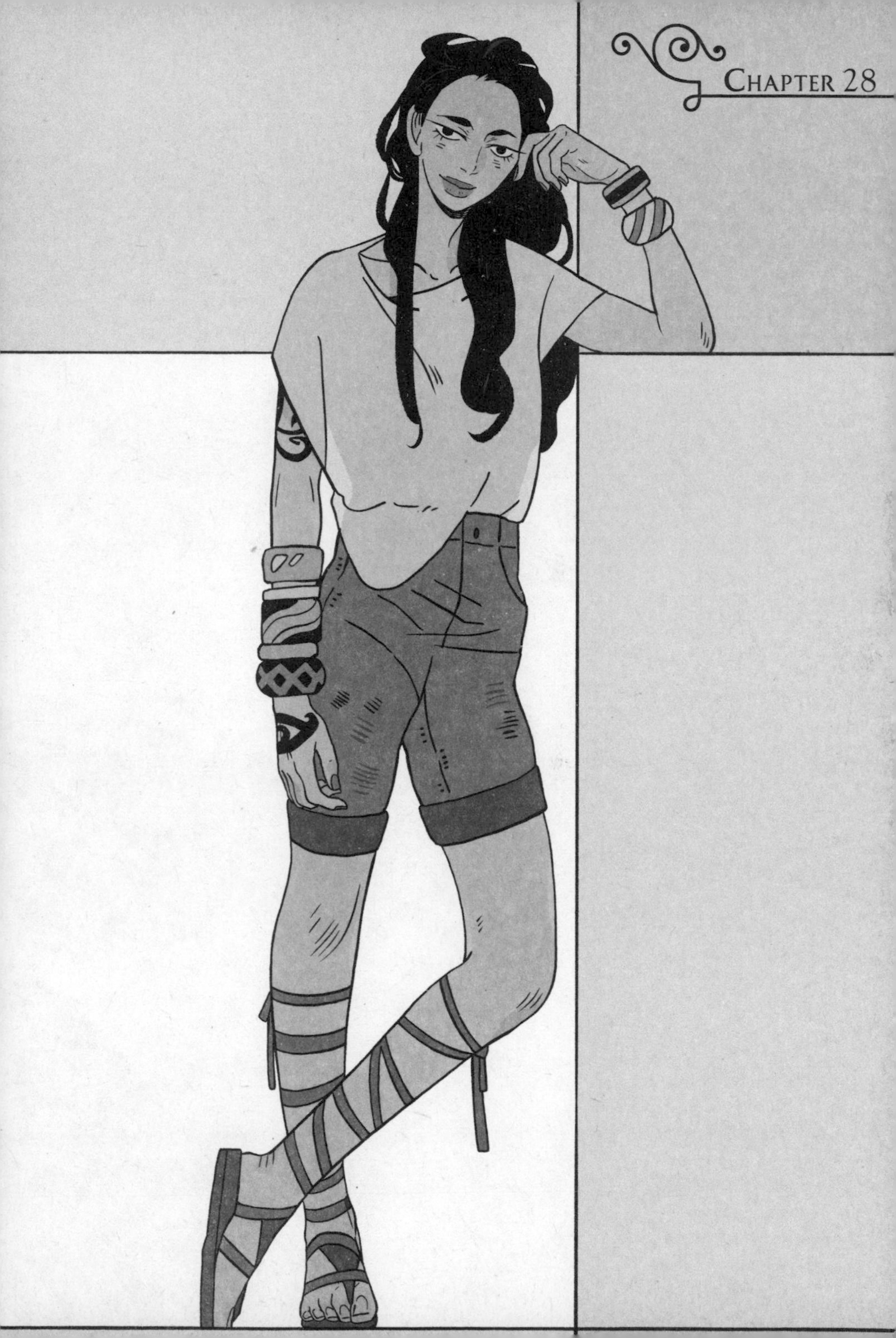

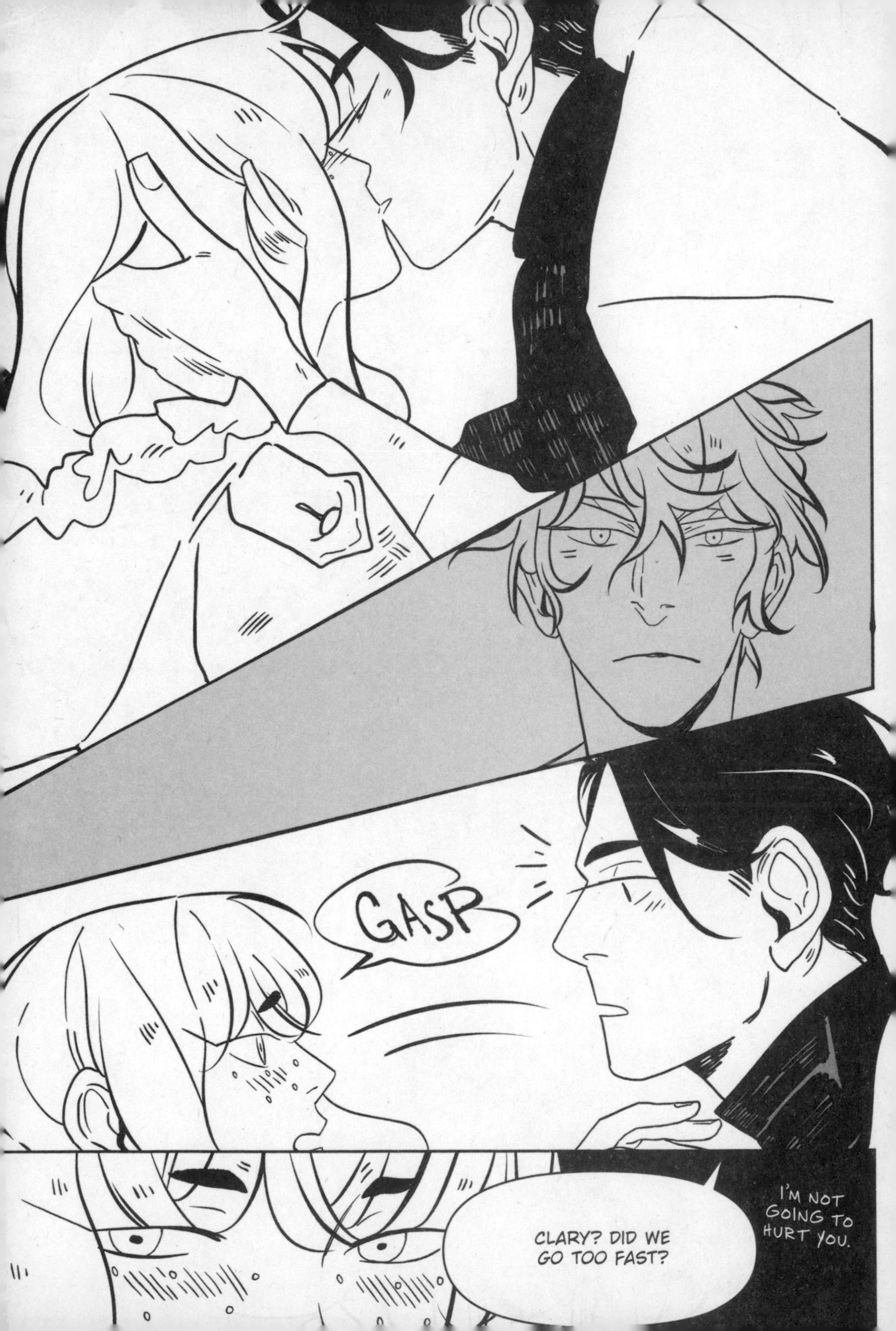
GASP
CLARY? DID WE GO TOO FAST?
I'M NOT GOING TO HURT YOU.

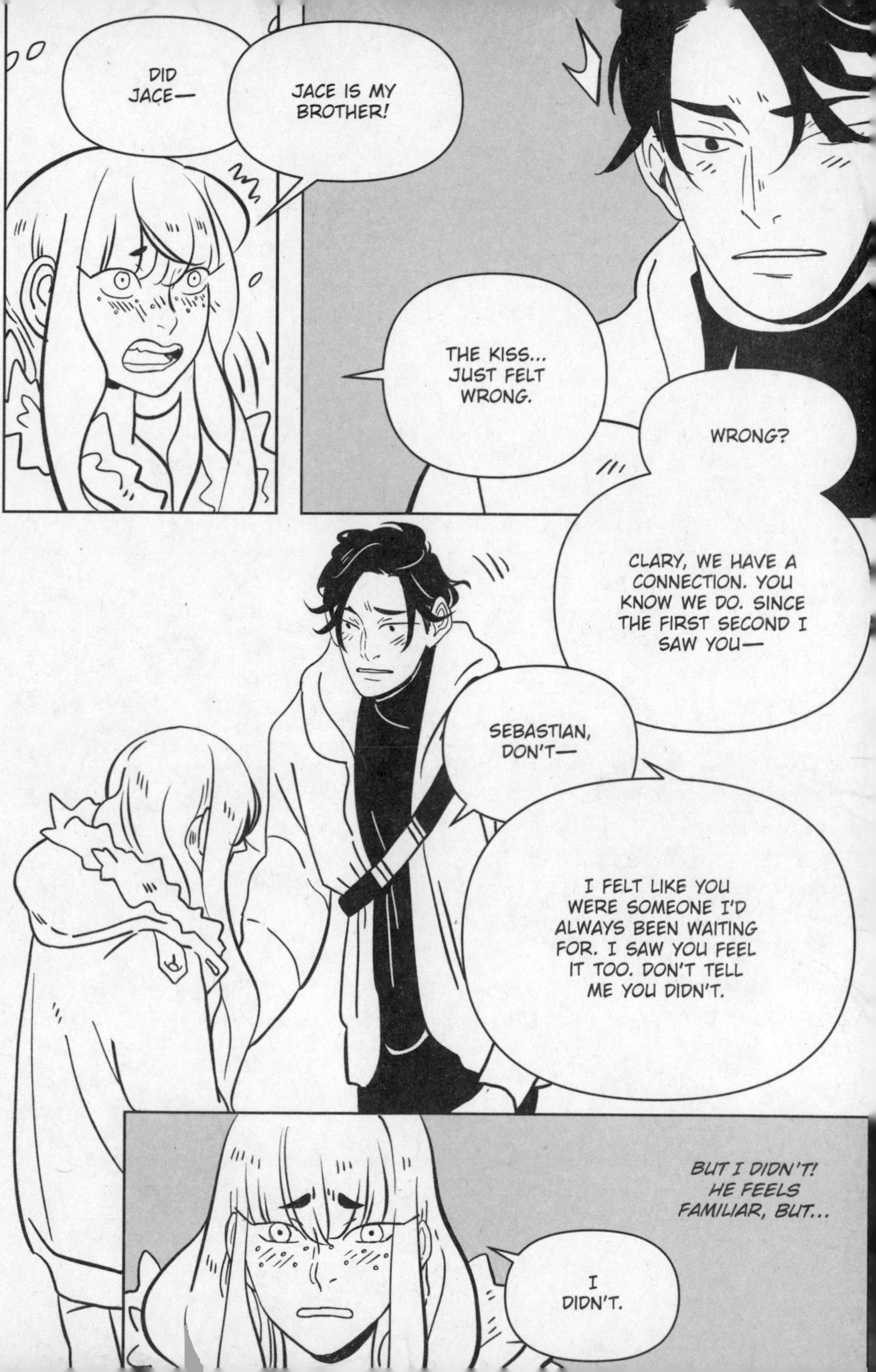
DID JACE—
JACE IS MY BROTHER!
THE KISS... JUST FELT WRONG.
WRONG?
CLARY, WE HAVE A CONNECTION. YOU KNOW WE DO. SINCE THE FIRST SECOND I SAW YOU—
SEBASTIAN, DON'T—
I FELT LIKE YOU WERE SOMEONE I'D ALWAYS BEEN WAITING FOR. I SAW YOU FEEL IT TOO. DON'T TELL ME YOU DIDN'T.
BUT I DIDN'T! HE FEELS FAMILIAR, BUT...
I DIDN'T.

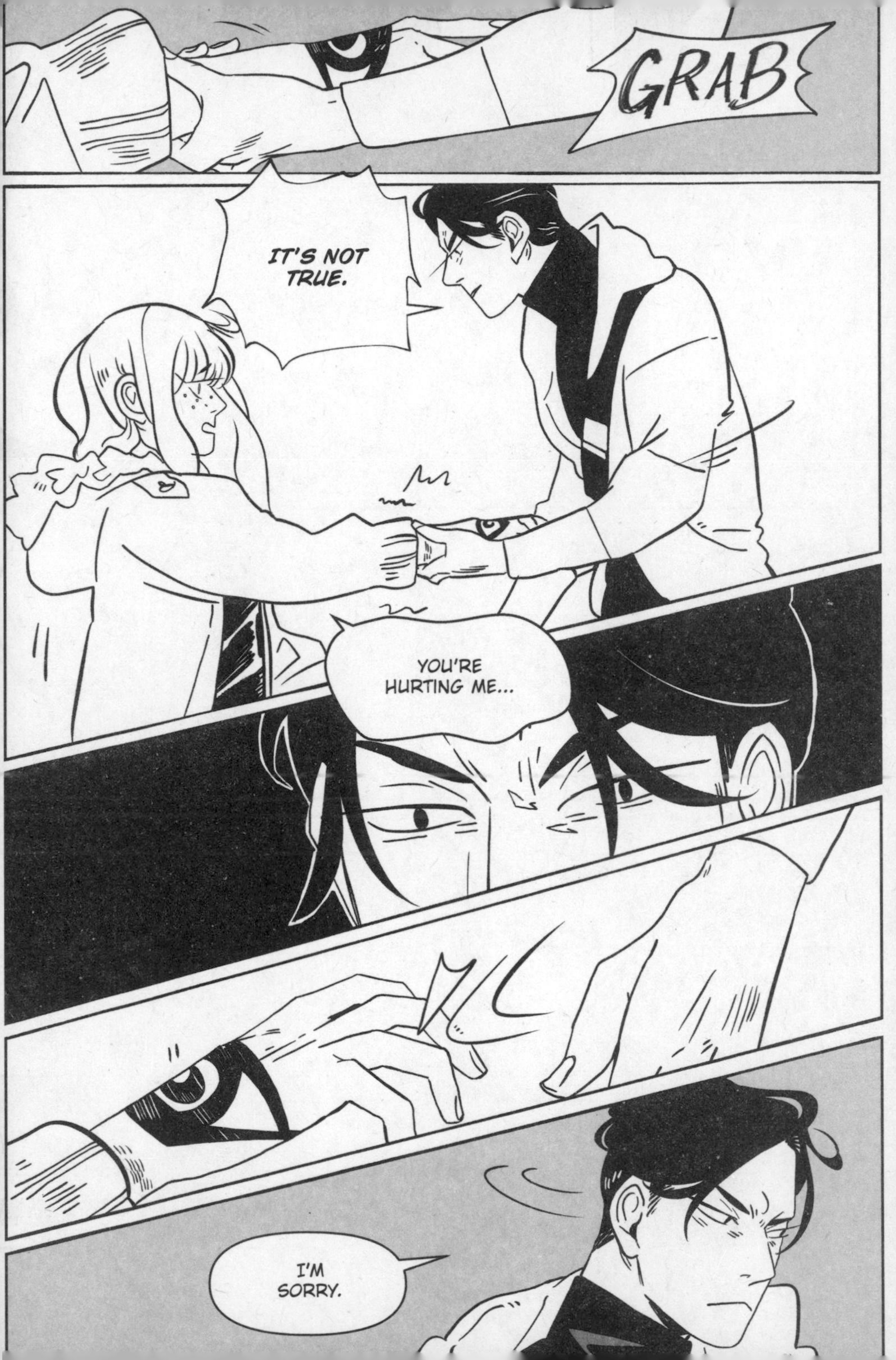
GRAB
IT'S NOT TRUE.
YOU'RE HURTING ME...
I'M SORRY.

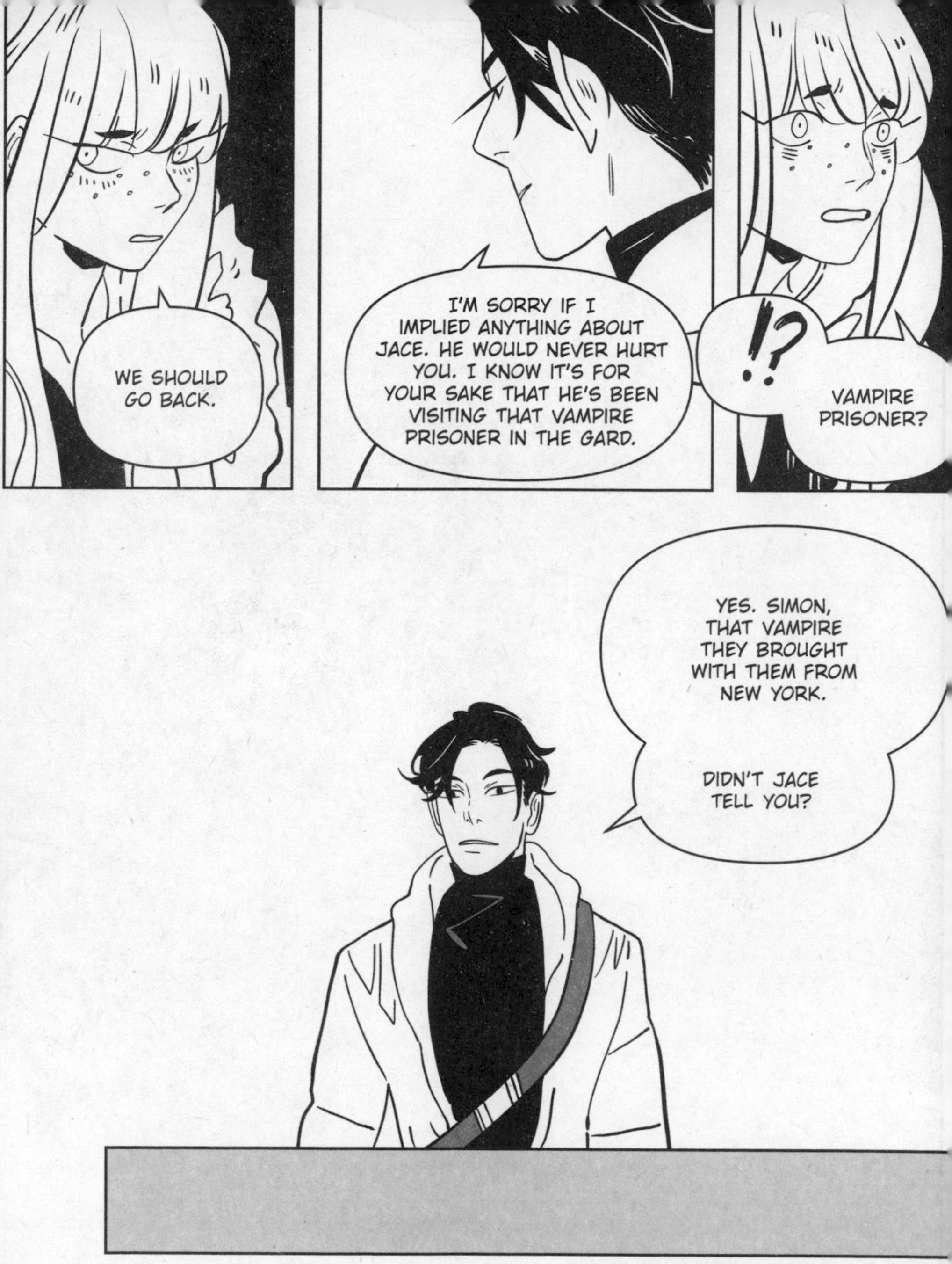
WE SHOULD GO BACK.
I'M SORRY IF I IMPLIED ANYTHING ABOUT JACE. HE WOULD NEVER HURT YOU. I KNOW IT'S FOR YOUR SAKE THAT HE'S BEEN VISITING THAT VAMPIRE PRISONER IN THE GARD.
!?
VAMPIRE PRISONER?
YES. SIMON, THAT VAMPIRE THEY BROUGHT WITH THEM FROM NEW YORK.
DIDN'T JACE TELL YOU?

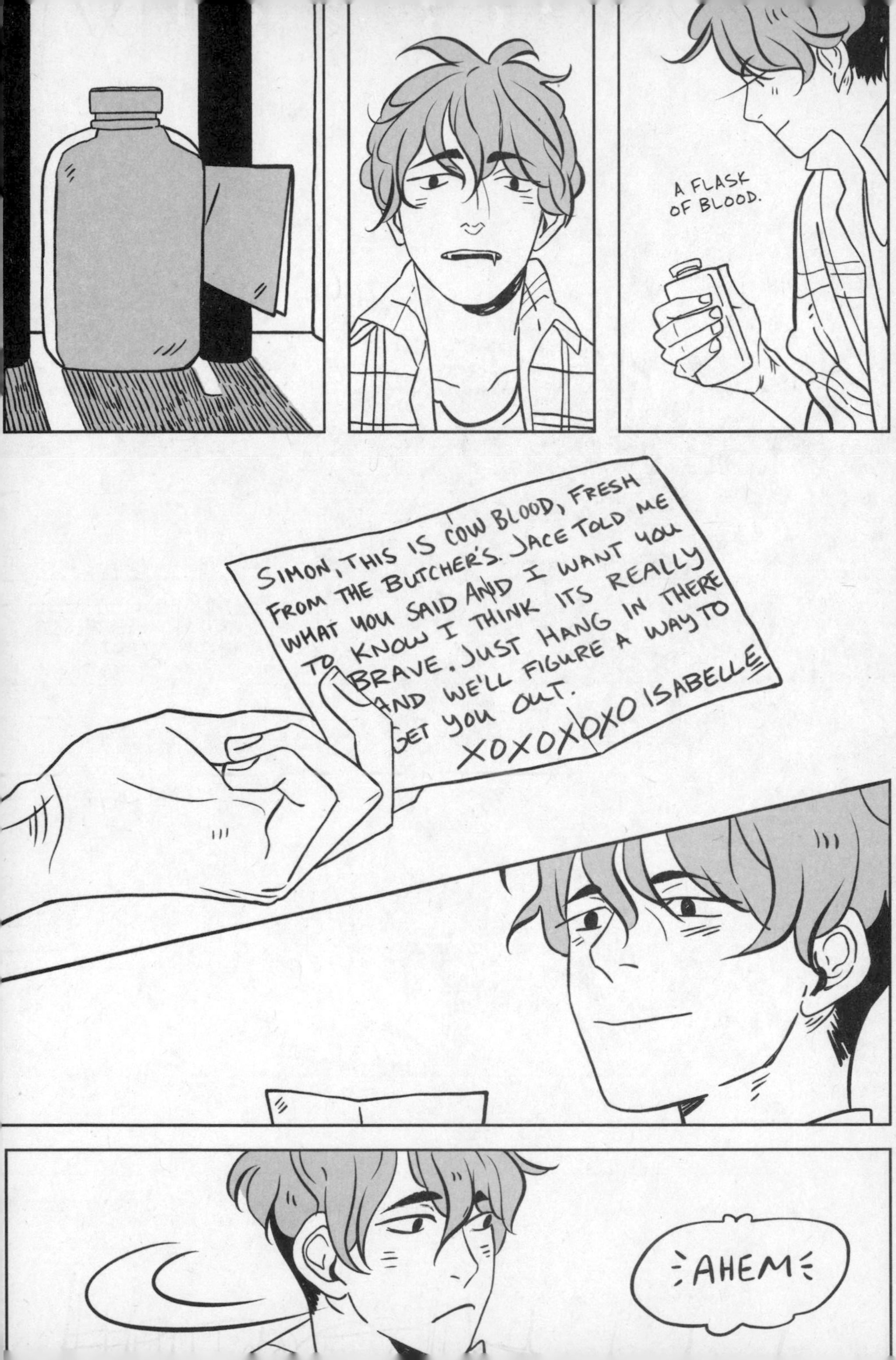
A FLASK OF BLOOD.
SIMON, THIS IS COW BLOOD, FRESH FROM THE BUTCHER'S. JACE TOLD ME WHAT YOU SAID AND I WANT YOU TO KNOW I THINK ITS REALLY BRAVE. JUST HANG IN THERE AND WE'LL FIGURE A WAY TO GET YOU OUT.
XOXOXOXO ISABELLE
AHEM

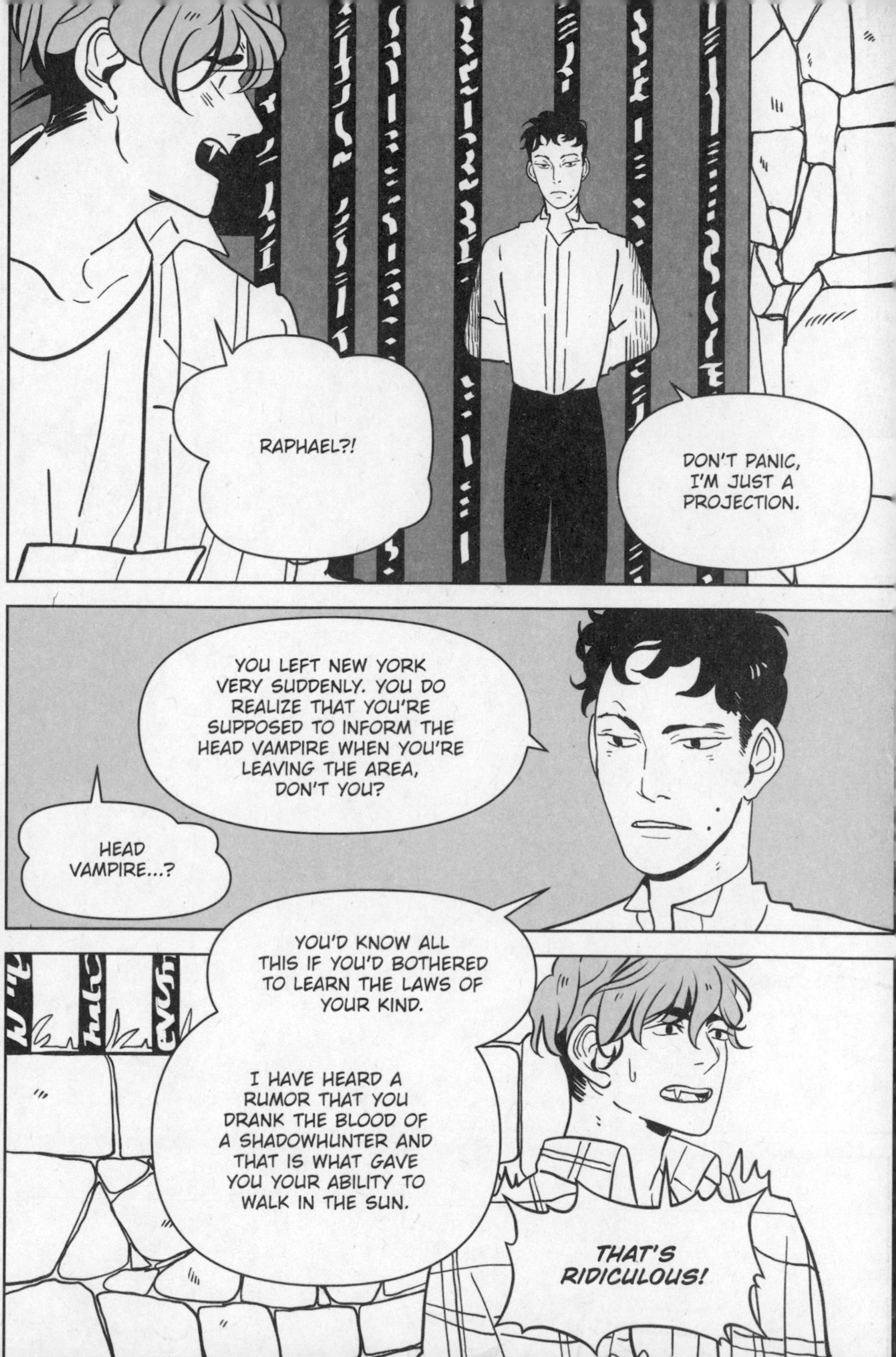
RAPHAEL?!
DON'T PANIC, I'M JUST A PROJECTION.
YOU LEFT NEW YORK VERY SUDDENLY. YOU DO REALIZE THAT YOU'RE SUPPOSED TO INFORM THE HEAD VAMPIRE WHEN YOU'RE LEAVING THE AREA, DON'T YOU?
HEAD VAMPIRE...?
YOU'D KNOW ALL THIS IF YOU'D BOTHERED TO LEARN THE LAWS OF YOUR KIND.
I HAVE HEARD A RUMOR THAT YOU DRANK THE BLOOD OF A SHADOWHUNTER AND THAT IS WHAT GAVE YOU YOUR ABILITY TO WALK IN THE SUN.
THAT'S RIDICULOUS!

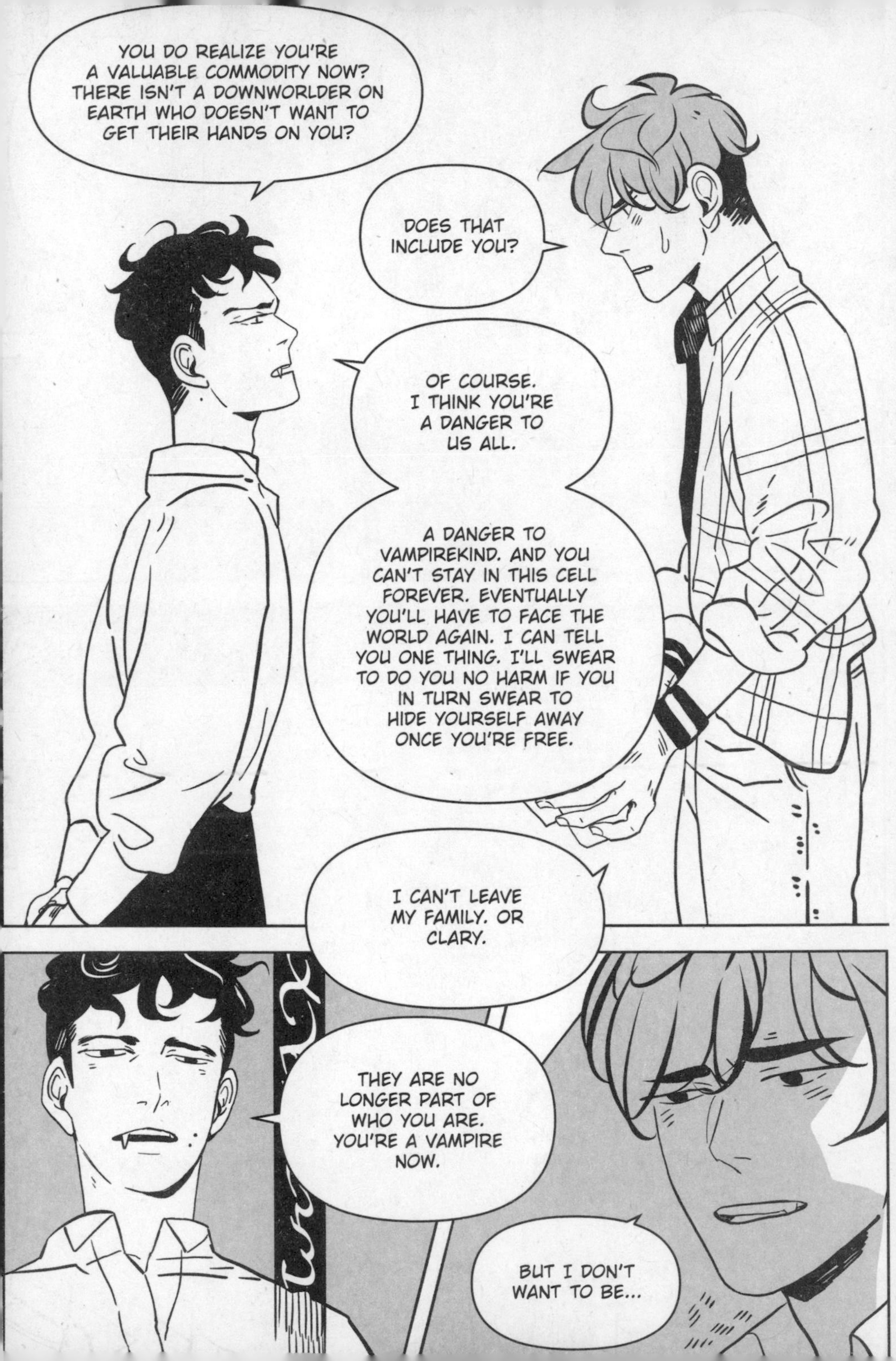
YOU DO REALIZE YOU'RE A VALUABLE COMMODITY NOW? THERE ISN'T A DOWNWORLDER ON EARTH WHO DOESN'T WANT TO GET THEIR HANDS ON YOU?
DOES THAT INCLUDE YOU?
OF COURSE. I THINK YOU'RE A DANGER TO US ALL.
A DANGER TO VAMPIREKIND. AND YOU CAN'T STAY IN THIS CELL FOREVER. EVENTUALLY YOU'LL HAVE TO FACE THE WORLD AGAIN. I CAN TELL YOU ONE THING. I'LL SWEAR TO DO YOU NO HARM IF YOU IN TURN SWEAR TO HIDE YOURSELF AWAY ONCE YOU'RE FREE.
I CAN'T LEAVE MY FAMILY. OR CLARY.
THEY ARE NO LONGER PART OF WHO YOU ARE. YOU'RE A VAMPIRE NOW.
BUT I DON'T WANT TO BE...

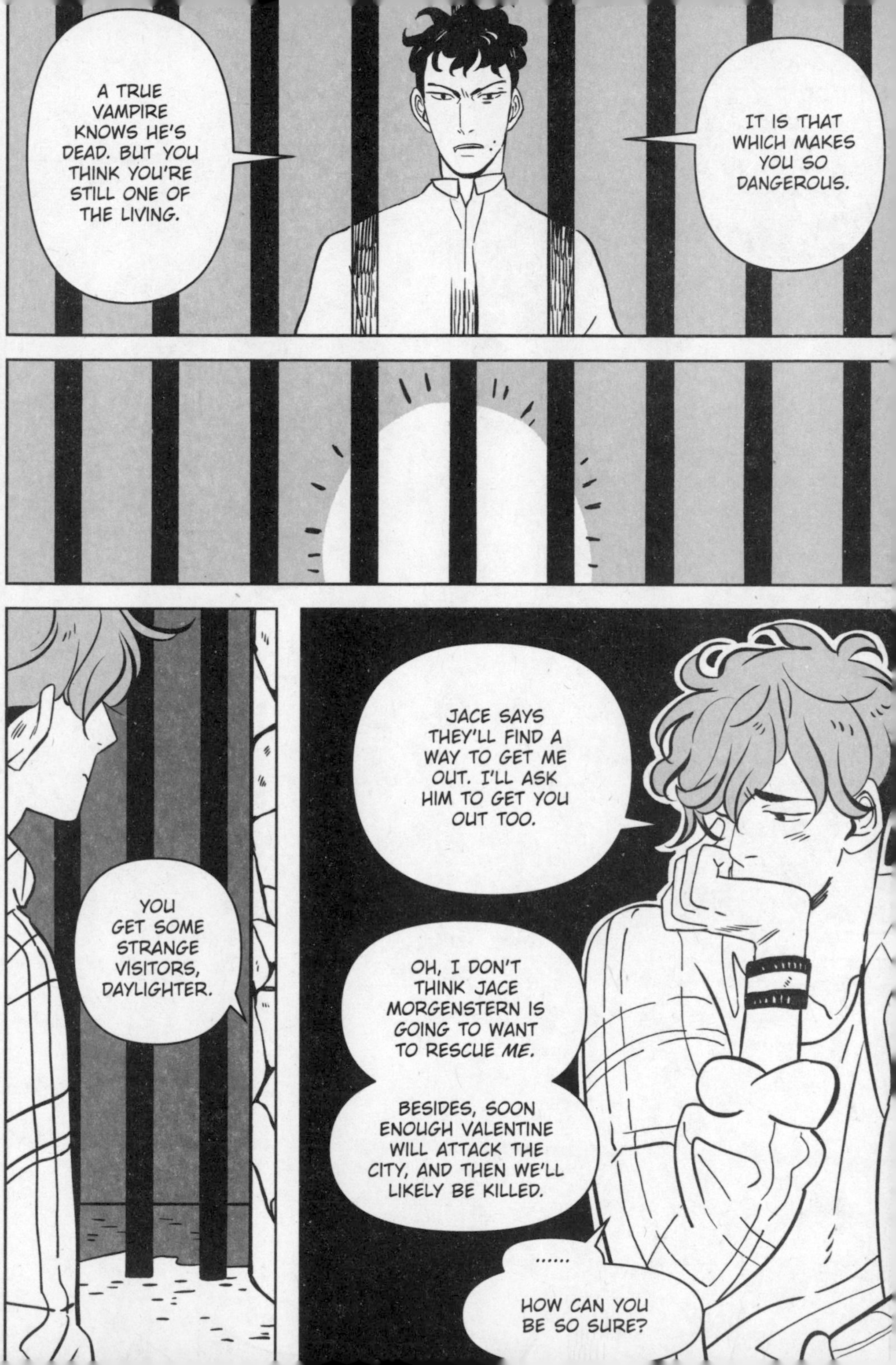
A TRUE VAMPIRE KNOWS HE'S DEAD. BUT YOU THINK YOU'RE STILL ONE OF THE LIVING.
IT IS THAT WHICH MAKES YOU SO DANGEROUS.
YOU GET SOME STRANGE VISITORS, DAYLIGHTER.
JACE SAYS THEY'LL FIND A WAY TO GET ME OUT. I'LL ASK HIM TO GET YOU OUT TOO.
OH, I DON'T THINK JACE MORGENSTERN IS GOING TO WANT TO RESCUE *ME*.
BESIDES, SOON ENOUGH VALENTINE WILL ATTACK THE CITY, AND THEN WE'LL LIKELY BE KILLED.
......
HOW CAN YOU BE SO SURE?

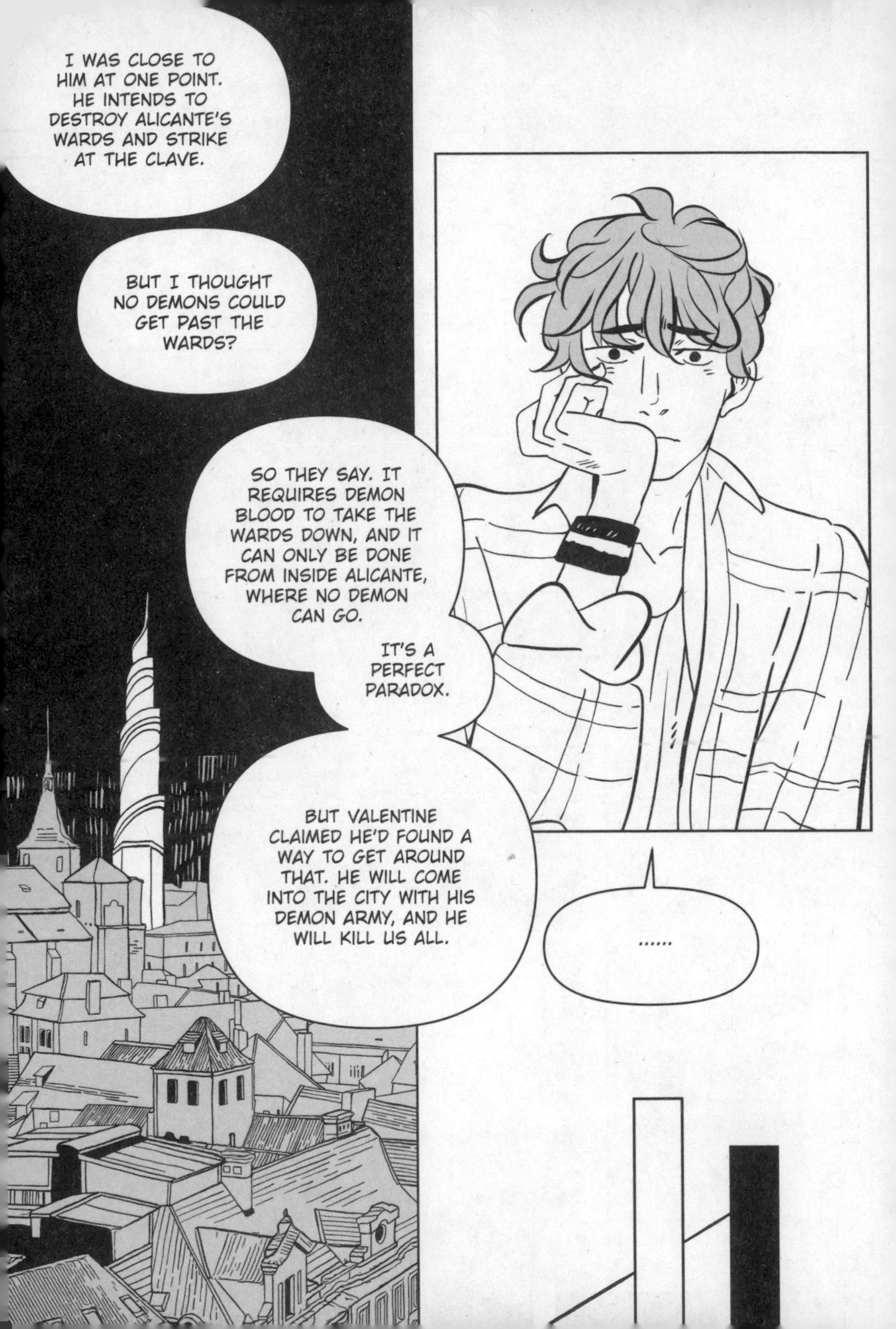

I WAS CLOSE TO HIM AT ONE POINT. HE INTENDS TO DESTROY ALICANTE'S WARDS AND STRIKE AT THE CLAVE.
BUT I THOUGHT NO DEMONS COULD GET PAST THE WARDS?
SO THEY SAY. IT REQUIRES DEMON BLOOD TO TAKE THE WARDS DOWN, AND IT CAN ONLY BE DONE FROM INSIDE ALICANTE, WHERE NO DEMON CAN GO.
IT'S A PERFECT PARADOX.
BUT VALENTINE CLAIMED HE'D FOUND A WAY TO GET AROUND THAT. HE WILL COME INTO THE CITY WITH HIS DEMON ARMY, AND HE WILL KILL US ALL.
......

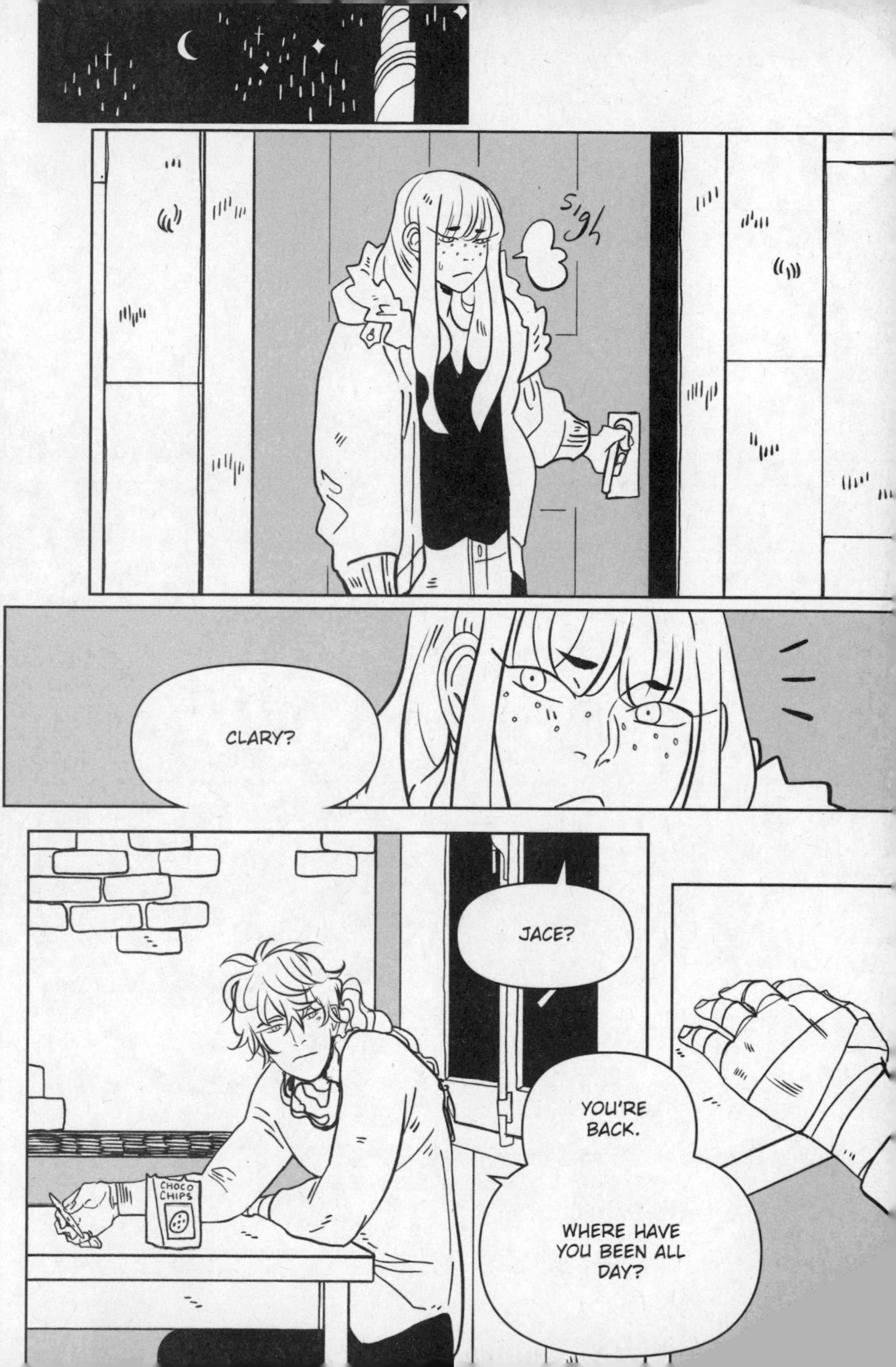
Sigh
CLARY?
JACE?
YOU'RE BACK.
WHERE HAVE YOU BEEN ALL DAY?
CHOCO CHIPS

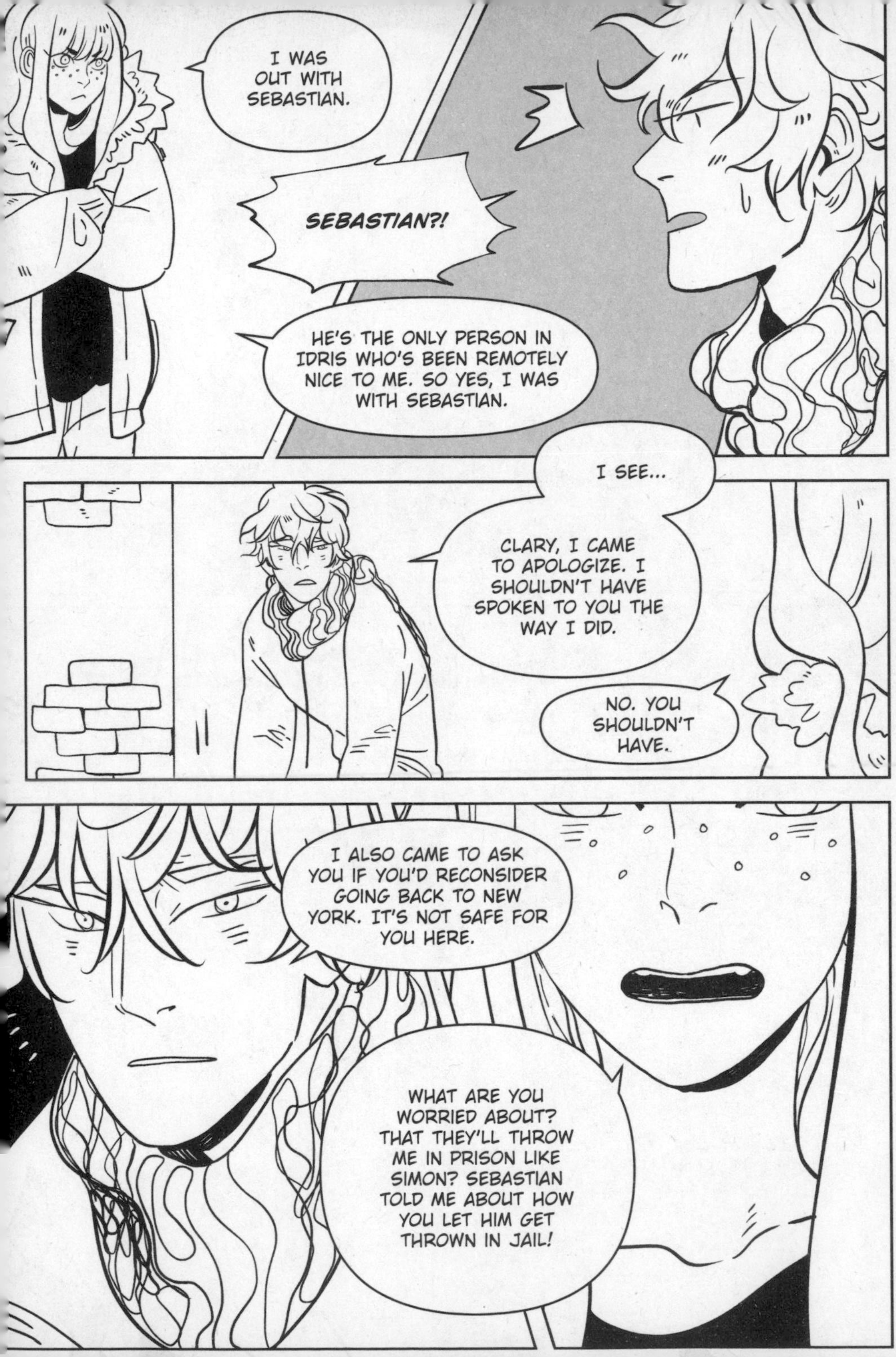
I WAS OUT WITH SEBASTIAN.
SEBASTIAN?!
HE'S THE ONLY PERSON IN IDRIS WHO'S BEEN REMOTELY NICE TO ME. SO YES, I WAS WITH SEBASTIAN.
I SEE...
CLARY, I CAME TO APOLOGIZE. I SHOULDN'T HAVE SPOKEN TO YOU THE WAY I DID.
NO. YOU SHOULDN'T HAVE.
I ALSO CAME TO ASK YOU IF YOU'D RECONSIDER GOING BACK TO NEW YORK. IT'S NOT SAFE FOR YOU HERE.
WHAT ARE YOU WORRIED ABOUT? THAT THEY'LL THROW ME IN PRISON LIKE SIMON? SEBASTIAN TOLD ME ABOUT HOW YOU LET HIM GET THROWN IN JAIL!

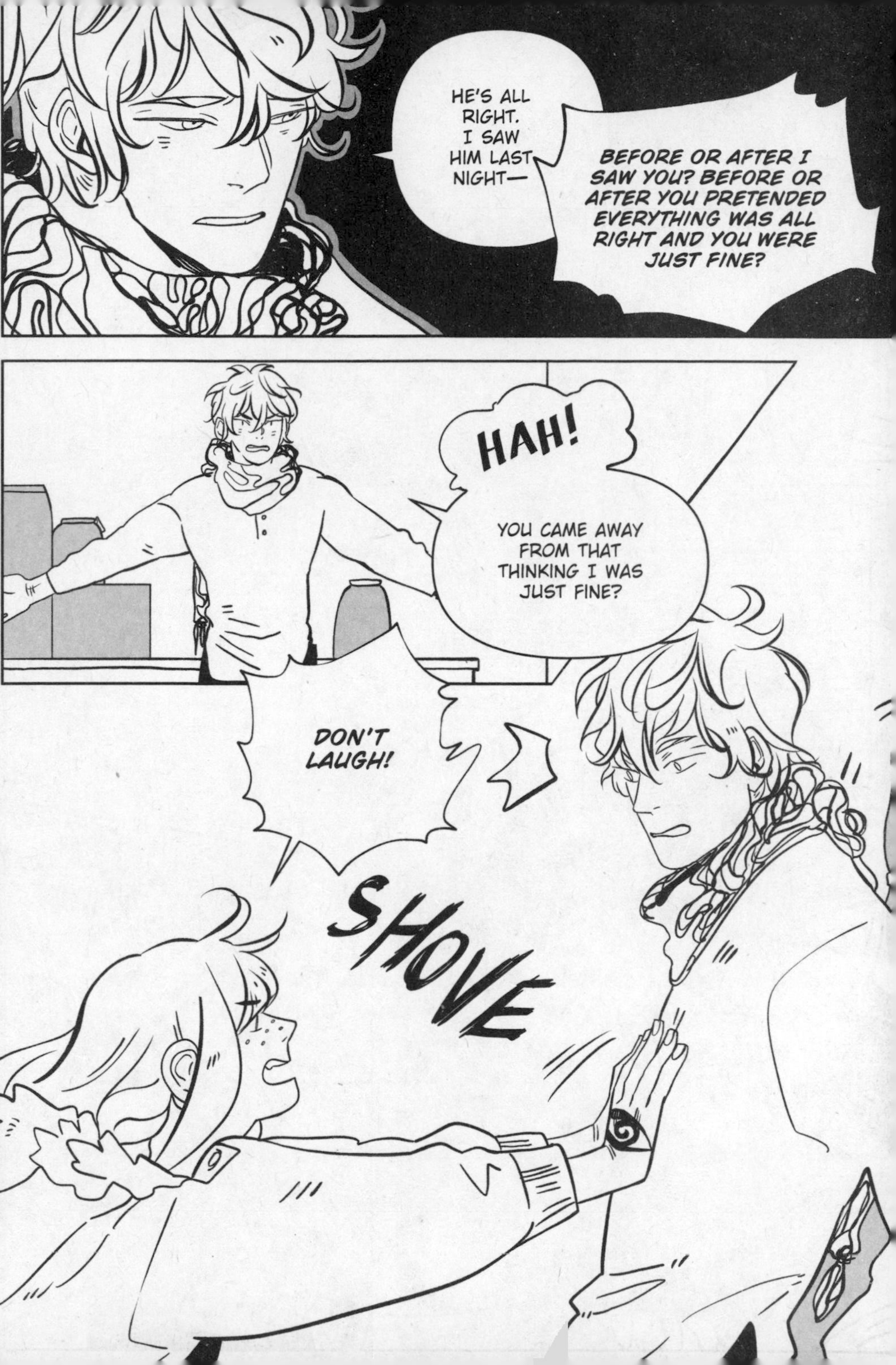
HE'S ALL RIGHT. I SAW HIM LAST NIGHT—
BEFORE OR AFTER I SAW YOU? BEFORE OR AFTER YOU PRETENDED EVERYTHING WAS ALL RIGHT AND YOU WERE JUST FINE?
HAH!
YOU CAME AWAY FROM THAT THINKING I WAS JUST FINE?
DON'T LAUGH!
SHOVE

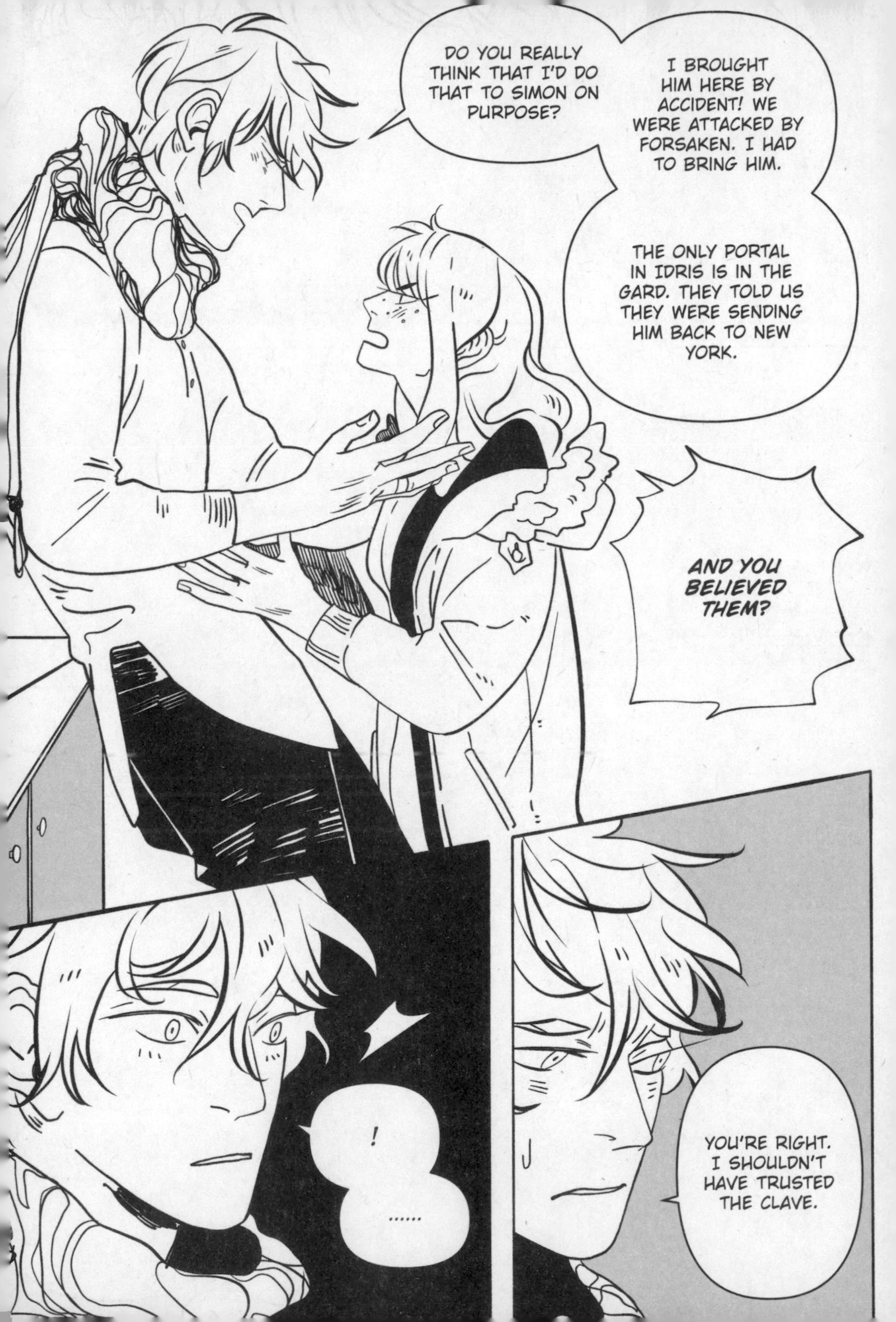
DO YOU REALLY THINK THAT I'D DO THAT TO SIMON ON PURPOSE?
I BROUGHT HIM HERE BY ACCIDENT! WE WERE ATTACKED BY FORSAKEN. I HAD TO BRING HIM.
THE ONLY PORTAL IN IDRIS IS IN THE GARD. THEY TOLD US THEY WERE SENDING HIM BACK TO NEW YORK.
AND YOU BELIEVED THEM?
!
......
YOU'RE RIGHT. I SHOULDN'T HAVE TRUSTED THE CLAVE.

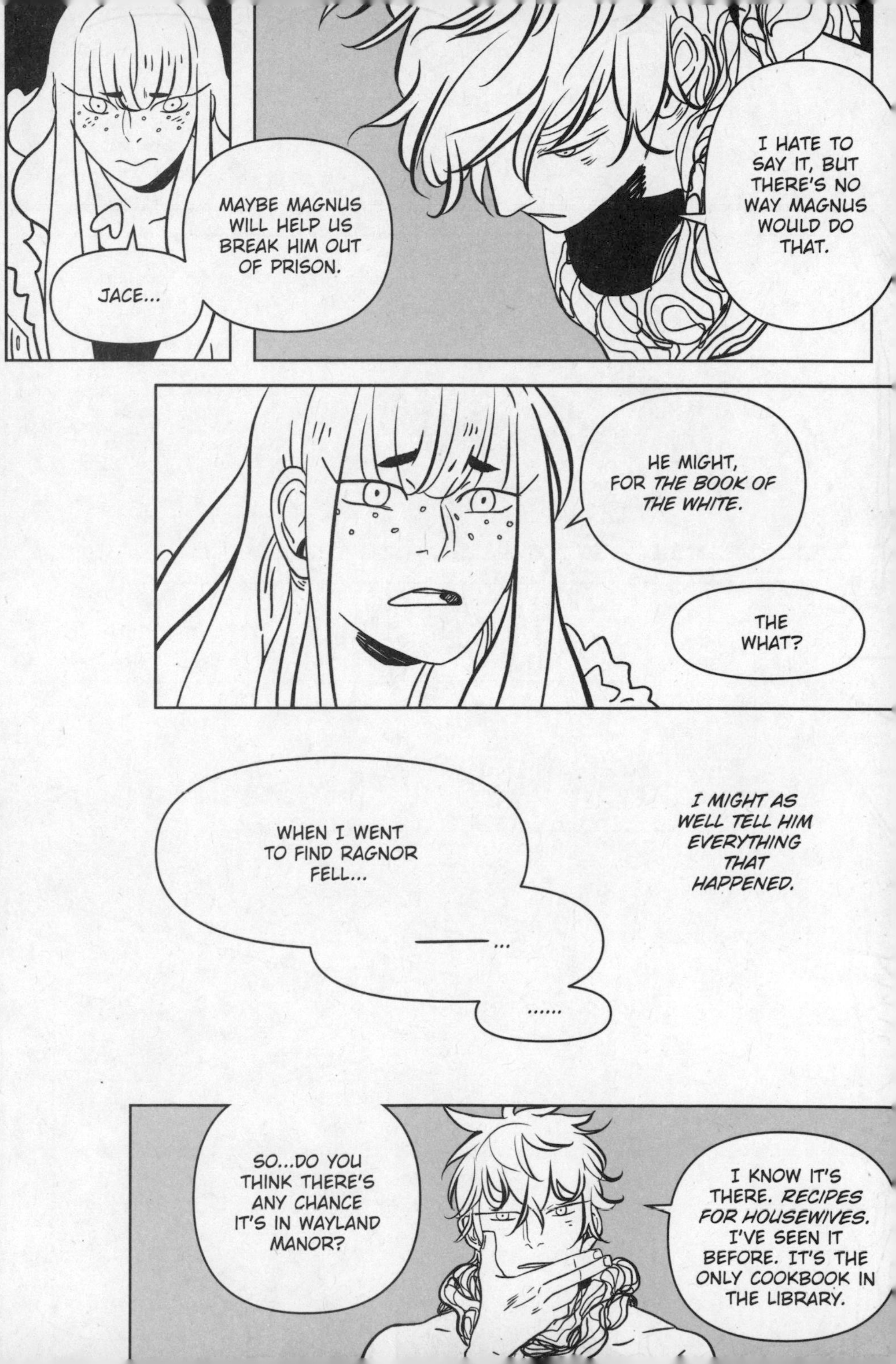
JACE...
MAYBE MAGNUS WILL HELP US BREAK HIM OUT OF PRISON.
I HATE TO SAY IT, BUT THERE'S NO WAY MAGNUS WOULD DO THAT.
HE MIGHT, FOR *THE BOOK OF THE WHITE*.
THE WHAT?
I MIGHT AS WELL TELL HIM EVERYTHING THAT HAPPENED.
WHEN I WENT TO FIND RAGNOR FELL...
———...
......
SO...DO YOU THINK THERE'S ANY CHANCE IT'S IN WAYLAND MANOR?
I KNOW IT'S THERE. *RECIPES FOR HOUSEWIVES.* I'VE SEEN IT BEFORE. IT'S THE ONLY COOKBOOK IN THE LIBRARY.

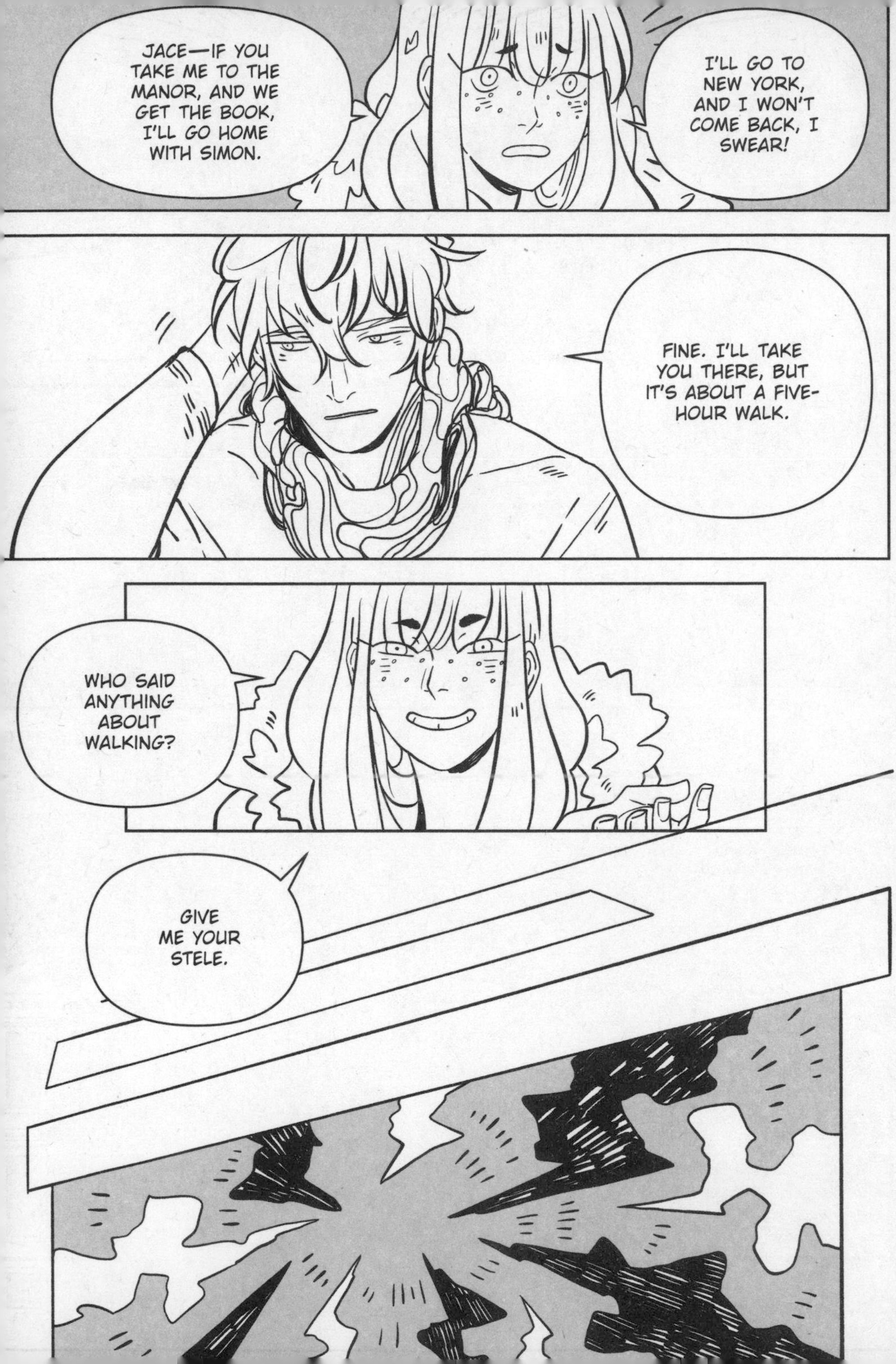
JACE—IF YOU TAKE ME TO THE MANOR, AND WE GET THE BOOK, I'LL GO HOME WITH SIMON.
I'LL GO TO NEW YORK, AND I WON'T COME BACK, I SWEAR!
FINE. I'LL TAKE YOU THERE, BUT IT'S ABOUT A FIVE-HOUR WALK.
WHO SAID ANYTHING ABOUT WALKING?
GIVE ME YOUR STELE.

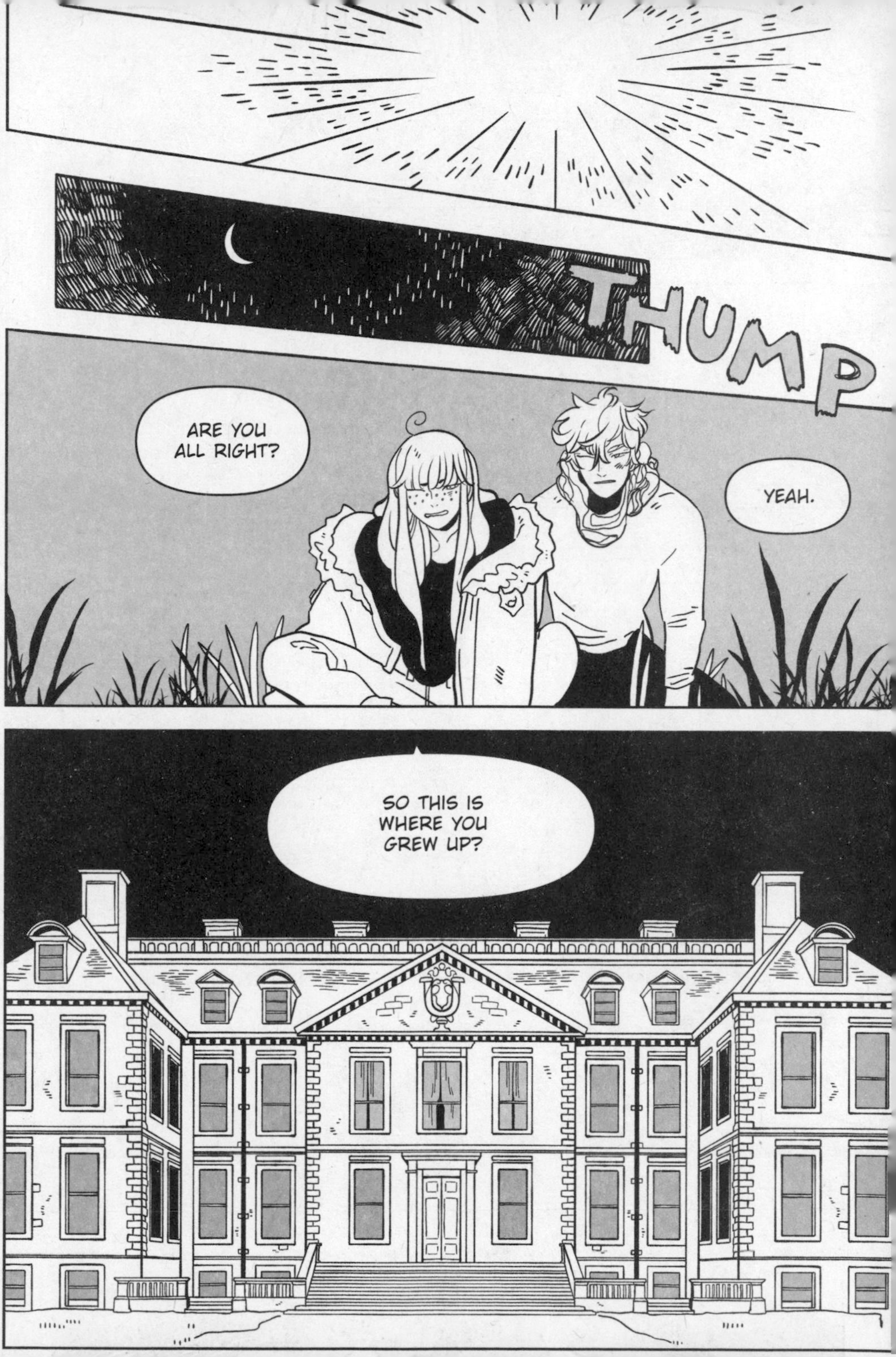
THUMP
ARE YOU ALL RIGHT?
YEAH.
SO THIS IS WHERE YOU GREW UP?

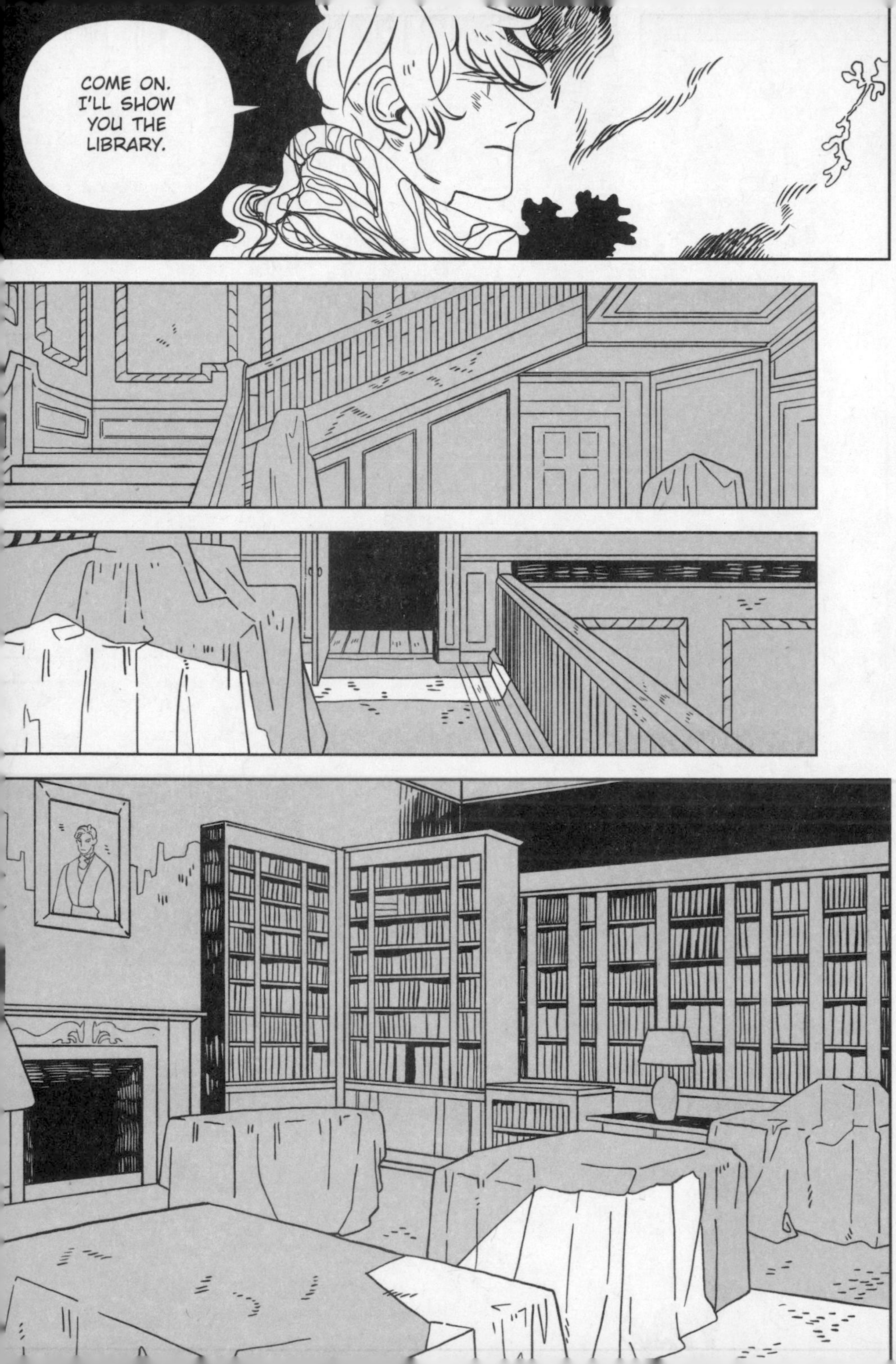
COME ON. I'LL SHOW YOU THE LIBRARY.

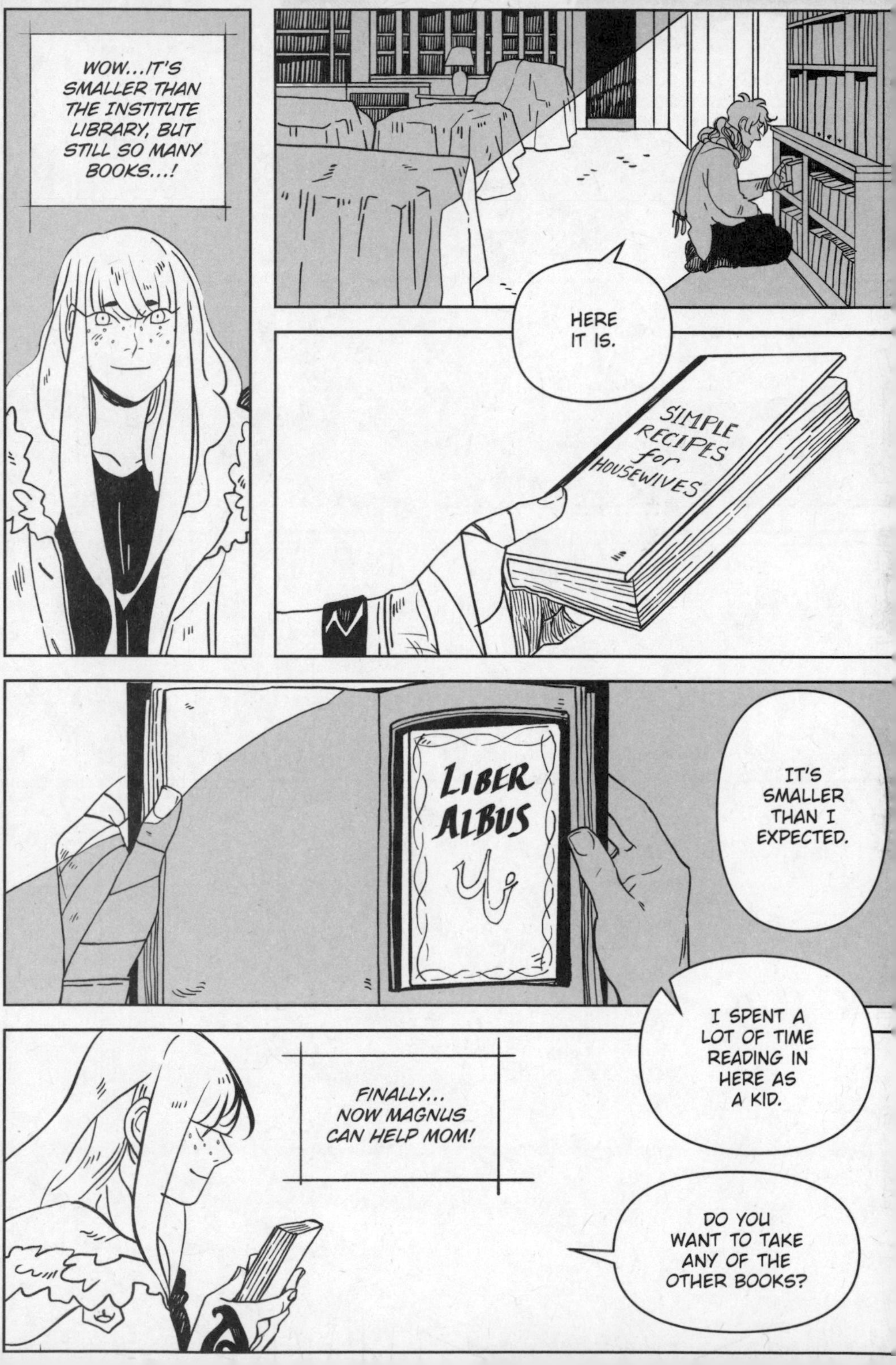
WOW...IT'S SMALLER THAN THE INSTITUTE LIBRARY, BUT STILL SO MANY BOOKS...!
HERE IT IS.
SIMPLE RECIPES for HOUSEWIVES
LIBER ALBUS
IT'S SMALLER THAN I EXPECTED.
I SPENT A LOT OF TIME READING IN HERE AS A KID.
FINALLY... NOW MAGNUS CAN HELP MOM!
DO YOU WANT TO TAKE ANY OF THE OTHER BOOKS?

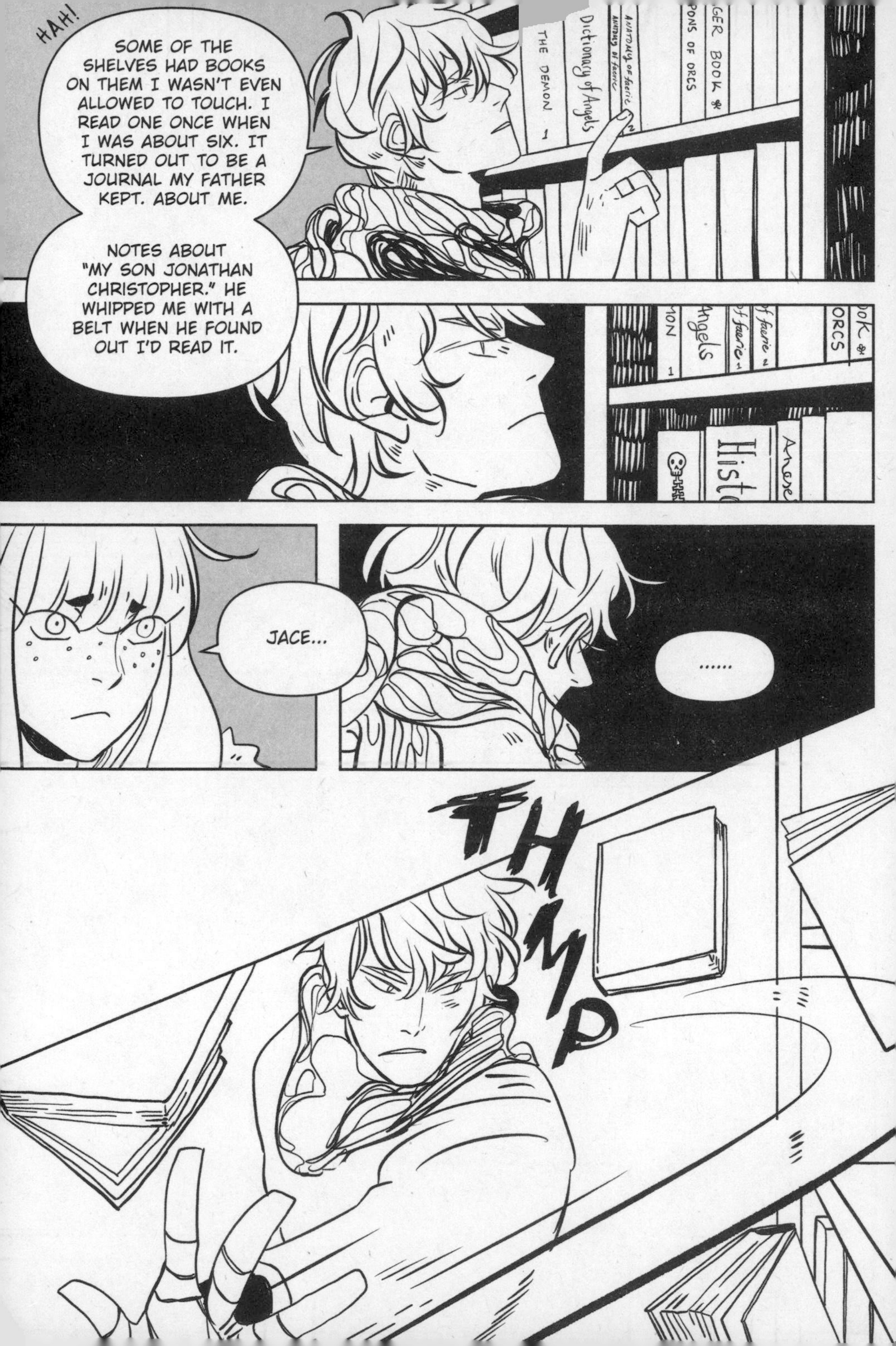

HAH!
SOME OF THE SHELVES HAD BOOKS ON THEM I WASN'T EVEN ALLOWED TO TOUCH. I READ ONE ONCE WHEN I WAS ABOUT SIX. IT TURNED OUT TO BE A JOURNAL MY FATHER KEPT. ABOUT ME.
NOTES ABOUT "MY SON JONATHAN CHRISTOPHER." HE WHIPPED ME WITH A BELT WHEN HE FOUND OUT I'D READ IT.
THE DEMON 1
Dictionary of Angels
JACE...
......
THMP

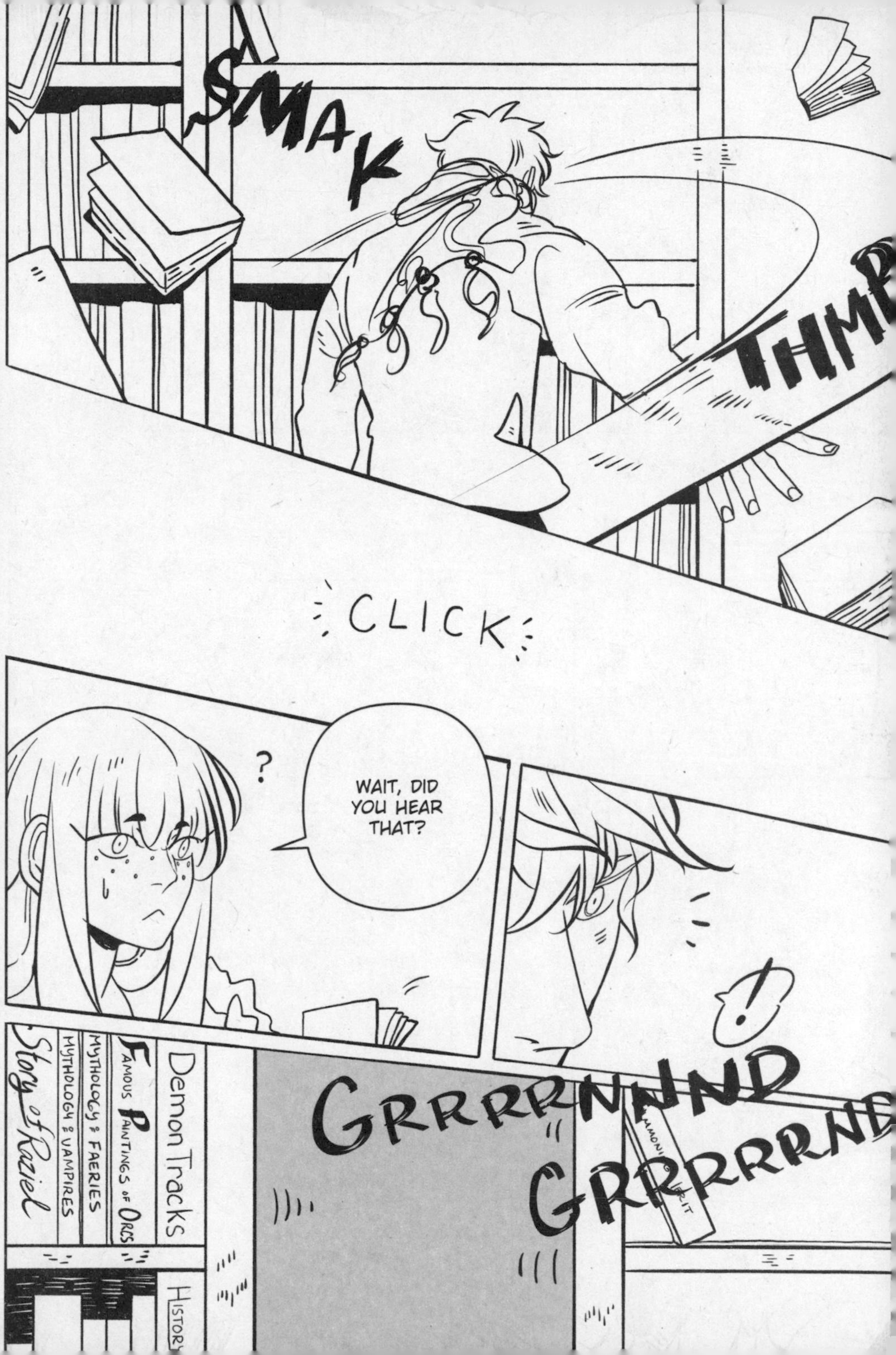
SMAK
THMP
CLICK
?
WAIT, DID YOU HEAR THAT?
!
Demon Tracks
Famous Paintings of Orcs
Mythology of Faeries
Mythology of Vampires
Story of Raziel
History
GRRRRNNND
GRRRRRND

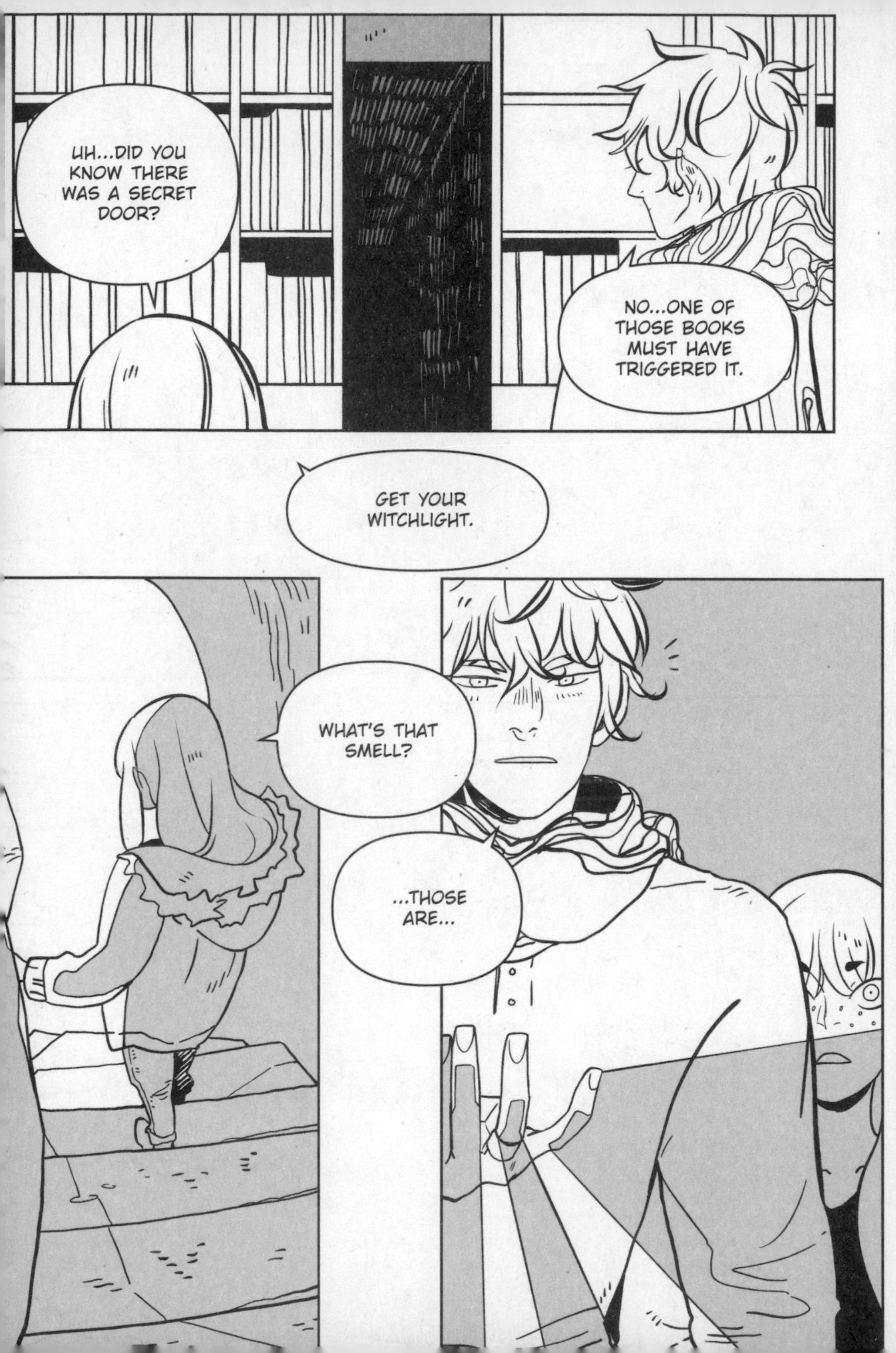
UH...DID YOU KNOW THERE WAS A SECRET DOOR?
NO...ONE OF THOSE BOOKS MUST HAVE TRIGGERED IT.
GET YOUR WITCHLIGHT.
WHAT'S THAT SMELL?
...THOSE ARE...

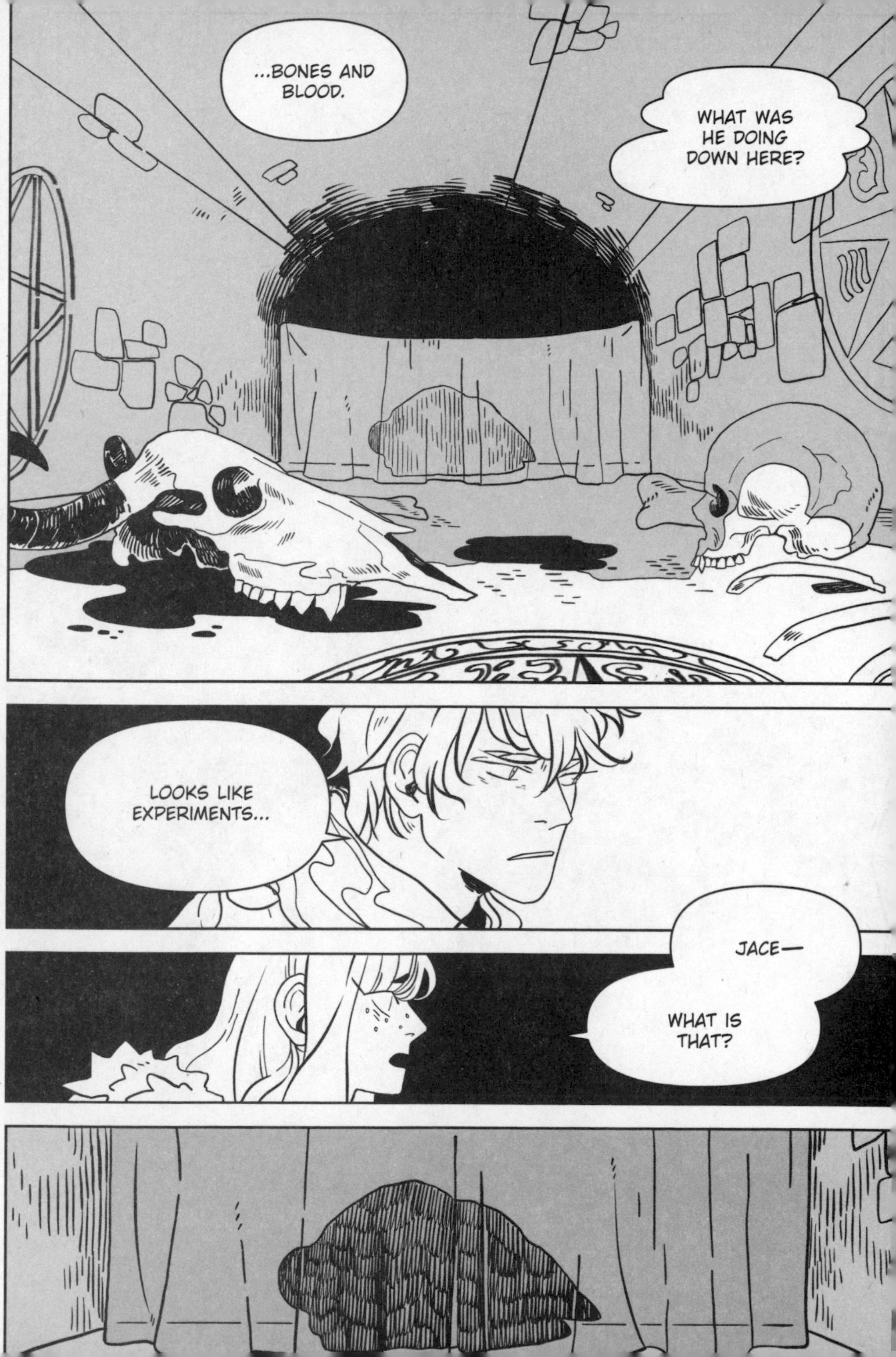
...BONES AND BLOOD.
WHAT WAS HE DOING DOWN HERE?
LOOKS LIKE EXPERIMENTS...
JACE—
WHAT IS THAT?

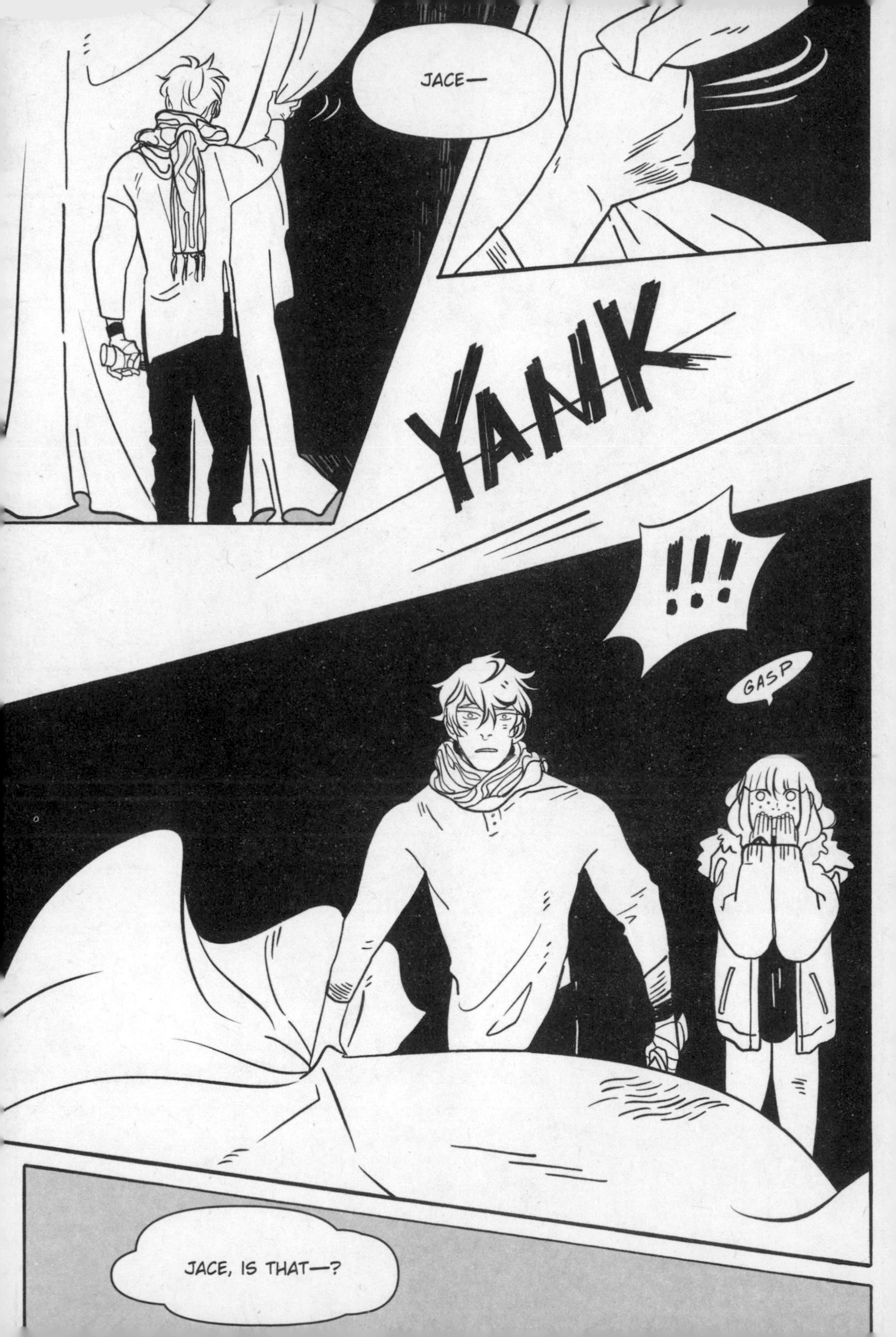
JACE—
YANK
!!!
GASP
JACE, IS THAT—?

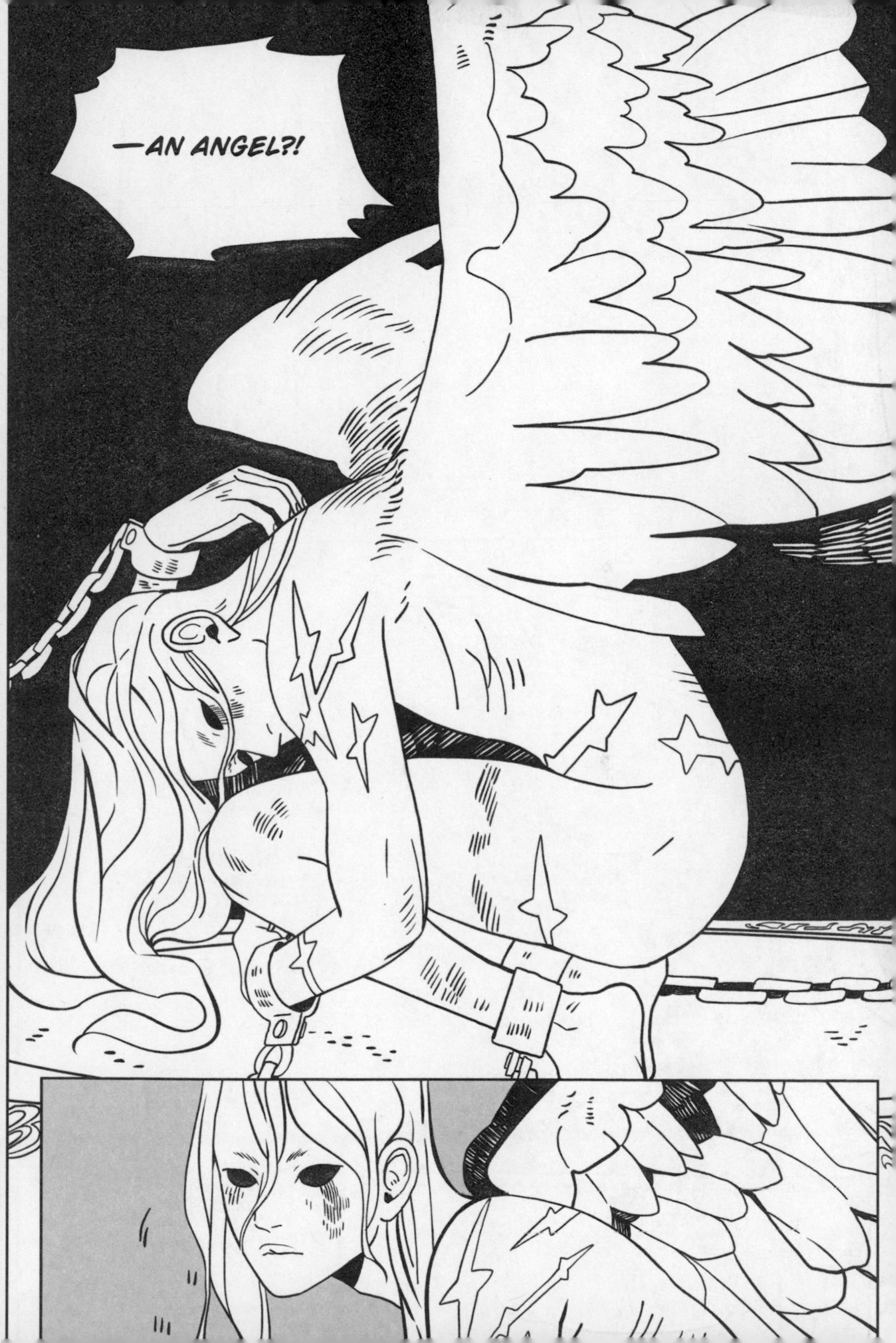
—AN ANGEL?!

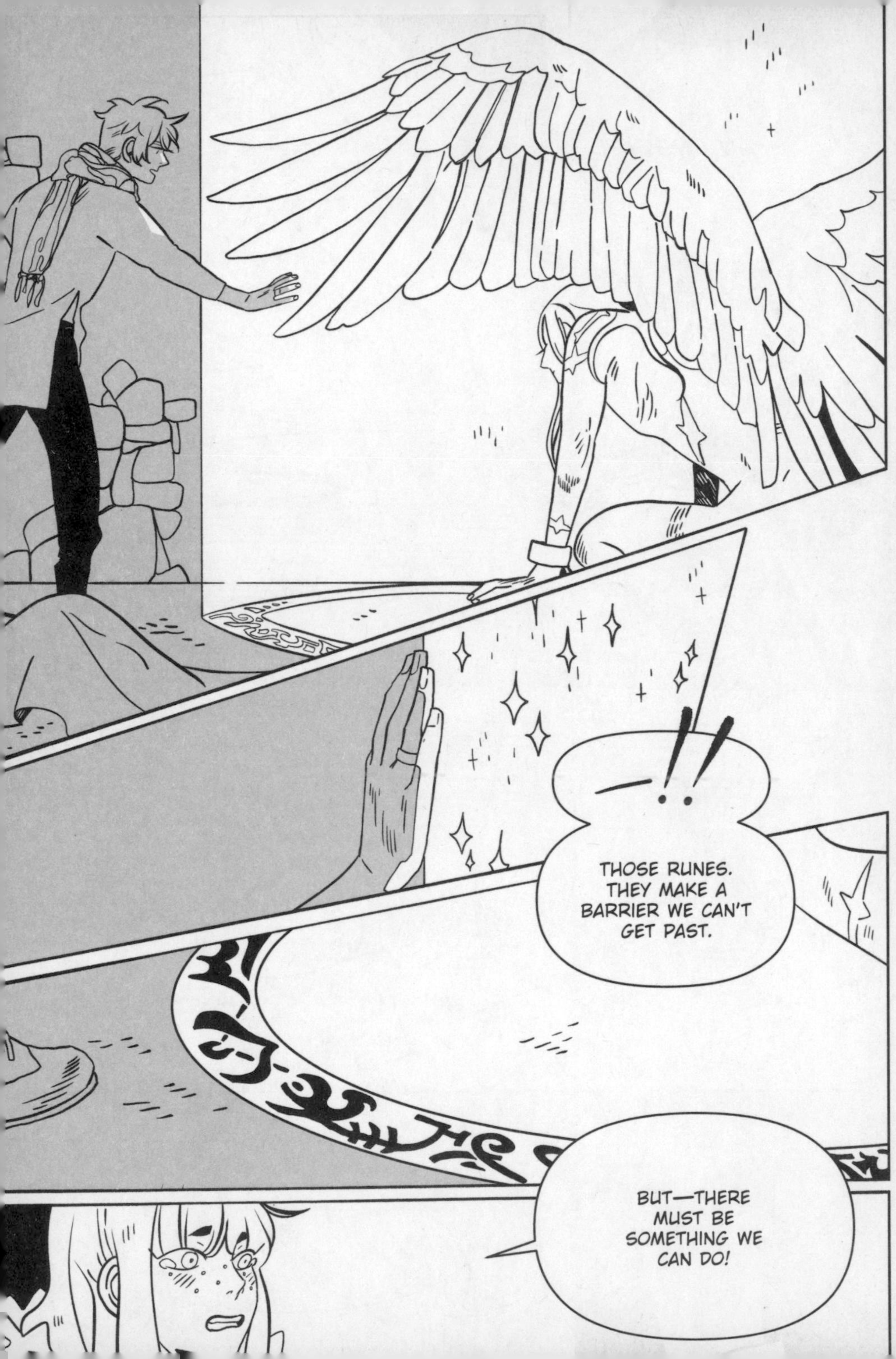
—!!
THOSE RUNES. THEY MAKE A BARRIER WE CAN'T GET PAST.
BUT—THERE MUST BE SOMETHING WE CAN DO!

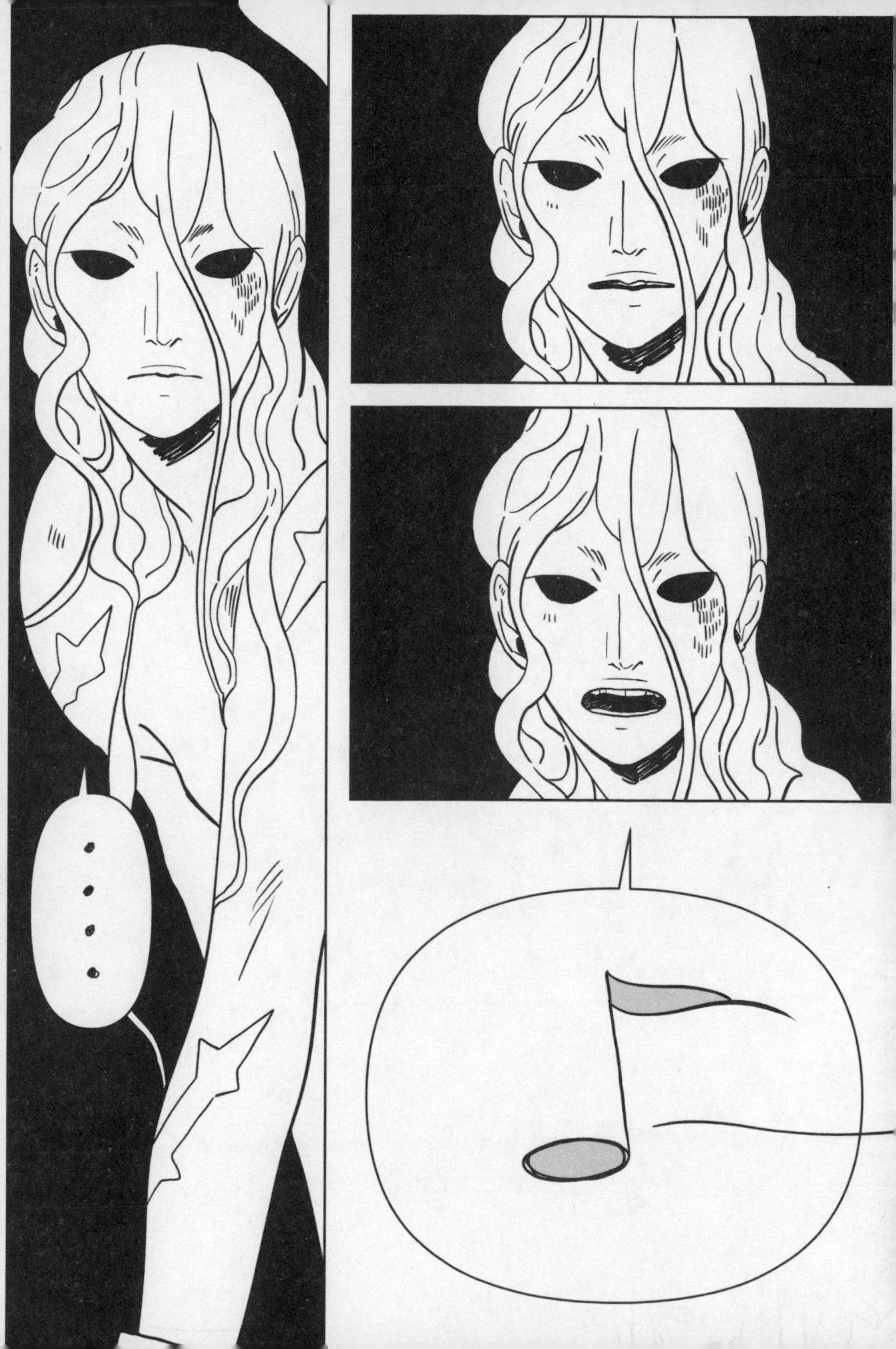
....

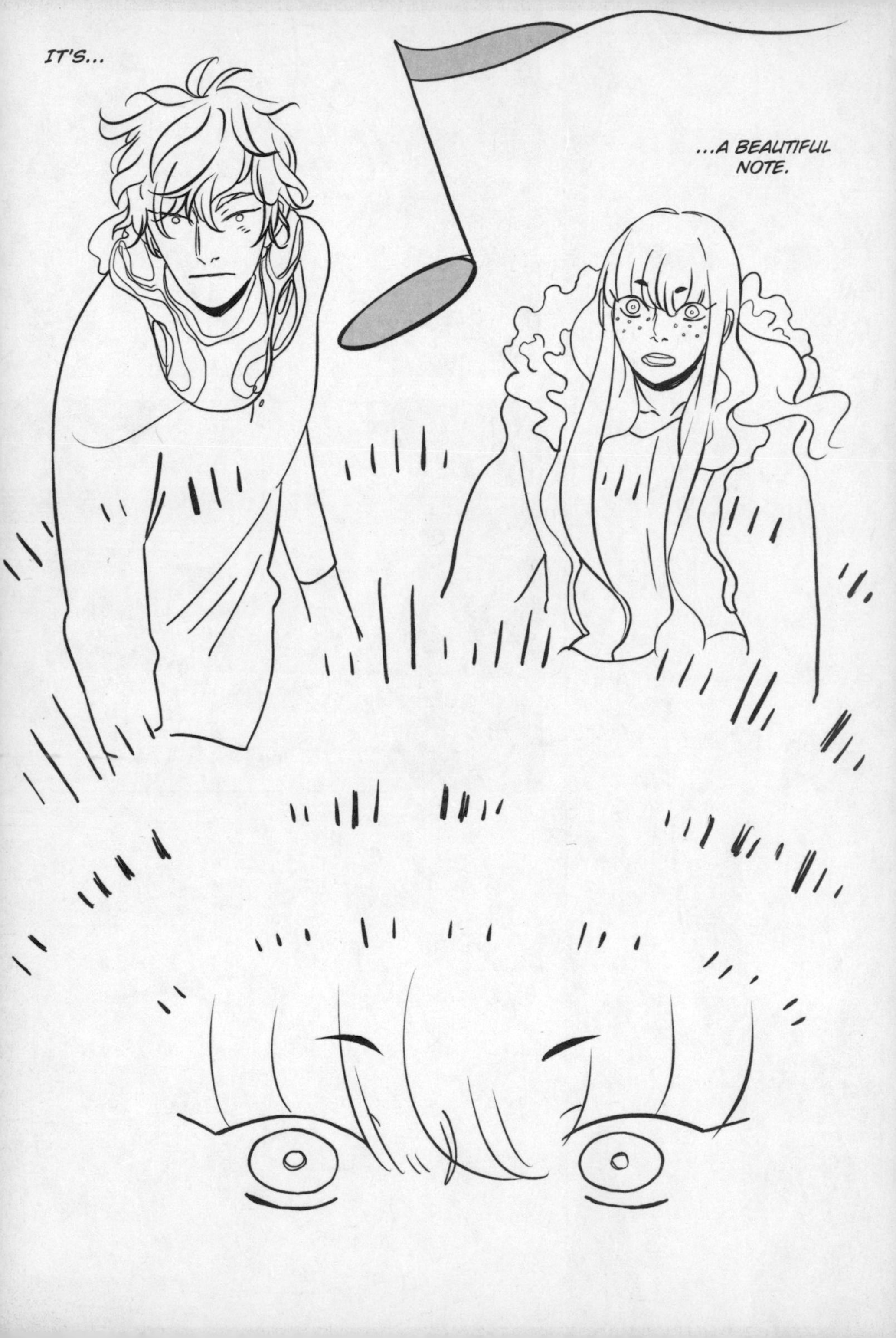
IT'S...
...A BEAUTIFUL NOTE.

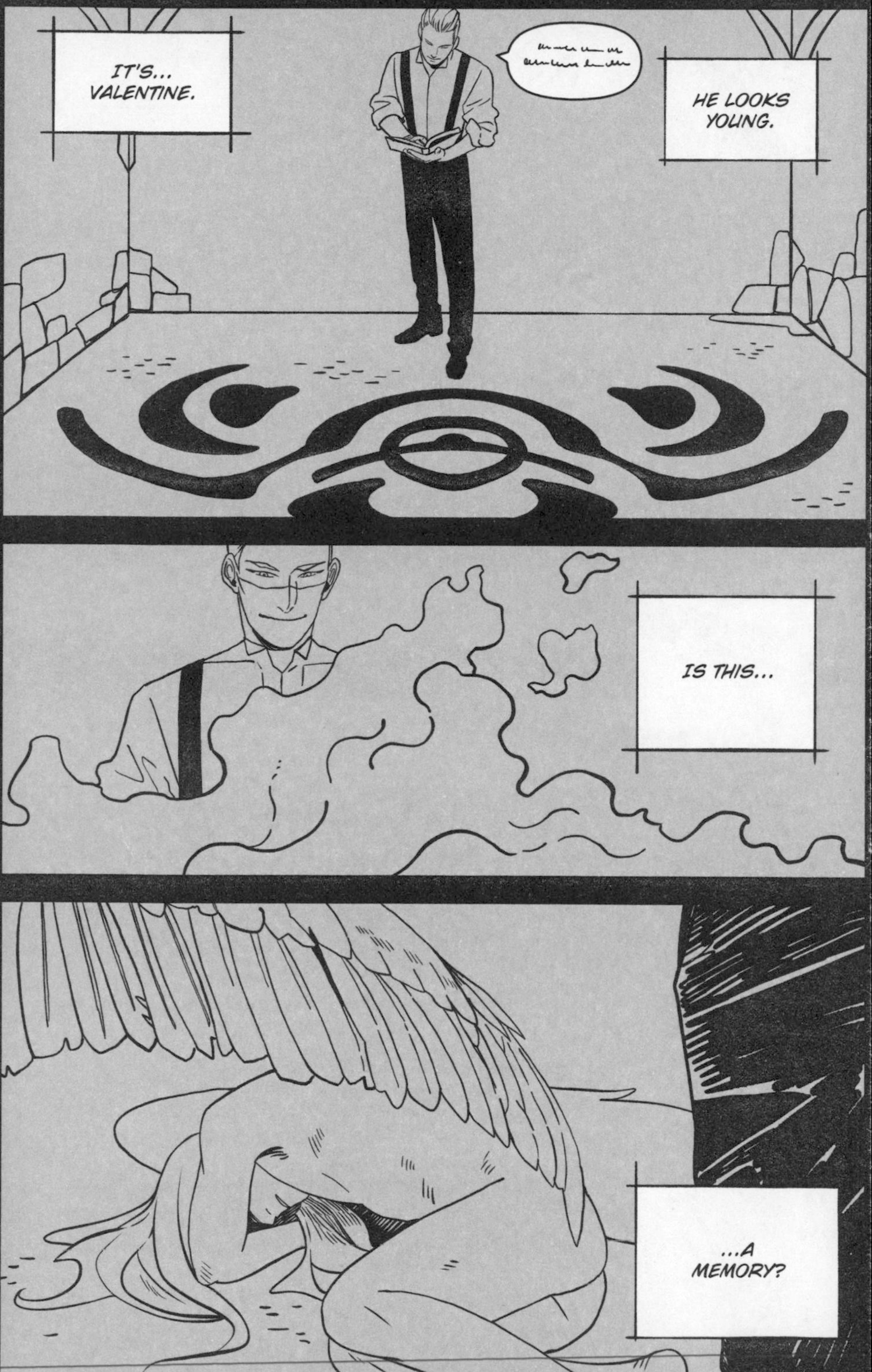
IT'S... VALENTINE.
HE LOOKS YOUNG.
IS THIS...
...A MEMORY?

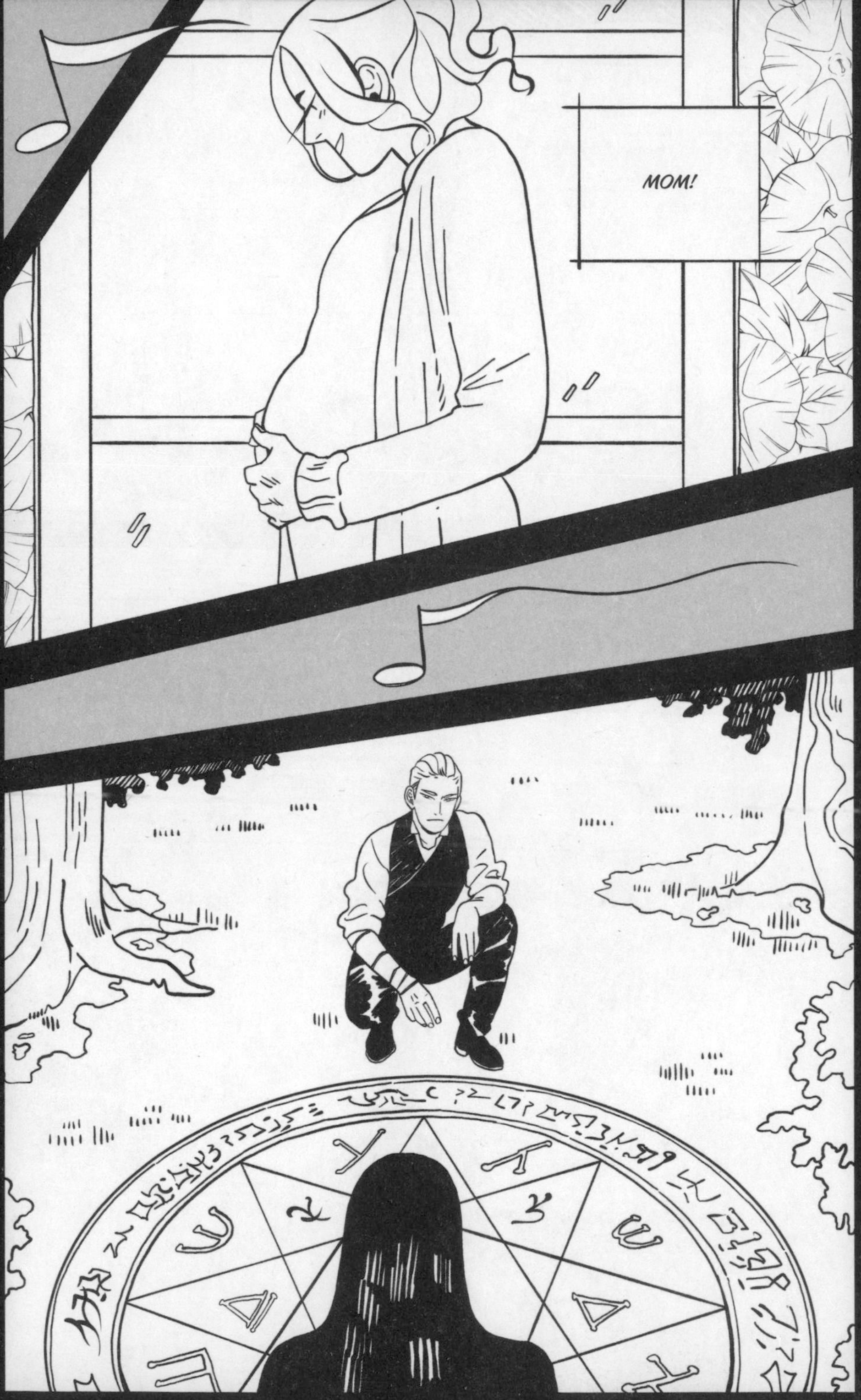
MOM!

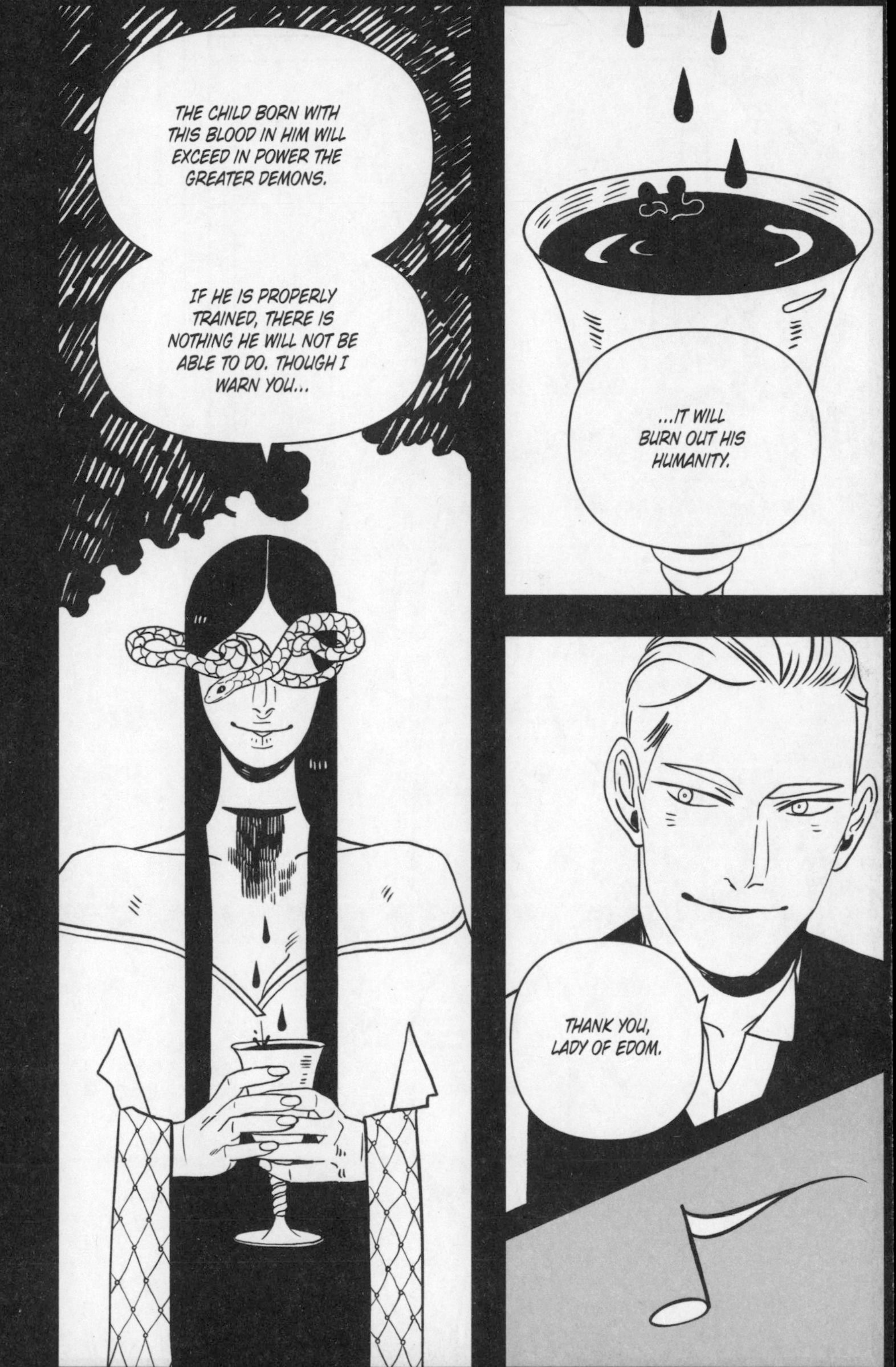
THE CHILD BORN WITH THIS BLOOD IN HIM WILL EXCEED IN POWER THE GREATER DEMONS.
IF HE IS PROPERLY TRAINED, THERE IS NOTHING HE WILL NOT BE ABLE TO DO. THOUGH I WARN YOU...
...IT WILL BURN OUT HIS HUMANITY.
THANK YOU, LADY OF EDOM.

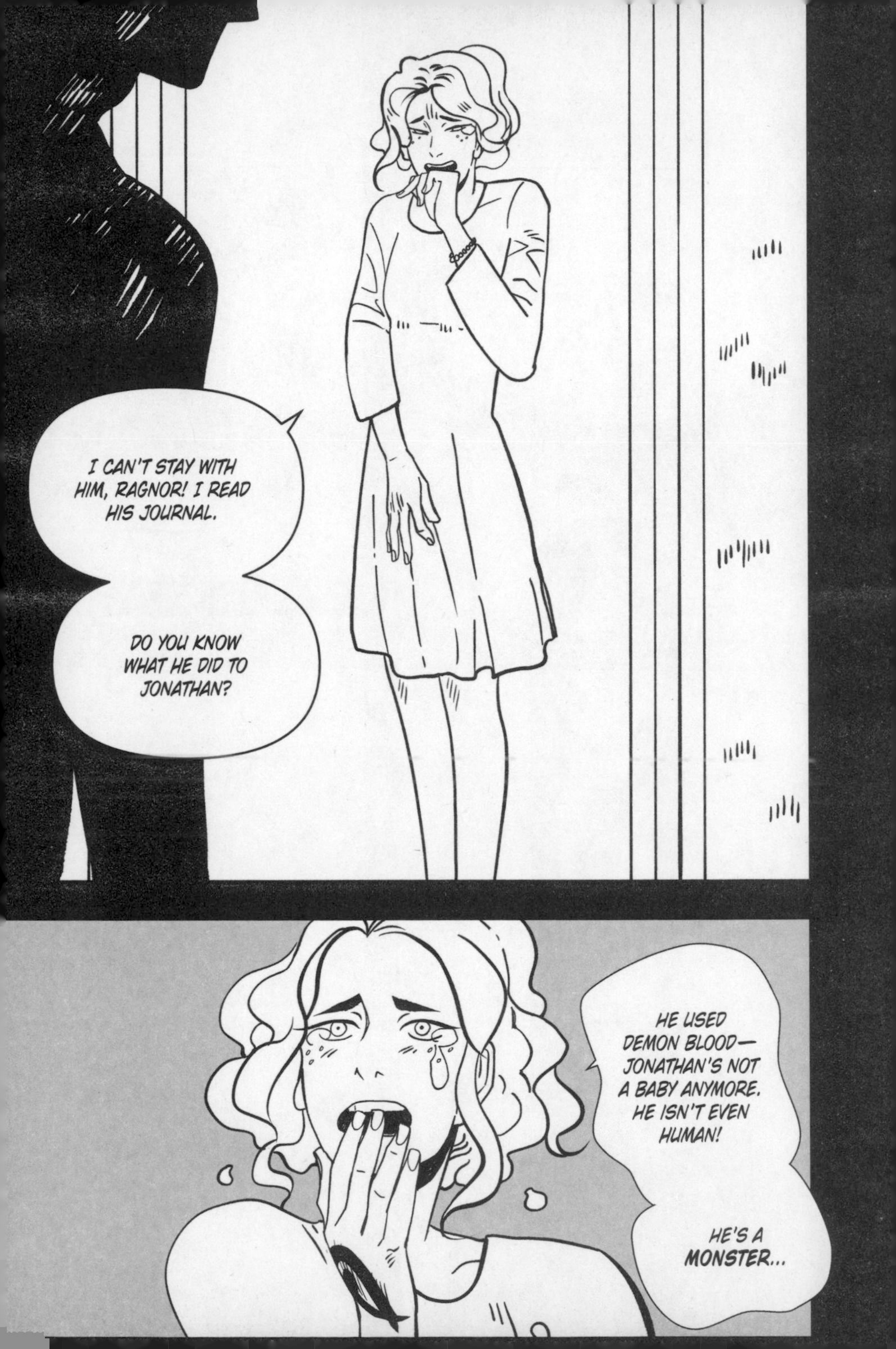
I CAN'T STAY WITH HIM, RAGNOR! I READ HIS JOURNAL.
DO YOU KNOW WHAT HE DID TO JONATHAN?
HE USED DEMON BLOOD— JONATHAN'S NOT A BABY ANYMORE. HE ISN'T EVEN HUMAN!
HE'S A **MONSTER**...

THE MORTAL INSTRUMENTS

THE GRAPHIC NOVEL

THE MORTAL INSTRUMENTS

THE GRAPHIC NOVEL

Chapter 29

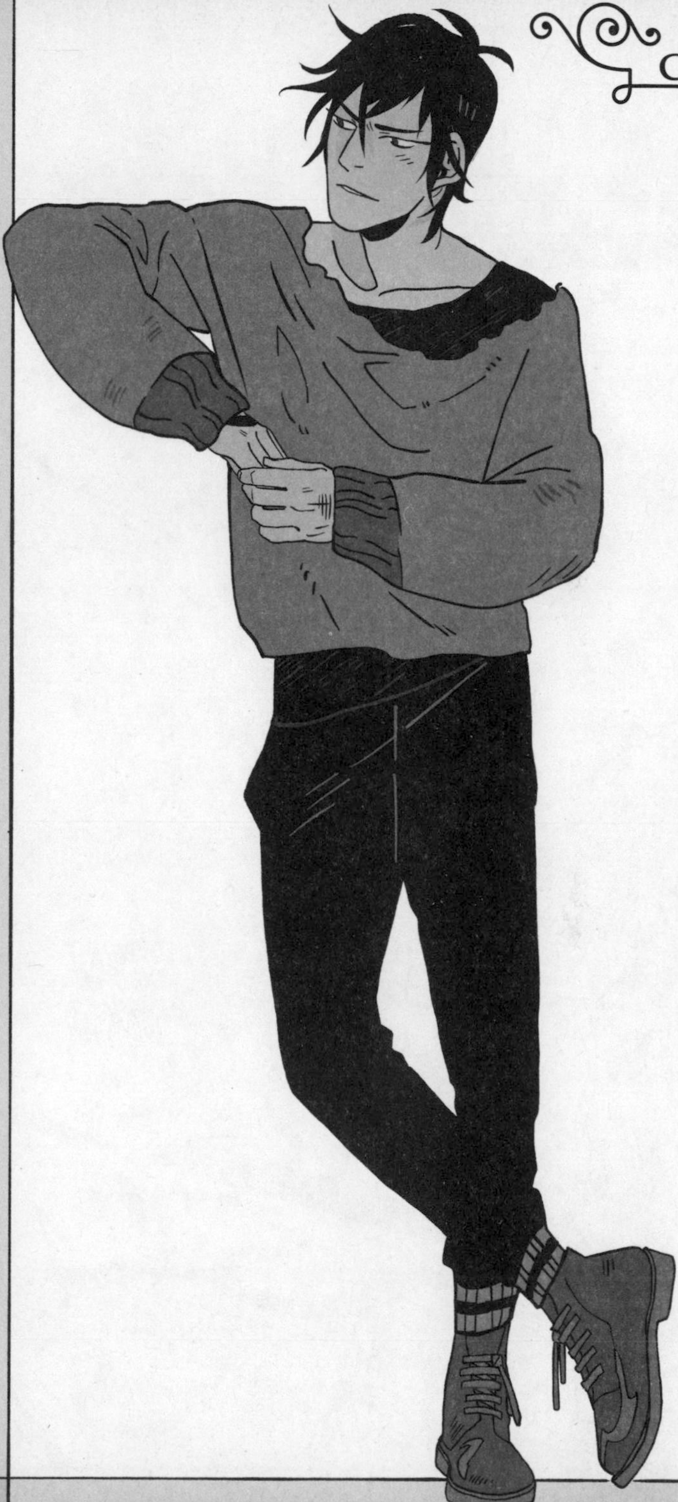

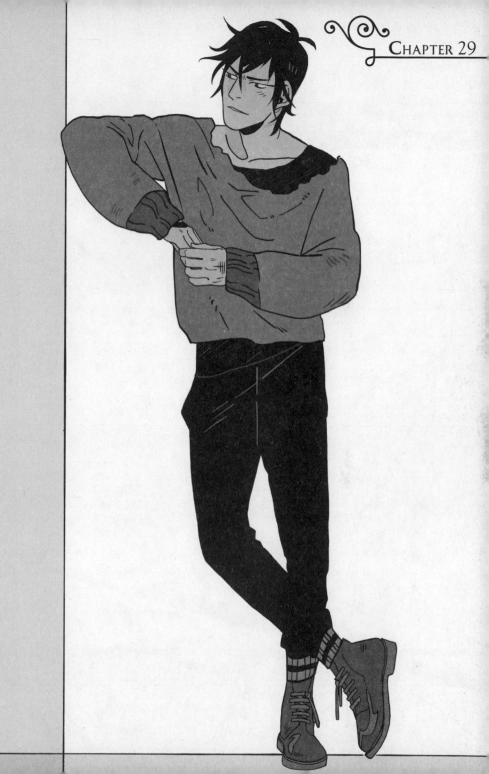

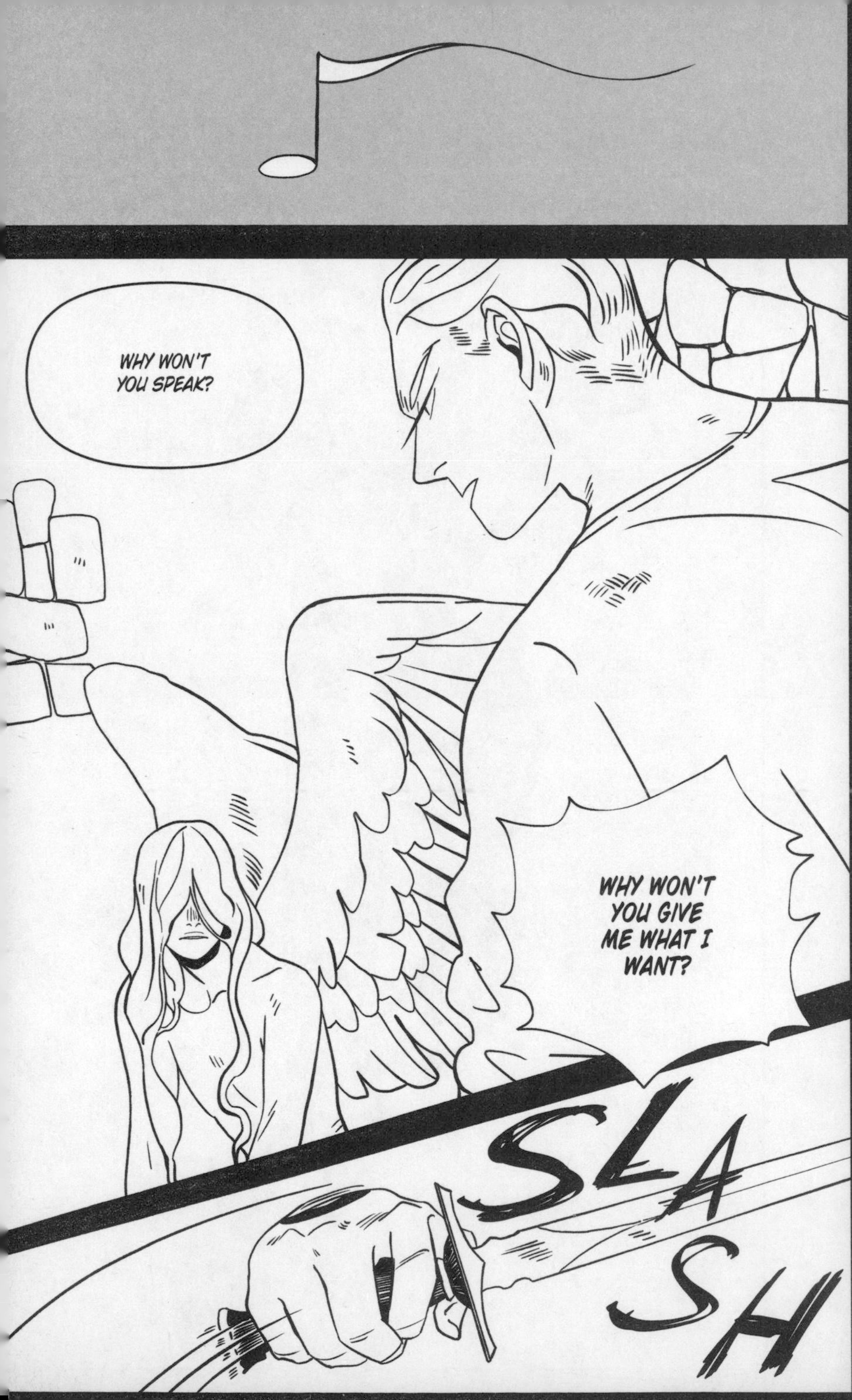
WHY WON'T YOU SPEAK?
WHY WON'T YOU GIVE ME WHAT I WANT?
SLASH

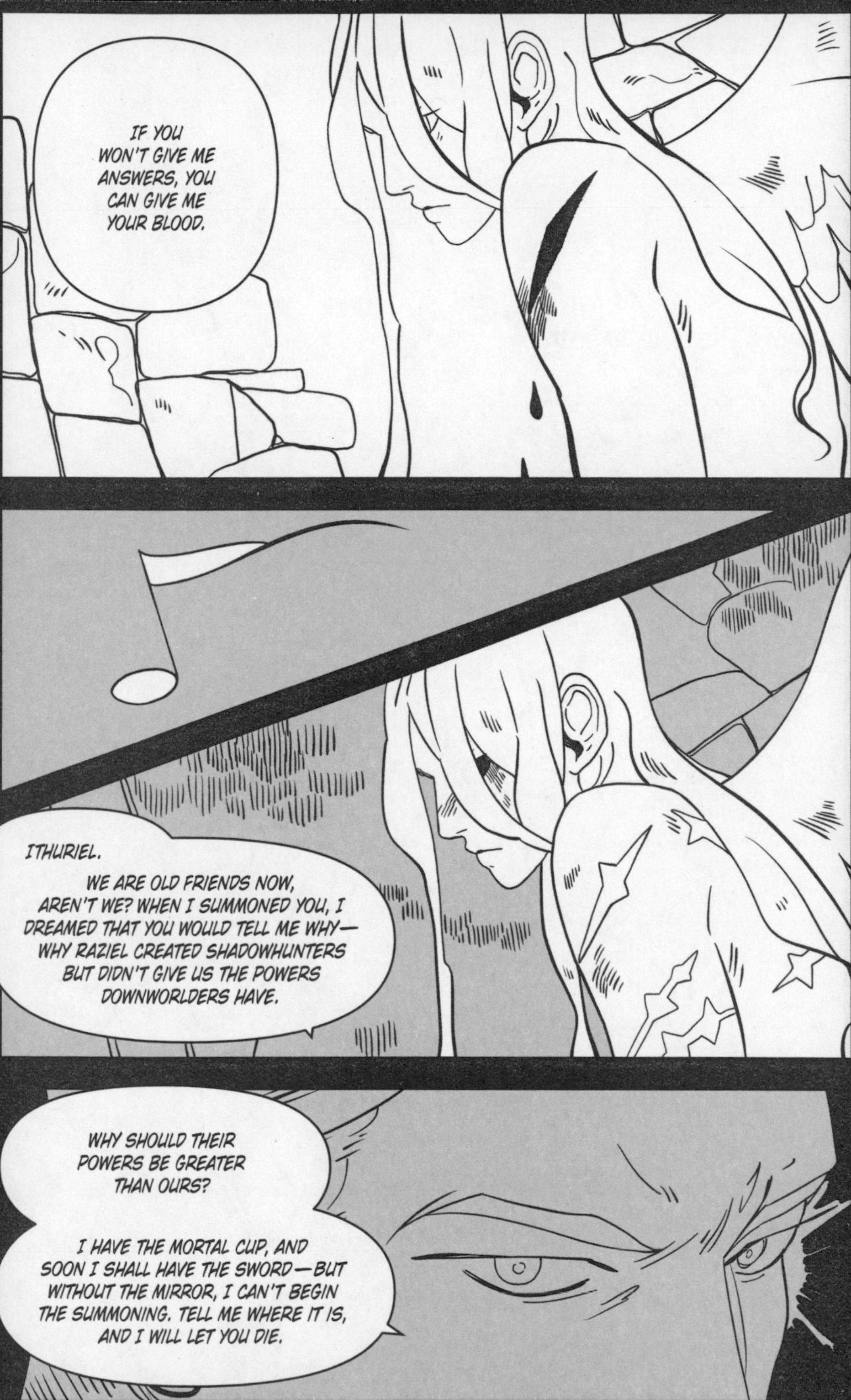
IF YOU WON'T GIVE ME ANSWERS, YOU CAN GIVE ME YOUR BLOOD.
ITHURIEL.
WE ARE OLD FRIENDS NOW, AREN'T WE? WHEN I SUMMONED YOU, I DREAMED THAT YOU WOULD TELL ME WHY—WHY RAZIEL CREATED SHADOWHUNTERS BUT DIDN'T GIVE US THE POWERS DOWNWORLDERS HAVE.
WHY SHOULD THEIR POWERS BE GREATER THAN OURS?
I HAVE THE MORTAL CUP, AND SOON I SHALL HAVE THE SWORD—BUT WITHOUT THE MIRROR, I CAN'T BEGIN THE SUMMONING. TELL ME WHERE IT IS, AND I WILL LET YOU DIE.

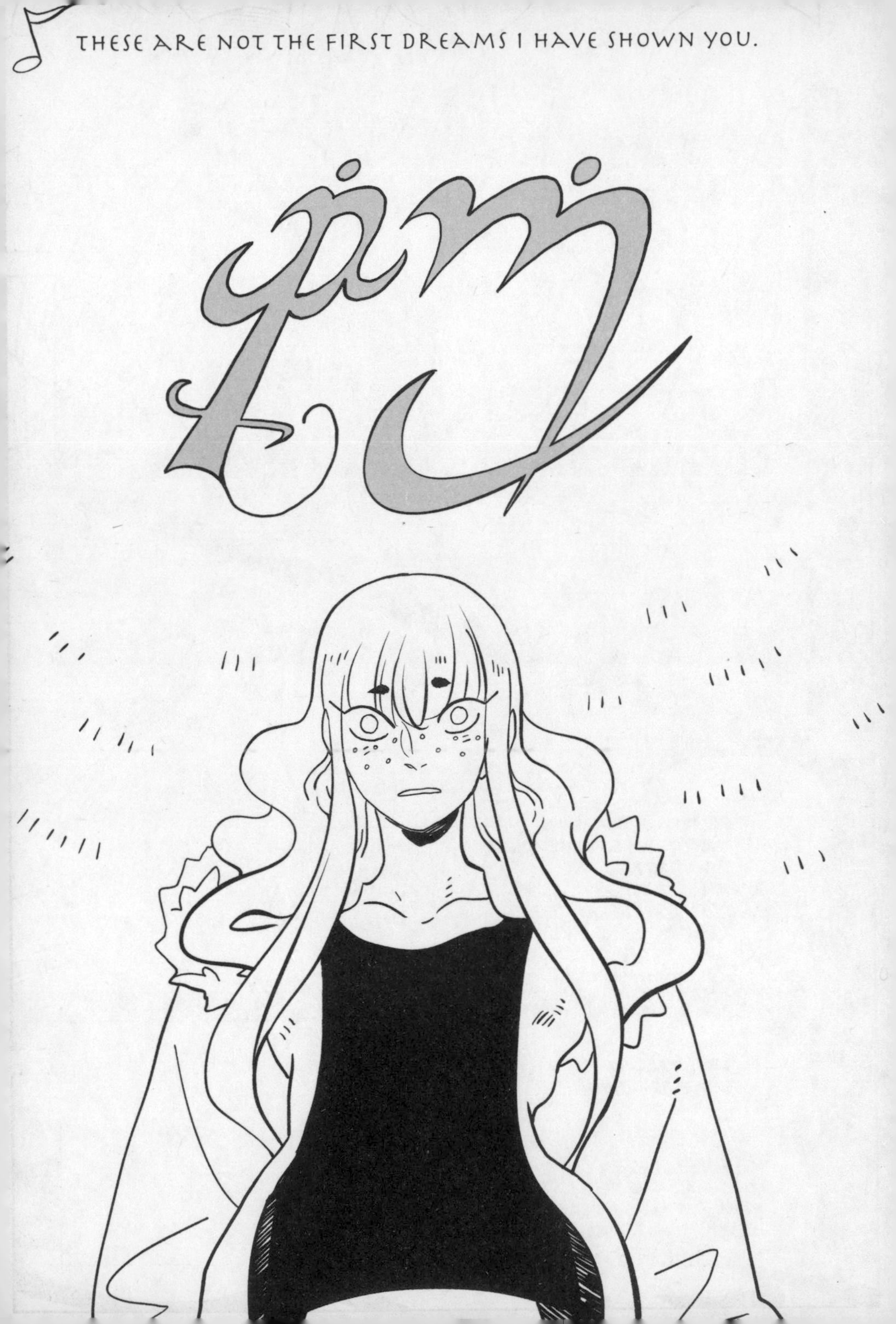
THESE ARE NOT THE FIRST DREAMS I HAVE SHOWN YOU.

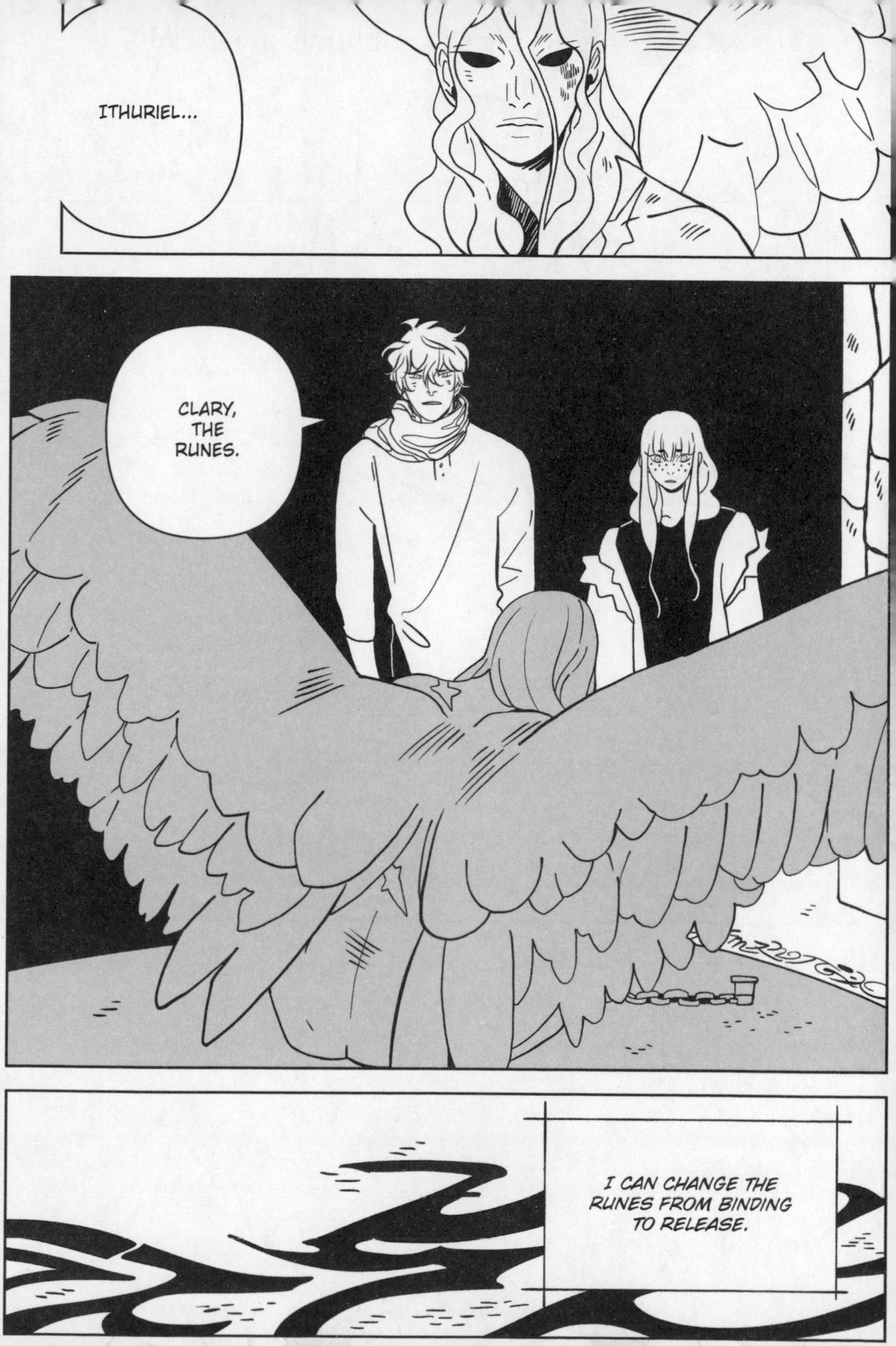
ITHURIEL...
CLARY, THE RUNES.
I CAN CHANGE THE RUNES FROM BINDING TO RELEASE.

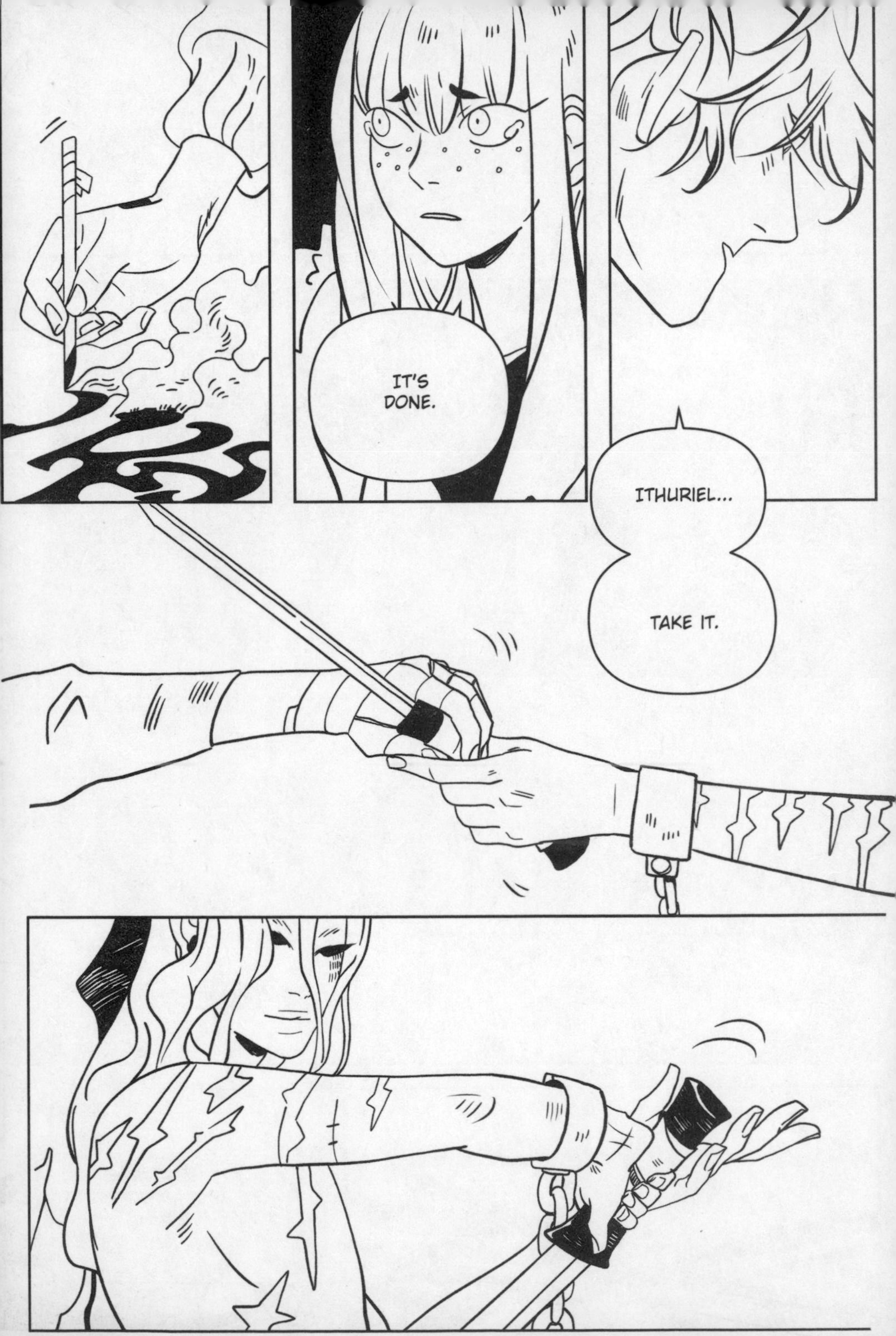
IT'S DONE.
ITHURIEL...
TAKE IT.

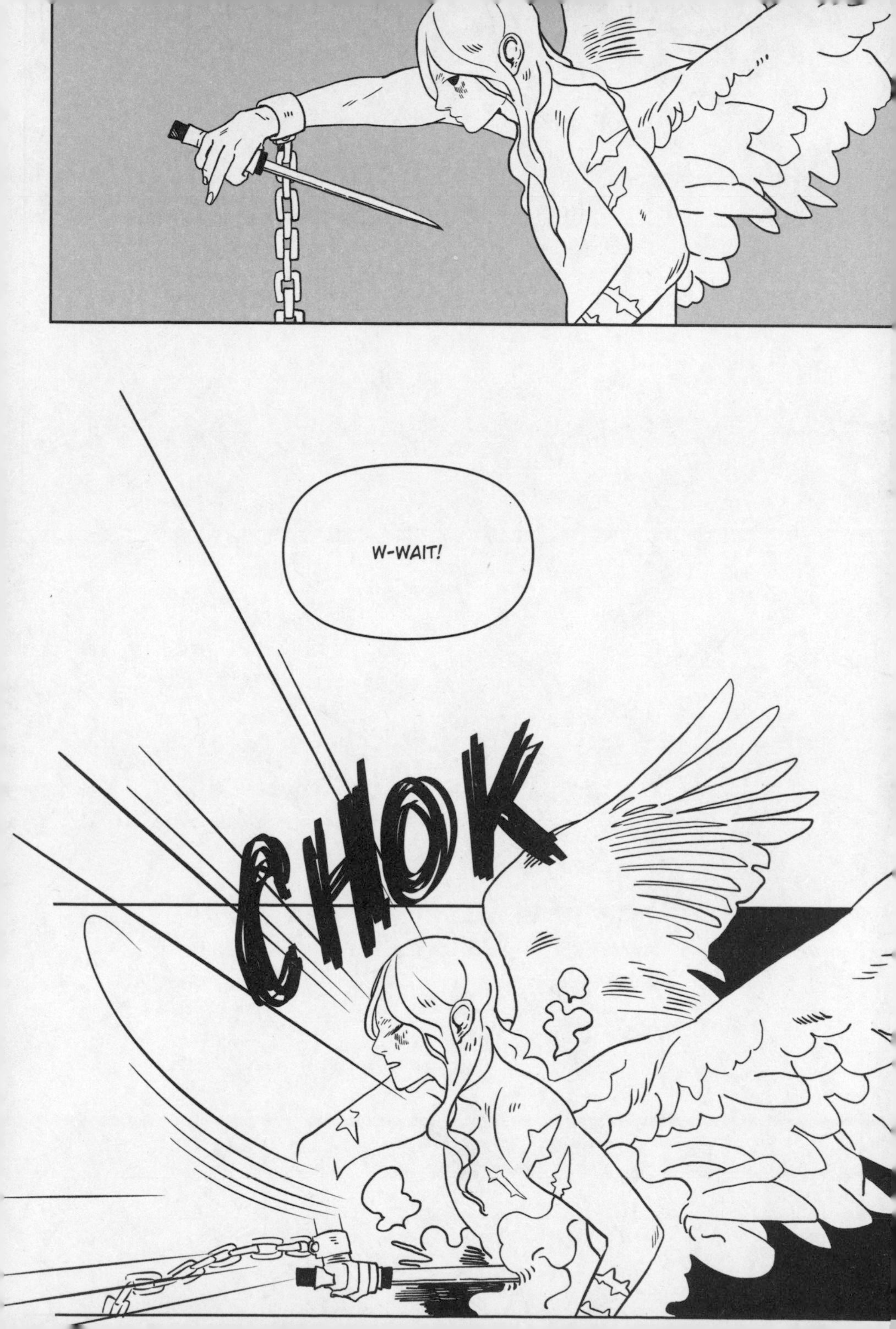
W-WAIT!
CHOK

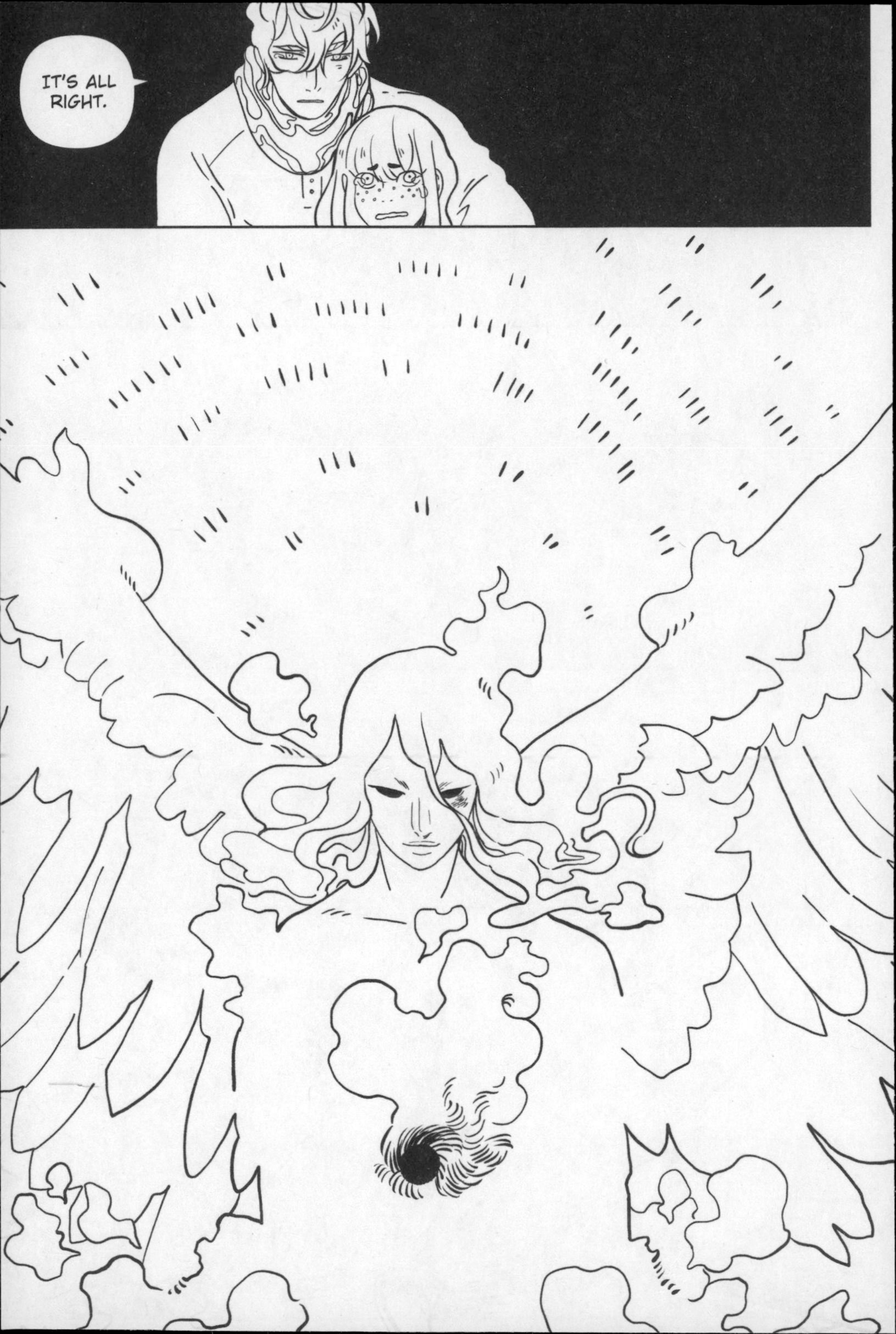
IT'S ALL RIGHT.

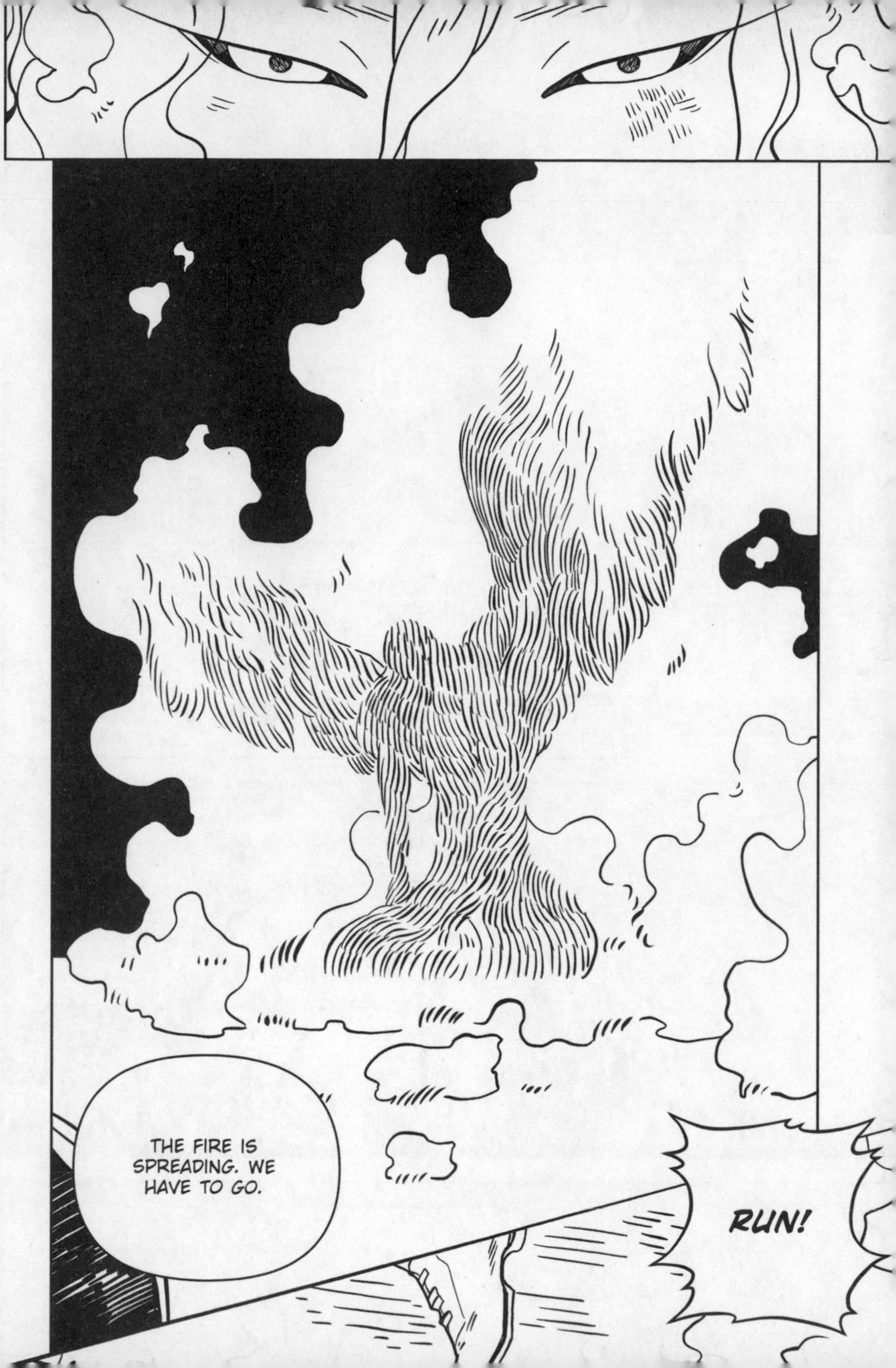
THE FIRE IS SPREADING. WE HAVE TO GO.
RUN!

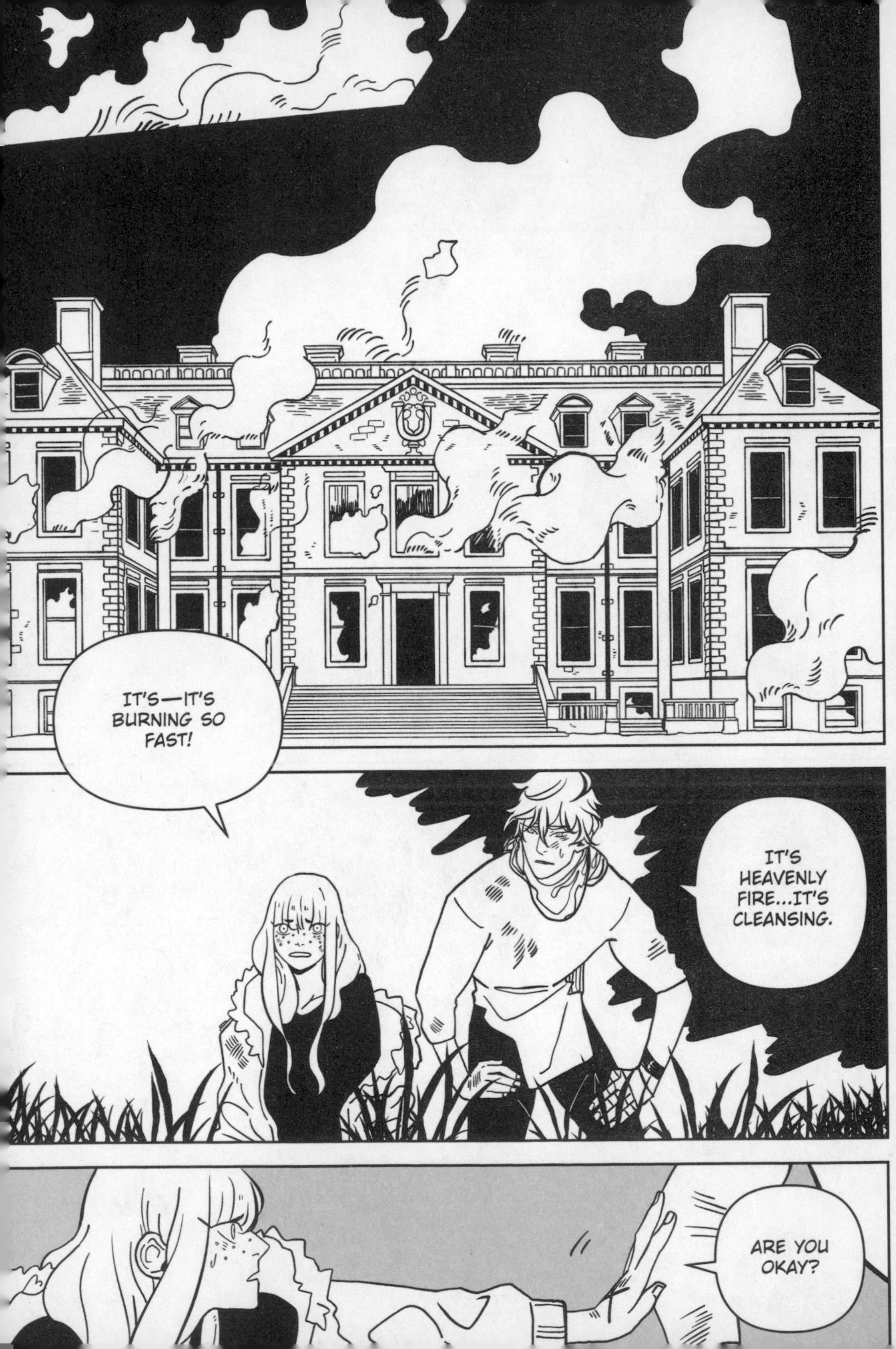
IT'S—IT'S BURNING SO FAST!
IT'S HEAVENLY FIRE...IT'S CLEANSING.
ARE YOU OKAY?

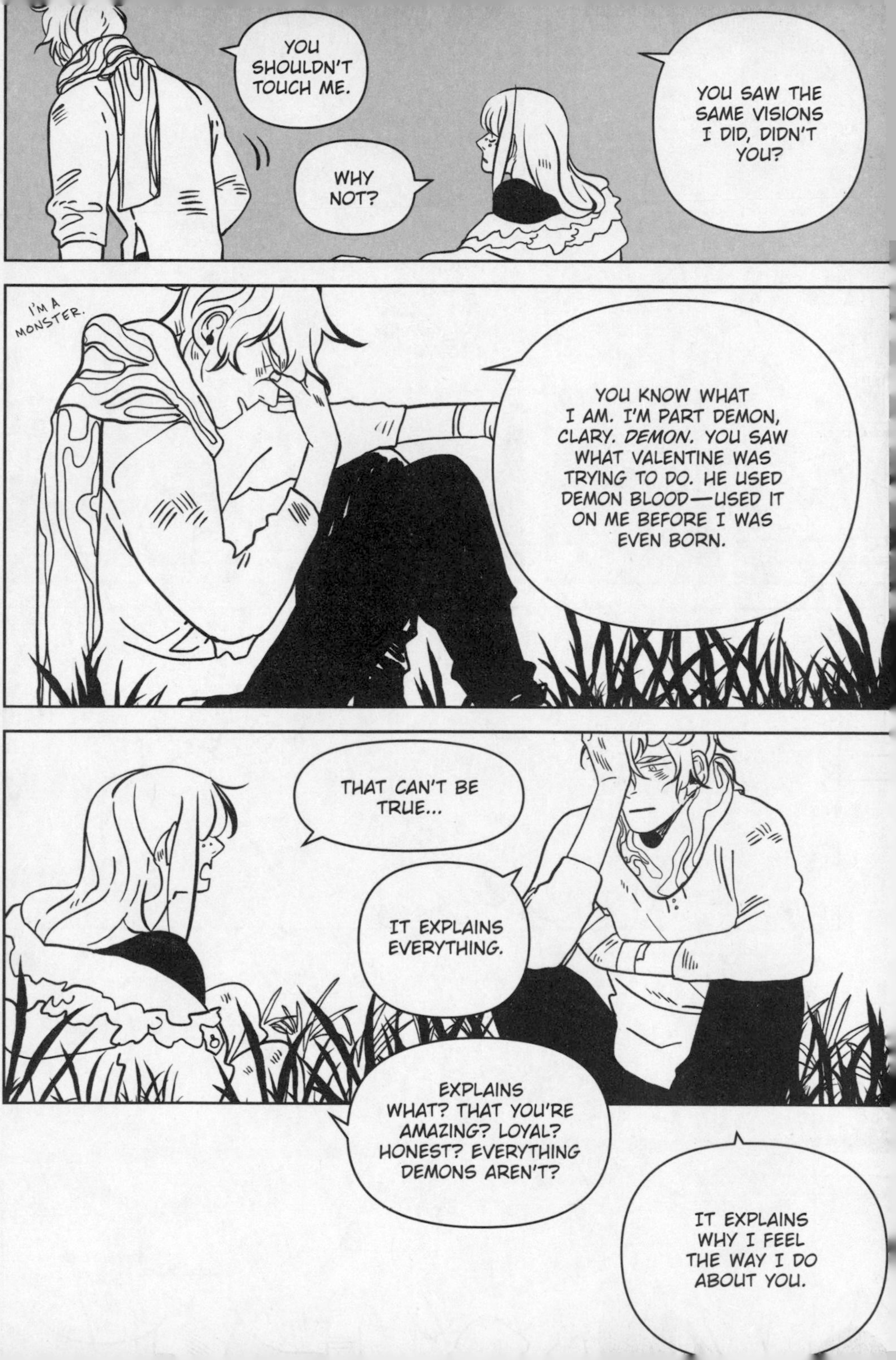
YOU SHOULDN'T TOUCH ME.
WHY NOT?
YOU SAW THE SAME VISIONS I DID, DIDN'T YOU?
I'M A MONSTER.
YOU KNOW WHAT I AM. I'M PART DEMON, CLARY. *DEMON.* YOU SAW WHAT VALENTINE WAS TRYING TO DO. HE USED DEMON BLOOD—USED IT ON ME BEFORE I WAS EVEN BORN.
THAT CAN'T BE TRUE...
IT EXPLAINS EVERYTHING.
EXPLAINS WHAT? THAT YOU'RE AMAZING? LOYAL? HONEST? EVERYTHING DEMONS AREN'T?
IT EXPLAINS WHY I FEEL THE WAY I DO ABOUT YOU.

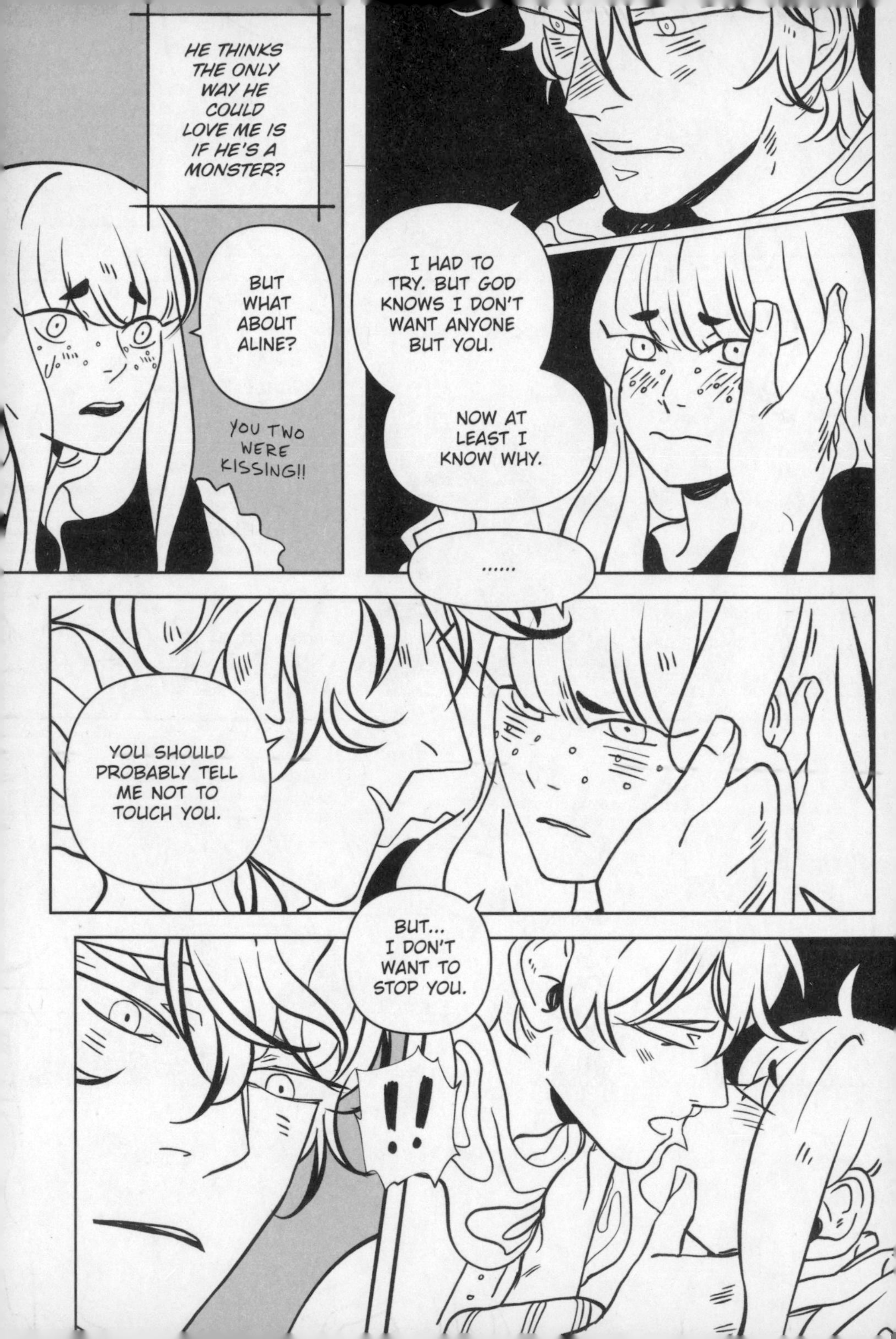
HE THINKS THE ONLY WAY HE COULD LOVE ME IS IF HE'S A MONSTER?
BUT WHAT ABOUT ALINE?
YOU TWO WERE KISSING!!
I HAD TO TRY. BUT GOD KNOWS I DON'T WANT ANYONE BUT YOU.
NOW AT LEAST I KNOW WHY.
......
YOU SHOULD PROBABLY TELL ME NOT TO TOUCH YOU.
BUT... I DON'T WANT TO STOP YOU.
!!

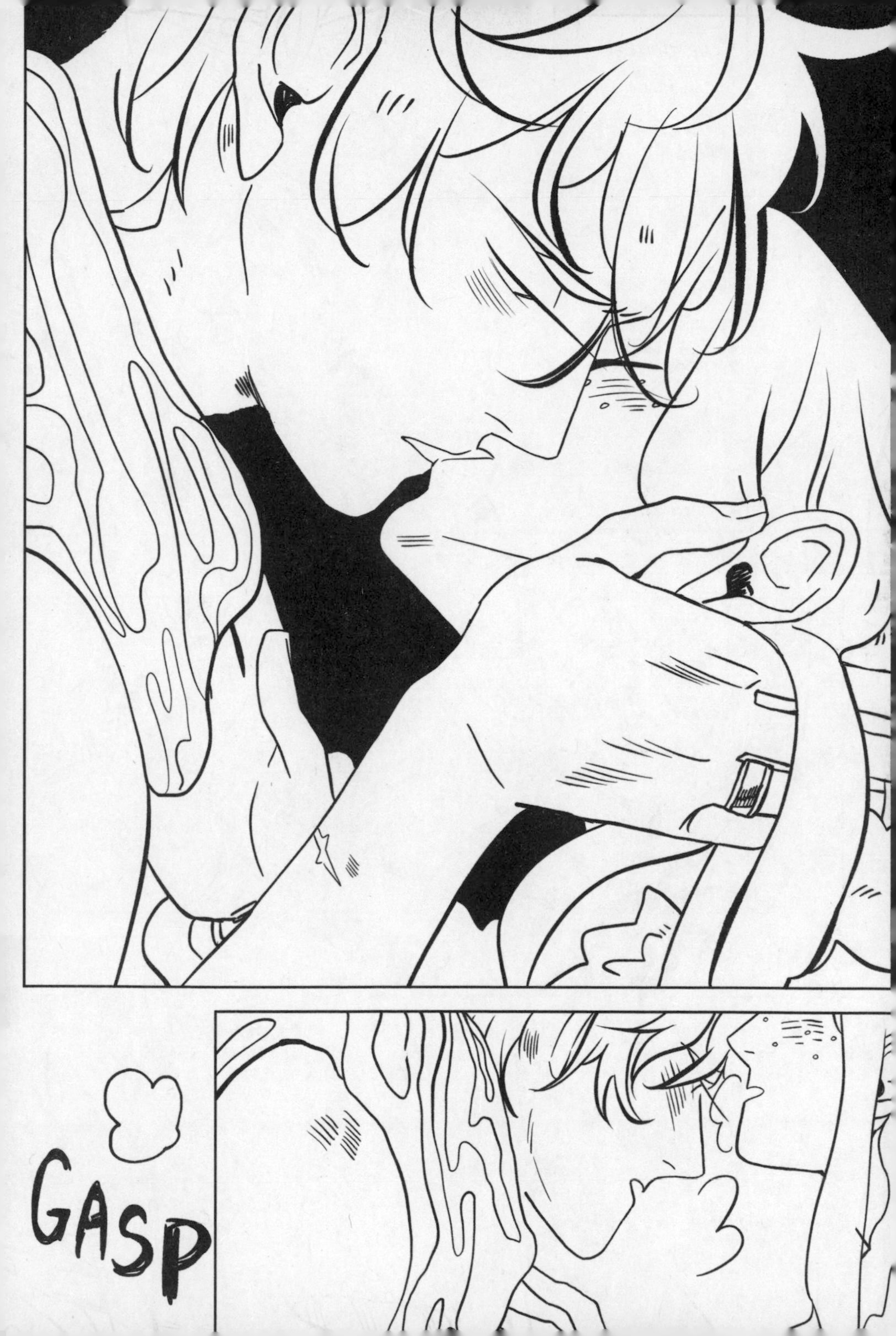
GASP

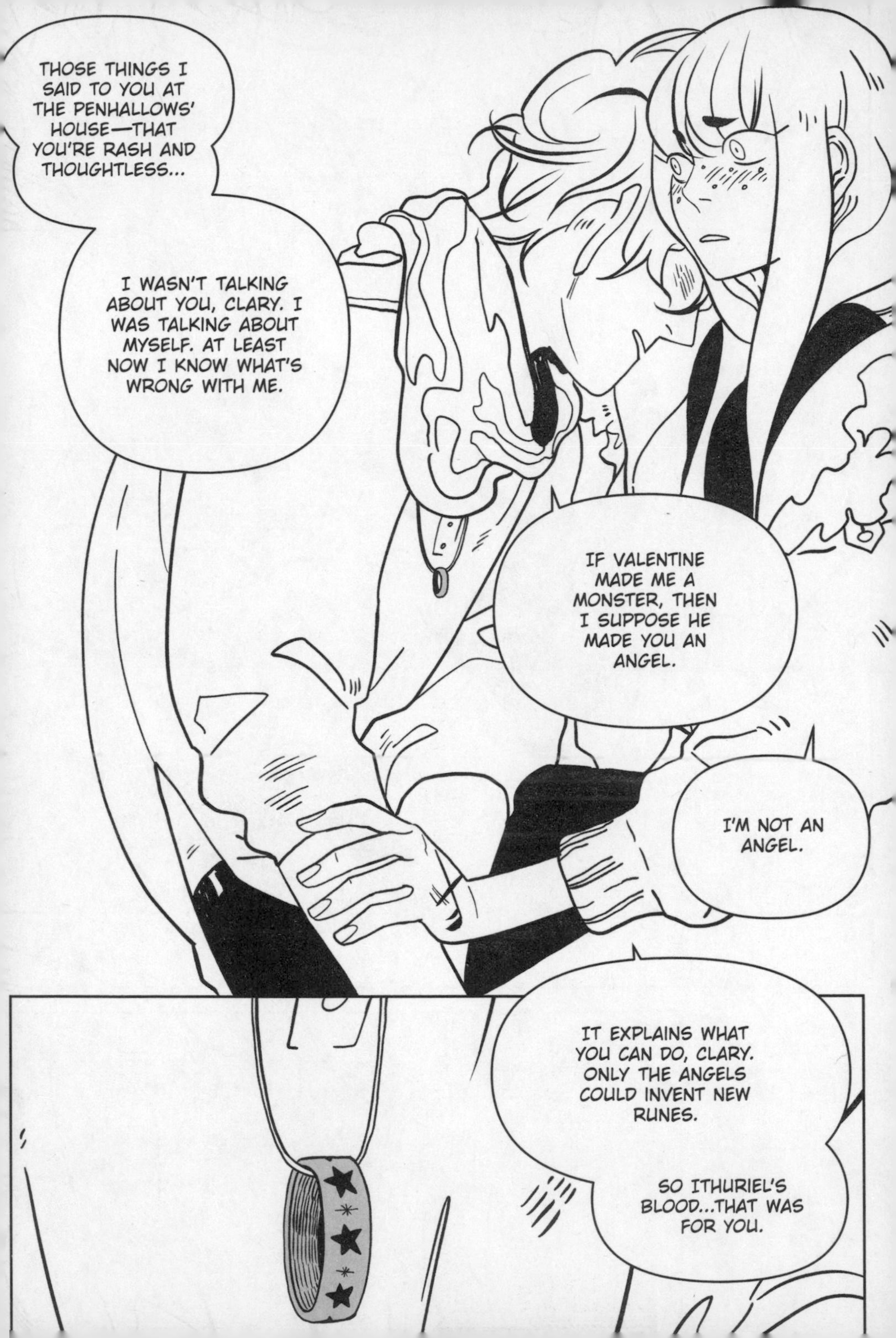
THOSE THINGS I SAID TO YOU AT THE PENHALLOWS' HOUSE—THAT YOU'RE RASH AND THOUGHTLESS...
I WASN'T TALKING ABOUT YOU, CLARY. I WAS TALKING ABOUT MYSELF. AT LEAST NOW I KNOW WHAT'S WRONG WITH ME.
IF VALENTINE MADE ME A MONSTER, THEN I SUPPOSE HE MADE YOU AN ANGEL.
I'M NOT AN ANGEL.
IT EXPLAINS WHAT YOU CAN DO, CLARY. ONLY THE ANGELS COULD INVENT NEW RUNES.
SO ITHURIEL'S BLOOD...THAT WAS FOR YOU.

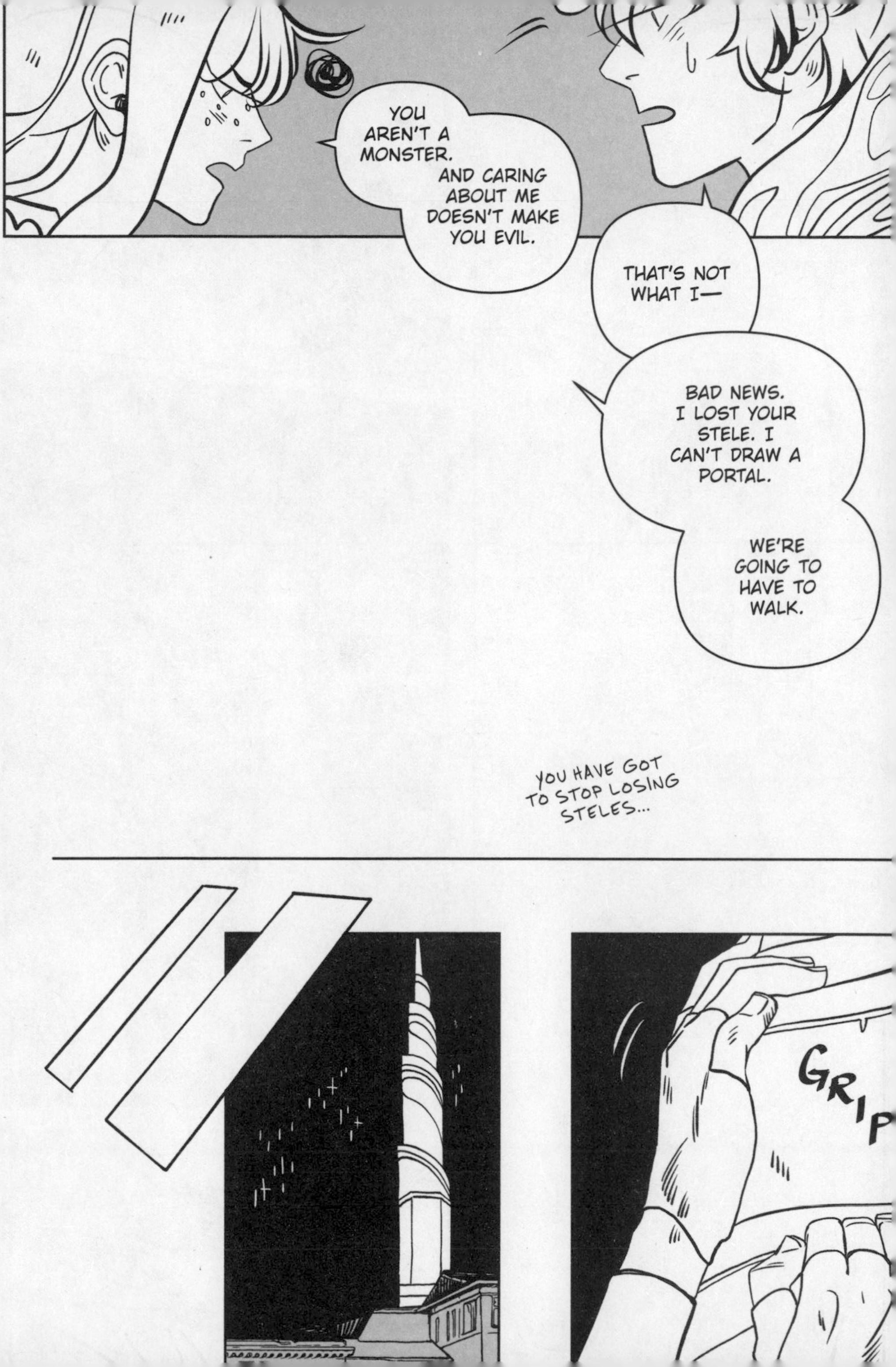
YOU AREN'T A MONSTER.
AND CARING ABOUT ME DOESN'T MAKE YOU EVIL.
THAT'S NOT WHAT I—
BAD NEWS. I LOST YOUR STELE. I CAN'T DRAW A PORTAL.
WE'RE GOING TO HAVE TO WALK.
YOU HAVE GOT TO STOP LOSING STELES...
GRIP

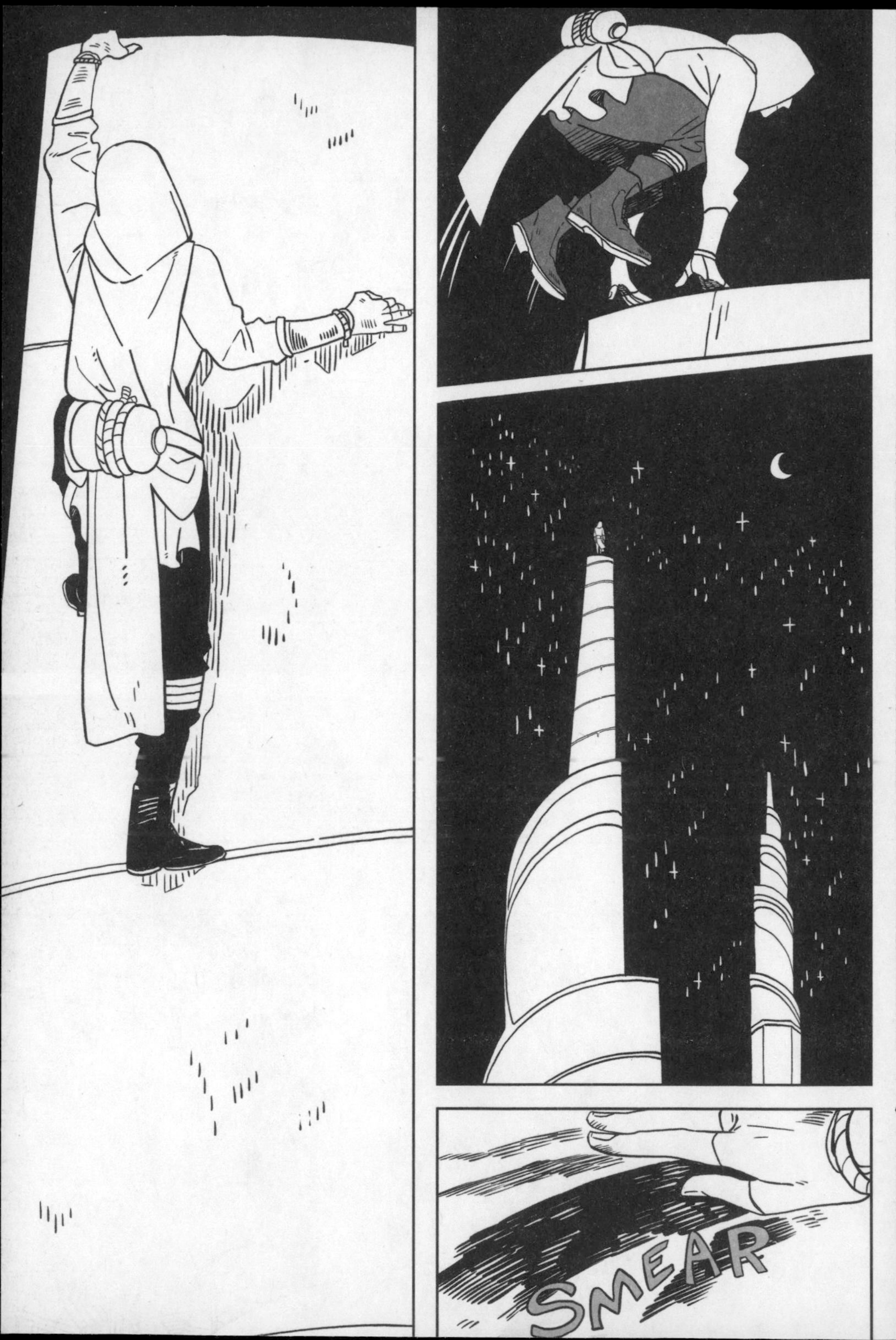
SMEAR

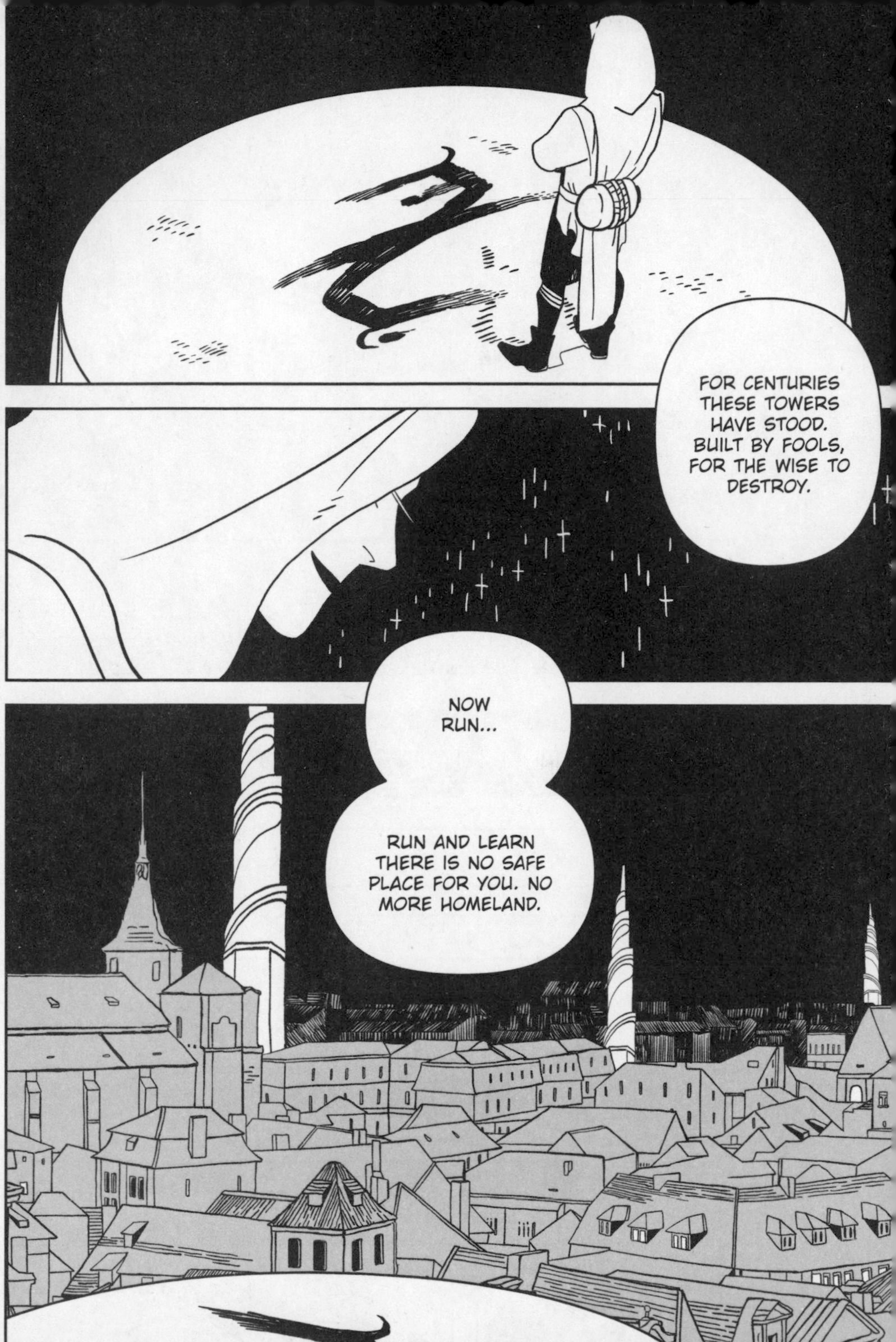
FOR CENTURIES THESE TOWERS HAVE STOOD. BUILT BY FOOLS, FOR THE WISE TO DESTROY.
NOW RUN...
RUN AND LEARN THERE IS NO SAFE PLACE FOR YOU. NO MORE HOMELAND.

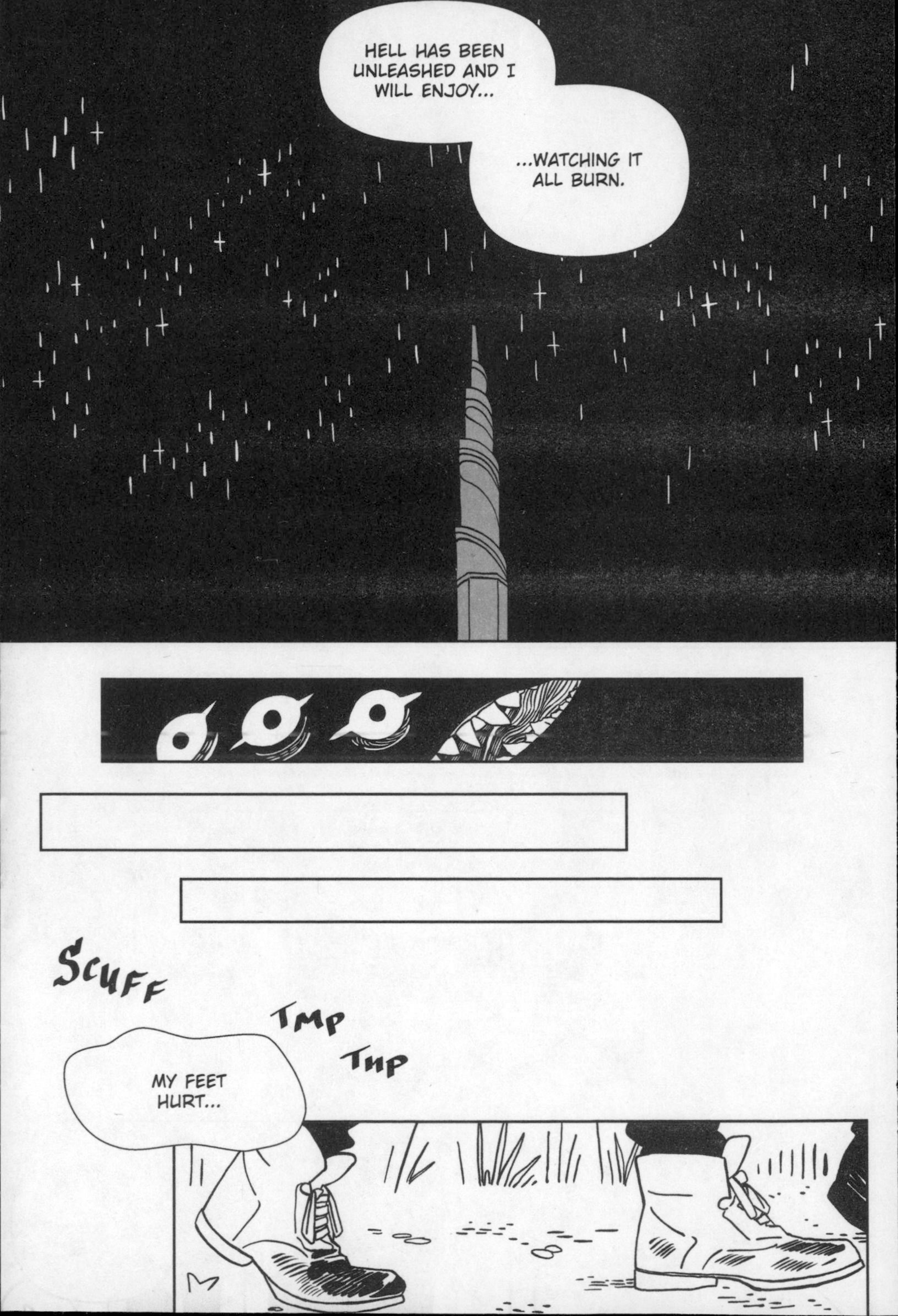
HELL HAS BEEN UNLEASHED AND I WILL ENJOY...
...WATCHING IT ALL BURN.
SCUFF
TMP
TMP
MY FEET HURT...

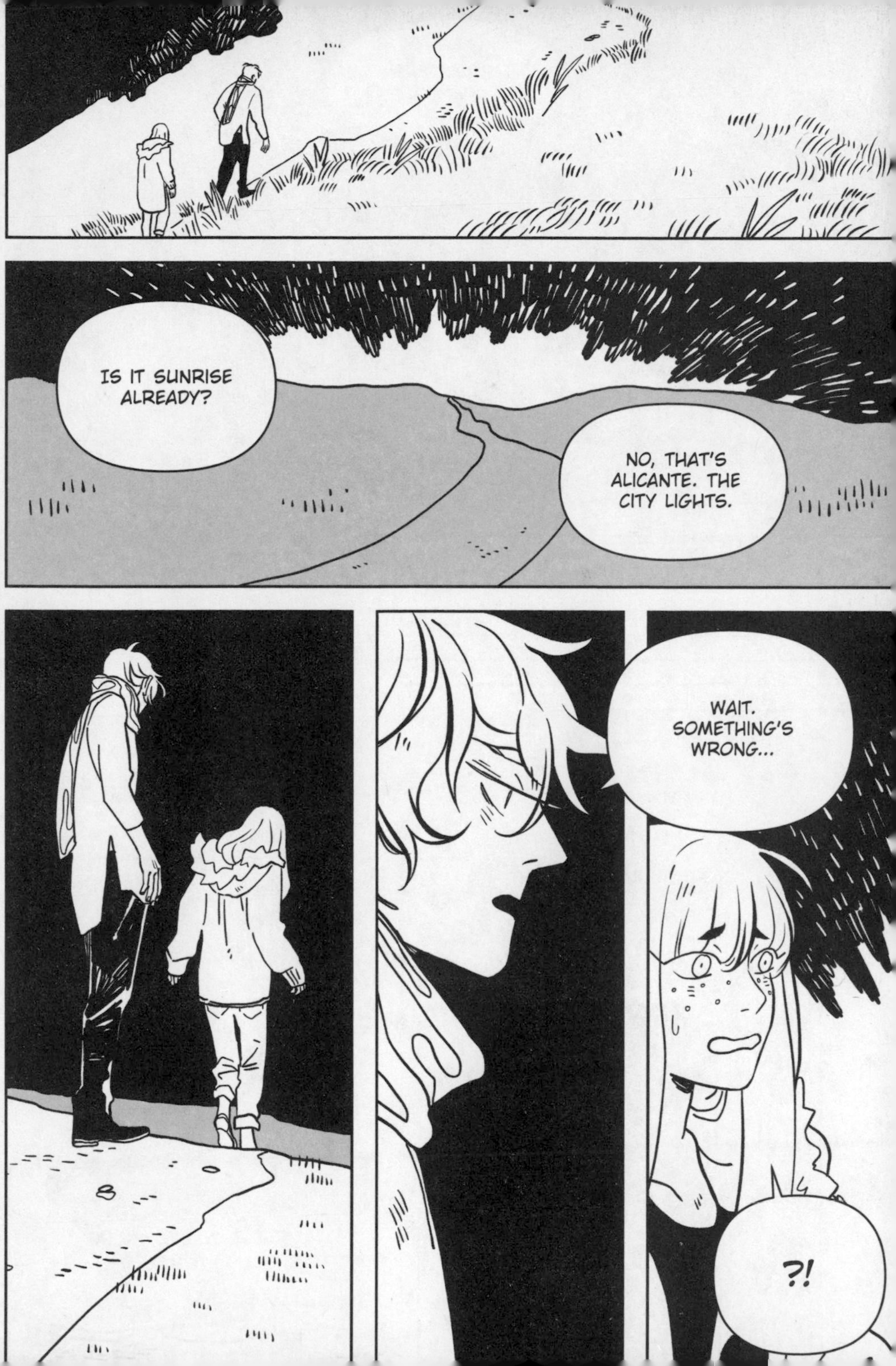
IS IT SUNRISE ALREADY?
NO, THAT'S ALICANTE. THE CITY LIGHTS.
WAIT. SOMETHING'S WRONG...
?!

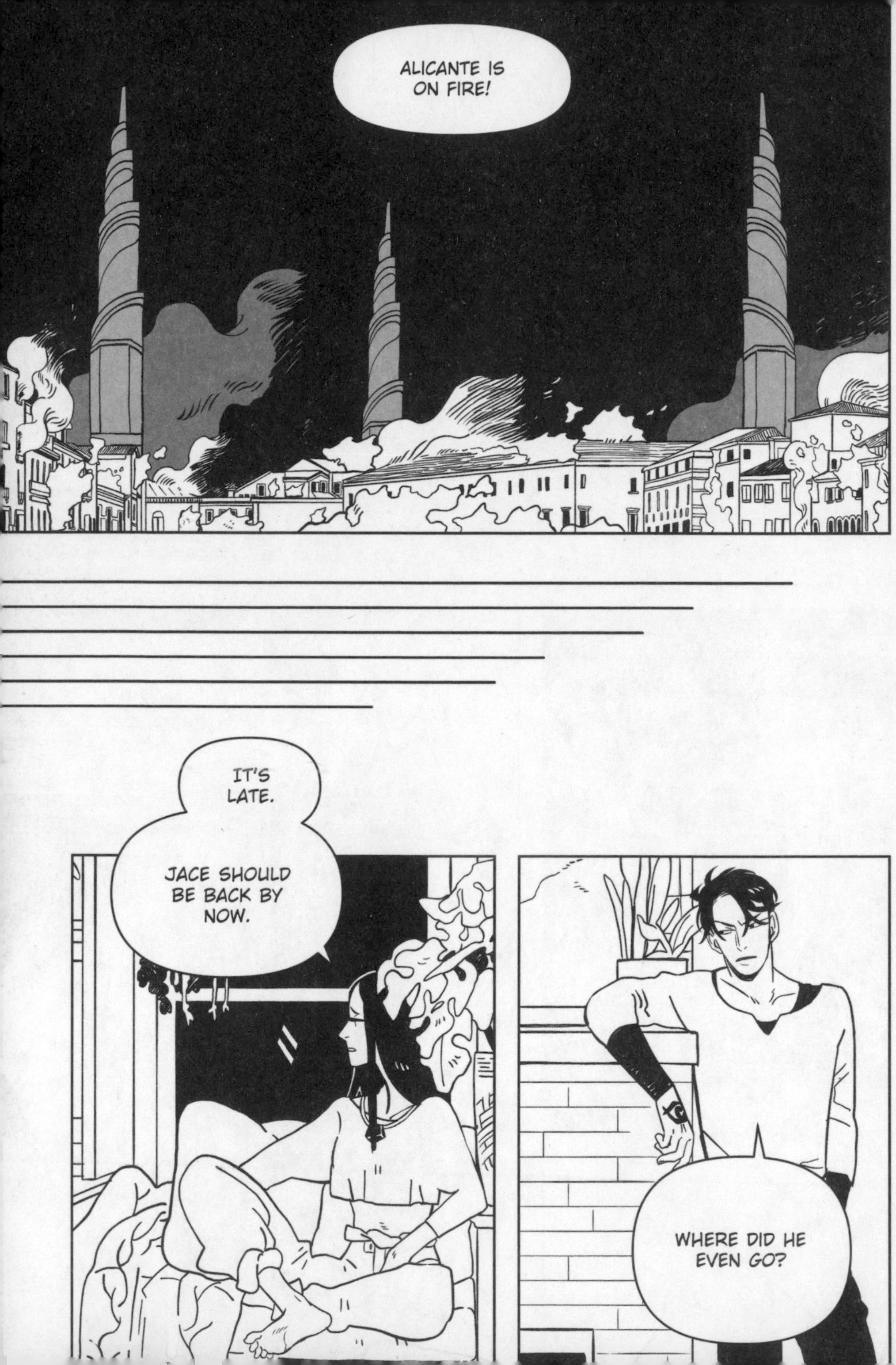
ALICANTE IS ON FIRE!
IT'S LATE.
JACE SHOULD BE BACK BY NOW.
WHERE DID HE EVEN GO?

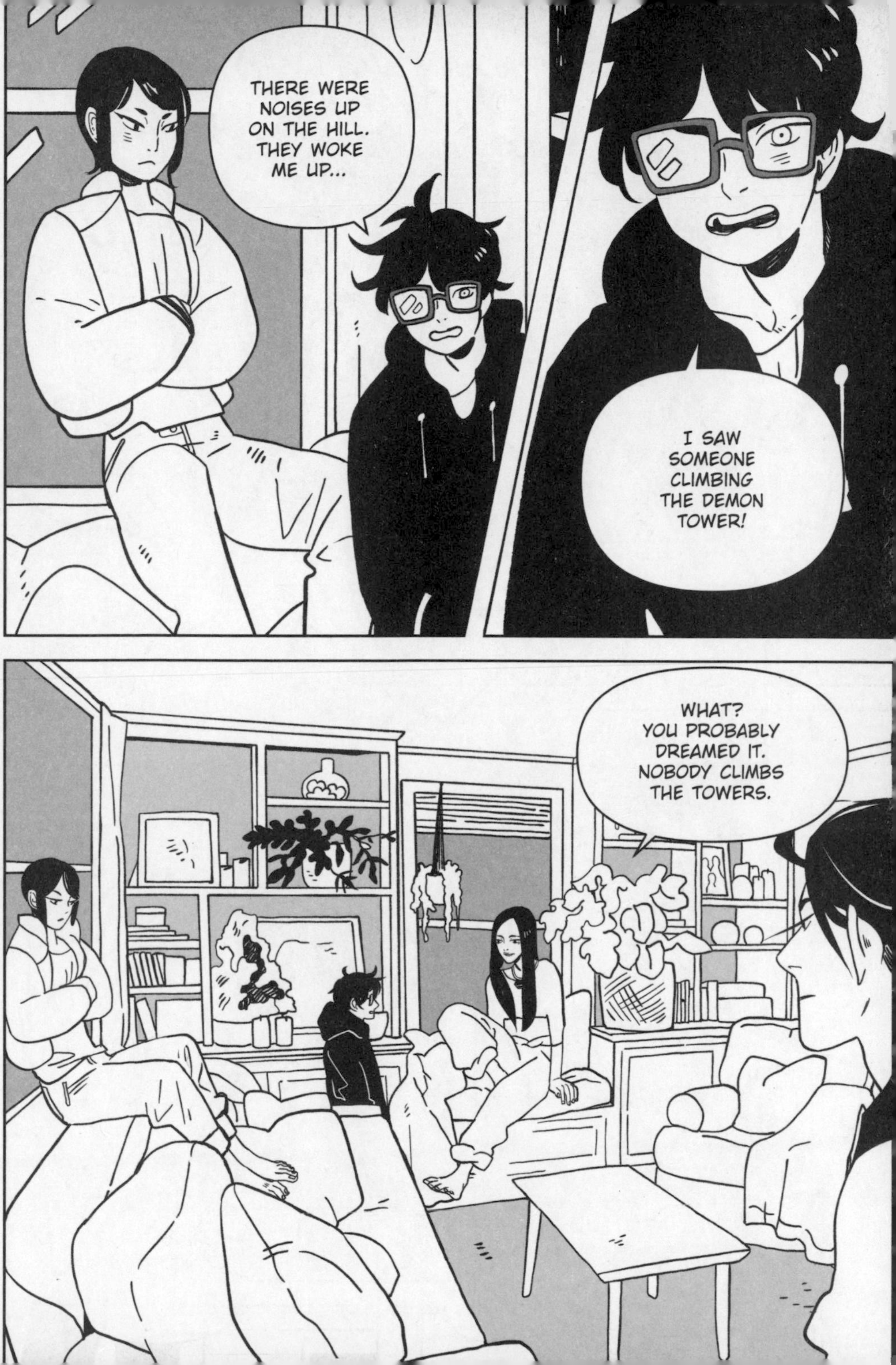
THERE WERE NOISES UP ON THE HILL. THEY WOKE ME UP...
I SAW SOMEONE CLIMBING THE DEMON TOWER!
WHAT? YOU PROBABLY DREAMED IT. NOBODY CLIMBS THE TOWERS.

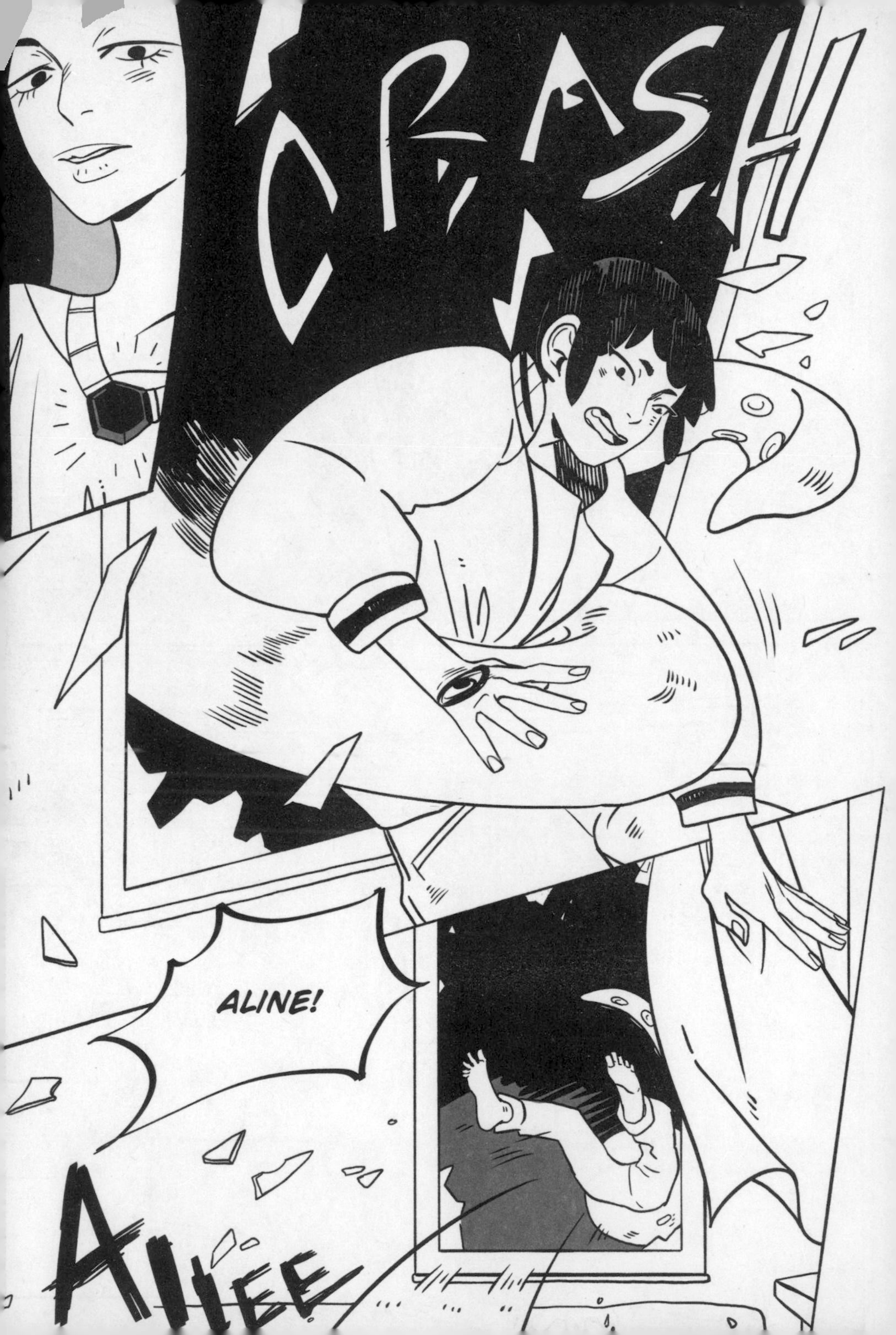
CRASH
ALINE!
AIIIEE

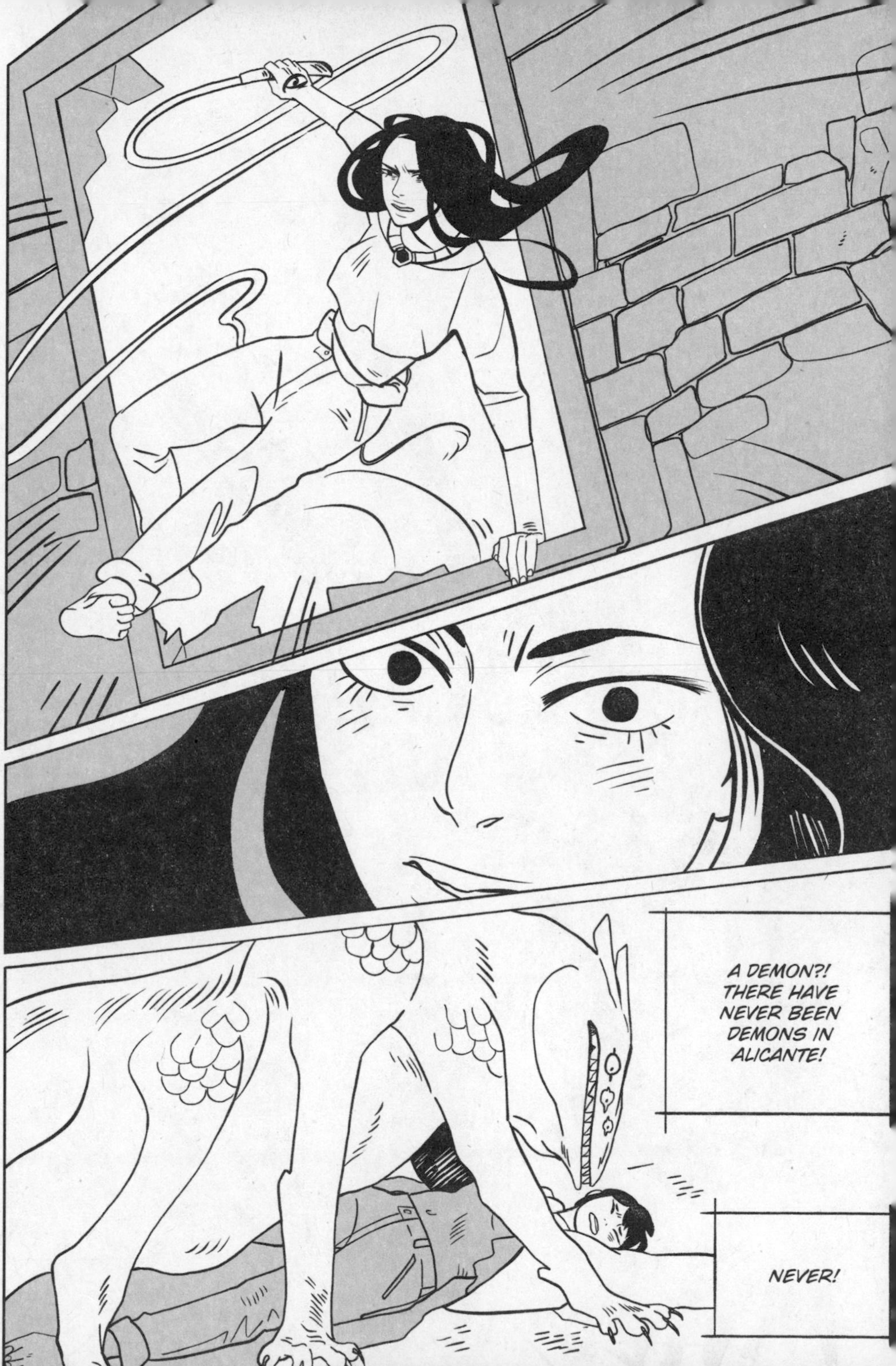
A DEMON?! THERE HAVE NEVER BEEN DEMONS IN ALICANTE!
NEVER!

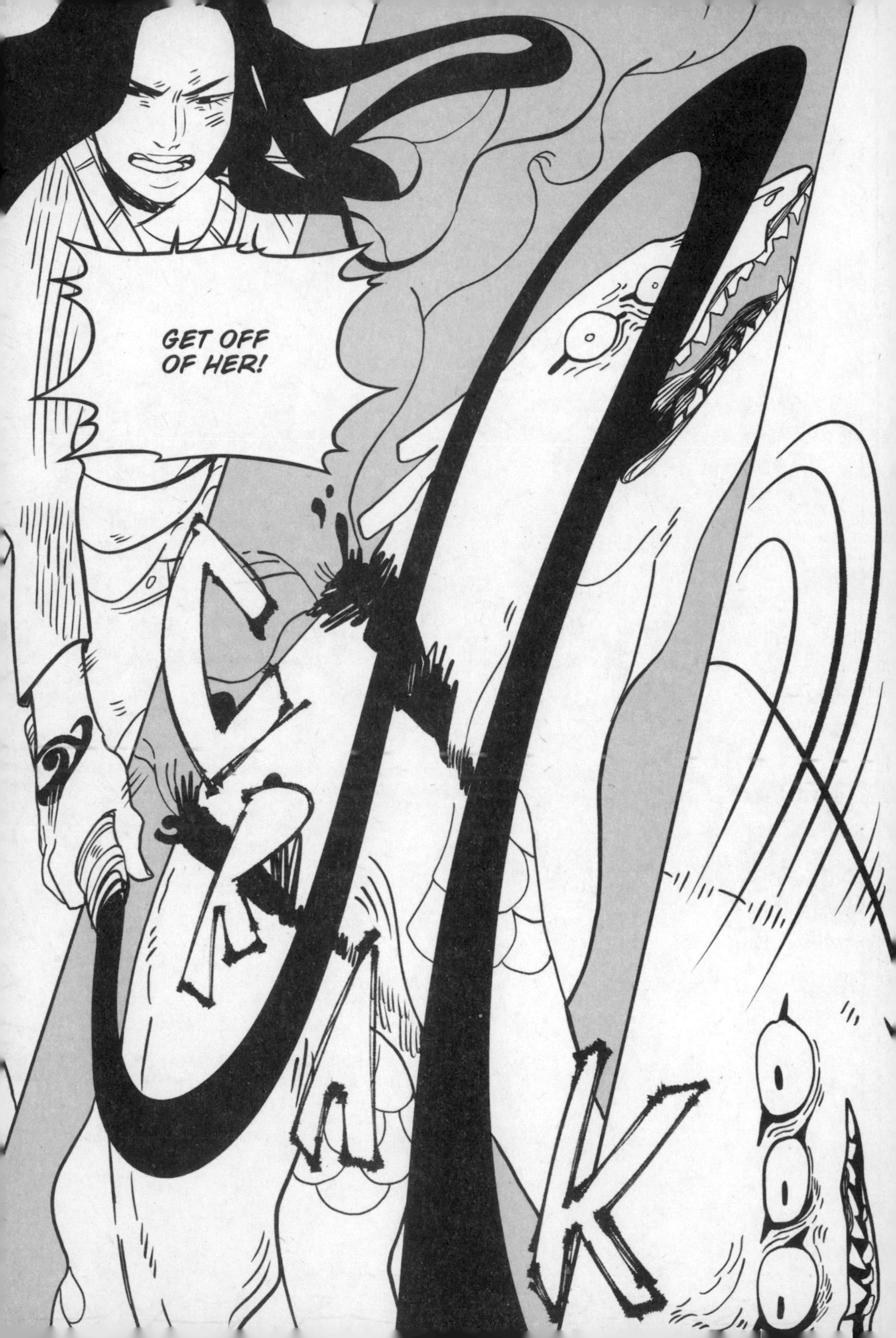
GET OFF
OF HER!

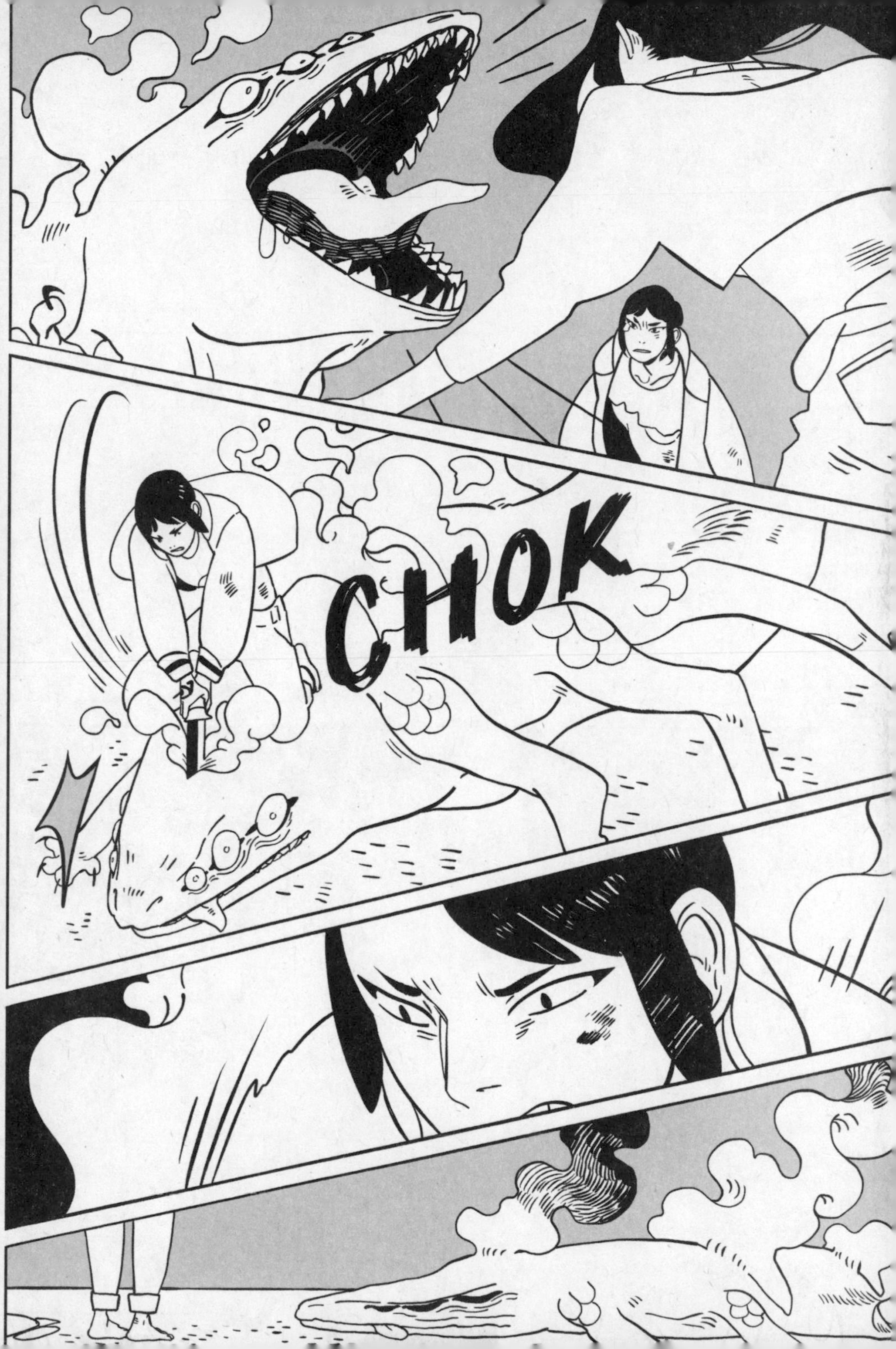
CHOK

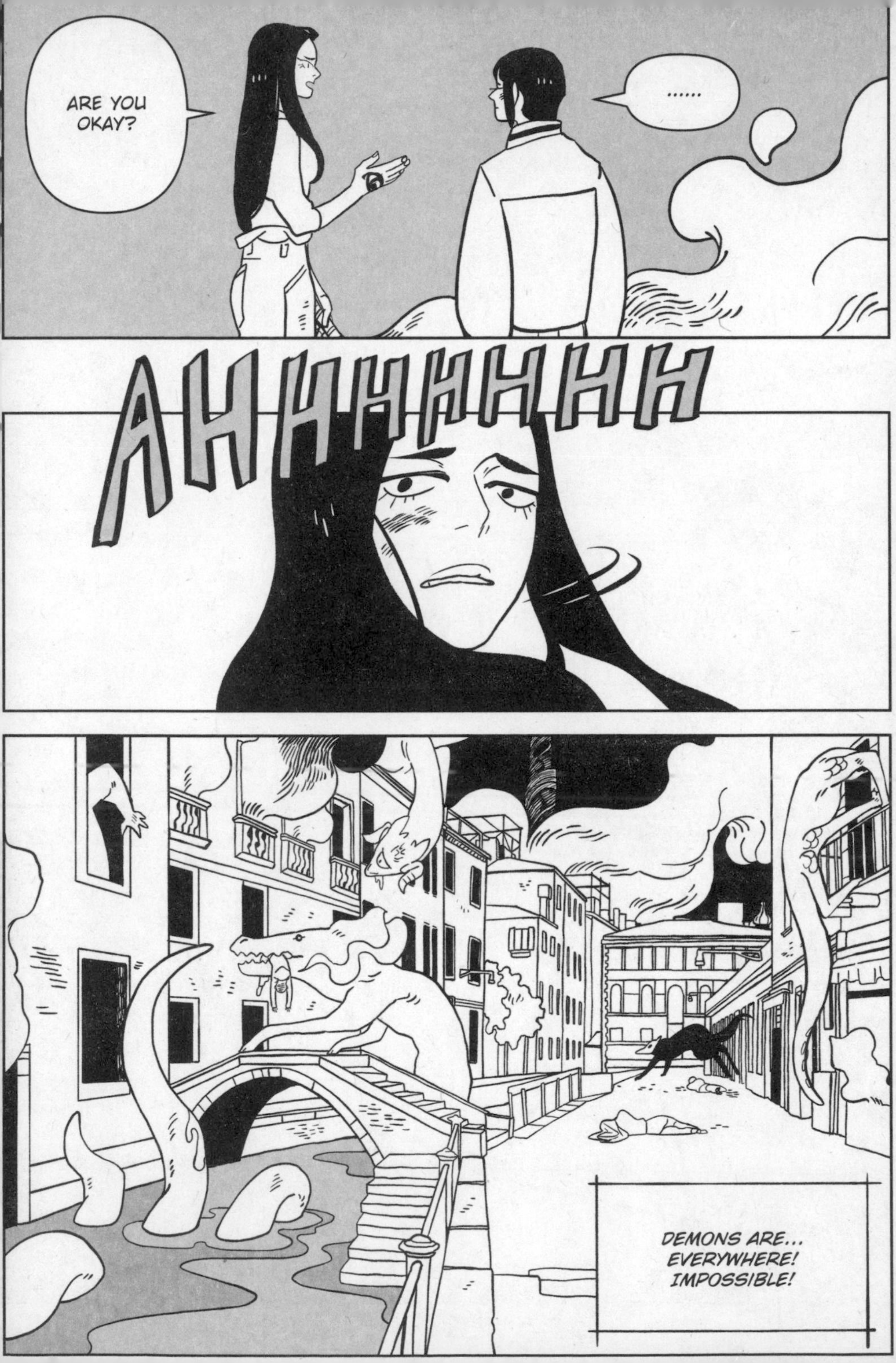
ARE YOU OKAY?
......
AHHHHHHH
DEMONS ARE... EVERYWHERE! IMPOSSIBLE!

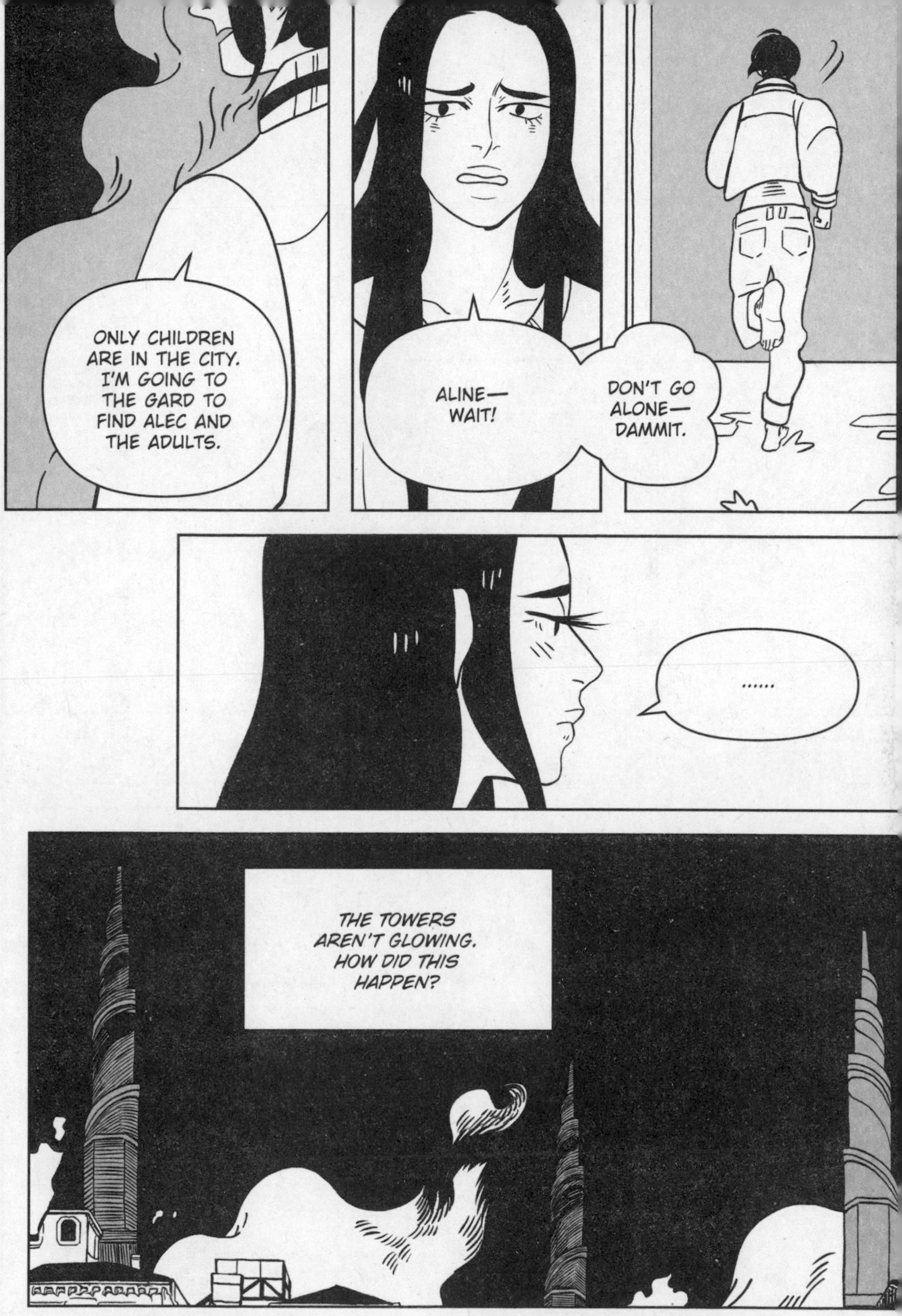
ONLY CHILDREN ARE IN THE CITY. I'M GOING TO THE GARD TO FIND ALEC AND THE ADULTS.
ALINE— WAIT!
DON'T GO ALONE— DAMMIT.
......
THE TOWERS AREN'T GLOWING. HOW DID THIS HAPPEN?

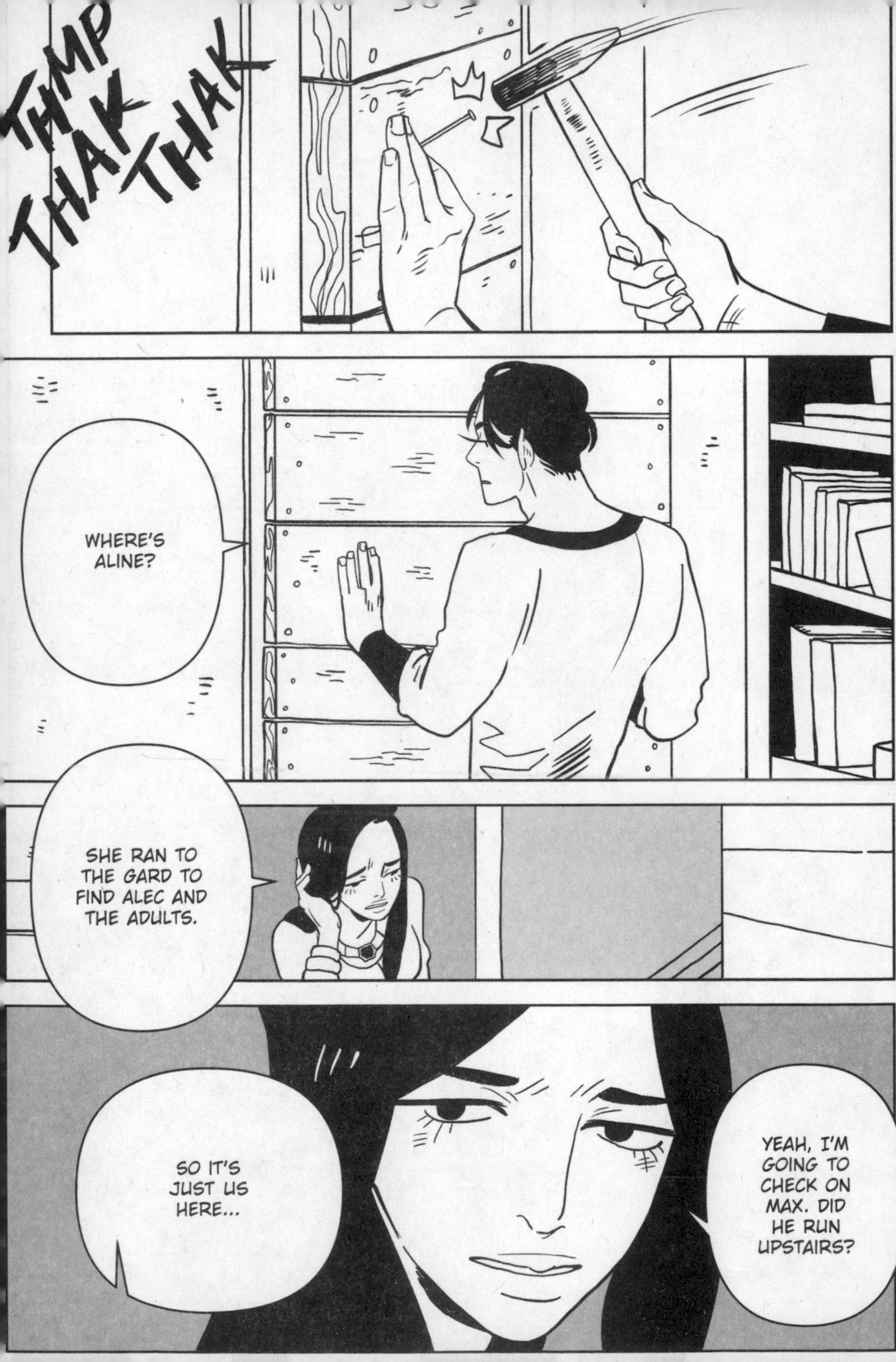
THMP
THAK
THAK
WHERE'S ALINE?
SHE RAN TO THE GARD TO FIND ALEC AND THE ADULTS.
SO IT'S JUST US HERE...
YEAH, I'M GOING TO CHECK ON MAX. DID HE RUN UPSTAIRS?

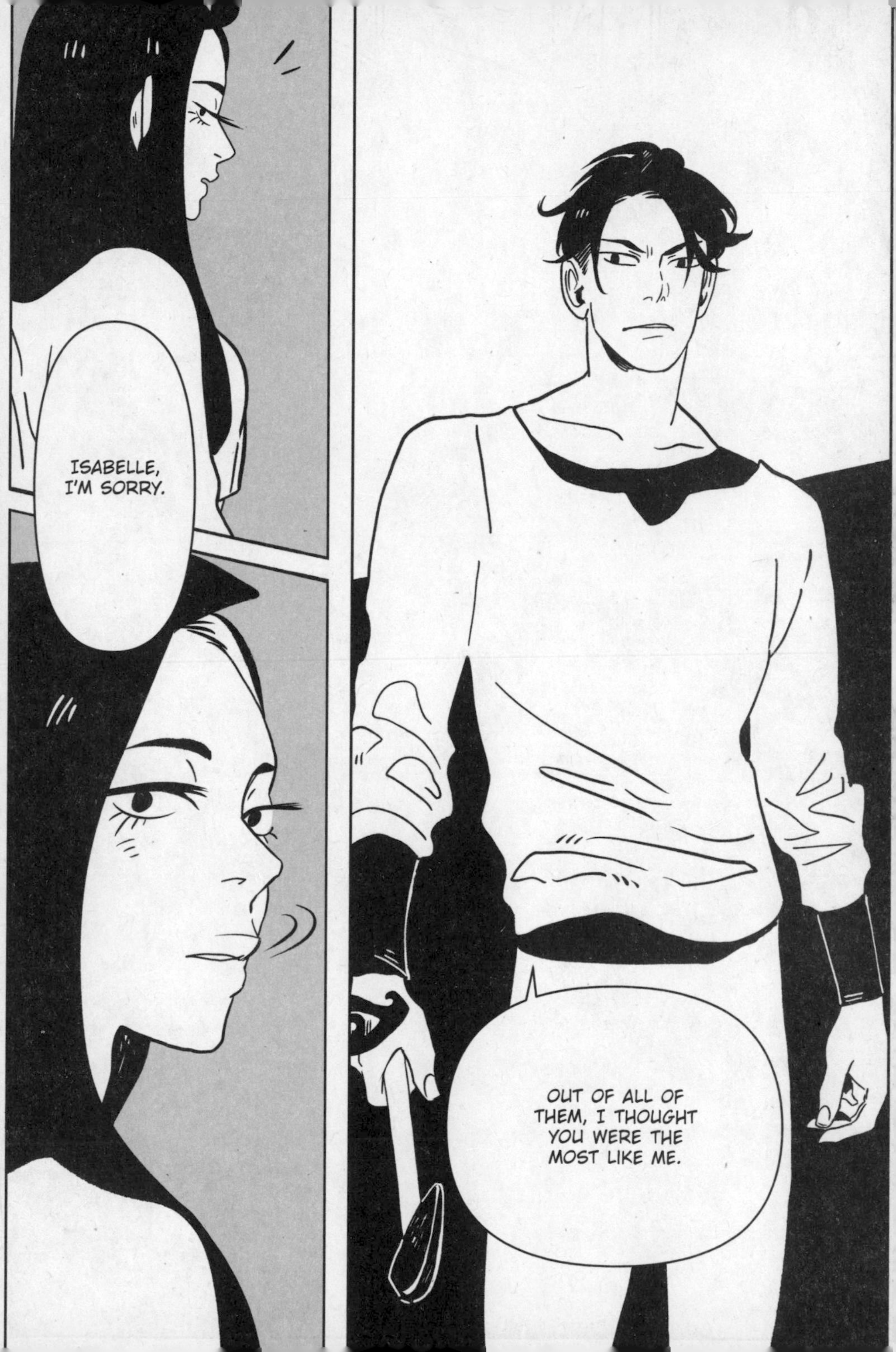
ISABELLE, I'M SORRY.
OUT OF ALL OF THEM, I THOUGHT YOU WERE THE MOST LIKE ME.

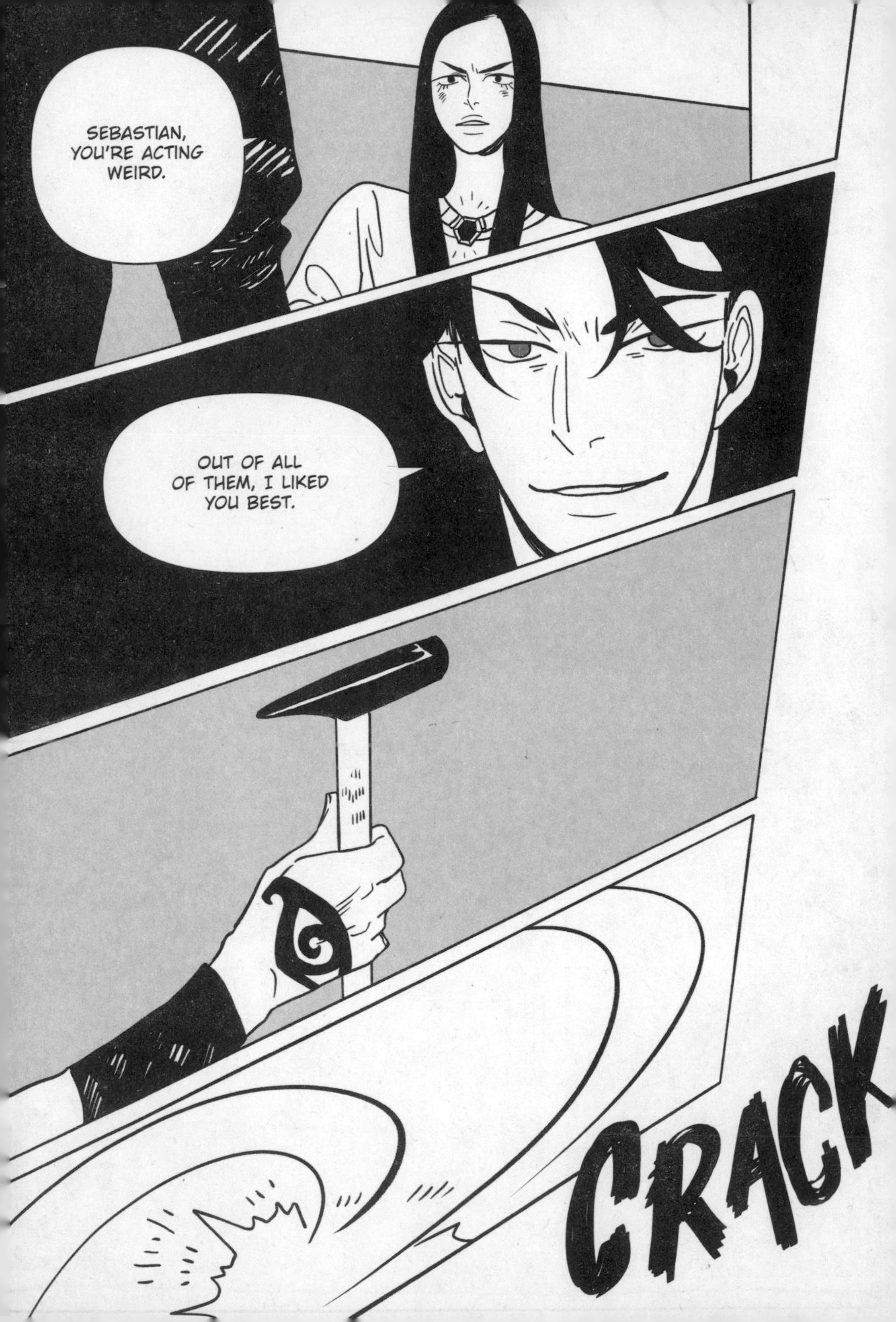
SEBASTIAN, YOU'RE ACTING WEIRD.
OUT OF ALL OF THEM, I LIKED YOU BEST.
CRACK

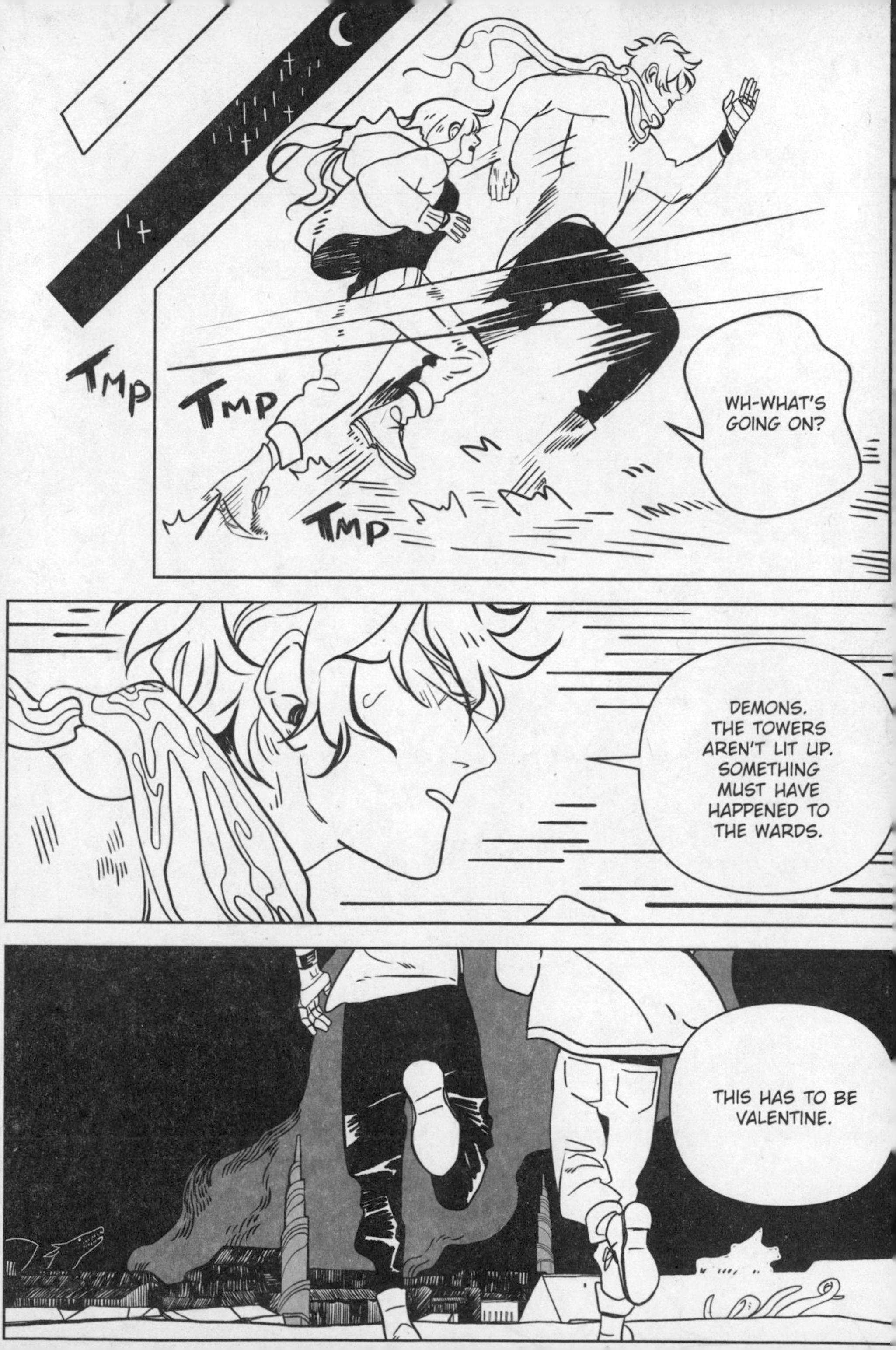
TMP
TMP
TMP
WH-WHAT'S GOING ON?
DEMONS. THE TOWERS AREN'T LIT UP. SOMETHING MUST HAVE HAPPENED TO THE WARDS.
THIS HAS TO BE VALENTINE.

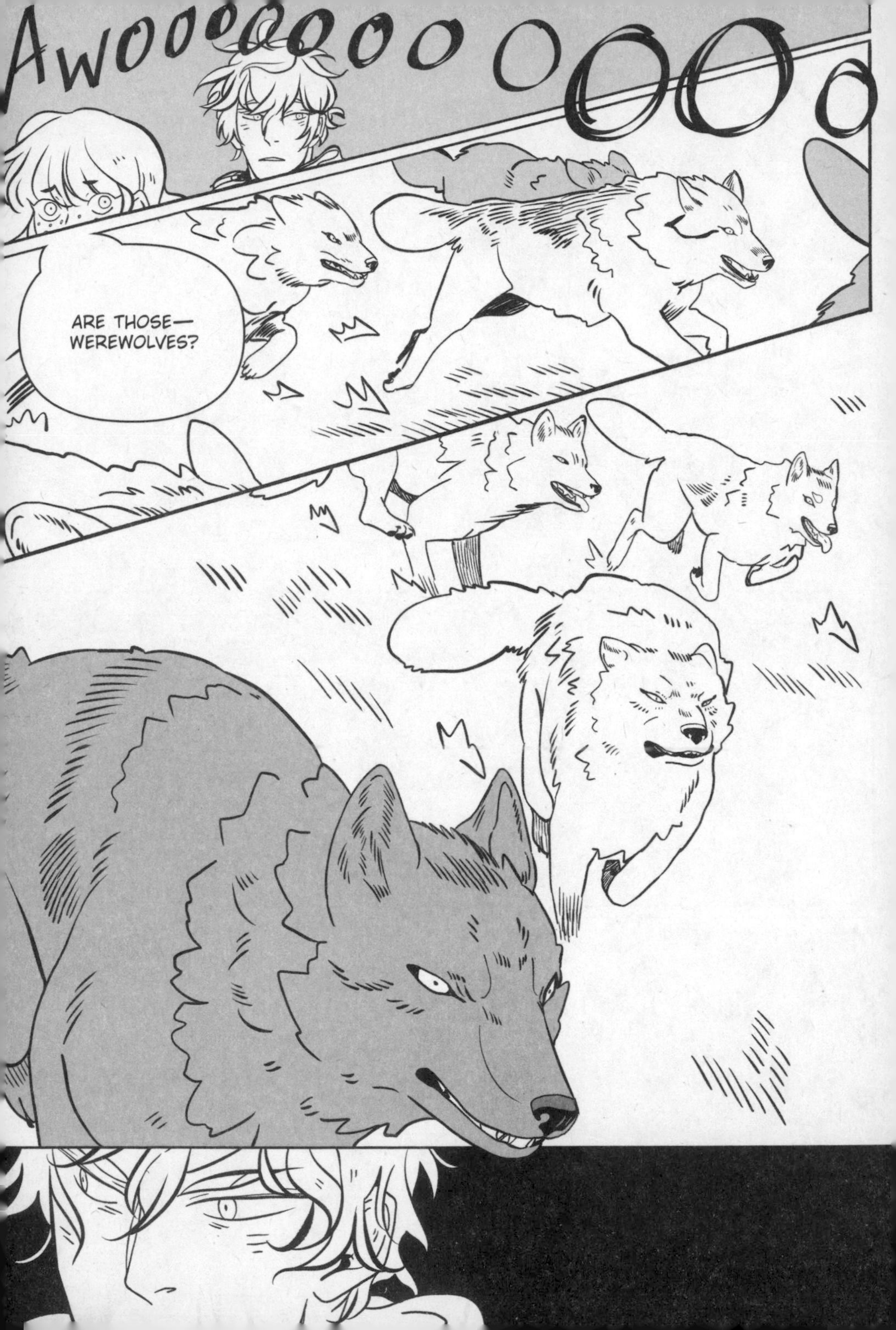
AWOOOOOOOOOOOOo
ARE THOSE—
WEREWOLVES?

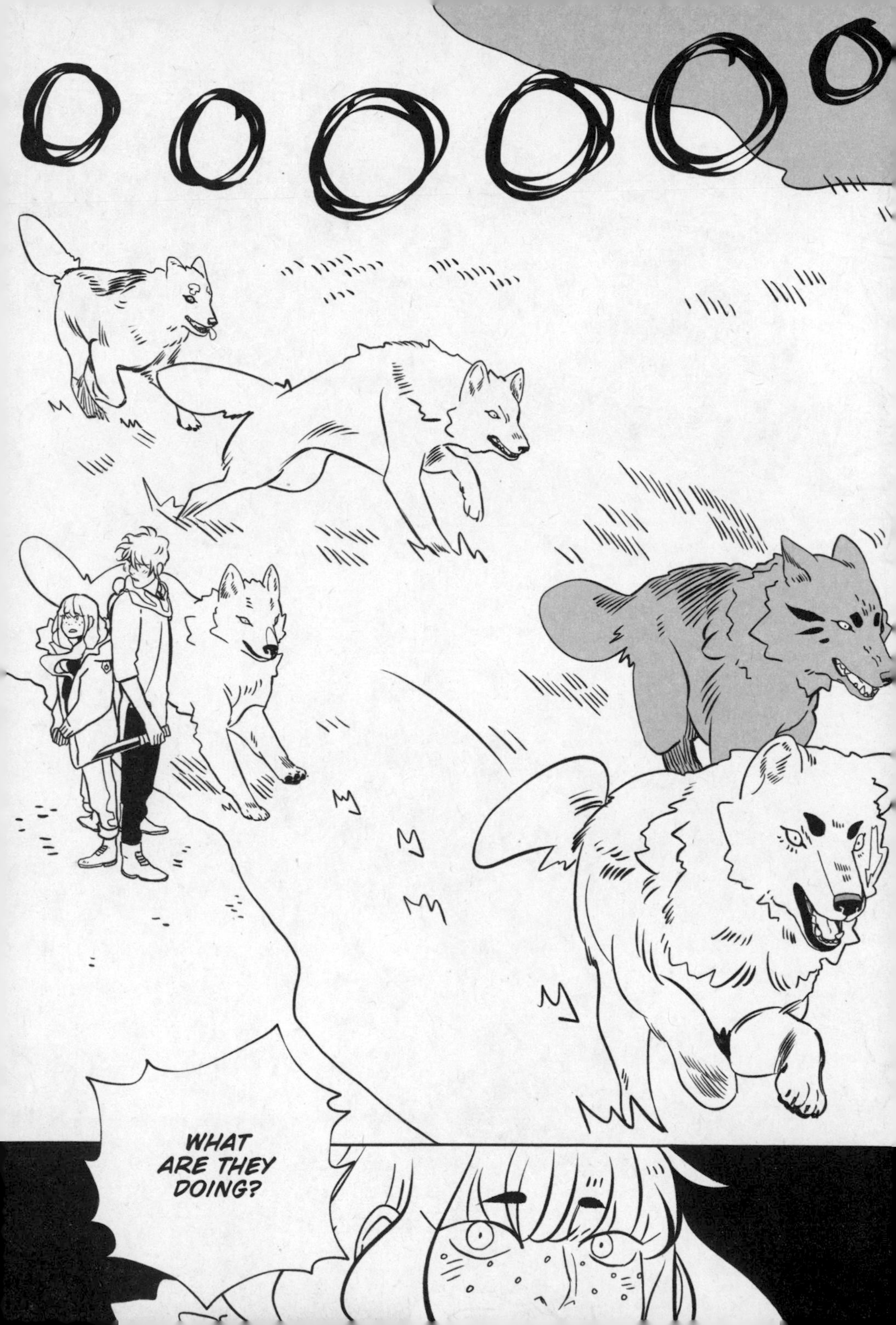
OOOOOO
WHAT ARE THEY DOING?

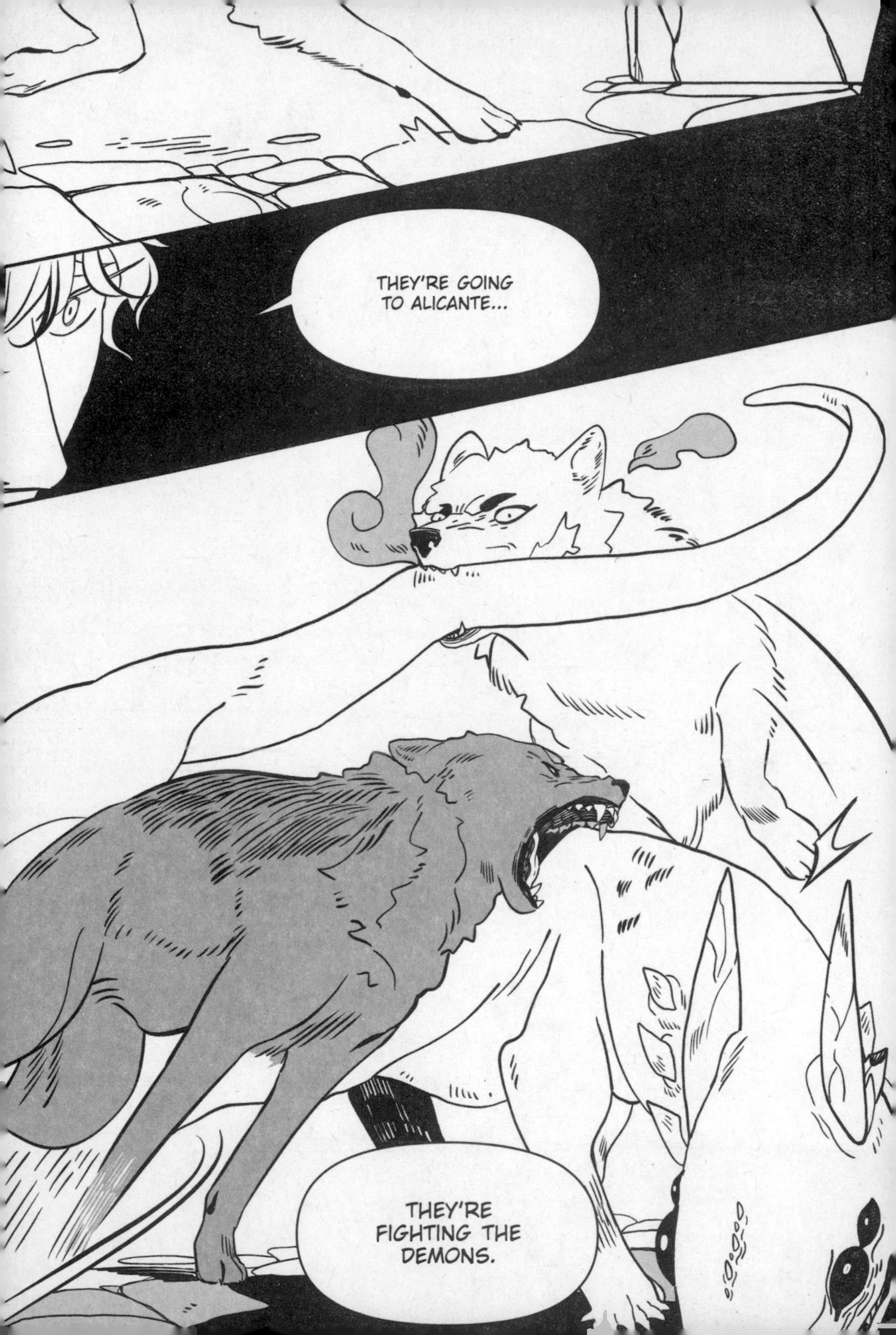
THEY'RE GOING TO ALICANTE...
THEY'RE FIGHTING THE DEMONS.

THE MORTAL INSTRUMENTS

THE GRAPHIC NOVEL

THE
MORTAL INSTRUMENTS
THE GRAPHIC NOVEL

Chapter 30

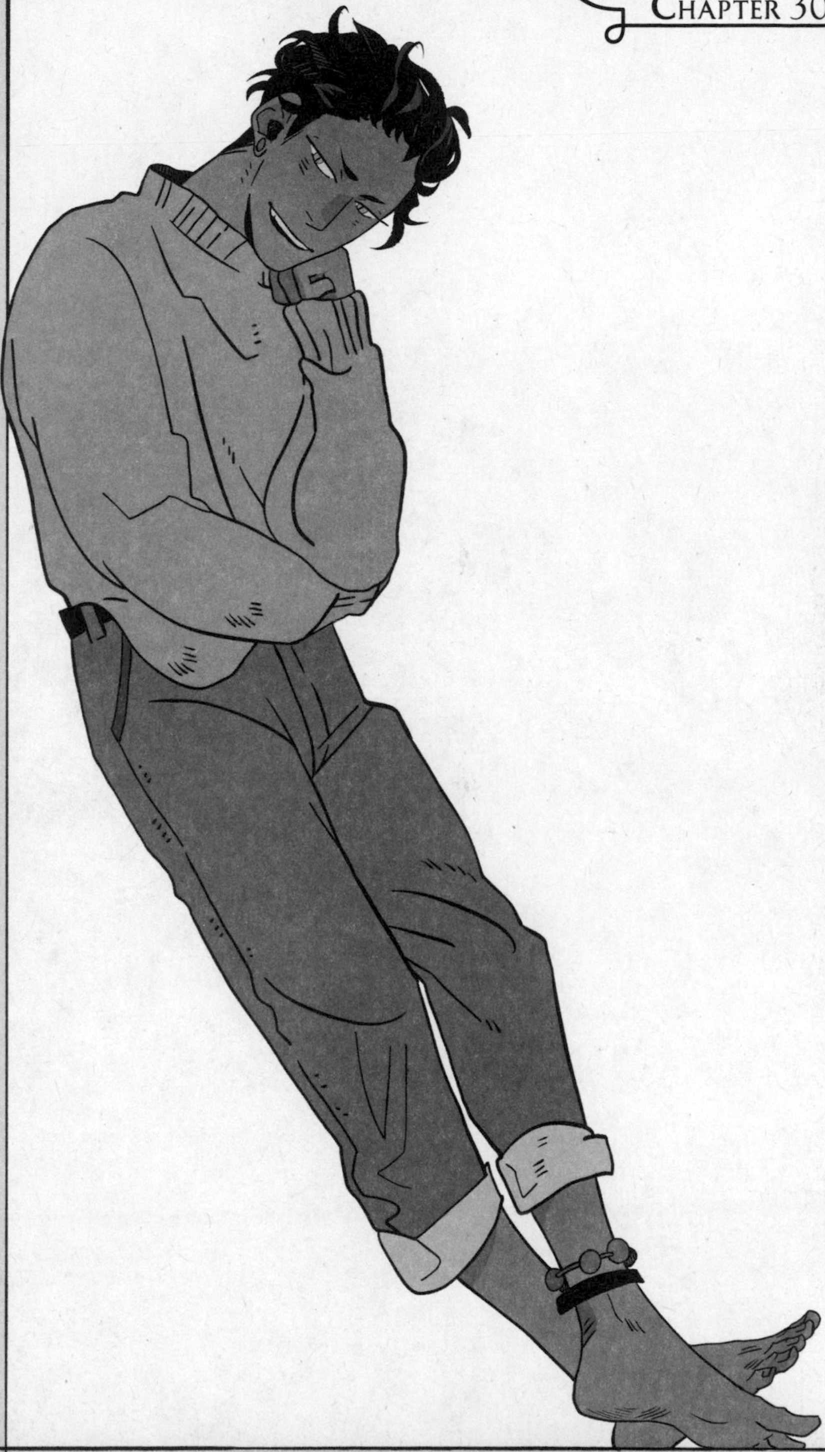

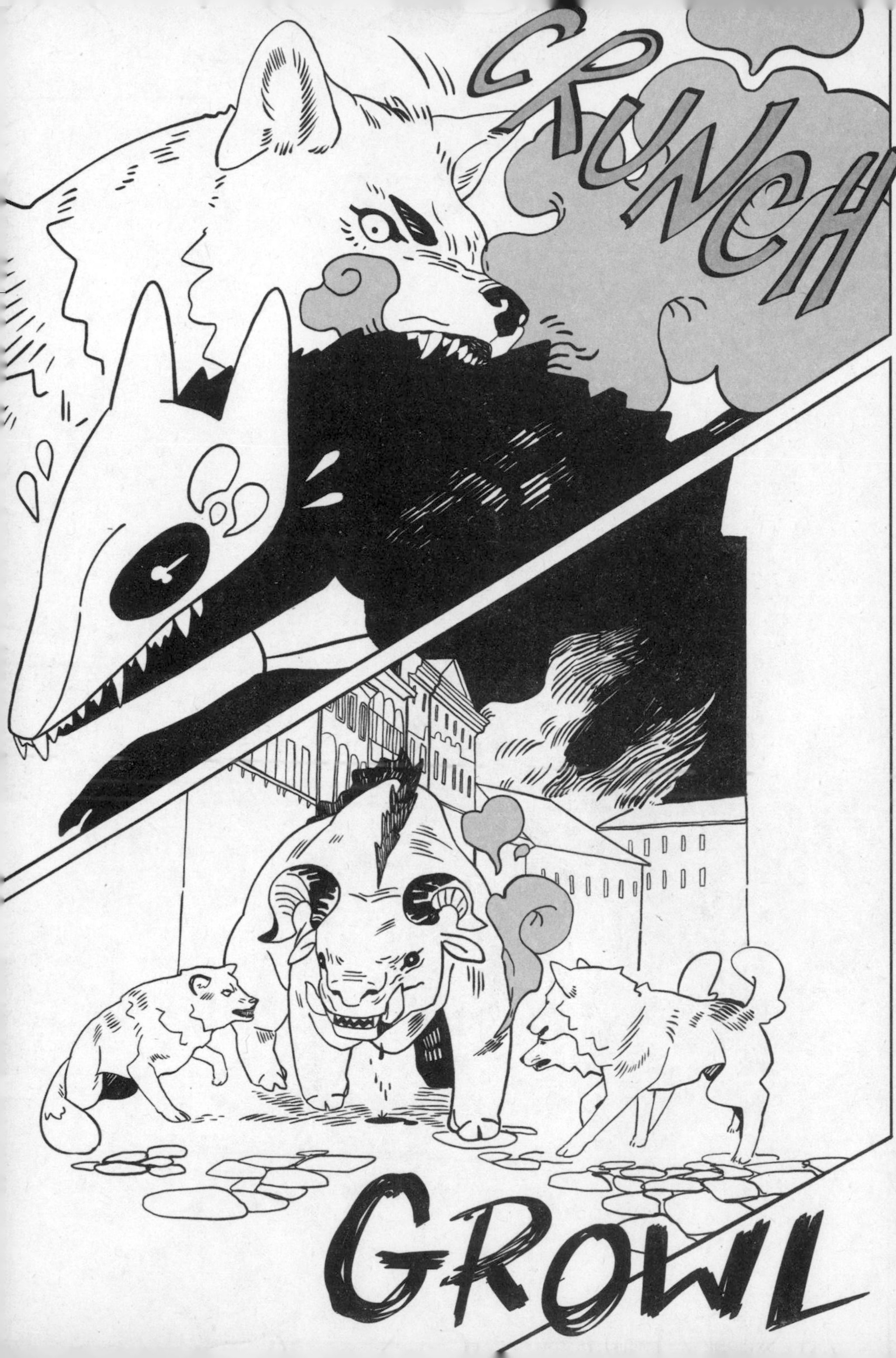
CRUNCH
GROWL

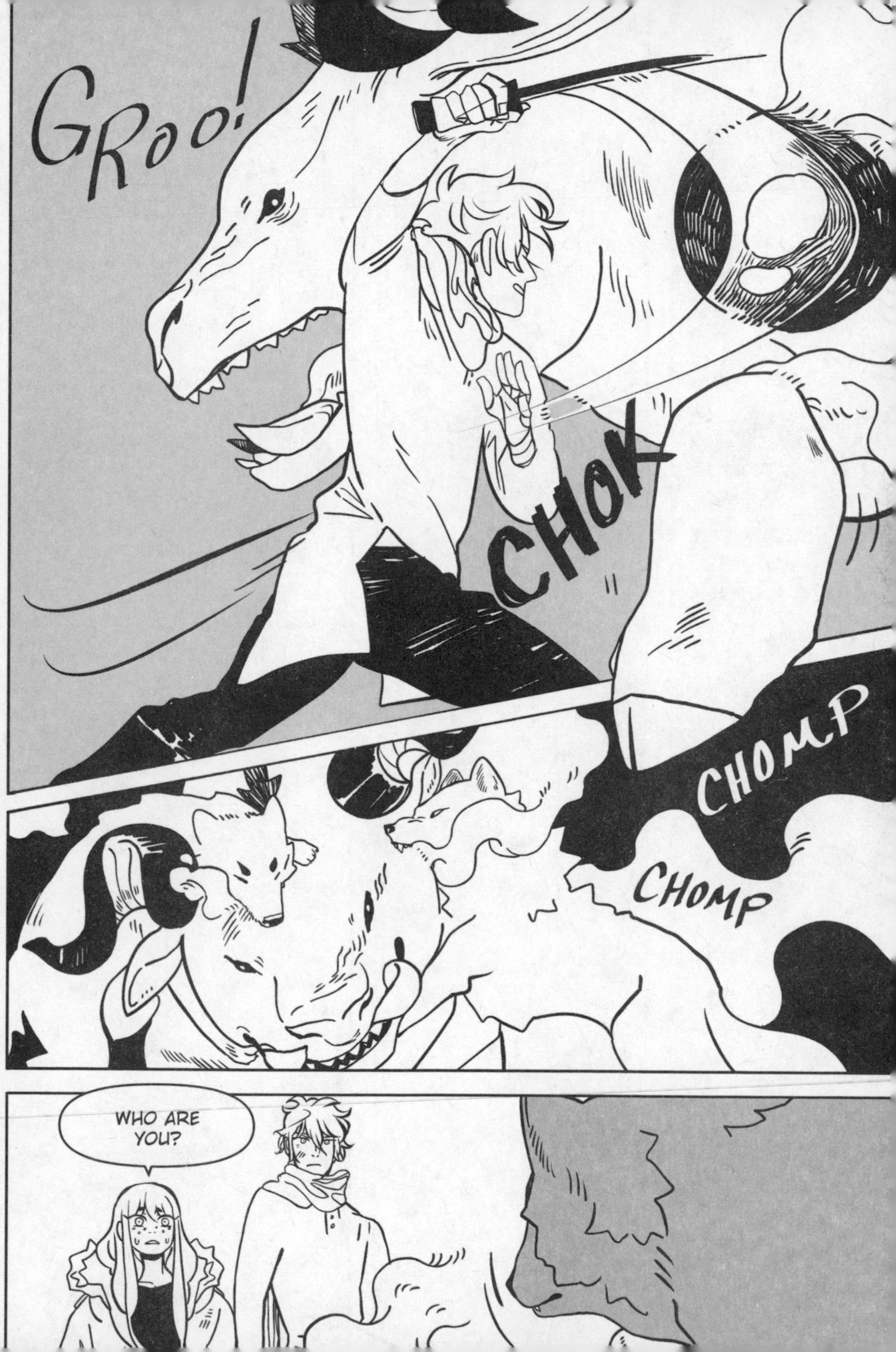
GROO!
CHOK
CHOMP
CHOMP
WHO ARE YOU?

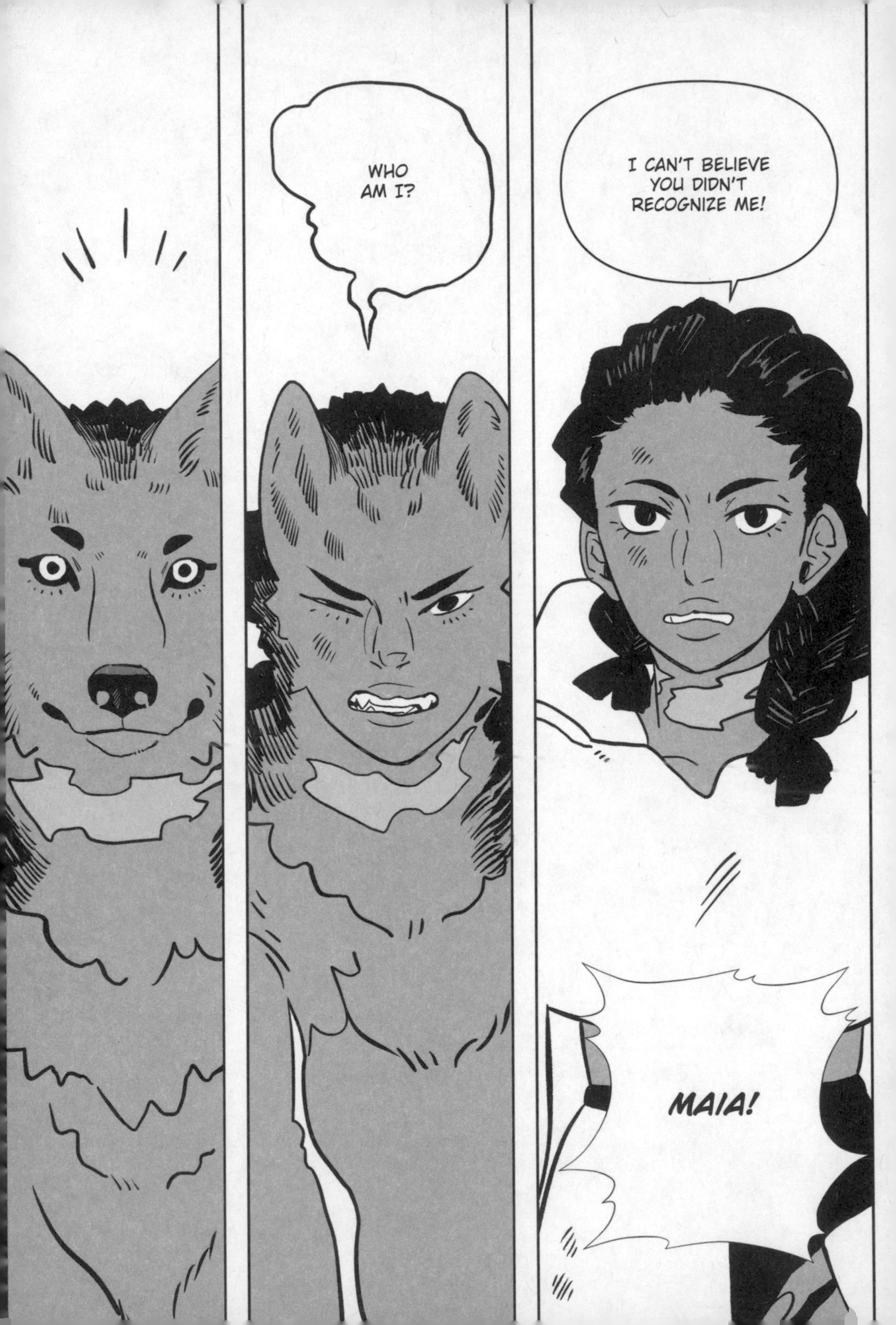
WHO AM I?
I CAN'T BELIEVE YOU DIDN'T RECOGNIZE ME!
MAIA!

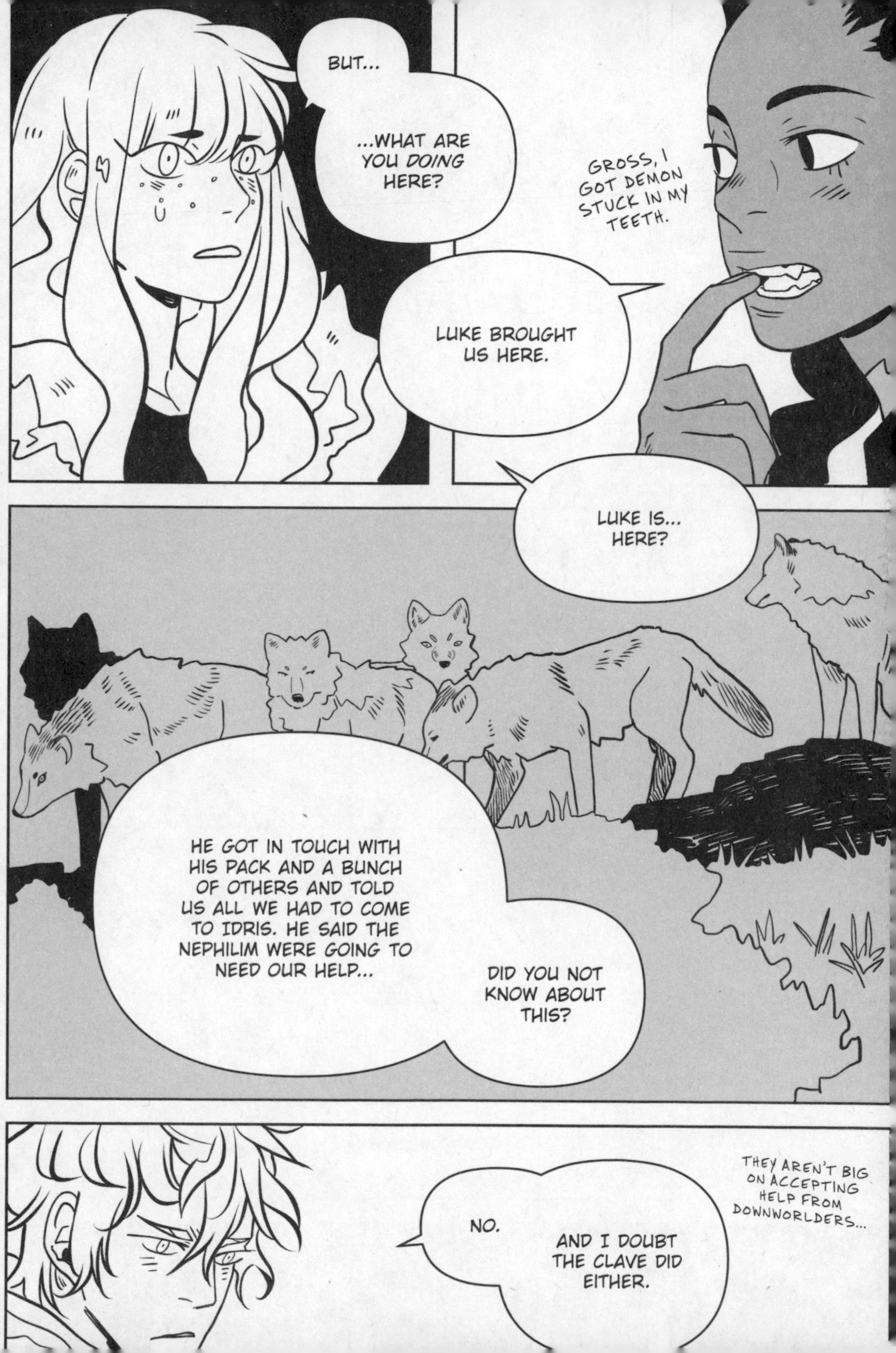
BUT...
...WHAT ARE YOU DOING HERE?
GROSS, I GOT DEMON STUCK IN MY TEETH.
LUKE BROUGHT US HERE.
LUKE IS... HERE?
HE GOT IN TOUCH WITH HIS PACK AND A BUNCH OF OTHERS AND TOLD US ALL WE HAD TO COME TO IDRIS. HE SAID THE NEPHILIM WERE GOING TO NEED OUR HELP...
DID YOU NOT KNOW ABOUT THIS?
NO.
AND I DOUBT THE CLAVE DID EITHER.
THEY AREN'T BIG ON ACCEPTING HELP FROM DOWNWORLDERS...

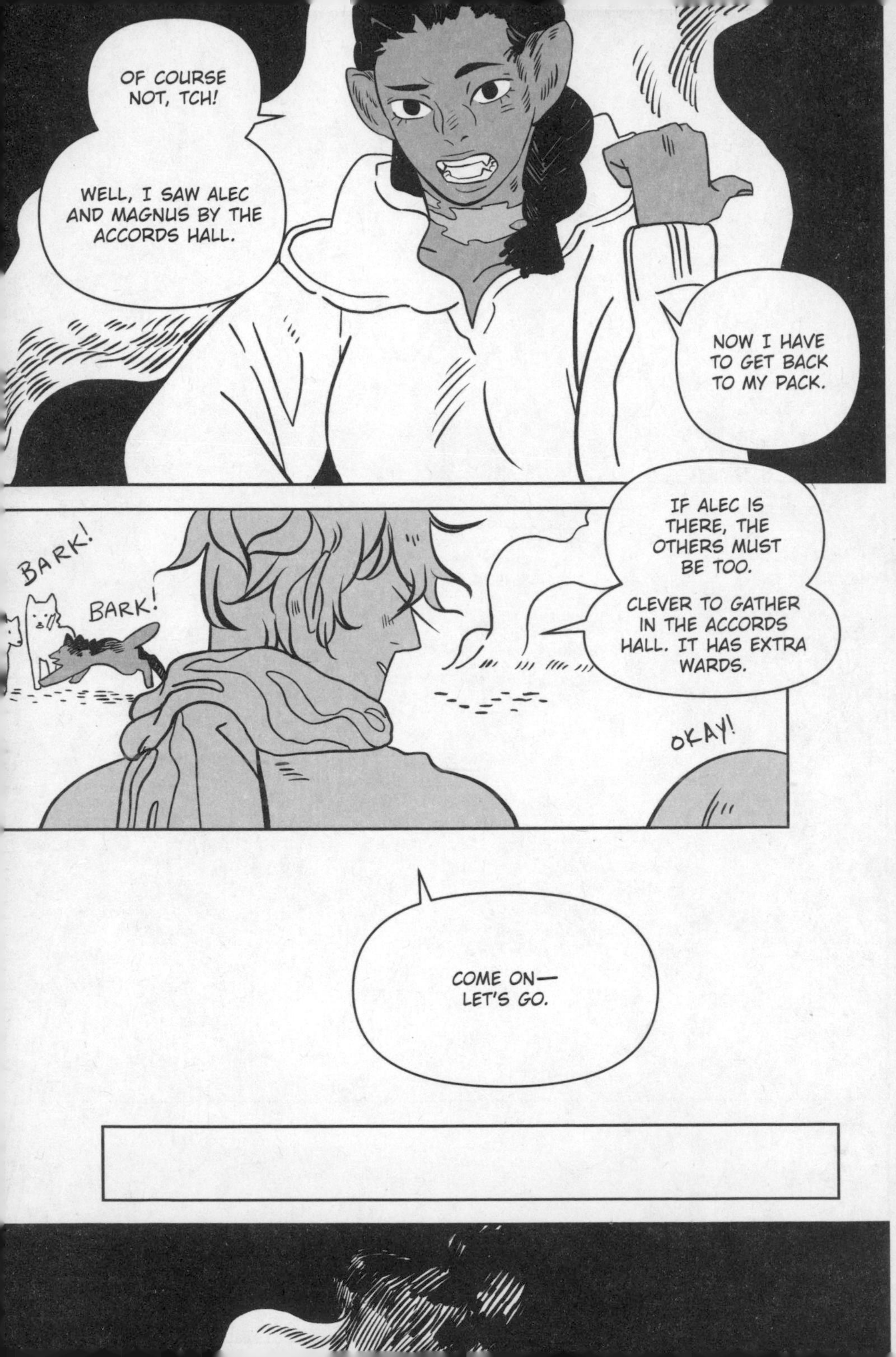
OF COURSE NOT, TCH!
WELL, I SAW ALEC AND MAGNUS BY THE ACCORDS HALL.
NOW I HAVE TO GET BACK TO MY PACK.
BARK!
BARK!
IF ALEC IS THERE, THE OTHERS MUST BE TOO.
CLEVER TO GATHER IN THE ACCORDS HALL. IT HAS EXTRA WARDS.
OKAY!
COME ON— LET'S GO.

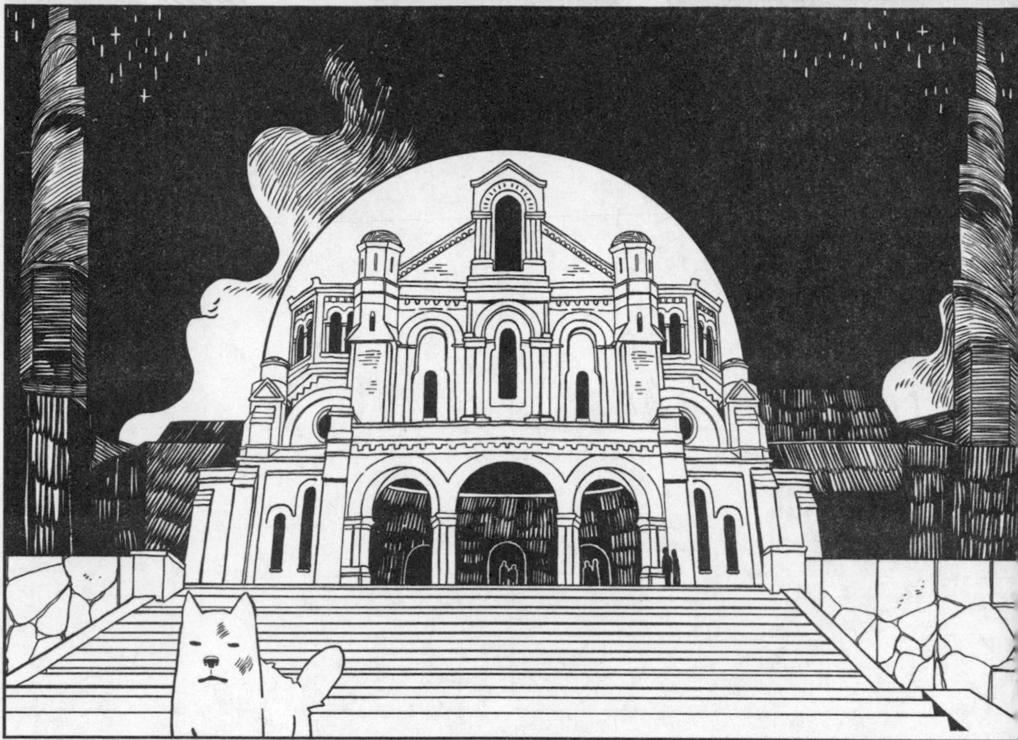

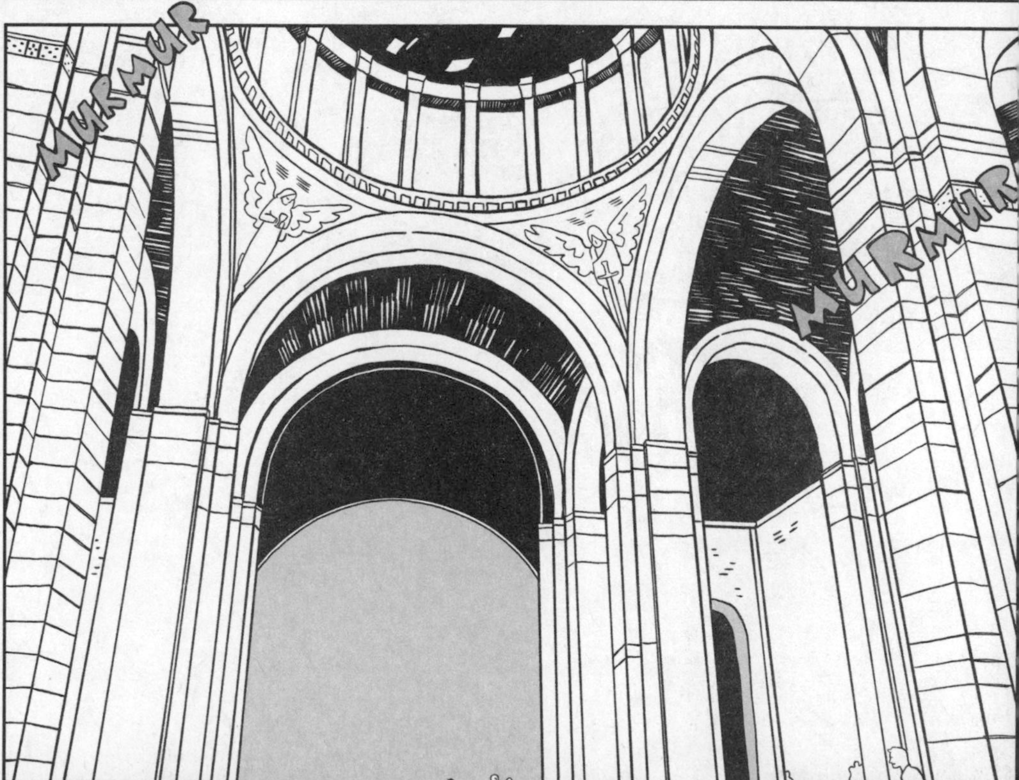
MURMUR
MURMUR

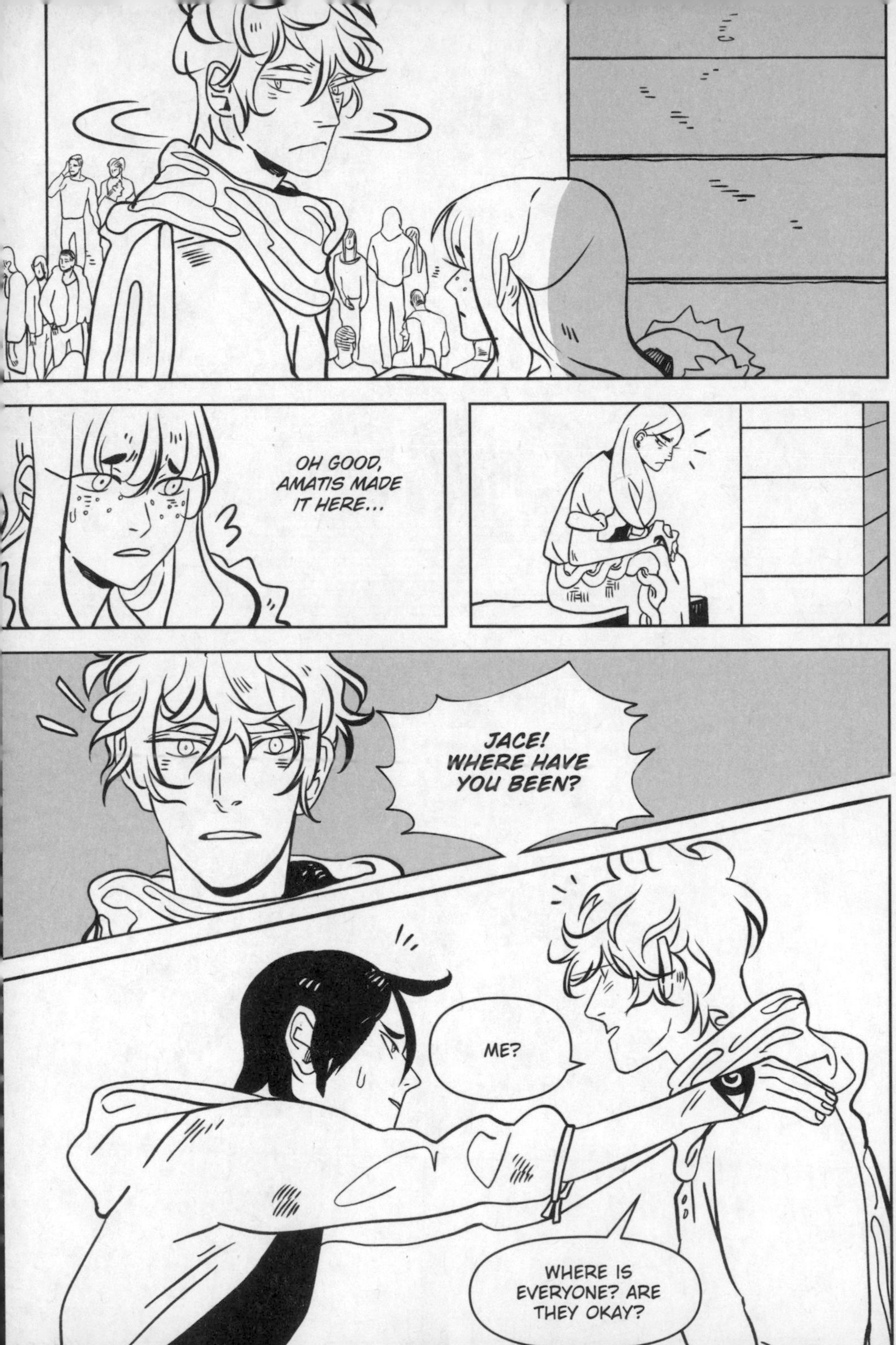
OH GOOD, AMATIS MADE IT HERE...
JACE! WHERE HAVE YOU BEEN?
ME?
WHERE IS EVERYONE? ARE THEY OKAY?

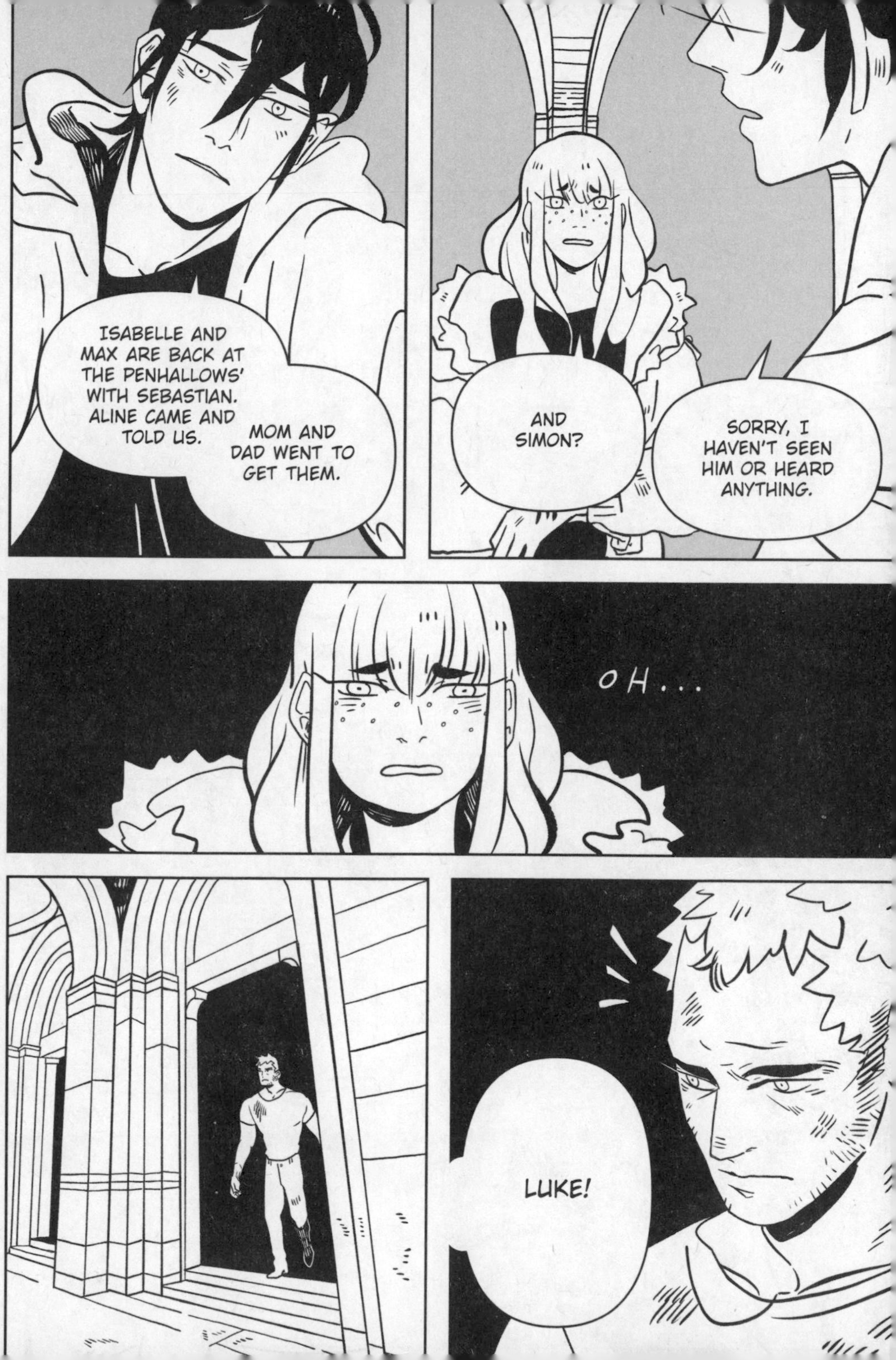
ISABELLE AND MAX ARE BACK AT THE PENHALLOWS' WITH SEBASTIAN. ALINE CAME AND TOLD US.
MOM AND DAD WENT TO GET THEM.
AND SIMON?
SORRY, I HAVEN'T SEEN HIM OR HEARD ANYTHING.
OH...
LUKE!

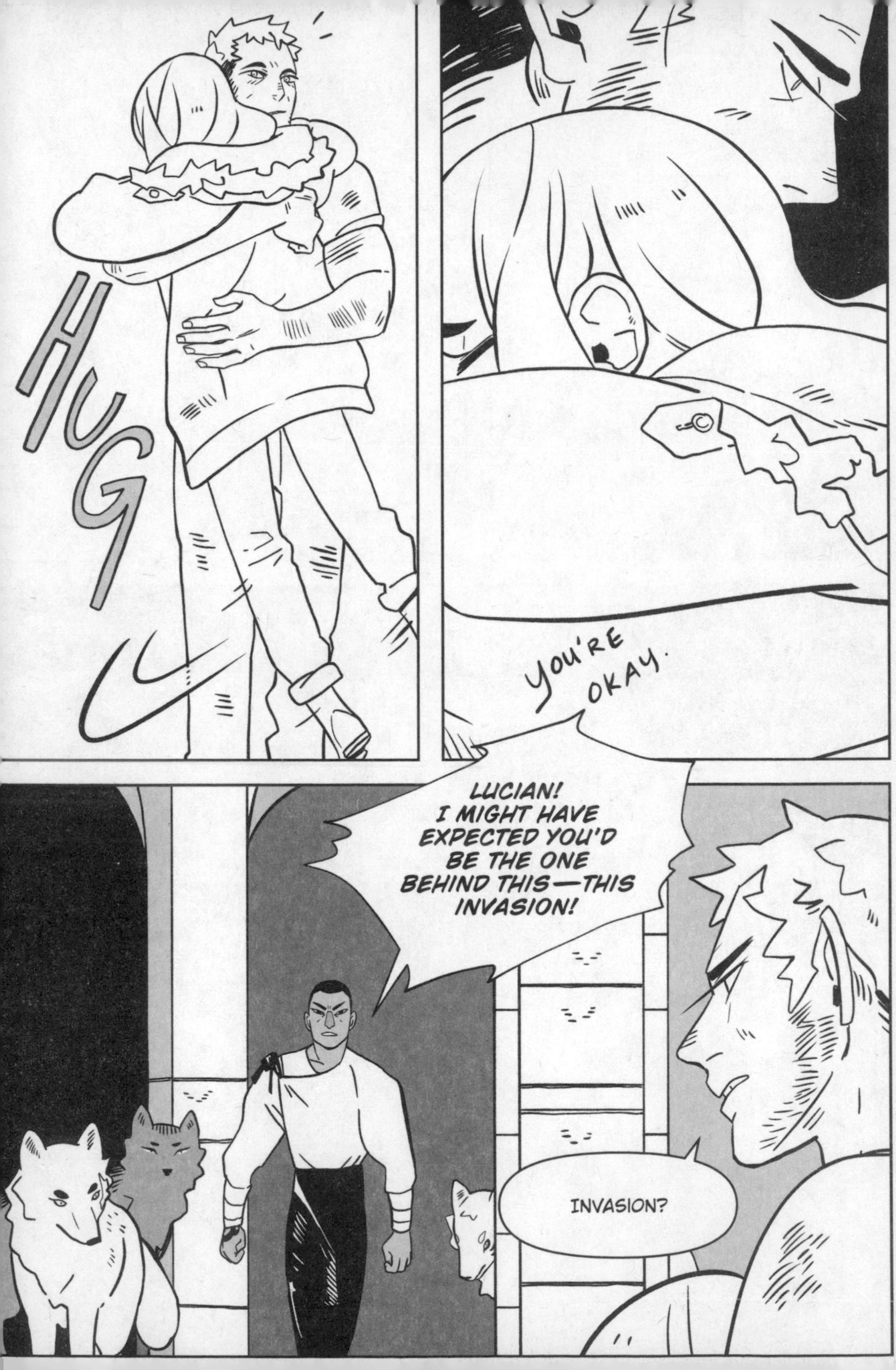
HUG
YOU'RE OKAY.
LUCIAN! I MIGHT HAVE EXPECTED YOU'D BE THE ONE BEHIND THIS—THIS INVASION!
INVASION?

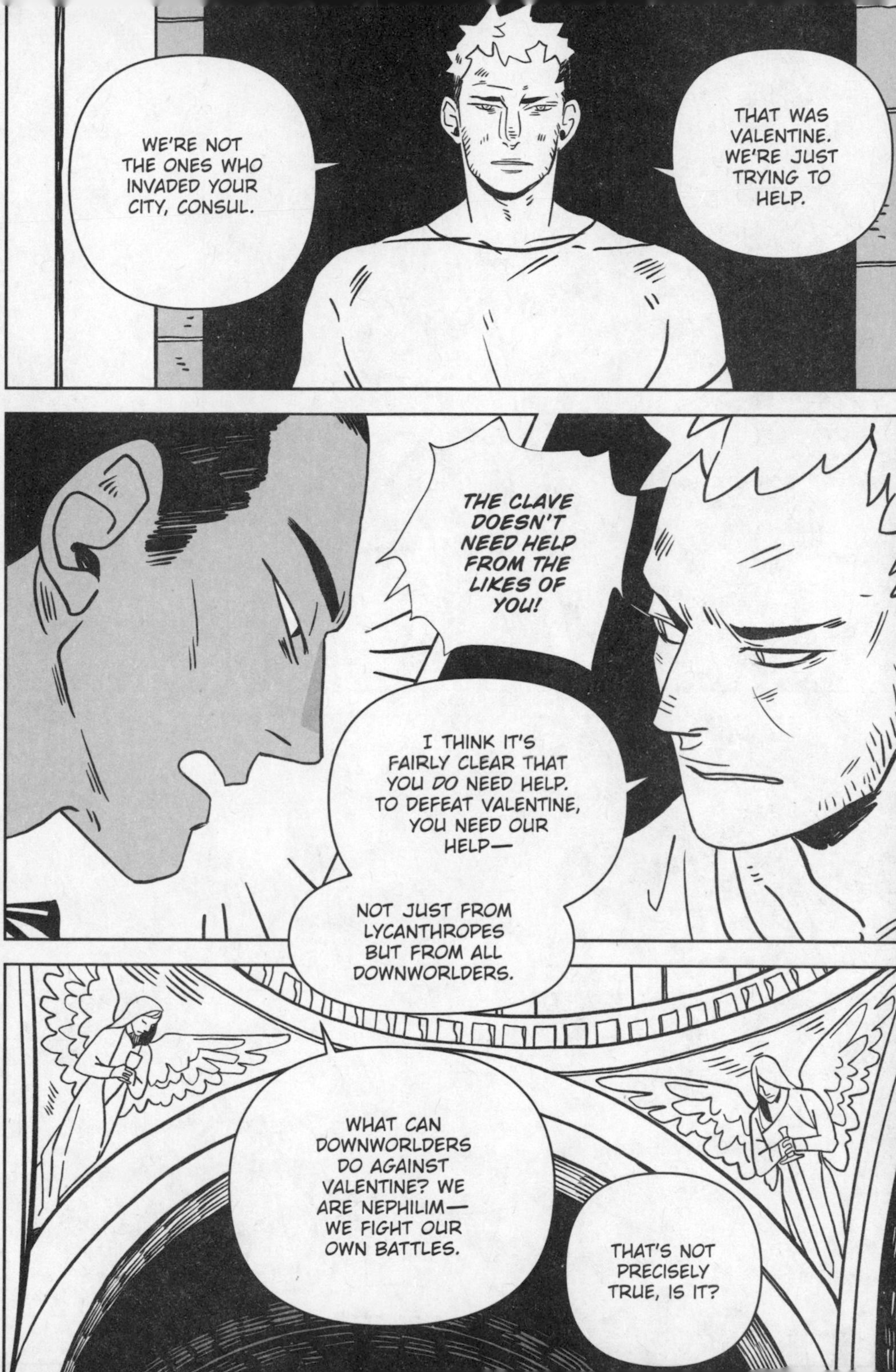

WE'RE NOT THE ONES WHO INVADED YOUR CITY, CONSUL.
THAT WAS VALENTINE. WE'RE JUST TRYING TO HELP.
THE CLAVE DOESN'T NEED HELP FROM THE LIKES OF YOU!
I THINK IT'S FAIRLY CLEAR THAT YOU DO NEED HELP. TO DEFEAT VALENTINE, YOU NEED OUR HELP—
NOT JUST FROM LYCANTHROPES BUT FROM ALL DOWNWORLDERS.
WHAT CAN DOWNWORLDERS DO AGAINST VALENTINE? WE ARE NEPHILIM—WE FIGHT OUR OWN BATTLES.
THAT'S NOT PRECISELY TRUE, IS IT?

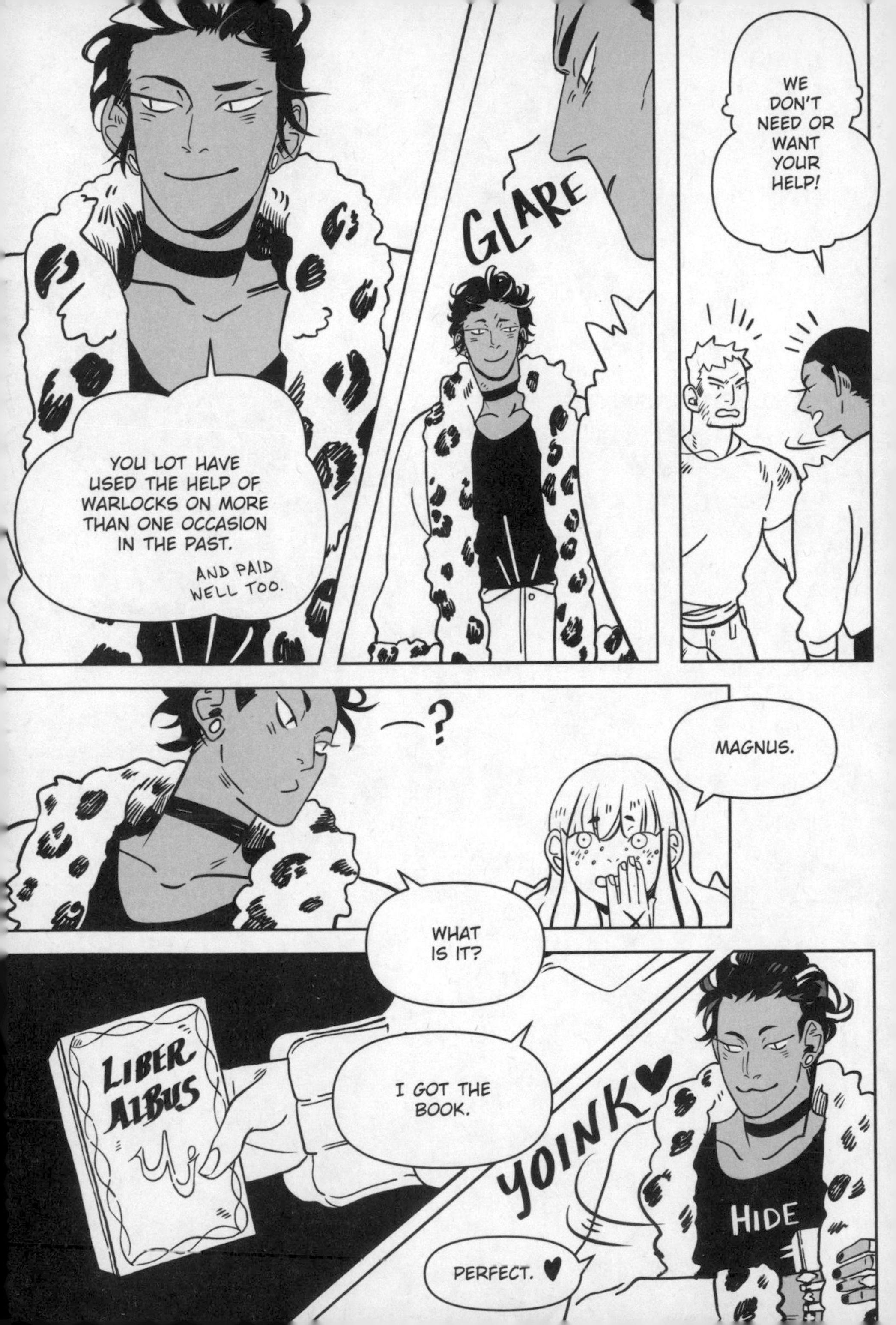
YOU LOT HAVE USED THE HELP OF WARLOCKS ON MORE THAN ONE OCCASION IN THE PAST.
AND PAID WELL TOO.
GLARE
WE DON'T NEED OR WANT YOUR HELP!
?
MAGNUS.
WHAT IS IT?
LIBER ALBUS
I GOT THE BOOK.
YOINK
HIDE
PERFECT.

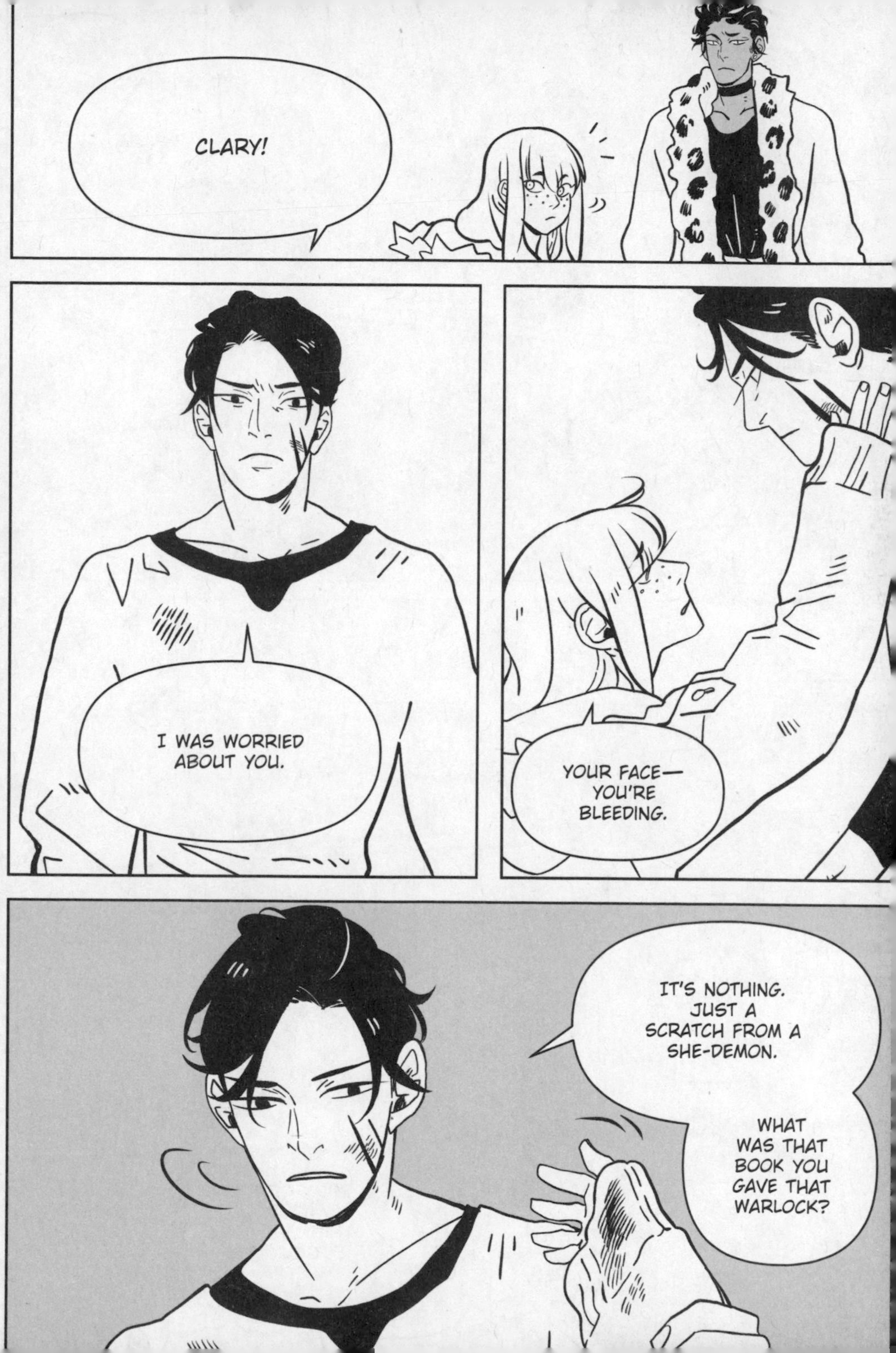
CLARY!
I WAS WORRIED ABOUT YOU.
YOUR FACE— YOU'RE BLEEDING.
IT'S NOTHING. JUST A SCRATCH FROM A SHE-DEMON.
WHAT WAS THAT BOOK YOU GAVE THAT WARLOCK?

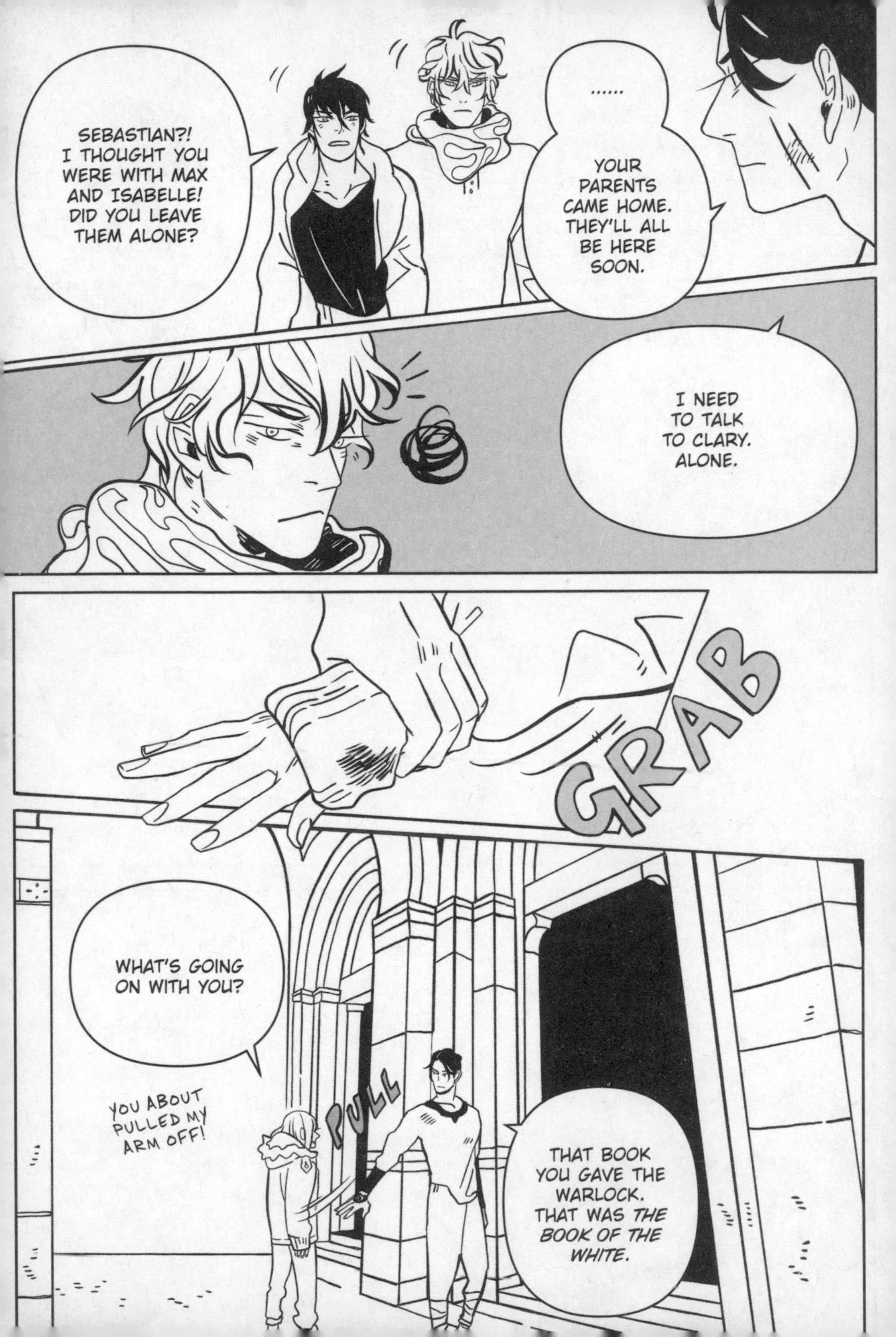
SEBASTIAN?! I THOUGHT YOU WERE WITH MAX AND ISABELLE! DID YOU LEAVE THEM ALONE?
......
YOUR PARENTS CAME HOME. THEY'LL ALL BE HERE SOON.
I NEED TO TALK TO CLARY. ALONE.
GRAB
WHAT'S GOING ON WITH YOU?
YOU ABOUT PULLED MY ARM OFF!
PULL
THAT BOOK YOU GAVE THE WARLOCK. THAT WAS *THE BOOK OF THE WHITE*.

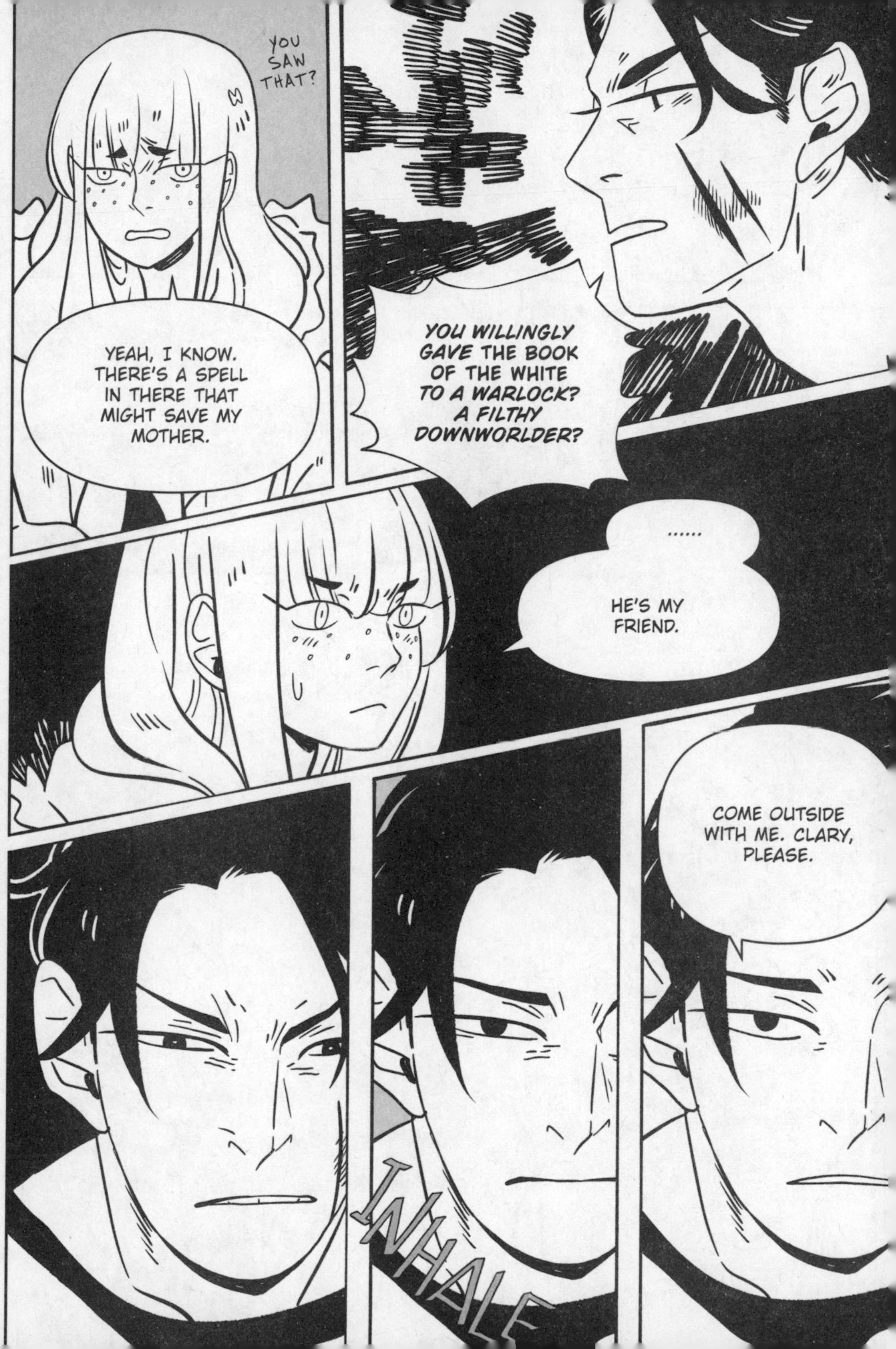
YOU SAW THAT?
YEAH, I KNOW. THERE'S A SPELL IN THERE THAT MIGHT SAVE MY MOTHER.
YOU WILLINGLY GAVE THE BOOK OF THE WHITE TO A WARLOCK? A FILTHY DOWNWORLDER?
......
HE'S MY FRIEND.
INHALE
COME OUTSIDE WITH ME. CLARY, PLEASE.

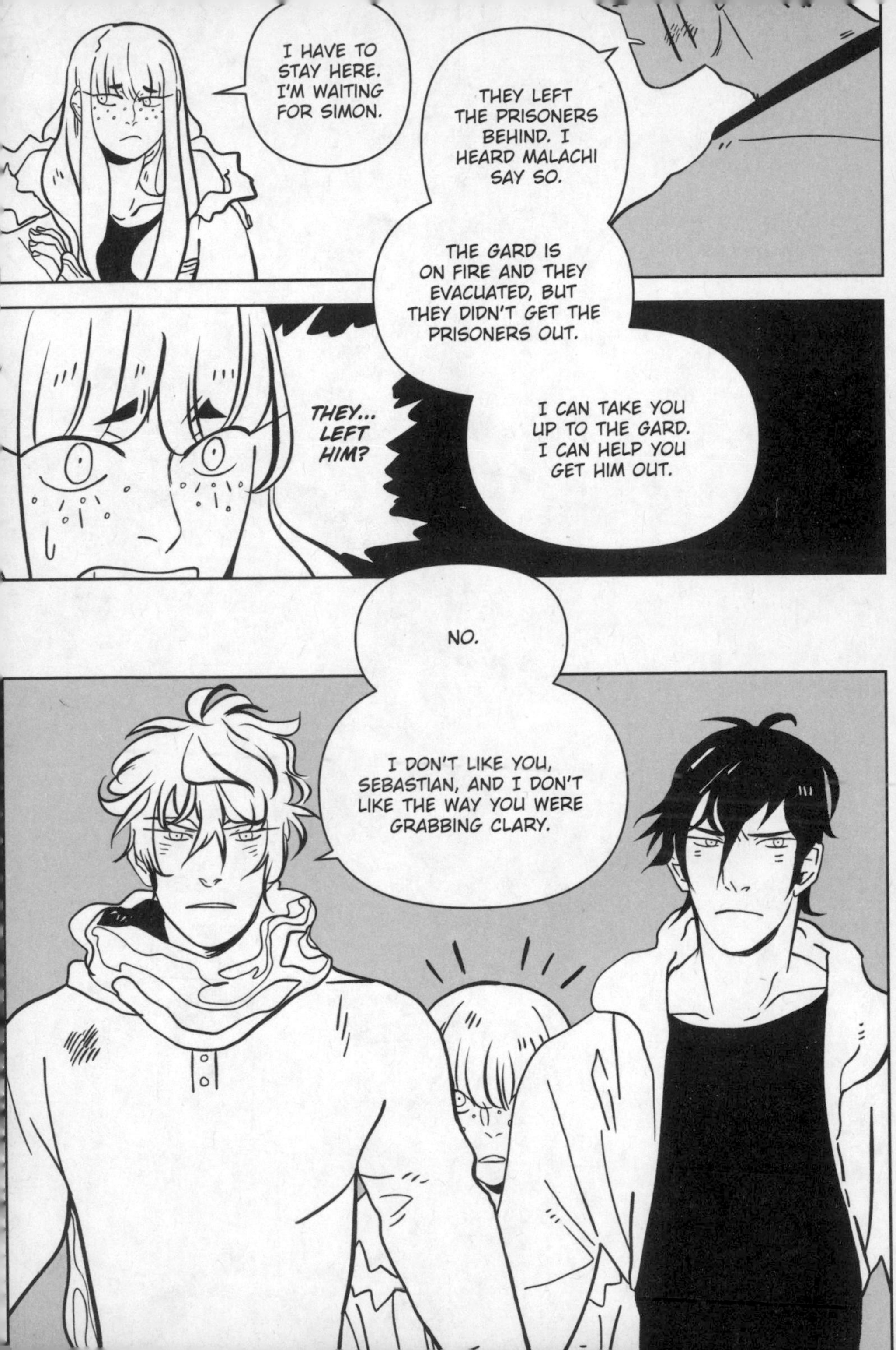
I HAVE TO STAY HERE. I'M WAITING FOR SIMON.
THEY LEFT THE PRISONERS BEHIND. I HEARD MALACHI SAY SO.
THE GARD IS ON FIRE AND THEY EVACUATED, BUT THEY DIDN'T GET THE PRISONERS OUT.
THEY... LEFT HIM?
I CAN TAKE YOU UP TO THE GARD. I CAN HELP YOU GET HIM OUT.
NO.
I DON'T LIKE YOU, SEBASTIAN, AND I DON'T LIKE THE WAY YOU WERE GRABBING CLARY.

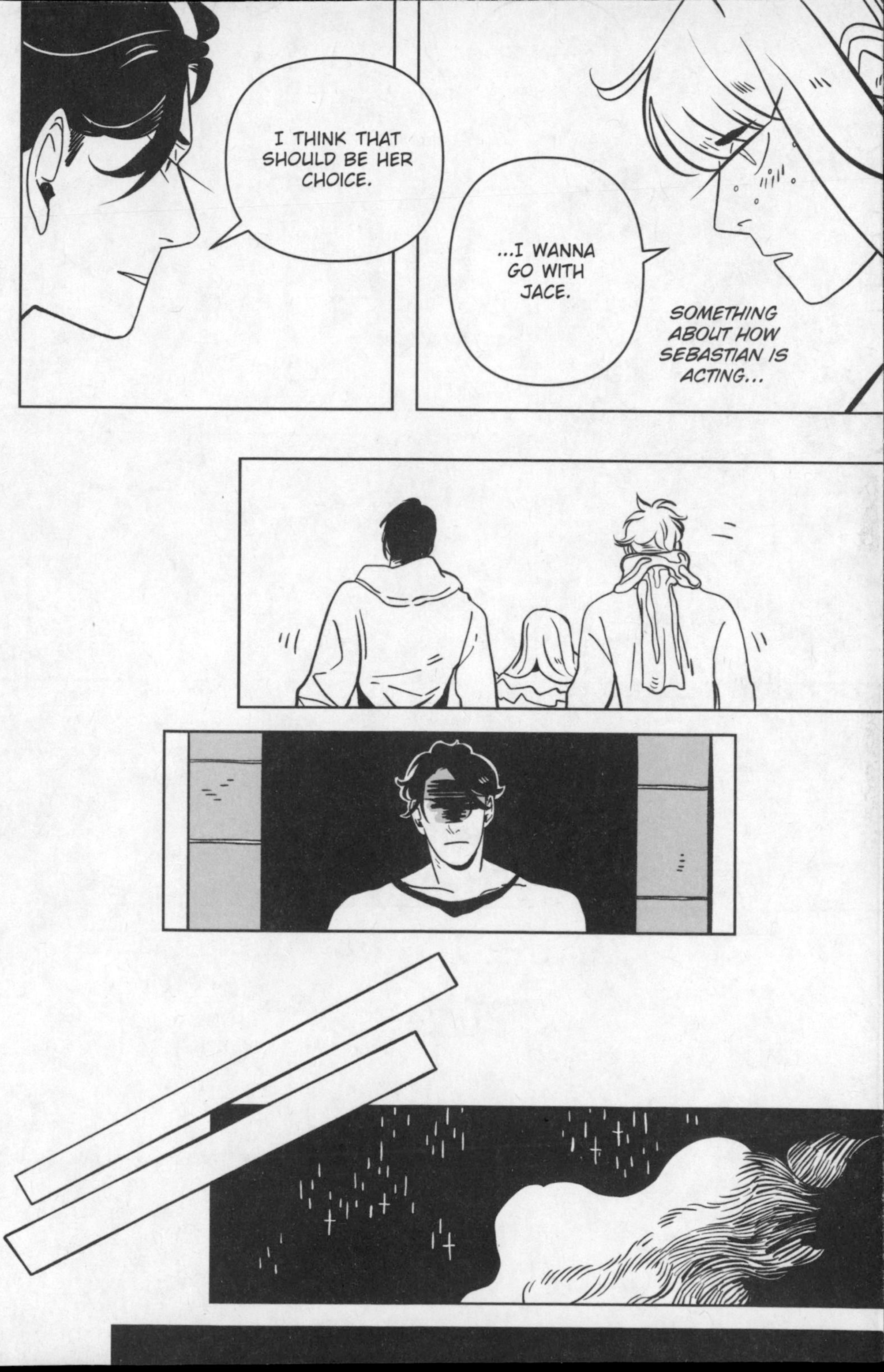
I THINK THAT SHOULD BE HER CHOICE.
...I WANNA GO WITH JACE.
SOMETHING ABOUT HOW SEBASTIAN IS ACTING...

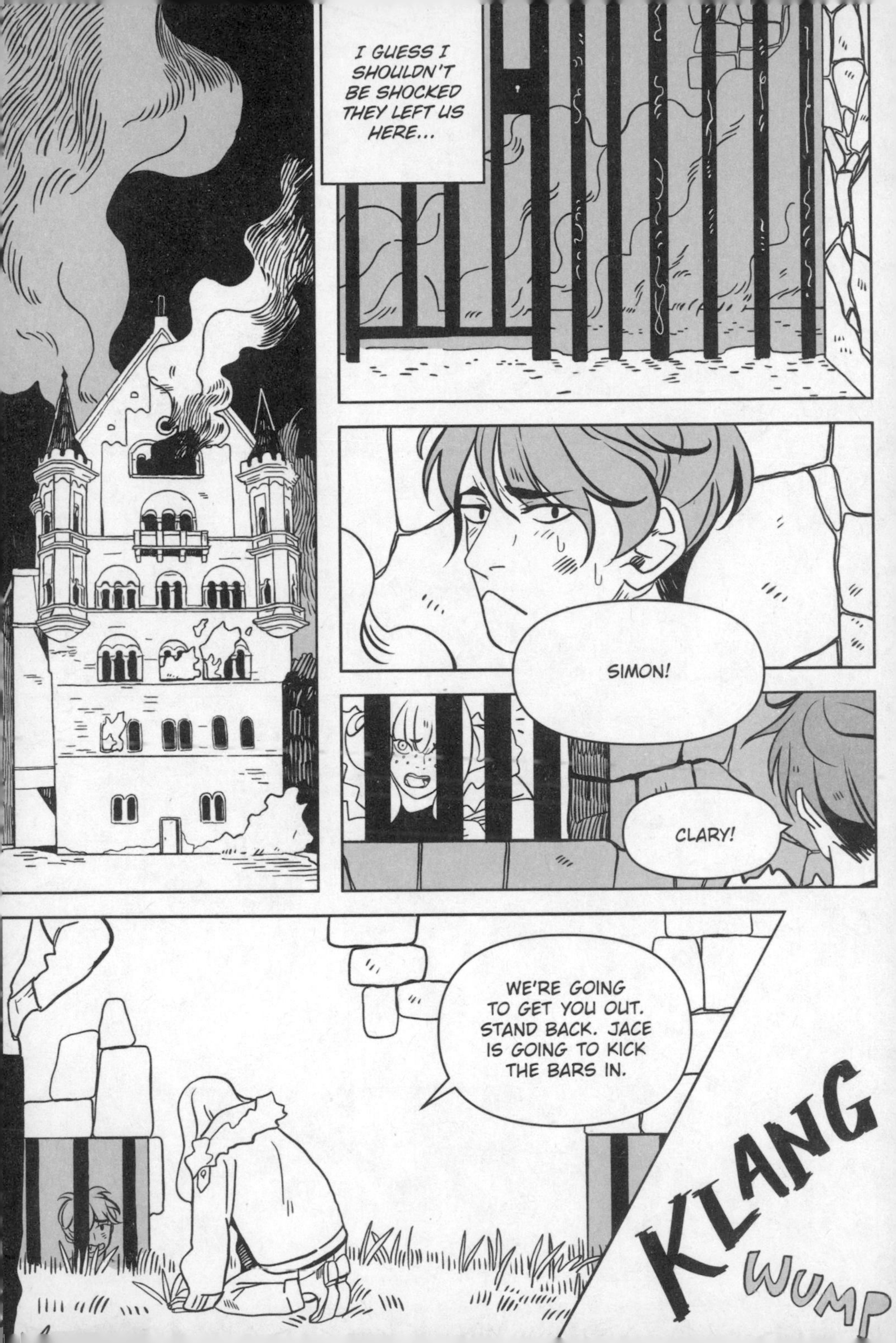
I GUESS I SHOULDN'T BE SHOCKED THEY LEFT US HERE...
SIMON!
CLARY!
WE'RE GOING TO GET YOU OUT. STAND BACK. JACE IS GOING TO KICK THE BARS IN.
KLANG
WUMP

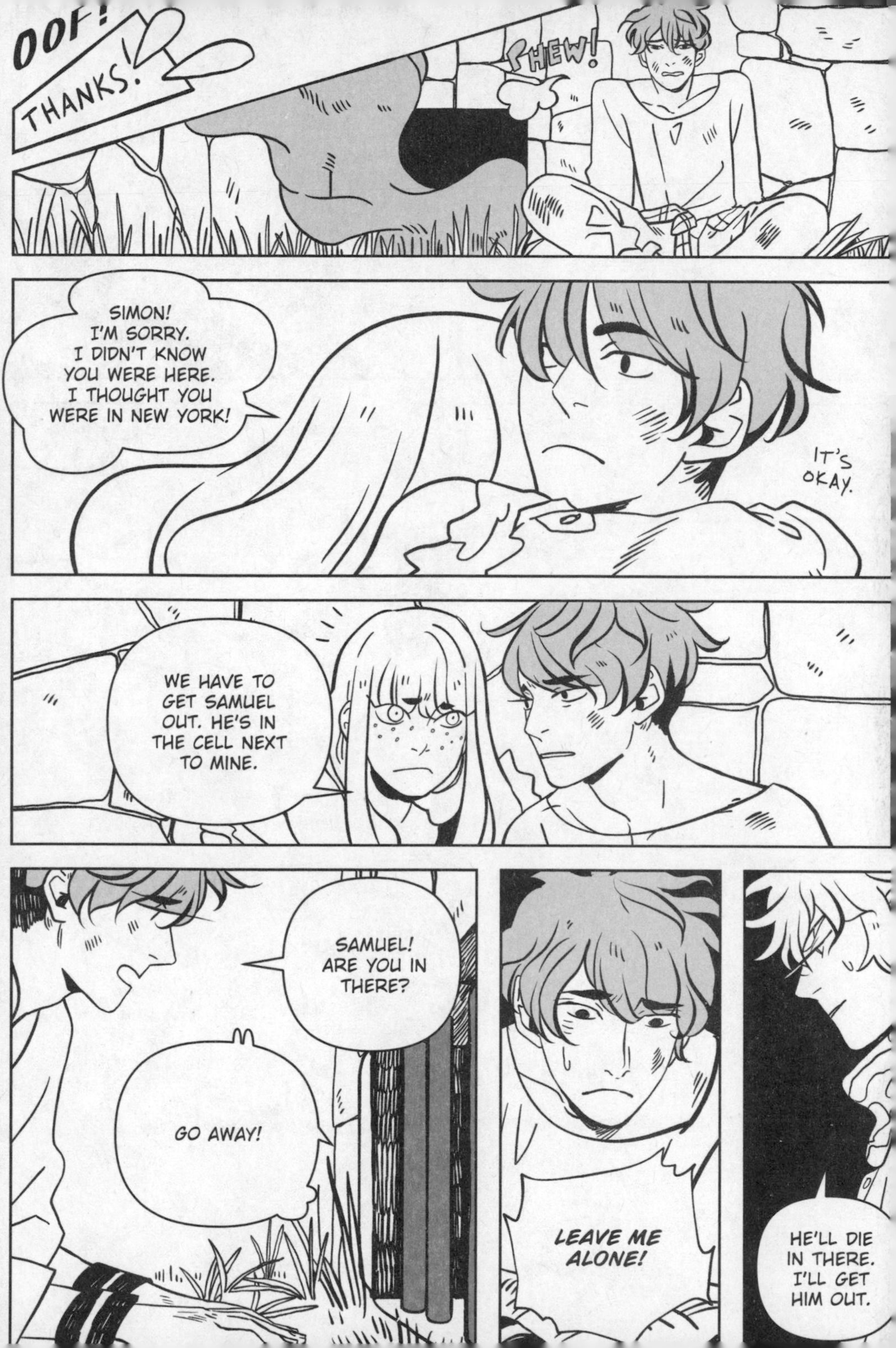
OOF!
THANKS!
SHEW!
SIMON! I'M SORRY. I DIDN'T KNOW YOU WERE HERE. I THOUGHT YOU WERE IN NEW YORK!
IT'S OKAY.
WE HAVE TO GET SAMUEL OUT. HE'S IN THE CELL NEXT TO MINE.
SAMUEL! ARE YOU IN THERE?
GO AWAY!
LEAVE ME ALONE!
HE'LL DIE IN THERE. I'LL GET HIM OUT.

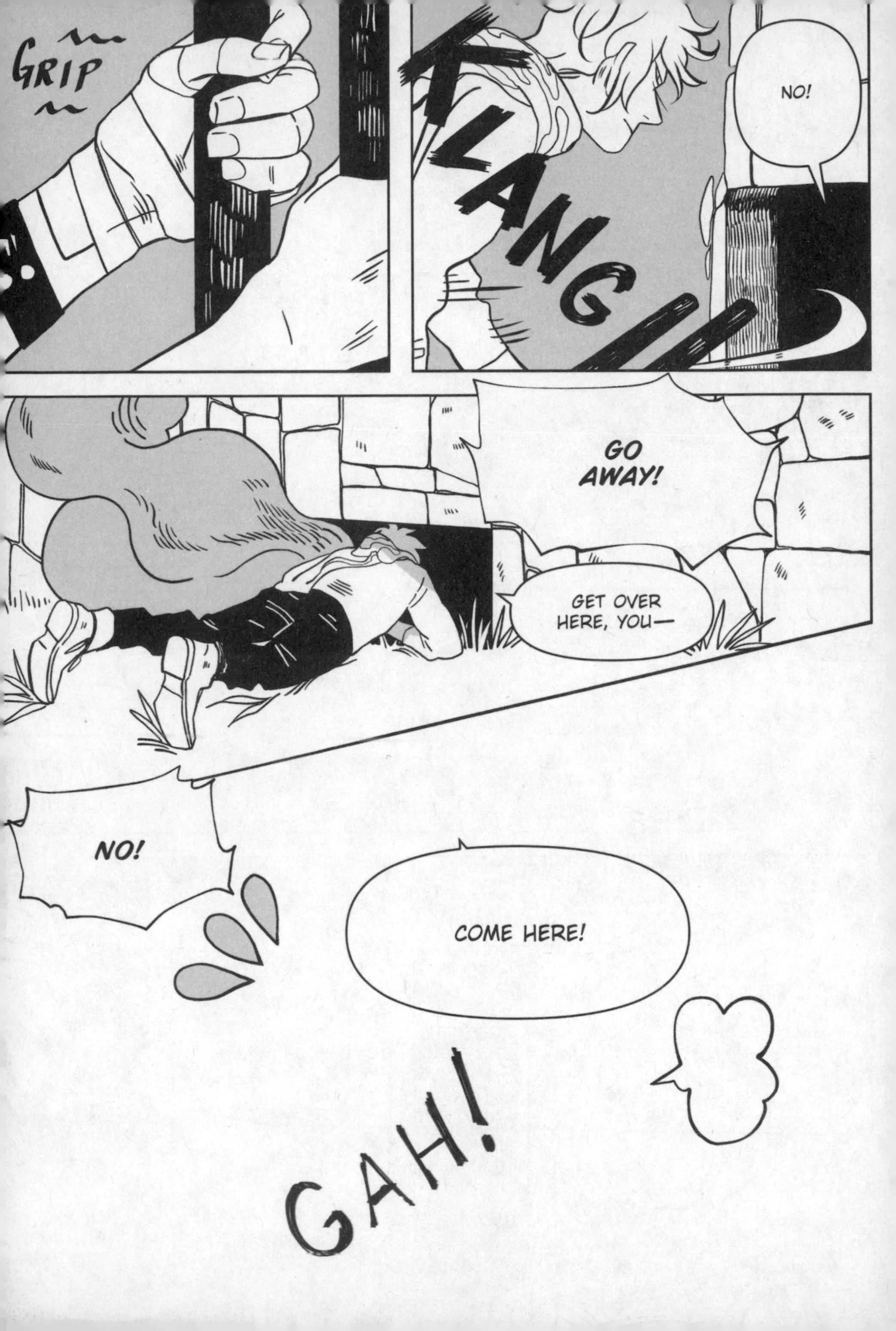
GRIP
KLANG
NO!
GO AWAY!
GET OVER HERE, YOU—
NO!
COME HERE!
GAH!

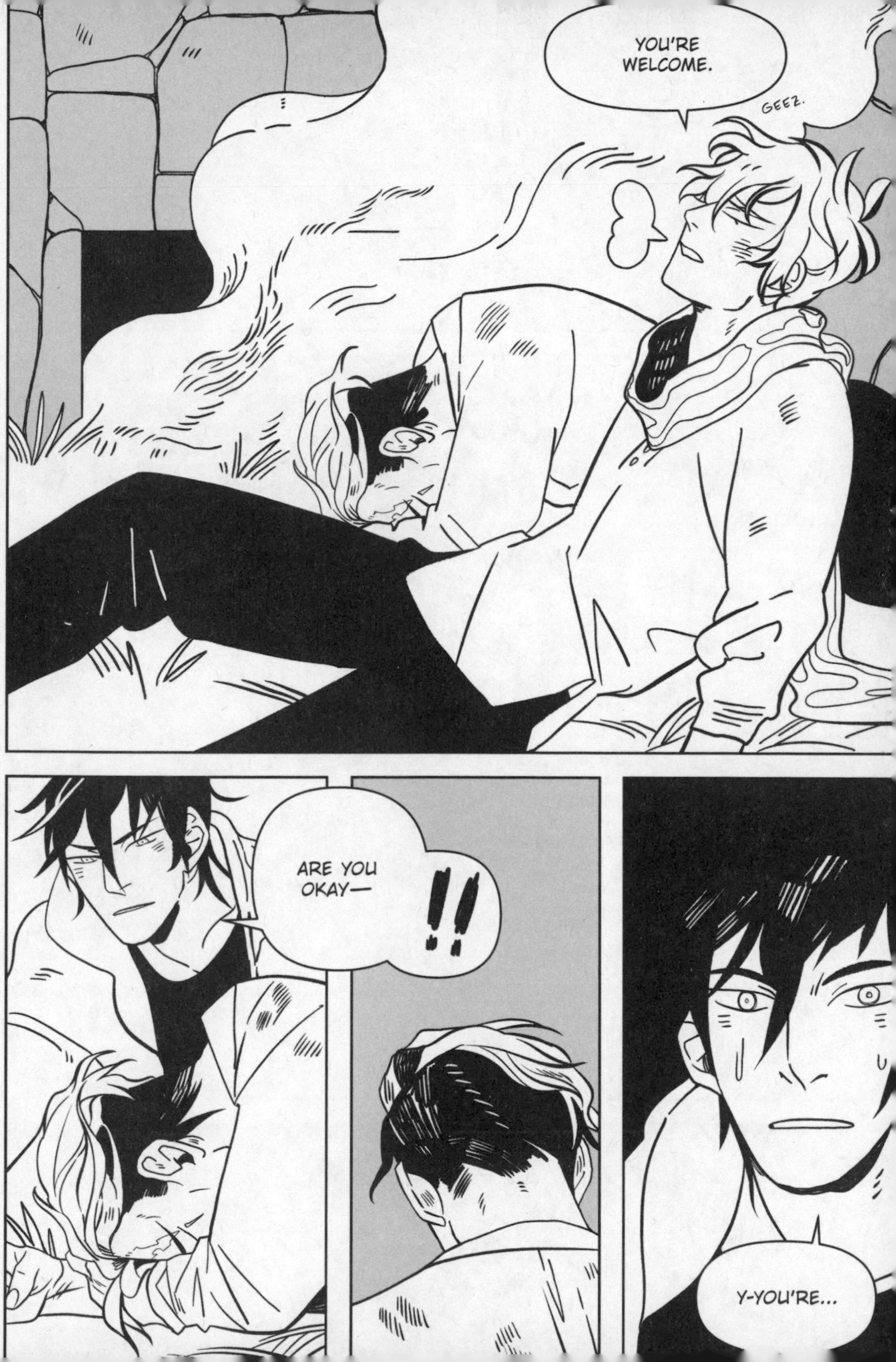
YOU'RE WELCOME.
GEEZ.
ARE YOU OKAY—
!!
Y-YOU'RE...

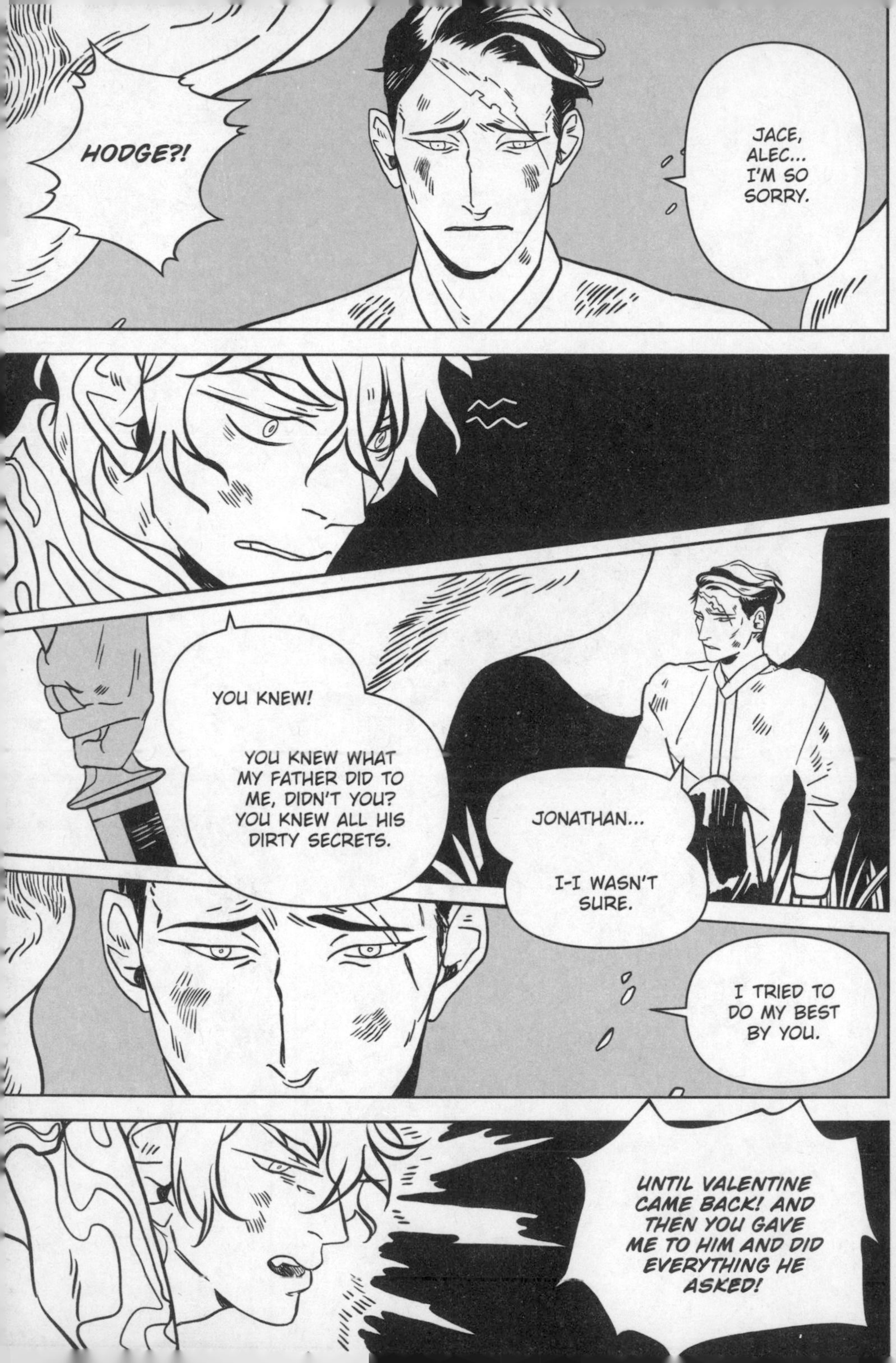
HODGE?!
JACE, ALEC... I'M SO SORRY.
YOU KNEW!
YOU KNEW WHAT MY FATHER DID TO ME, DIDN'T YOU? YOU KNEW ALL HIS DIRTY SECRETS.
JONATHAN...
I-I WASN'T SURE.
I TRIED TO DO MY BEST BY YOU.
UNTIL VALENTINE CAME BACK! AND THEN YOU GAVE ME TO HIM AND DID EVERYTHING HE ASKED!

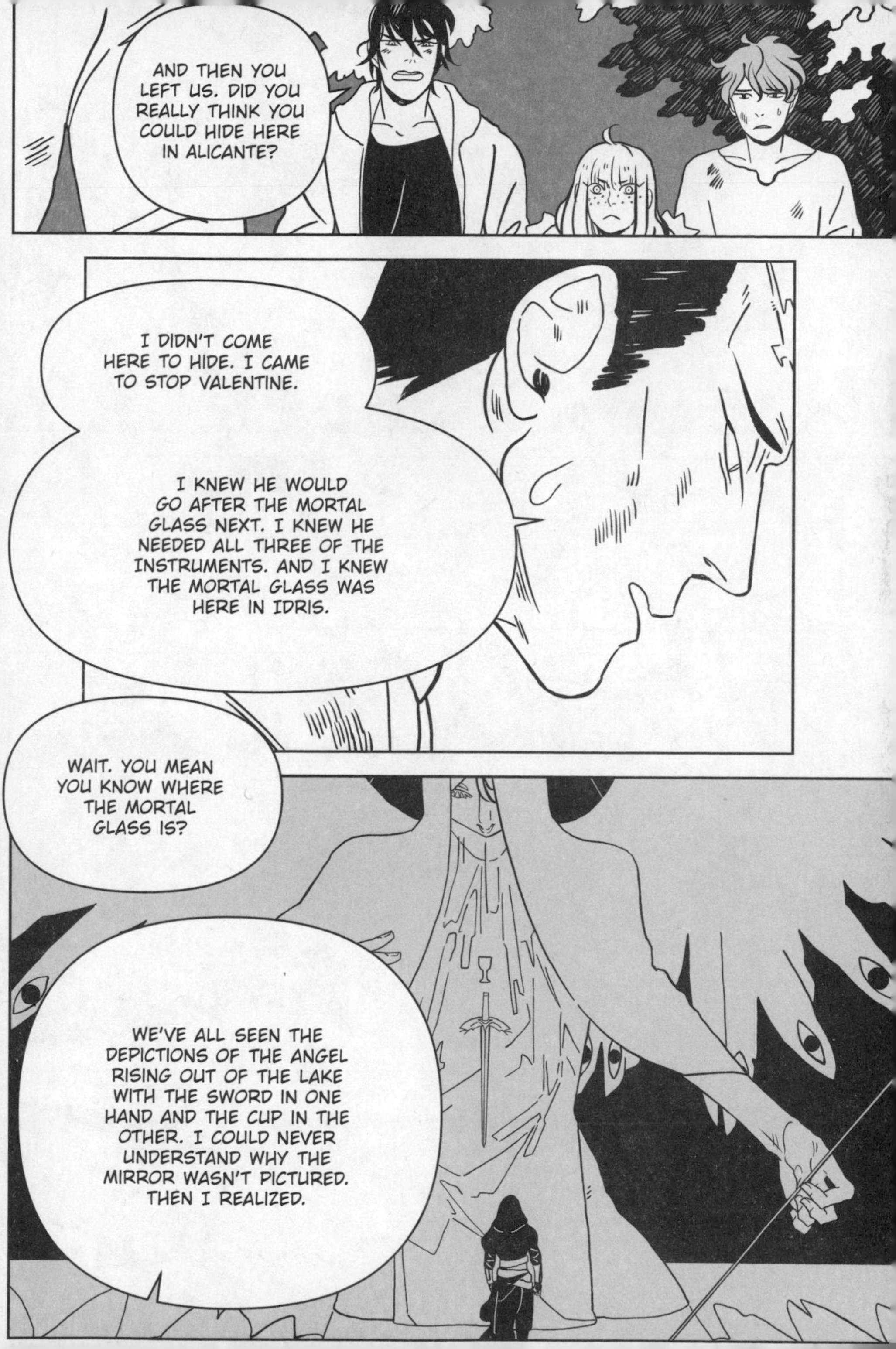
AND THEN YOU LEFT US. DID YOU REALLY THINK YOU COULD HIDE HERE IN ALICANTE?
I DIDN'T COME HERE TO HIDE. I CAME TO STOP VALENTINE.
I KNEW HE WOULD GO AFTER THE MORTAL GLASS NEXT. I KNEW HE NEEDED ALL THREE OF THE INSTRUMENTS. AND I KNEW THE MORTAL GLASS WAS HERE IN IDRIS.
WAIT. YOU MEAN YOU KNOW WHERE THE MORTAL GLASS IS?
WE'VE ALL SEEN THE DEPICTIONS OF THE ANGEL RISING OUT OF THE LAKE WITH THE SWORD IN ONE HAND AND THE CUP IN THE OTHER. I COULD NEVER UNDERSTAND WHY THE MIRROR WASN'T PICTURED. THEN I REALIZED.

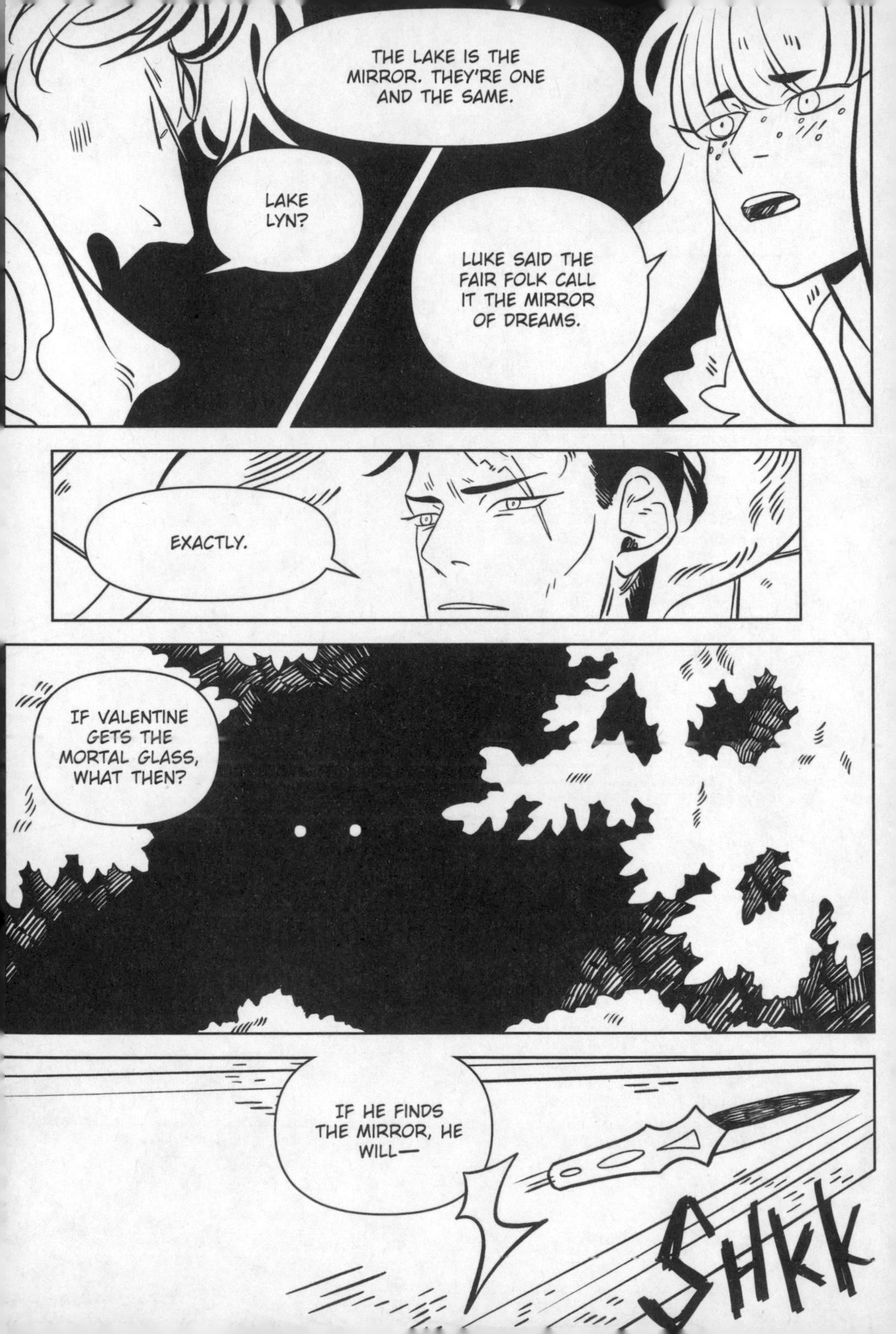
THE LAKE IS THE MIRROR. THEY'RE ONE AND THE SAME.
LAKE LYN?
LUKE SAID THE FAIR FOLK CALL IT THE MIRROR OF DREAMS.
EXACTLY.
IF VALENTINE GETS THE MORTAL GLASS, WHAT THEN?
IF HE FINDS THE MIRROR, HE WILL—
SHKK

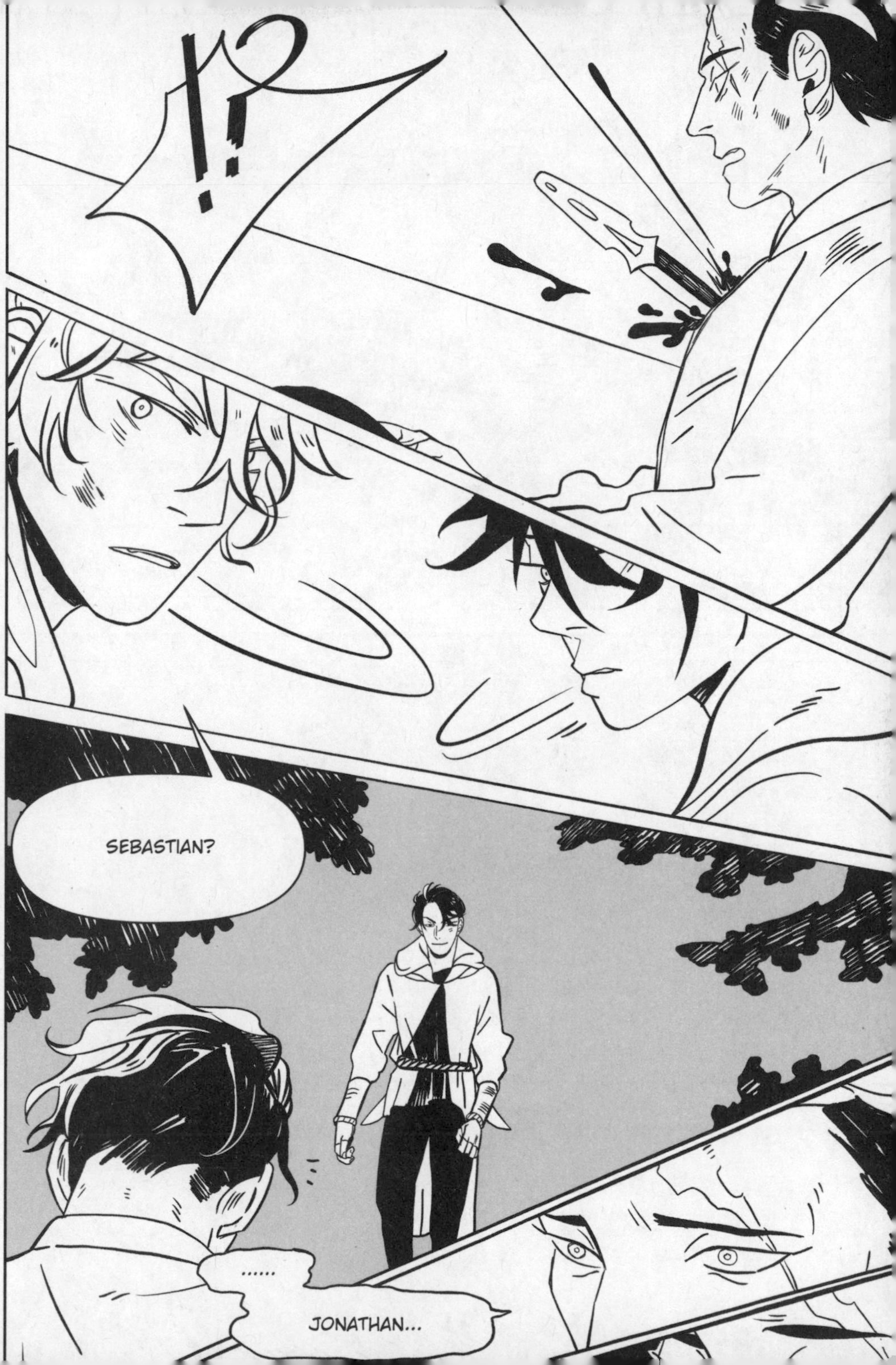
!?
SEBASTIAN?
......
JONATHAN...

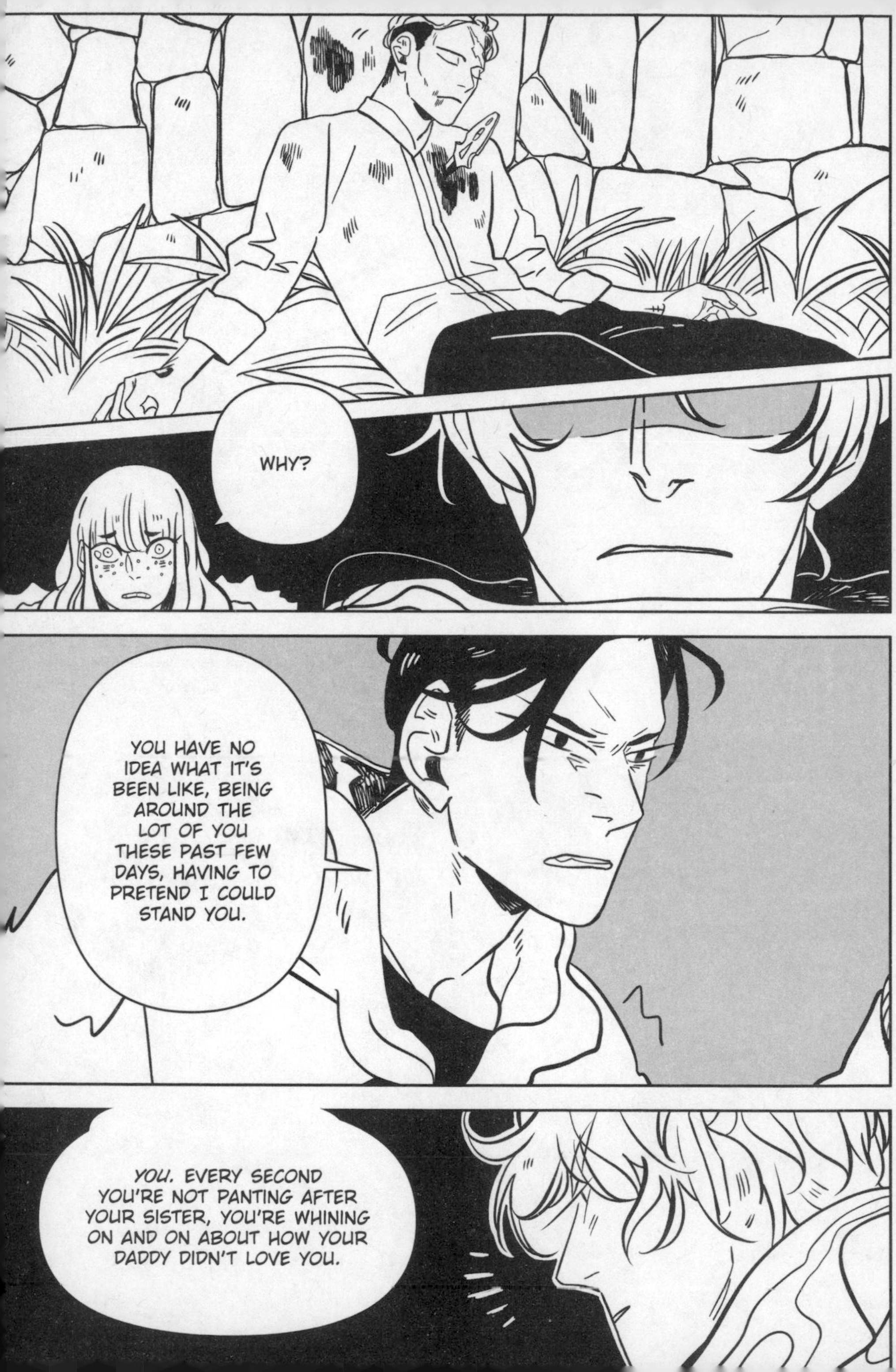
WHY?
YOU HAVE NO IDEA WHAT IT'S BEEN LIKE, BEING AROUND THE LOT OF YOU THESE PAST FEW DAYS, HAVING TO PRETEND I COULD STAND YOU.
YOU. EVERY SECOND YOU'RE NOT PANTING AFTER YOUR SISTER, YOU'RE WHINING ON AND ON ABOUT HOW YOUR DADDY DIDN'T LOVE YOU.

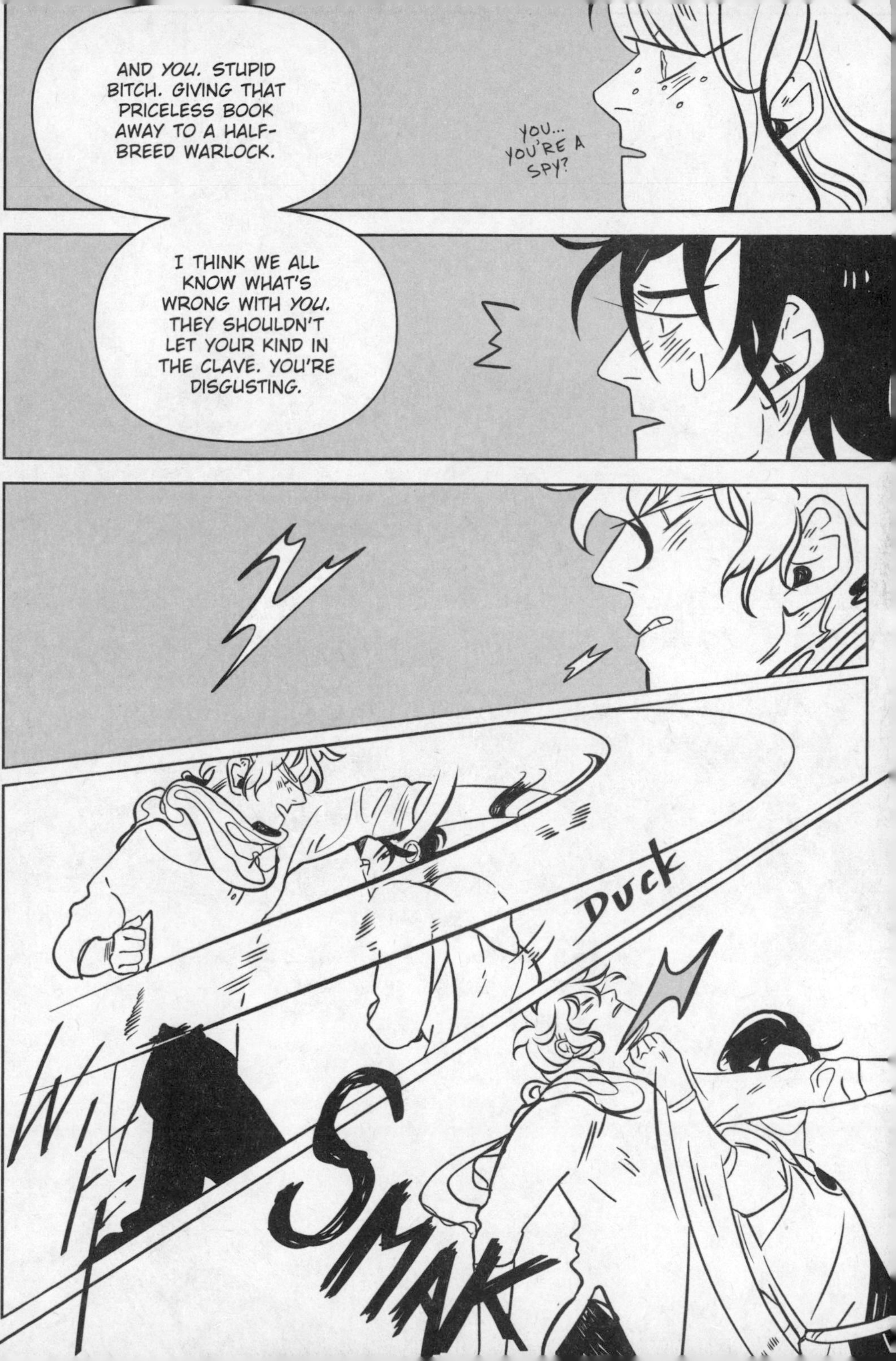
AND YOU. STUPID BITCH. GIVING THAT PRICELESS BOOK AWAY TO A HALF-BREED WARLOCK.
YOU... YOU'RE A SPY?
I THINK WE ALL KNOW WHAT'S WRONG WITH YOU. THEY SHOULDN'T LET YOUR KIND IN THE CLAVE. YOU'RE DISGUSTING.
Duck
WHFF
SMAK

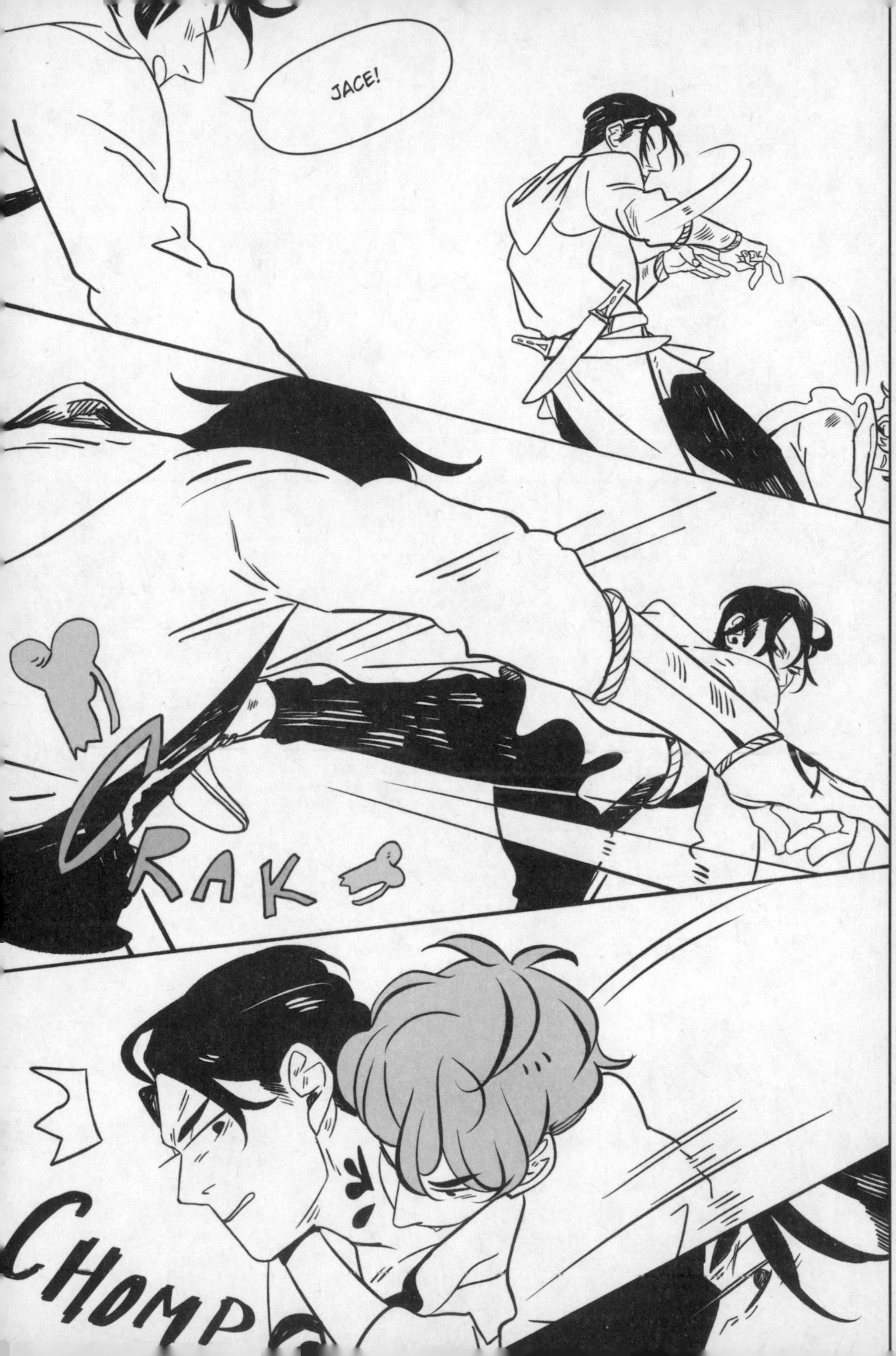
JACE!
CRAK
CHOMP

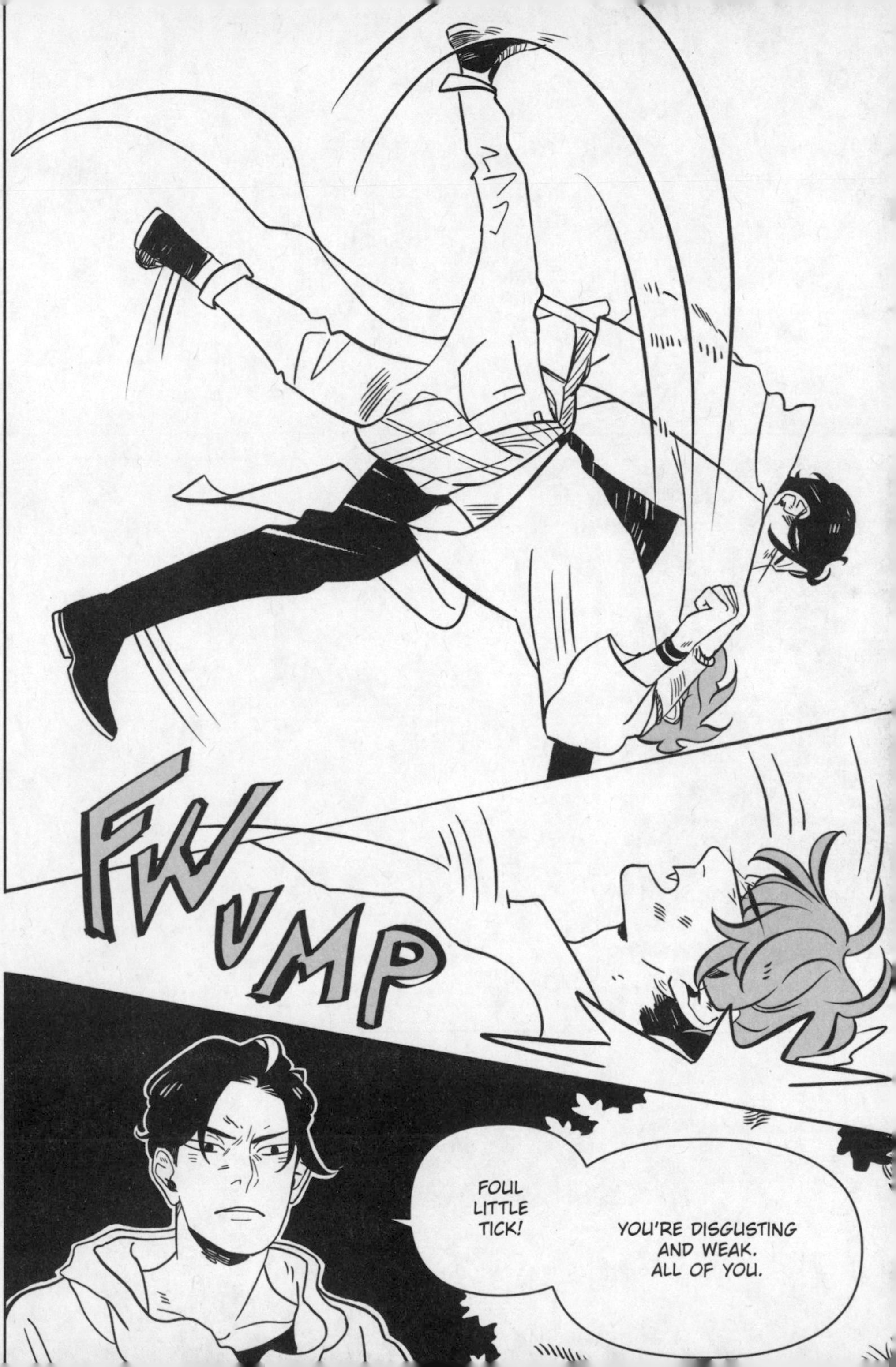
FWUMP
FOUL LITTLE TICK!
YOU'RE DISGUSTING AND WEAK. ALL OF YOU.

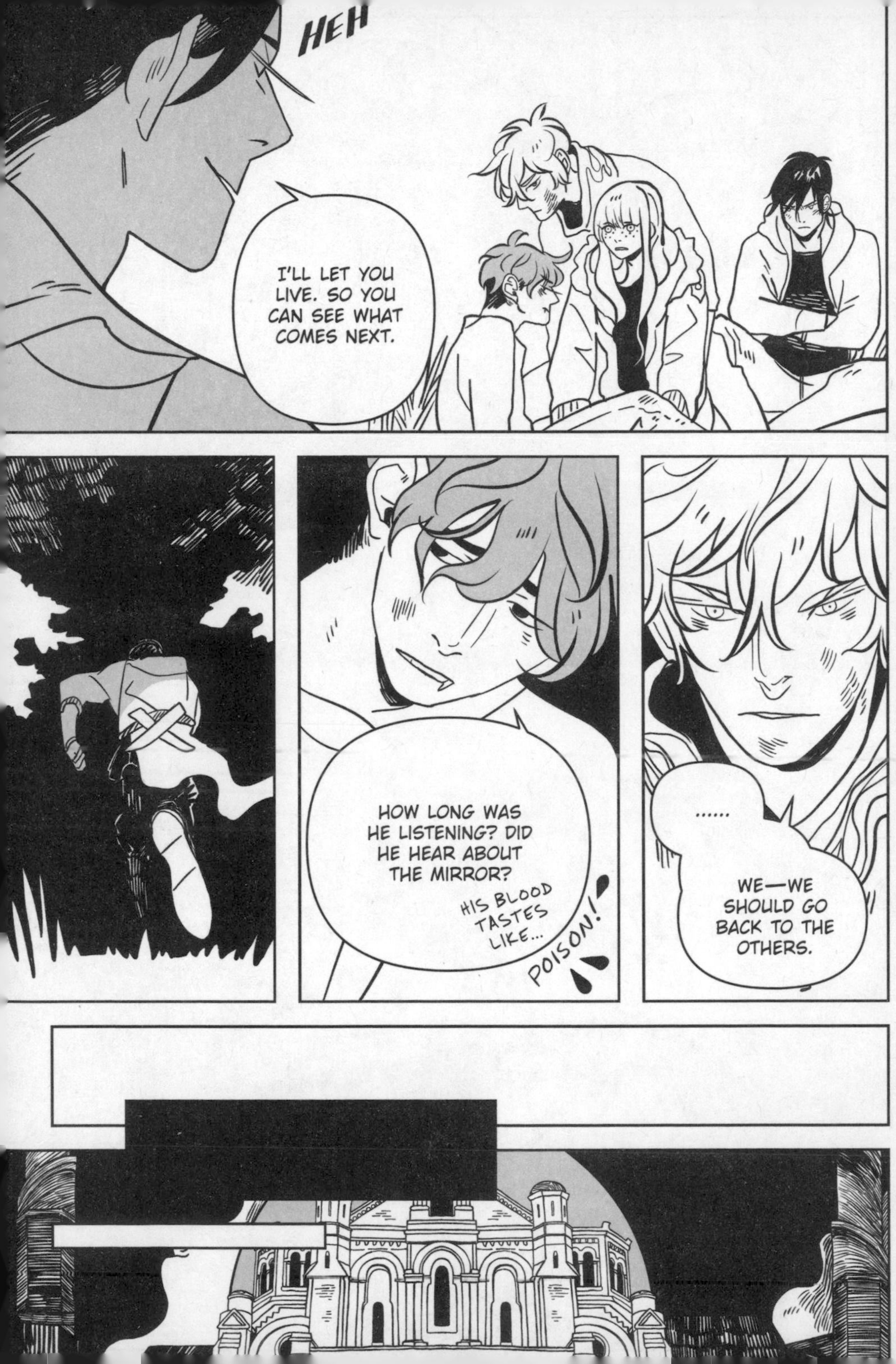
HEH
I'LL LET YOU LIVE. SO YOU CAN SEE WHAT COMES NEXT.
HOW LONG WAS HE LISTENING? DID HE HEAR ABOUT THE MIRROR?
HIS BLOOD TASTES LIKE...
POISON!
......
WE—WE SHOULD GO BACK TO THE OTHERS.
[redacted]

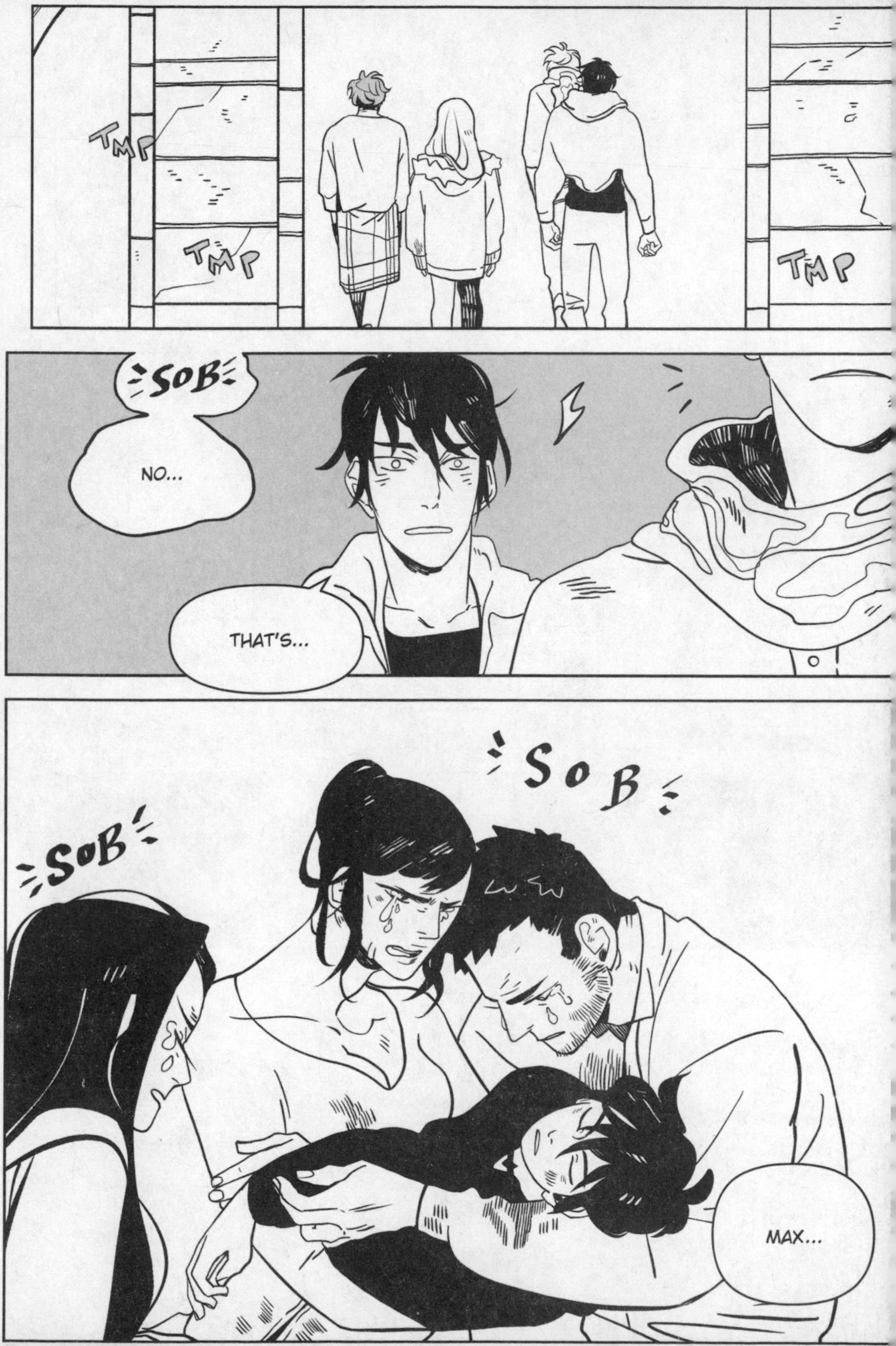
TMP
TMP
TMP
SOB
NO...
THAT'S...
SOB
SOB
MAX...

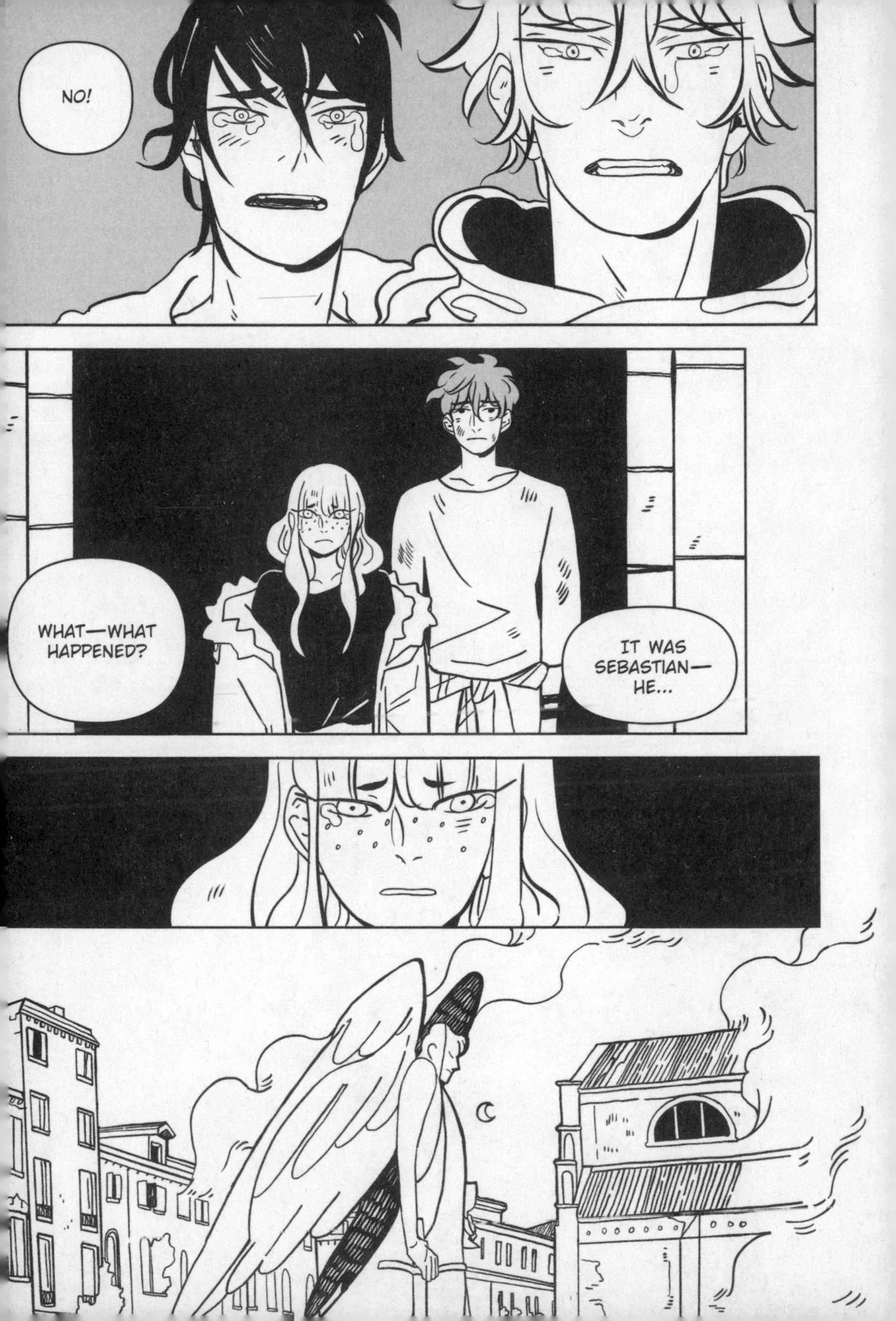
NO!
WHAT—WHAT HAPPENED?
IT WAS SEBASTIAN—HE...

TO BE CONTINUED IN THE SIXTH VOLUME OF

THE MORTAL INSTRUMENTS
THE GRAPHIC NOVEL